A
Paradigm
of
Earth

Also by Candas Jane Dorsey

Black Wine

A
Paradigm
of
Earth

CANDAS JANE DORSEY

TOR®

A TOM DOHERTY ASSOCIATES BOOK

NEW YORK

A PARADIGM OF EARTH

This book is printed on acid-free paper.

Edited by David G. Hartwell

Design by Heidi Eriksen

A Tor Book
Published by Tom Doherty Associates, LLC
175 Fifth Avenue
New York, NY 10010

www.tor.com

Tor® is a registered trademark of Tom Doherty Associates, LLC.

Library of Congress Cataloging-in-Publication Data

Dorsey, Candas Jane.
    A paradigm of earth / Candas Jane Dorsey.—1st ed.
        p. cm.
    "A Tom Doherty Associates book."
    ISBN 0-312-87796-X (acid-free paper)
    1. Human-alien encounters—Fiction.   2. Infants—Fiction.   3. Canada—
Fiction.   I. Title.

    PR9199.3.D56 P37 2001
    813'.54—dc21

                                                                2001034767

First Edition: October 2001

Printed in the United States of America

0   9   8   7   6   5   4   3   2   1

...every heart, every heart to love must come, but like a refugee...

—LEONARD COHEN, "ANTHEM,"
THE FUTURE

❃   ❃   ❃

Dedicated to the memory of

F. Jack Dorsey
December 30, 1914–September 17, 1997

and

Jaclyn M. Dorsey
November 18, 1943–December 24, 1997

and to all those
who helped my heart on its refugee journey,
most especially and always my belovéd Timothy

A
Paradigm
of
Earth

Prologue

Morgan isn't ready for the aliens to arrive. Occam's Razor has not yet cut deep enough. She must be pared to the minimum, and although she thinks her life is bleak now, there is much more that she can lose.

It is a conceit to think that the universe is preparing her specially, like a medieval saint, by these cruel trials, for her future role. The cosmos is random, and reaching for more randomness. She is thoroughly a part of it, and thus a part of its pains. The further truth: she is nothing special. Her value lies in her membership in the world.

Occam's Razor is sharp. Morgan bleeds real human blood.

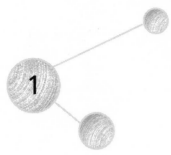

Morgan among the gargoyles

Every day Morgan moved among the living gargoyles.

Asam was seven. He had come for a new face. The surgeon would break his skull in half a hundred ways, would put him back in a shape his mother, thank goodness, wouldn't recognize. His mother had lived with and loved that face everyone else feared. Now it was Morgan's turn. Morgan held him in her arms, rocked him in the rocking chair.

"Will it hurt?"

"I think it will, Asam. Not during the operation, 'cause you'll be asleep then. But after, it will hurt for quite a while."

"I'm gonna be brave, I won't cry. Big boys don't cry."

"Big boys do so cry. Crying is good for you. If somebody says big boys don't cry, it's just 'cause they're scared of crying themselves. You cry all you need, okay?"

Pause. "Okay." Pause. "Will I be pretty after the operation?"

"I don't know. But you'll look more like other people."

"Will I still look scary?"

"No." It was useless to say he wasn't scary now. He knew what the kids in the hometown said. He knew the grimaces of adults on the street. He didn't know that when his mother, who was the repository for all his trust, first saw him after birth, she was sick and screaming with horror and disbelief. After that she had loved him fiercely, protective but not overprotective. Her husband (he didn't like to think of himself as the boy's father; it frightened him. "Big boys don't cry," he'd told Asam when he'd moved out of Asam's mother's life) had reacted calmly, but left after four years of calm, fathered another, very healthy child on another, younger woman. His wife was pregnant when he'd left; that is probably why he went. Asam's sister was a beautifully regular child, who loved her brother's face. She would probably cry when he came home, not to know him any more. Asam's half sister had never seen him. Her father didn't want her frightened.

Morgan rocked his wrecked head against her shoulder, sang a lullaby. His perfect hands held her sleeve desperately, unconsciously. She was for that moment as good as his mother, and closer.

"Will I have bad dreams?"

"Tonight?"

"When I'm asleep for the operation."

"I don't know. I don't think so. Let's ask the sleep doctor when he comes tomorrow. He's called the anesthetist, really. Can you say that?"

His palate made it a struggle, but he managed a facsimile.

"Good for you. He'll come tomorrow morning to see you and tell you what he does. When he comes, ask him about it. He'll know."

This boy had a tenderness and a strength which touched Morgan more than most. His mother had taught him a sturdy self-reliance. He forgot his face, some days. He had even learned a smile, which those who didn't know him would have found a horror. When Morgan saw it, her heart lifted with energy. She felt that despite the risks he must live. He is a survivor, like her.

journal:

Teaching the activities of daily living to the long-time and the newly handicapped: twisted, ill-made, malformed, mutated, burned, scarred, maimed, shocked, blinded, deafened, they are relentless: so am I.

One after the other comes, is terrifying at first, becomes usual, familiar, beloved. Then the people in the streets look bloated, obscene, like dolls, with their wide blank eyes, flat features.

Have mercy on the untouched ones, with our lonely perfection. We are united here in thoughts of pain and triumph.

The cat Marbl watches with wide blank eyes as I sift the litterbox with the tiny plastic shovel, my hands efficient, terrifyingly so after the hands of my loved ones; my skin moving like, better than, the supple pink plastic covering the microcircuitry of their prostheses. I dream of maimed kittens, clawless, pawless, hunchbacked, gargoyles, all needing to be taught how to scratch and shit, lick and purr, crunch and leap.

Today Asam, my newest patient, arrived, a gargoyle child, a rarity ("which Klaus of Innsbruck cast in bronze for me"?) in this day of repairable birth defects, seven years old, brought by his mother a thousand miles to this: O my heart. I had already loved him astonishingly as soon as I read his chart; after I met him I went away and vomited privately, in atonement for my smooth skin, my fine bones. Guilt is the friend of all we selfless, unscarred ones. A calm home with the perfect and beautiful is all the self-indulgence I allow myself. I don't work with animals, teaching them to scratch, I said to myself—and remembered the dream, while I was heaving and puking up nothing.

"It's not as if we're the first lovers to part," said Vik, putting a comforting hand on Morgan's shoulder. Morgan didn't turn. She would like to have continued the habit of receiving comfort from Vik, but the decision they had just made removed that option. She found a small apartment that day, moved the next, stored her boxes and big furniture, set up a barren and functional campsite in the small high-rise rooms. Said goodbye to the house and yard, the trees and flowers she had planted, the stained-glass window in the stairwell, the things she and Vik had bought together which she is leaving as she leaves Vik. Said goodbye to Vik.

"Will we see each other again?" Vik asked in a moment of nostalgia, as they hugged, remembering how it had been better.

"I don't know," said Morgan, remembering that they are not the first lovers to part.

✿   ✿   ✿

The night shift was coming on, chattering over report while Morgan read aloud to them the letters to the editor. "Listen to this," she said to Penelope. " 'If impressionable young men and women are exposed to these unnatural pleasures before they have had the opportunity to make a commitment to a spouse and family, society risks losing any chance to reproduce itself.' " The debate was over a proposed law to make twenty-five the legal age of consent for same-sex sexual activity. The bill had received first reading.

Penelope laughed. "As if that will do it!" Pen's mother was a lesbian and Pen was a member of ChoQ (Children of Queers).

"What's wrong with that?" said Jo-anne as she shrugged into her uniform jacket and looped her stethoscope around her neck. She was an LPN but she liked to look like a nurse, so she wore the same style of fatigues as the nurses did, but in white.

Morgan laughed, then she saw that Jo-anne wasn't joking. "Do you really think . . ."

"I can see why *you* wouldn't agree," said Jo-anne. "You people can't have children, so you recruit them."

Penelope guffawed. "I wish my mom could hear you."

Jo-anne looked hurt. "Say what you like," she said, "but it's not natural."

Morgan went home and looked at her empty apartment, no pictures on the walls. Only the day before, she had taken the accumulated journals from her early adulthood and presided personally over their shredding. If anything wasn't natural, it was bric-a-brac. She preferred her life undecorated at the moment, she thought. Be careful what you wish for, the Universe said quietly.

✿   ✿   ✿

Morgan was unable to suppress her relentless intelligence even though her father was dying. Convincing the others to go down for food, out for a walk, she sat holding his hand, noting every detail of the machinery of living to which they had him connected. Or, in this case, as she well knew but her mother tried hard not to believe, the machinery of death.

Morgan's profession for many years had taken her into rooms like this, and she was grateful for small differences—though her father could no longer talk, he awakened enough to clasp his hand around hers, her brother's, or her mother's. For now, that kept him immediate, and so she could not think of him as a case study. Much as she feared his dying, she was stuck with it.

✧   ✧   ✧

The next day Morgan went over to Personnel, in the main building of the hospital, to re-arrange her tithes and beneficiaries.

"Constance Morgan Shelby. Okay, here you are. Beneficiary Vik Pearce," said the clerk. "You'll be removing him from your insurance *and* your tithes?"

"Her. Yes."

"Her? You had a same-sex beneficiary?" The woman's gaze sharpened. Her "Contented Employee" button identified her as "Chelsea".

"Yeah, so?"

"You're the last one, then," said Chelsea, putting on her bifocals to squint at the computer screen. "I hate these things," she said. "I used to have contacts, but I can't afford bifocal contacts. They make the bottoms heavier so they stay in your eyes the right way up, you know."

"Have they de-insured them too?"

"Yeah. I'm going to tithe for them, but it takes time. I'm still paying off the dental surgery I had. Who's your new beneficiary?"

"Put down my brother Robyn for now." Morgan spelled his name.

"What about the tithe?"

"Direct it to savings. Did you know *tithe* means one-tenth?"

Chelsea laughed, an astonishingly loud snorting bray that made her co-workers in the open office smile: they'd obviously heard it before. "One-*tenth?* That's more like what's left over! Really?"

"Yeah, it's old English. There was even a deal where ten people used to live in the same place and be equally responsible for upkeep and behavior."

"Like a co-op? My parents lived in co-op housing."

"I guess."

Chelsea was still filling in the blanks on the database. "You broke up, huh?"

"Yeah."

"She getting married?"

"What?"

"Most of the other same-sexes, they're all getting married now. It's not easy being, you know . . ."

"Queer?"

"Geez, I haven't heard that in ages. Everybody says *that way* around here!"

Morgan grinned. "And you? Are you a friend of Dorothy's?"

Chelsea had barrettes in her greying hair. Morgan was teasing her, but to Morgan's surprise Chelsea blushed. "That's even older," she said. "My mom used to say that. Yeah, I used to be, but I sold Dorothy down the river about three years ago. I can't afford to take tea with Dorothy any more, the way things are."

"I'm sorry," said Morgan. "Anything I can do?"

"Nah, I'm dating a guy from Supply and Services. It's all right. It's bearable. I got the promotion. I'll be in an office with walls next week."

"Worth it?"

"No," said Chelsea, "but I was getting too old for the bar scene anyway, and I couldn't go to the Community Center, the surveillance would have told my boss. So . . ."

Morgan nodded. "Well, 'Dorothy' and I split up, yeah, but she's not getting married. She's just getting out. I always could date anybody, but . . . I'm not dating right now. My dad's in hospital . . ."

"Mine died last year," said Chelsea. "It's rough. That why your folks aren't on the beneficiary line?"

"Guess so. . . . Oh, well, never mind."

"Had a friend used to say that, when I was a kid. I'd forgotten. You been asleep for twenty years or something, you know all the old ones?"

It felt like it, but Morgan smiled. "Nah, just resting my eyes," and was rewarded with another snort of laughter.

"You're cute," said Chelsea. "Too bad I gave it up."

"It is too bad," said Morgan, "but you gotta live in this world, right?"

"Too right," said Chelsea. "There, I changed it so they can't go back and find Vik. Safer that way, these days, don't you think?"

"You can *do* that?" said Morgan, impressed.

"I was quite a computer geek in my youth," said Chelsea. "Why do you think I'm getting promoted?"

"Well," said Morgan, "have a good life."

"Yeah, you too. And if you ever see me again, ignore me." Chelsea was smiling, but she meant it.

"That dangerous, huh?"

"I work in a government office," said Chelsea. "You bet."

"Good luck," said Morgan. She probably should have been bitter about the woman's naked sell-out, but she only wished her well. Hard times required hard solutions.

      ✢   ✢   ✢

Morgan thought of her father as the sort of person others called "a sweet guy". Devoted to his family, kind, gentle, he worked all his life to ensure the comfort of his beloved wife, his daughter and son. Against her will, Morgan loved him dearly: against her will, because his sweetness seemed to her a parody of himself, of what he could have been if his wit, his grace had been in the service of something more than suburban life. *He coulda been a contenda,* she mocks herself, but even as he lies dying, consumed with the rebellion of his immature cells, she is impatient with his choices.

The resident reading the chart was new to the case. "He was a businessman?"

"Yes," said Morgan. "And he was in service clubs, and volunteered at the AIDS Network, and coached soccer."

Her brother had been listening, sniffling a little, staring at the erratic monitor screens, and now he said strongly, "He had an immense reverence for life—other people's and his own." And he went on to describe for the resident's benefit—the tag said "Murray" but the young doctor had introduced himself as Tom, and Morgan absently noted yet another person with a name made up of first names, like herself—their father's relentless history of goodness. The resident submitted to the flood.

"He sounds like a fine person," he said weakly, as Morgan's brother wound down.

"Yeah," said Morgan. "He's a real sweet guy."

❖　　❖　　❖

Her father's death was so quiet that they hardly noticed until the nurses and doctors ran in from the nursing station where alarms rang when the machines flatlined. Morgan would much later be glad they were all there, surrounding him. Her mother's tears gave way to screams, and the doctors finally had to sedate her. "How will I get by alone?" her mother sobbed. "How will I live?" Morgan understood the truth of another cliché: Morgan's heart went out to her mother. *Goes out, gets lost, cannot find its way back,* and instead, Morgan thought: *how we all live?* One breath, one pointless breath at a time.

❖　　❖　　❖

When the police came with the news, Morgan was first angry before afraid. One more body blow felt to start with like just a low blow, and she was at the morgue identifying her mother's body before she realized how alone she now was. Surprisingly, considering the violence with which she had died, her mother's face was unscarred and serene. As if she had faced death with respect.

What do you know about death and disaster? she thought as the benevolent flock of locustlike paramedics, police, and ambulance drivers who had clustered around the barely living body, failing to save her, now made their clumsy apologies to Morgan. *What caused the event. The people on the street who materialized from nowhere and watched with detachment. The tension built.*

When it is someone you love. When it is someone who is going to die. When it is someone who dies. The tension breaks.

"Yes, that is my mother," Morgan said, and, "I'll call you about the arrangements."

At the hospital where her father's body still lay, she met her brother. He was holding the diary in which their mother had scrawled: *I can't hold up without him. It's too much. The babies will be alright, but I have nothing. . . .* Morgan spells it *all right*, edited it in her thoughts, her anger flared at the word "babies", the idea that she and Robyn were nothing to their mother in her grief. But she saw the ruin of Robyn's emotions in his face, and long years of training had taught her to save souls.

"It's not conclusive," she said. "She could have just been driving badly."

Morgan was lying: she understood death's appeal, but she was trapped here helping her brother stay alive. She was fairly certain her mother wasn't so considerate.

When Morgan had the time, she would decide what she felt about that. As a rule, she suspected clichés.

After that, routine rescued them from too much thought. The police looked at the diary, but in context, in the midst of an entry that is an incoherent outpouring of raw grief, the lines Robyn had pointed out to Morgan seemed inconsequential, and they wrote "accident" on the form. *If they knew how much the insurance was,* thought Morgan savagely, *they wouldn't be so kind.* Out of honesty, she tried to say something to the corporal, but he shook his head. "I won't be part of an insurance investigation against a

21

dead woman," he said. "You've reported it, I've put it in the report—but look: it was raining, the street had oil on it, and the witnesses say she took the corner too fast. The guy in the car she just missed said she looked shocked. And your brother and you both say she wasn't the kind to take innocent people with her. The road was crowded, and it's pure luck that three other cars didn't get hit. It was an accident."

He looked at her kindly. "Don't be angry at her," he said. "It was an accident."

Morgan was not so sure, but the others forced her to accept that she would never be sure.

❧   ❧   ❧

Morgan's aunt was the executor of the wills. She called Morgan and Robyn to her crochet-intensive home to read them the instructions.

"Dear, please don't play with those."

Morgan put down the blown-glass poodle she was examining and turned to her aunt, expecting her next to offer cookies and milk. No such luck.

"Of course these bits don't apply: *if my wife should predecease me*—here's the gist of it. He left it all to her except the sentimental bequests: here's a list. It's your mother's will that matters to you now. She left you the house in town, Robyn, but of course she left Constance the other place."

"Other place?" Morgan looked at Robyn but he was equally puzzled.

"The old house. It's been empty since last fall. She had it rented to a religious group, you know."

"Auntie," said Robyn, "what are you talking about?"

"Oh," said their aunt, blushing faintly, "I forgot. She never told you. It's the place her mother left her, but there was never any money, of course. She hated it, anyway. It's where the school was."

"School?" It transpires that their grandparents, of whom they have been told little, had founded, and operated for a period of some years, a private charter school located in an old, historic mansion gone to seed, in the prairie city west of theirs. Her mother had now left this house to Morgan.

"I spent five years at university in Edmonton, paying rent, and she had a *house* there?"

"It's not a house per se, my dears. It's more of a . . . mansion. The church people's lease was for twenty years, anyway."

"She doesn't say a word all our lives, and now she leaves it to *me?*"

"She thought you might make something of it. She was talking to me about it just after your father died, you know."

"So she was planning this."

Her aunt was shocked. "Oh, you must never say that, dear. Such a terrible accident would never be her choice. She wanted to tell you about it finally. I convinced her it was the best thing. Whatever we felt, children deserve to know about their family history. But I suppose it doesn't matter now, really. What matters is that there is no tenant. It's perfect. You can sell it right away and buy something better."

"No," said Morgan. "I need a place to live. That will do as well as any."

❂   ❂   ❂

In the darkness the night before the funeral, contemplating the deaths of her parents, Morgan was suddenly bathed in light: icy, blue, fluorescing with meaning: an invisible light coldly revealing to her that she was wrong. She had been wrong about almost everything. About her parents, about Vik, about her name, herself, her brother . . . Only in her work had she found and held to the truth. Asam waited tonight for his surgery, Morgan waited for her parents' funeral—but it seemed she was scheduled for surgery too.

Under the relentless light of truth she was prepared by a wash of dread, made naked, wheeled to her own judgment. The surgeon whose knives would flay her was either the unfeeling cosmos or her own broken spirit, finally ready to admit defeat. Exposing under the relentless light of the operating theater the gargoyle face of Morgan's soul, peeling back the skin to reveal the deformities, the failures of structure.

Vik, the slightest of those. Some friends are not meant to be lovers. Morgan, knowing this much sooner than Vik, should have given her the courtesy, if nothing else—good manners, if not love—of the truth. But Morgan had lied to herself, said, I can expect no better: my passions are not realizable—and because of that lie had waited years for Vik to get sick of the deficits and find anger, with that anger to prise herself from Morgan's ruthless charity.

From a childhood adoration which had been boundless and unassailable, Morgan had grown in adulthood to despise her father for being good. Why is good hated, and by what? Good is hated by failure, by evil, by despair because it cannot be sullied. Morgan hated him for being successful at kindness, where she always failed, and so she had let him slip away without telling him the central and more real truth, that she loved him desperately and that his kindness had kept her alive.

What Morgan had seen as neurotic, unhealthy, soft these last few days, responding to her suspicion that it was her mother's unbelievable preference to run her car into a bridge rather than stick around to do what was expected of her, to live, Morgan now understood to simply be love: love for a simple man who chose not to be intellectual from a simple, strong, quiet woman. The yielding she had seen as his frailty was his strength, a strength Morgan didn't have, had never had; her mother's grief was the artifact of that same love, and Morgan had mocked it. Now she saw her own smallness instead.

The surgeon of the Universe is relentless and in this cold night she welcomed that decisive cautery. It did not occur to her to seek a second opinion, a more kindly practitioner who might have told her that extremities of grief are not always the best spotlights on the truth. Instead, she felt freed of all her unsavory attachments, like a conjoined twin whose other half is finally cut away.

Through her father's long dying she had thought like one of the machines which tended him. She had responded to his last,

tender conversations (that saying-of-what-had-to-be-said imperative) but not wholeheartedly: she had chosen to be safe: safety
was petty in the face of the absolutes, but she had valued it more.
Through her mother's great grief and loss Morgan had stood in
judgment, thinking cool irritated thoughts about over-
dramatization, about excess: reacting with ego to the realization
that her mother prized her father over her children: unwilling to
believe that such a great grief could exist, because unwilling to
accept the love underlying it.

If I could love someone like that, Morgan groped her way to
understanding, I could feel that; as it is I can only scorn it. She
felt grubby and dishonest. She imagined that her mother, after
death, had heard her crabbed, sour thoughts and had had one
more source of grief: her daughter's betrayal. *I am sorry,* Morgan
offered up uselessly—while she believed in the wheel, she didn't
believe her words mattered now. Only what she did and withheld:
her love withheld, her intense belief that her mother and father
were the pillars of the Universe—and finally, held back in denial
for all those wasted years of distance, she had come up to and
accepted the grave catalog of her stupidity, ignorance, and cruelty.

Her name was part of the betrayal she had lived. In the world,
she had always gone by Connie, Constance, but she was not constant. She was withholding, fluid, elusive, evasive. She had come
over the years to a state where she gave nothing which cost her
anything. Everything came from the surface and nothing from a
loving heart, a heart which could love. *I will not be Constance, a
constant lie, any more,* Morgan thought, and she turned to the
name by which she had often thought of herself, her secret central
name, Morgan, the name of the witch who betrayed. If in the
depths of magic there was a true-hearted Morgan le fay about
whom the Christian world had constructed a lie, our Morgan had
not met her yet.

She thought of herself as the witch, thought of who the witch
was: a sour, twisted, externally beautiful sorcerer who used the
flesh of others for her binding spells, who fucked her brother
Arthur: Morgan has not imitated her with Robyn in the bodily
sense of the word, but now decides she had in the old slang sense

fucked him over. By being that elder sister and not loving him as she could have, she had withheld something vital, some heart of love without which he grew into less than he could have. For a moment she saw how it could have been, her arm around the small body instead of holding him apart: the gifts she could have given him of protection, of song, of support, of acceptance: instead he had been blinded, blanded by his unimportance, had sought out insignificance and tried to live inside the lines. Perhaps even if she had tried he would have slipped away into mediocrity—but she didn't try.

It took more time to record these reassessments in her journal than it did to have them. Morgan started by crying, but she immediately condemned the impulse as false, the tears as crocodile tears—as false as her grief, which seems only the costume of a vast disinterest. She had the right only to desolation until she learned to love those she kept at arm's reach. She was empty and shorn of illusions. In an older time she would have cut her hair to accept it, and gone on, but she kept her desolation instead as a kind of secular penance—she didn't think that word because she was not from that Roman Catholic tradition, even from any Christian tradition which would exact penance. She felt instead remorse: a vast repetitive wasteland of remorse, wheeling like an Einsteinian curved universe to surround her every way she looked, except one thin path back to Asam, the only being she had properly—that is to say objectively, unselfishly—loved, even a little, on the face of the whole earth.

In the years with the gargoyle children, symmetry had been the goal of countless observed surgeries, and Morgan's cold epiphany was in this tradition. She did not question it, or the breakage needed to effect it. She would have to leave here, find a place where she could do no harm, where perhaps she could learn to improve a little eventually. Tomorrow after the funeral she would go to see Asam one last time, and before she could betray him (she knew this as a conceit, and easily upturned into another betrayal—that of desertion—by a certain acrobatics, but she can't see another way) she would say goodbye. Then she would take her inheritance—born of the love of others—and use it to try to make recompense, living in the daily memory of her failure to understand.

Do no harm was the mantra by which she finally put herself to sleep, curled into herself in misery, Marbl—steadfast and concerned—perched on her hip. It didn't occur to her to think that her plans were actually to do good, to act, to be active. Even if she weren't too tired to think of it, she would not have allowed herself that hubris. At the moment humility was a fetish she had hung around the overblown neck of her recalcitrant ego as the carcase of the duckling is hung around the neck of the predatory farm dog: she understood nothing of its worth or its distortions. She was tired, she was invisible—

She was asleep: and she had no dreams.

        ✿   ✿   ✿

Morgan's brother stood beside her through the brief ceremony. At one point he buried his face in his hands, then shook himself and stood upright again.

"Go ahead," Morgan whispered automatically. "You'll feel better." She herself was far away, thinking about Asam in his little room, the machines pumping. She had to think that machines can keep some life going.

The twin white coffins were grotesque and macabre. She wished her aunt had some good taste. Then she thought, with cunning and detachment, *well, it's so people can mourn better.* The waxed faces were arid. She walked almost past before she realized she had better look while she could. Standing beside her father's coffin, she gazed at the face, trying to find something. The skin was tight over the fine bones, but of course he was the color of bad stage make-up, and nothing was left of his integral tension, what made him real. Not a new thought, but what could she think? She had had no practice in last words.

She turned to her mother's body, put her hands on the side of the coffin, leaned over slightly to look at the frail skin bolstered by make-up for the last time. She wanted to make some final gesture but she only managed to fumble and drop her damp, crumpled handkerchief into the coffin where it lay flamboyantly on the red silk. Her mother would have laughed at that. Morgan had for herself too an insane desire to laugh, insane because she knew if she laughed she would never stop, they would put her in a little room like Asam's but softer, where she would scream and pound her thoughts out on the padded hinges and never get anywhere any more. She must stay in the void where it was safe. She picked up the handkerchief and put it in her pocket.

She had to get out of there. The rest of the relatives were waiting to file past. She turned to her brother. He was unselfconscious now about the tears that rolled down his face.

"I'm going now," she said curtly. "I can't stay here. I'll call you."

He reached a hand for her in protest but she walked away, out of the perfumed chapel into the dull sunlight. The forest fires in the north were sending a pall of smoke across the city. She thought, *that's appropriate for the burning-day.*

Home, she looked around the modern apartment, where she had taken comfort in its increasing emptiness, then walked to the basement storage room to get her suitcase. It was big and made of leather; it had belonged to her mother, who used to travel on business. She quickly packed the few belongings left there. Her trunk and furnishings had already been picked up by the shippers; the cat now went into the carrier, she handed the keys in to the manager with no regret. Morgan took the bus to the hospital, a route she had ridden twice or more every day for longer than she liked to think. The driver knew her and nodded sympathetically.

"Sorry to hear about your folks," he said. "You must be feeling pretty bad."

She nodded wordlessly. He can't tell, she thought. I suppose it doesn't show. She supposed it was melodramatic to believe she didn't exist any longer but she in fact knew that was true.

At the hospital she left her suitcase, and Marbl in her carrier, with the porter, went up to Asam's room. The machines were silent, rolled back and hooked to nothing. The carbolizing team was making up the bed. The maid knew her, looked for a moment at her, then jerked her head aside. *Gone,* she meant.

There was only one place he could go. Morgan had just sent her parents there.

The supervisor was surprised to see her, and solicitous. "Are you all right to be back at work so soon?"

"No, I quit," Morgan said.

There were a few more words but she thought as they were said, *that's the end of* this *story.*

"Bye-bye, Connie," the porter said as Morgan hefted the suitcase.

Bye-bye Connie, thought Morgan. She thought the smoke must have been irritating her eyes more than she knew, because she felt tears start. She walked toward the bus stop, her body twisted with the unevenly balanced weight of the luggage, her tears out of her control. She thought, *I have come to the end of the route;* she thought, *there's no transfer.* Still she had considered somewhere else to go, had decided she would go somewhere, so she snorted at the foolishness of her own melodrama.

She would go where she had planned to go, to live in the basement flat of her parents' house until the estate was executed, and then to this strange new home the Universe had thrust upon her. It was apparently huge, big enough to share with other orphans and failures. She would subject herself to service, and routine, and she would ignore herself as much as possible. After all, she thought, there must be a reason she was still breathing. Every thought told her to stop, every instinct perpetuated breath. She put one foot in front of the other.

She had nothing left to do but that. *It should be,* she thought, *all I desire.*

Now, Morgan was a fugitive from the war with life. She had escaped from the world of the damned, the red brick hospital where the twisted bodies and tortured souls of the gargoyles and other ruined ones were sent to live and sometimes to die. She had escaped the wake of torment after the death of her parents. She had escaped the minor needs—to care, be cared for, to live with happiness. They were all irrelevant to her: she, her suitcase and her cat fading away into the distance rather romantically, although really it was more than a month before she could put herself on a Greyhound bus, and the journey was mundane, even ridiculous: infants crying in their mothers' arms, large countrymen with their tractor caps cocked back on their balding heads, fussy old people insisting on the seats near the driver, pre-teenaged children with a gross sense of importance traveling alone for the first time, and Morgan.

❋   ❋   ❋

Morgan can see that she is not human. It is clear. She has kept the external shell, but everything has been scraped out, there is a void there, an alien void, outer space made internal, and she wonders whether she will ever have the courage, or energy, to explore it. As the poet said, *the energy needed to live / alone is so great.*

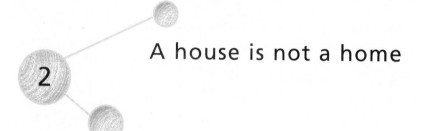

A house is not a home

Morgan dragged her heavy suitcase out of the car while the driver unloaded the cat carrier, and stood looking at the huge house. It looked like a mansion; in fact, it had not been a family home since before the days of her grandparents' school, and they had told her it had most recently been used as a monastic community of some kind. Morgan hoped that the peace still lived there, even though the godly did not. She was so tired. The weeks of dismantling her parents' lives were over now, the estate divided, and her share (both realized and expected) sunk almost completely into the essential refurbishing of this great shaggy lumbering Edwardian dormitory, a shabby relic a hundred years old and counting, where she hoped to do some good, eventually.

The house stood inside an overgrown yard surrounded with a rusty wrought-iron fence. It faced south, fronting onto a cul-de-sac avenue along the edge of the riverbank. Morgan left her suitcase by the gate, took the cat carrier and walked across the narrow street to the ribbon of grass boulevard. In front of her a dramatic drop two hundred feet to the river was staged by a small shelf of greenery alongside the water, where bicycle paths and picnic tables attested to the urban parkland vision—but the picnic tables were weathered from green into grey, and up on the grass, the bench overlooking the river had been carved deeply with graffiti. She showed Marbl the view, but the cat was complaining loudly, and turned her back like Gertrude Stein.

Morgan smiled without humor. "Guess you're telling me not to avoid it any more," she said, and the cat was silent at last. They returned to the gate and Morgan lifted the latch. It was stiff, and caught briefly, then released with a musical pop. She kicked the gate shut behind her, climbed up the three stairs to the wide veranda, and unlocked the heavy wood door with the leaded-glass central oval.

The house was still entirely empty but for the jumble of her belongings, stacked haphazardly in the living room by the moving company. She left her suitcase and Marbl's carrier in the sun-drenched hall where the stained glass and prisms of the door panel cast rosy blocks and rainbow patterns over the scratched wood paneling and chipped plaster.

The huge living room was on the left of the door. A dining room mirrored it on the other side. Both were separated from the hall by leaded-glass doors. Behind the living room, a smaller room, completely wood-paneled up to a picture rail, and with piano windows of stained leaded glass, had been converted to an office with telephone and data lines. Morgan nodded. This would be hers, a kind of household command center.

The dining room was separated from a huge kitchen and pantry by pocket doors. Behind the kitchen was a mud porch, a utility room, and a small bedraggled greenhouse with broken panes. Two other doors led toward the center of the house. Hearing Marbl's howls begin again and echo in the empty hall, Morgan left these rooms unexplored, returned to her annoyed pet.

"It's okay, sweetie," she said soothingly, "we'll find a place to sleep." She made sure the door was latched.

In the back of the hall there was an ancient brass-fitted elevator with a telescoping metal door. She walked up the stairs behind it.

One of the rooms had long windows looking out onto a small balcony littered with fallen leaves. Hanging against one of the windows on a leather thong was a small dusty metal ring filled with a colored glass mosaic. At the wind of the opening door, it bumped gently against the window like a moth trying to get out. Small, inside it, was the image of the prairie, with its warm clear light sky, rendered in epoxied shards with an artistry not slavish to detail but for that even more exact. Morgan, seeing it for the first time, was momentarily paralyzed. Then her eyes blurred with tears.

She didn't know she had tears any more. She went to the hall and got her suitcase. The hollow bang as she set it down in the prairie room was a punctuation mark. This would be her place. She brought the cat carrier up, closed the door behind her, and opened the carrier. Marbl came out wondering into the empty room and, seeing refuge, dived for the closet where she crouched, her complaining *miaouw* echoing.

The stained glass was like a raindrop caught in the curve of metal, a lens making the landscape tiny. Or a teardrop? She laughed shortly at her own conceit.

❖   ❖   ❖

The best house computer she could afford was old and clunky, with no virch and no smart-chip capability, upgrading the hundred-year-old house to the minimum standard of smart, but it was adequate. After a few days, Morgan found herself in a habit of late-night game playing: always the repetitive, patterning games to put her in trance.

The night she found herself playing the game and weeping, she took all the games off her partition and the common area. She might not have been good at grieving, but she was damned if she was going to let the machine do it for her.

Instead, she decided, she would revive and keep her journal, write in it every night. A journal on paper, not in the machine. She had enjoyed, or at least found release in, journal writing before; now it was a survival device and she approached it as a discipline, the same way she had the requirement of her previous profession to write daily report: doggedly, and with a cool documentary flavor.

She wrote about the renovations, the recurring real estate administrivia, the way the cats were eliminating the mouse problem, the motion of light on the surface of the river, or the sweep of an advertising spotlight across the sky. She didn't include in the diary her frustration at how the constant low-level business torment that remained as the final detritus of her parents' wills was made more difficult by the necessity to either see or avoid her brother—she chose avoid, usually—and if she mentioned it at all on the pages of the journal, she tried to be dispassionate about the cool anguish of her restless nights.

She took her duty as a recorder seriously. Some details were not important.

❀   ❀   ❀

Morgan's room was plain, almost barren, a habit into which she settled. A low wide platform in one corner was the bed, covered with, and with pillows of, plain-colored and Indian-print cottons. Against one wall were the desk and the short oak filing cabinet she had taken from her father's office. A woven Cree rug near the bed covered part of the hardwood floor. The white walls were bare except for the colors cast by the sun through the tiny piece of stained glass.

Soon she was no longer completely unencumbered. In a few weeks, she gathered some moss—of the human sort. Delany, her close friend all the time in university and fitfully since then, had been living in adapted housing that had just been "discontinued": the polite word for sold out from under her to the highest bidder. Morgan made her the first of the tenants in her penitential boarding-house. Then, by chance in the Swedish prefab-furniture store, she met Russ, back in the city from Indonesia and looking for a house to share: she recognized him despite the beard and the heavy tan—and the streaks of white in hair and beard. A friend of Russ's, Jakob, recommended because he was a dancer and needed a studio and Morgan's house had big rooms, turned out to be someone she had worked with years ago in an art therapy program, canceled during funding cuts.

Jakob discovered (with suitably dramatic shrieks of joy) the tiny gymnasium the school had long ago created in the attic when converting the brick house, and immediately claimed it for a practice room. At one end there was a loft which became his sleeping place. He hung it about with silk scarves and gaily-colored cloths. His bed was a pallet on the floor, spread with a brocade throw. He was putting up mirrors on one gym wall, and a *barre*, had rented a sander to smooth the floors. From his area outward, all the surfaces in the house were starting to be covered with a layer of fine wood dust, dotted with the pawprints of cats.

Russ was moving into the small room upstairs, at the back. Nothing was there right now but cardboard boxes containing the modular furniture, ready to be assembled, that he had been buying when he and Morgan happened on each other. He had gone hiking: would really move in next week, he'd said.

Delany chose the room beside the elevator. She was in angry revolution against ground-floor living after years in the handicapped-people's-housing complex; the elevator allowed her to take this second-floor room with the big north-facing windows giving her an elevated perspective of the deep ravine behind the house. The room's ell shape had been formed decades ago by removal of walls between three smaller rooms—in the school, it had been a common room for the teachers. In one arm of the ell was her special bed; in the other, in the light from the biggest windows, her paints and easel. The rest would arrive on the weekend, when her brothers were going to help her move. From that room, for three days, had come plaster dust and paint fumes from the renovations, while three grumpy workers had taken only an hour to install a wheel-washer for Delany's wheelchair in the mud room at the side door.

Morgan looked into doorways at random, walking through and through the house, wearing down her paths. Occasionally she encountered one of the cats doing the same. Marbl, the one she had brought with her, was five years old, lonely and tentative. Dundee and Seville, the five-month-old marmalade twins they had all gone together to pick out at the SPCA, were exuberant and raucous. Morgan felt a kinship to Marbl, who stayed close to the walls, hissed when the twins tumbled into her full-tilt on one of their rampages. What was she doing filling with all these beings a house meant to be quiet and insulating?

Then why didn't I sell the house and buy some solitary apartment with no room for anyone but me and my cat? her interior voice mocked her. *Methinks the lady doth protest too much . . .*

Morgan settled in the kitchen, where big windows looked out over calm trees in the back yard, the tumbledown garden shed, and the weathered ramshackle fence along the lane. The rain clouds that had threatened all day had loosed into a sheet of soft grey silk whipping across the greenery. The air blowing through the open screen smelled damp and alive.

Morgan knew she was alive because she slept and woke, ate and shat, still trembled at infinity. But she experienced the rain as everything else, like the cat in the hallway, looking through open doors at the real universe. She was waiting for something to teach her to go there. To invite her to go there. She couldn't go without leave. She didn't live there any more.

✿   ✿   ✿

Morgan wanted the world to end. She sat on the riverbank in the clear dusk and wished the glittering buildings along the curve to explode, wanted the towers of commerce to topple, not from economic but from physical decay, a decay like that in her heart, she thought, and seeing the towers intact after all that destructive thought she smiled with the same anger at herself, wondering if she would want to be on top of such a falling edifice, thinking it might be an interesting way to die, wondering if any dying can be interesting, wanting the world to die and leave her senseless.

How maudlin of me, she thought, and the word started her considering Maudlin and Bedlam, their close relationship, the prisons of the mad: she thought of the old English song *Mad Maudlin goes on dirty toes, for to save her shoes from gravel. . . .*

Mad Morgan, she thought, *how I wish it were so.*

The mad have an easy time of it, she thought; *they can let go. They can let the towers of their own minds crumble with no resistance. They are free of whatever damning necessity keeps me sane, keeps me in this prison of my body, this quiet madhouse, this disguise. Where do they get the courage? Just to go crazy, to leave their old world behind, without caring who they leave there crying?*

Like the dead, she thought, *they are free to desert us.*

I wonder what it takes to make me into one of those people who just disappear one day, she asked herself. *I quit my job, brought the cat with me, didn't just go out to the store one night and vanish, sadly missed by loving family, only to be found ten or twenty years later, found by accident, in New Zealand or somewhere, with a new name.* Usually also they have a new spouse, more kids, another job, she remembered. Changing your life isn't easy.

She thought about the big leather suitcase she packed in her tiny apartment. She thought about the time she spent packing her parents' belongings, dividing them into categories, what to take, what to keep, what they wanted whom to have, what to give away, what to leave in the basement for her brother Robyn to sort when he had become accustomed to living in the house he inherited.

She thought that those who desert us leave us a terrible burden of which to dispose. She remembered the cartons and green plastic garbage bags readied for the Goodwill truck to collect, the furniture carried out to its merciful maw by two amiable, slow-witted men who knew how to be kind, so much kindness that she wondered how used they were to taking away the furniture of the dead, comforting the living. How many graveyards did they dismantle every day? She thanked them for their work, and their kindness, then left the ravaged house, put the key back through the mail slot for Robyn, and fled.

For the first time she thought of it as flight, but she sidestepped that thought too, and stood up from her cramped seat on the bench, went back to the house, where she had left the desk light burning in her ascetic room, where dusk was coming persistently in at the windows but was kept at bay by the yellow skirt of light. She lay down on the cotton-covered bed and went suddenly to sleep, like a baby.

✧　　✧　　✧

She dreams of the six o'clock news, telling her that the aliens have landed, the aliens have her parents' calm dead faces but she is not afraid. "What do you want?" she asks. "It's not easy to go away without packing anything," her father replies. Her mother says, "We'll be in New Zealand if you need us." The skyscrapers are impossible icicles of flesh; they fall slowly and silently and never break against the ground. There is an indigo mist around them, and it forms into a clutch of faces. Her parents' bodies are blowing away, leaving only their smiles, like the Cheshire Cat—

❖   ❖   ❖

—and she wakened with Marbl sleeping on her bed, purring a little.

As Morgan woke the purring faded, the cat went more soundly to sleep. It was full night and despite the room warmth Morgan was shivering. She stumbled up from the bed and into the cone of light where she sat down like a prisoner, tears drying on her face: the interrogation was not a success, where were you on the night of the—

—and the cat Marbl, wakened too by Morgan's upheaval from the bed, raised her head and meouwed once, then put her head on her crossed paws and watched with an unblinking stare while Morgan weathered the agony of not weeping.

❖   ❖   ❖

Finally the sawdust was all vacuumed away, the varnish smell aired out enough to be background, the last contractor's bill paid with the last of Morgan's inheritance, and they had the house to themselves. Morgan walked the corridors at midnight, checking that the windows were latched and the doors locked.

The house felt empty despite the people working or sleeping behind each door. Morgan realized she missed her dead—but in a distant way: she too was missing, presumed dead. She was a set of behaviors without a person inside. Since her night of self-scourging established a baseline of self-loathing, she had not allowed herself to go searching for the missing self. She did not yet believe she needed anything she had lost that night. But the truth was coming for her, stalking her through the silent corridors of her life as softly as the cat Marbl who followed her on her rounds.

One night as she passed Delany's room, Delany opened the door. "Tea time?" she said, wheeling herself out into the corridor and toward the elevator. Marbl ducked into the room behind her, and Delany laughed. "You'll get paint on your paws again, you silly thing!"

"Do you want me to get her out of there?"

"Sure. Last time she left little prints on the new floor. Teal, very fetching and old-fashioned; I'm gonna leave them there— but perhaps best if not continually augmented in other colors. I'm working in tiger yellow today."

"That's the same combination I have in that Simpson water-color," said Morgan. "I should leave her to it." But she was chasing Marbl as she spoke.

Marbl was a fluid cat, always had been good at getting under the furniture. Morgan hadn't been in this room since the renos were done and the furniture came, and she saw it from lower than her usual eye level, bent over to look for the cat, which meant perhaps at Delany's usual eye level. The furniture was wood, and old, and had been ruined with paint. It looked, not like family hand-me-downs, but like some theater set seen up close: spattered and textured with paint and stain; what from the corridor looked like a patina of age seemed from three inches away to have been engineered that way from a standing start. Morgan was uneasy with its falsity.

"Like the antiquing," she said to Delany. Delany wheeled back in, startling Marbl out from under the only easy chair in the room—which was stacked with art magazines and painting materials. The walls were still bare, white and smooth.

"Yeah, my brother and his ladies did it. Got the idea from one of those back-to-the-twentieth-century home decor mags. I plan to reverse it as soon as I can afford to get it stripped. The original finish was a beautiful rich dark brown. Fumed oak. Can you believe it?"

Morgan laughed. "I am *so* glad you said that. I was wondering if you'd had an aesthetics transplant since university!" She lunged for Marbl, who, emerging from behind a stack of canvases with their faces turned to the wall, was poised to leap up onto the painting table, and caught her just as she left the ground. One paw had indeed been leaving tiger yellow prints already, and Morgan wiped it with a paint rag. The cat protested with a tiny plaintive mew, and Morgan hugged her and petted her in apology.

Marbl hated cuddling, pushed away from Morgan with soft paws, her claws retracted. Morgan scratched under her chin and she half-purred, still struggling. "Ach, ye poor beastie!" Delany crooned, laughing. "Doomed to have affection lavished upon you."

Morgan wasn't listening. She was struck by the image on the easel, the only image in the room. The rich yellow light, created with rays of the "tiger yellow" which was almost saffron where the thick smears of paint had folded, cascaded behind a dark figure which, though small, dominated the canvas. In front of the figure, however, in a reversal of traditional road images, there was only darkness, and it was clear that the figure itself saw none of the light outlining it. Below the feet of the figure there was a brown tabby cat, realized in meticulous detail, almost as if it had been created hair by hair. Though the painting was clearly unfinished, it already had a disturbing, raw challenge about it.

"Marbl! You're a star!" Morgan said, and Marbl, as always when her name was spoken, meowed a fierce alto response. Morgan and Delany laughed together, and Morgan reluctantly drew away from the image. Delany waited for her to go out, wheeled through the door, and then turned to pull the pocket door shut.

"It's very good," said Morgan.

"She comes in and models now and again," said Delany, and Morgan was not sure if Delany misunderstood accidentally or on purpose. Morgan let Marbl go, and the cat poured down from her hands to the stairs and leapt away, vanished through the open door of Morgan's room.

"Hmph," said Morgan. "She doesn't think much of our company!"

"She only loves me for my paints," said Delany, and wheeled ahead to the elevator.

Morgan watched her, and something readjusted in her mind. When Delany said, "I need room to paint," Morgan had unconsciously supplied her laughing, joking, physically-limited friend with a talent for minor landscape watercolor, hobbyist pap, or at best the kind of interchangeable scenic painting loved by the decorators of show homes. She should have known better: the Delany she knew in university was wild and angry: her meticulous good manners, obviously learned since, had misled even Morgan.

Delany turned. "Coming?" Morgan, startled, hopped into the elevator after her, and they went down.

✿   ✿   ✿

Morgan sat at the house terminal in the house office, working out budgets. She was setting up the monthly funds transfer to the teenager who had the recycling route, and sighing at the bank balance, when Russ breezed in to pay his rent.

"Here, I'd like to pay for six months right now," he said, "while I have it. You know how I am." Morgan opened an entry port into her bank account into which he could direct his deposit.

"I won't even argue about what a bad money-management choice that is," said Morgan, hitting the *enter* code. "I need the money. Look at this. All that insurance, and I still am going to have to get a job."

"The insurance paid out?" He perched on the edge of her chair to enter his password, and the transfer flashed as complete. "There," he said with satisfaction.

"Yes, there was no way to prove that her diary was a suicide note. Robyn got on their case. I wouldn't have, but hey, now I have a house, right?"

"Don't be bitter, sweetie, it doesn't suit you."

She turned her bleak look on him, but he glared back, and finally she smiled slightly.

"Fine. I have a house. But the settlement was spent before it

41

arrived. Now there will be no money for food or utilities, unless I get work soon. When did all these laws get passed, anyway?"

"Laws?"

"New death duties. Inheritance taxes on top of those. The dead pay, the living pay. Taxes on insurance pay-out, despite the policy. Property tax surcharges."

"They passed while you were fighting the sex laws and human rights code violations, and I was fighting racism and the tightening of immigration. We were busy. And face it, did you ever think you'd have to worry about the joys of having money?"

"Problem is, I don't really have money. The truly rich pay almost nothing at all. The accidentally fortunate, with no long-term capital to buffer expenditures, are dinged just like the working poor. Well, I've had a windfall, like some perverse lottery of the damned, and paid the price of it, and here I am."

"You might find a good job. Something fun."

"If I can wait for one I like. I may not have time to be picky."

"How long can you hold out?"

"About three more months and I'll be on my face."

"And such a lovely face it is too."

She glared at him and he laughed. "That's what I heard my boss say to the supervisor of engineering yesterday," he said. "I thought she'd kill him. But, unfortunately, she didn't."

"How's it going there, anyway?" Russ had returned to the government office where he worked before his "sabbatical" overseas; he spent his days now programming computers and creating net interfaces to inform or, as he darkly grumbled, mislead the public. Morgan figured he'd last a year, two at most.

"I'll survive."

"Don't we all." But she knew that the answer to that was *no: we don't all survive.*

❀   ❀   ❀

The sky was dark blue in summer intensity when the aliens arrived. In the park down by the river the cyclists on their intricate machines crisscrossed the bicycle trails. Above them on the bluff, looking down over the river toward the towers of the city, sat Morgana le fay, home from the wars.

If ever a vessel sat empty, scoured by sand and fire, it was Morgan then as she sat looking over the city. Sun's heat only accentuated her inner chill; she watched the cyclists with the detachment of despair. If suicide had been a word in her lexicon she would have been spelling it, but it was not, so she sat on the riverbank looking out without emotion across the valley.

She had come from a long distance, and she felt the distance, every moment of it, as she waited for the story she did not know was about to happen.

Though that day the aliens had arrived, she didn't know it then, could think of little but her twisted gut. The wind was blowing all the day, out of the south-east, blowing the sky clean of clouds and scouring it dark, blowing as if to wipe the city away. A day or three ago something she ate was wrong, coursed through her body, migraine headache this day and the day before, then suddenly, after she had retreated from the riverbank gale, as she sat reading the newspaper, but starting from the back page as always, the knot loosened in her belly, into a rush of gas and diarrhea, barely controlled, and she missed the front-page news until hours later. Then Russ came in, excited, to her room where she sat on the bed, leaning on the wall at its head, knees up, writing sporadically at a letter between runs to the toilet.

"Fantastic, eh?"

"What?"

"The big news!"

"What?"

"You don't know? Haven't you seen the paper? Heard the news? It's practically being shouted in the street!"

"So what, already? I've been sick half the day. I can't stand the noise when my head aches."

"The alien, the spaceman who's come to see us! We really are not alone!"

She shouldered him aside, tangentially remembering her dream as she did so, and ran for the discarded newspaper, and sure enough, front page and whole first section said it:

We Are Not Alone!
Man From Outer Space Lands in Zurich!
Alien Makes Visit to Peace Talks!

The blurry photo could as easily have been anyone, though the color balance was all wrong for human skin. The blue aliens in her dream had had her parents' faces: that was obvious symbolism; this was just coincidence. She was too ill to read the small print. She went back to bed.

❖   ❖   ❖

Someone left the newspaper open to the help wanted ads, and Morgan saw there—she thought Russ must have marked it for her—a child care job. Teaching certificate required. Working with disadvantaged adult clients. A child care job with adults? Must be low-IQ, thought Morgan, as she printed out a résumé and sent it off.

Getting an interview was unexpected. Her application had been so perfunctory that it was almost worse than no effort at all; clearly, her subconscious had hoped to sabotage the process. But now there she was, walking through the door of an unlabeled government building. There were decontam procedures at the entry, strong security. She thought the interviews must be far from the job site: who would keep kids in a place like this? But inside, the building opened out into a giant atrium, with huge trees and running water in a courtyard big enough to hold—holding, in fact—a couple of smaller buildings.

She was placed in a waiting area with benches, under one of the clusters of trees. Small birds flitted through the branches. Morgan felt itchy, watched. She looked up, around, irritated at herself for the cliché: if she was thinking about surveillance, why not use her mind, rather than the hair on the back of her neck? But there were no cameras. She turned impatiently, and under the thick branches of the tropical mini-forest there was someone crouching, watching.

Adult body, to be sure, but certainly childlike pose and gaze. She had just met one of the "clients", she thought, unsurprised. In the green shadows under the boughs, the pale skin looked blue.

"Hello, person," said the being, sounding like a recording. Autism sometimes presents this way, Morgan thought, and waited for more evidence.

"Hello, person to you too," said Morgan.

" 'You too you too you too.' That's okay, just stay right there while I look at you.' " The second imitated voice was deeper and differently accented: Mennonite Manitoban? Morgan thought. There were many causes of this kind of imitativeness.

"I'm not going anywhere," Morgan said. "Are you going to come out and let me look at *you*?"

The being sighed exaggeratedly, another imitation, and crawled out from the jungle.

The skin *was* blue.

Morgan was looking at one of the aliens.

"Blue," she said, involuntarily.

"Blue," it said. "Blue blue blue blue?" The face was blue, but blue in a thick undertone to ivory, an undertone that took no life away from the rich texture of the skin. The eyes were dark. The hair was long, and knotted behind the head, carelessly through itself. Strands were loose. They were a dark blue, close to black, the way dark brown is close to black. Gleaming dark strands. Morgan's own long hair was tied in a knot; she wondered who had taught the visitor that trick, not foolish enough to believe that such details are universal.

"That about covers it. What's your name?"

"Blue."

"My name is Morgan. What is your name?"

"Blue. Blue. My name is—Blue." In Morgan's voice.

This was very silly. Not at all like in all those SF books. Exactly like. What was she doing here? This was stupid.

Another voice, from another being this time: "You're hired."

"Say what?"

"You're hired." A grey man—no, thought Morgan, a man in a silver-grey suit, a man with prematurely white-grey hair and grey eyes, figures of speech could too easily become real around here—stood on the path behind them.

"I haven't even had my interview yet."

"Yes you have," and he gestured at Blue. "Blue hasn't responded to any of the other candidates. Hasn't talked, answered, approached. You have clearly been chosen."

"Some selection process."

"Yes, well, I'm not too keen on it myself, but we've done all the screening we can do at our end," Mr. Grey said grimly. "We had to have someone the . . . *Blue* would work with. *Blue*'s been on a work-to-rule campaign lately."

"Is this the first time Blue has named . . . um, itself?"

"Yes."

Morgan had a job. It almost interested her.

❀   ❀   ❀

The dream is a murky sea of waterlike air or airy water, hazy and dark blue as the sky at dusk on a winter's day. Morgan is swimming. She alternates between a sense of freedom and a terrible drowning panic. Below her, she sees a dark form curled into a fetal position, sinking slowly, spinning. She calls sharply, and dives. When her hand grasps the naked, livid shoulder, which despite her expectation of cadaverous cold is hot under her fingers, the motion of grasping—

—woke her. Her hand was in the air above her, fingers still reaching for the drowning victim.

That's pretty obvious, she said to herself. Nonetheless, each time she returned to sleep that oppressive yet liberating presence is there, the rescue continues in ever more surreal surroundings. Finally she spoke to the house for some light, and in the sudden glare blinked at Marbl. She got up and, downstairs, made herself a cup of hot chocolate without turning on the light. Outside, she thought she saw a shred of motion behind a nearby hedge but when she looked out cannily, concerned with safety for the house, there was no lurking shadow. Shaking her head at her paranoia, she went back to bed, this time to sleep.

✣   ✣   ✣

In the shadows the silver-haired man in the grey track suit turned away, satisfied with the night's surveillance. As he walked toward the dark car waiting in deeper darkness under the arching trees beyond the property, he thought, *strange bunch of people. And she has insomnia. I wonder why.*

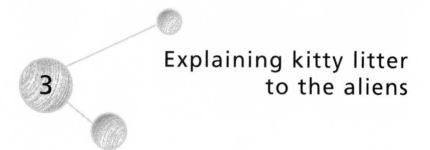

Explaining kitty litter
to the aliens

Call him Mr. Grey, as Morgan had done. That was the premature state of his hair, that was his favorite color and attitude. There was more to him than met the eye but not many were allowed to see that. He had worked himself up the law enforcement ladder far enough to be a bureaucrat, but not far enough to lose his anonymity or his power. His wife died birthing a second, late child, who also died; their first daughter grew up rebellious against authority in ways he luckily had had no cause to question: they were a fine young nuclear family once, but fission set in: one of the reasons he secretly cheered his daughter as she crusaded for social justice, personal freedom, safe alternatives to nuclear energy. He was all for fusion or even sunshine, whatever warmed the heart.

What rebellion was in his own heart was carefully curbed and directed into channels. He knew all about channels. So when the alien came into the world of humankind, flowed down the channels into our consciousness, he was in the way. In the way, but whether he was swept away or not was a matter of opinion. Eventually he was questioned by his superiors, even mentioned in Parliament, but he was kept on the job. That's the test of a bureaucrat's security, if not efficiency. So Mr. Grey managed to keep his footing when all around him were losing theirs, without having to be a Man or have a son, and the alien was initiated into human values in ways no politician could have visualized.

If this was good, we have him to thank. If we don't like what he did, we can lay traps for him, write letters to our Member of

Parliament, demand in the popular press that Mr. Grey be demoted.

He might have cared about that once, but he looks at his work differently now.

      ✿   ✿   ✿

What does a career policeman think when first he walks into the room where an alien is crouching quietly, watching everything? Does he think perhaps of the soft color of blue smoke drifting above mountain valleys, the color of a gust of rain on a grey day, the fog of punctuation marks that measure out his life? For the alien is a blue color such as might inhabit his dreams, a dusky soft blue as human skins can be a dusky soft pink or a dusky soft tan or a dusky soft brown, and the alien's hair which is long and unbound is a dark dark blue of midnight.

The grey man thinks nothing, but he is struck by some stunning astonishment of heart. He wants to reach out and touch the face of this being, reach into this being's beginning and find the mystery, reveal the source, invent the common language. This being makes him hungry for things he hasn't been seeking since his youth. He remembers his cheap telescope, he remembers the yellow-covered novels he used to read and trade with his Boy Scout companions before they all graduated to serious adulthood, he remembers his discomfort with their insistence he belonged only to their club, he remembers reading Stoltenberg and trying to understand why the world told him he must be a Man when he only wanted to be a human being. Now this new being makes being human something exclusive, also. He is afraid for Earth, but his job will not allow him to be rough with the alien who curls in the posture of an infant.

"Can I help you?" he says reflexively, then curses himself internally for a fool.

But of all the aliens only one had spoken, only once, and not a word from any of them since. He had seen the tape.

On the tape, the first alien had said, "To learn from you. Yes. That is the assignment."

"What do you mean, assignment?" the astonished diplomat, prepared with all the right greetings, had said.

"Earth is needed to know. So one is sent to know Earth."

"And that one is you?"

"Yes. That one is you."

"We too must study and understand. We want to ask you questions, examine you, find out where you are from."

"To find out from this one is not to happen. This script is complete, and will erase. Do not erase the recording you make. This bodies will stay. It will not much known. But to learn and take knowledge back. An assignment."

The eyes blanked, the body fell. After that moment, as he now knew too intimately, watching through the one-way glass, all the alien bodies had been like newborns: helpless, incontinent, and without language. As if, the grey man thought, a recording had self-destructed after being heard by the necessary people. Mr. Grey knew that trope from reruns. We, he thinks wryly, old enough to remember this allusion, are the I.M. Force, whether we choose to accept it or not.

Assignment. Whatever the alien's assignment was—and it seemed peculiarly clear that human beings were now expected to educate these empty beings starting at the very beginning—the grey man had his too.

❊   ❊   ❊

It was the grey man who decided that the alien should be moved, and where. He established security and arranged that the alien be taught. The alien had no more language, just a nonfunctional eulalia, so could not supply a name, and upon examination was demonstrably neither male nor female, but similar to both. When the child care worker was finally hired, for a baby now toddling and graduated to eulalic phrases from syllables, she called the alien "Blue". Or, she said, that the alien had chosen to be called that. Whether or not it was true that the alien had named itself, "Blue" sufficed.

✿   ✿   ✿

"We want to start your orientation with the first-contact film," said the tall woman in the green flowered dress with the smoothly-pulled-back hair. She had introduced herself as a staff sergeant in charge of training for the Canadian Security and Intelligence Services, then fussed about making Morgan a cup of hot chocolate with a couple of biscotti on the saucer. Almost milk and cookies: Morgan grinned to herself. Morgan, who had dressed in her usual neutral black-leather skinsuit, felt as warmed as she was intended to feel by the old-fashioned motherly image of this senior-management otter. She knew CSIS's brief and reputation, suspected that the ease with which she played auntie meant that the woman was hard as nails and could as easily play bad cop in more serious CSIS interviews, but Morgan allowed herself to go with the reflexively returned smiles her body produced.

"I saw it on TV," she said.

"This is the director's cut," said the woman. Without further signal, the room went dark and a vid began to play on what had formerly seemed to be a mirror wall, back-projected onto the one-way glass. Morgan was reminded that in facilities like this, everything is secret but nothing is private.

The familiar speech, replayed hundreds, maybe thousands, of times by TV stations, vid programs, netcasters, played out. The blue alien said primly, "To learn from you. Yes. That is the assignment." The astonished diplomat had said something unscripted, and the alien went on, "Earth is needed to know. So one is sent to know Earth."

"And that one is you?"

"Yes. That one is you."

The tapes always stopped there. But this one continued. The diplomat spoke soothingly about studying and understanding the alien too, and the alien said cryptically, "To find out from this one is not to happen. This script is complete, and will erase. Do not erase the recording you make. This bodies will stay. It will not much known. But to learn and take knowledge back. An assignment." Then it seemed to snap into some fugue state, and fell sideways from the chair. The confusion afterward did not arouse it. After a moment the otter woman raised her hand and the film stopped on the scene of bureaucratic shock and chaos. The lights faded up in the interview room.

"That's not ours, of course, it's the one at the UN. Ours appeared curled up on the floor of the Senate Chamber. If they were trying for Parliament, or the Prime Minister's Office, they missed. Anyway, this was all any of them have ever said," she said. "We never heard another word out of them until Blue started imitating us. It's possible that is happening elsewhere in the world. So far we know of twelve other aliens. They likely all came in this vegetative—well, call it infantile—state."

"Possible? Likely? You aren't in touch with the other . . ."

"Like our government, the other governments hosting the aliens believe that discretion is the better part of valor." The quiet, ironic voice from behind her made Morgan jump despite herself. She turned to the grey man—for it was indeed the man she had seen so briefly several days ago—and met his eyes. He's pretty, she thought, like some kind of bird. Raptor, she modified her thought as she saw him tilt his head at the otter-mother and the woman moved to a side chair to allow him to sit. Behind the grey man, a large, untidy man in a rumpled blue suit and a younger, sharp-faced junior in perfect corporate gear—the kind that Morgan thought of as a "boy wonder"—crowded into the room.

"Sorry I'm late," said the grey man. "Glad you started, Flora. Go on."

"All we can determine is that they have the ability to learn," Flora went on. "We've tested ours as much as we can, given that from the start it fought like a panther if we tried to get samples"— she pulled up her sleeve to show bruises and several long, healing scratches, and made a moue of frustration—"and it appears to be a newborn in everything but body size and strength. Our doctors suggested that we treat it like an infant, 'raise it' like an infant. It grows fast, developmentally. It's walking, eating solid foods, and babbling already."

"What is its metabolism? What does it eat?"

"It eats our food. What it wants of our food. As far as we can tell, it is a human clone. We don't know why the blue color," Flora replied.

"Unless their TVs are out of adjustment," said the Boy Wonder.

"As far as you can tell?" said Morgan.

"It still fights when we try to take tissue samples or do tests. We tested its wastes. Mostly leftovers from what went in. Different trace elements every time. As if the body is learning too," said the man in the blue suit. He glanced at his boss. "As far as we can tell."

"I thought it best not to traumatize Blue by pressing the issue," said the grey man. "I've taken some flak for that decision."

Filing that for further reference, Morgan went on, "They've been here for three months. This is all you—"

"No," interrupted the grey man, "we know a great deal. But none of it is—what they want, or where they come from, or how to unlock any memory from that beautiful blue head. We have to assume that what we have here is a *tabula rasa*. An infant. We teach it, we train it. There are indications that the ship will be back in somewhere between two and five years. Depends on which theory you believe about their drive capacity. Maybe by then they will expect their data shells to be full."

"Creating a paradigm of Earth," said Morgan.

"Elegant phrase. Yes. That's our theory."

"Your theory, Mac," said the Boy Wonder.

"Yes, well," said the grey man mildly, smiling, "but I rank high enough that I'm allowed to have a theory. When you rank me, you can have a theory too."

The CSIS agents all laughed politely. Morgan didn't laugh. She looked at the freeze-frame on the wall, a blue body curled fetally on the floor of an office, surrounded by an almost comic array of panicky UN officials, security staff, and medics, crammed into the frame like the Marx Brothers in that scene from *A Night at the Opera*.

The grey man stood up beside her. At a touch from him the image cleared and in its place was "her" alien, the beautiful Blue, in its nursery room, combing its hair and humming eerily, like the Siren. As if it could see them, it looked up toward the camera and smiled.

"I have decided," said the grey man quietly, "that it is better if you don't know too much. We know everything, and we know nothing. We want you to teach Blue, and to learn, and we will all watch and learn, and if you can give it a good image of Earth, a kindly one, all the better."

Flora began to speak, coughed, shook her head, and turned her gaze to her sleek shoes. The untidy large man cleared his throat and said, "Rahim, maybe you and I could . . . ," and went out, the Boy Wonder following him. Flora looked at Mr. Grey.

"Sure," he said, though she had said nothing. "Check back with me if you find anything." Flora too left the room.

"Blue doesn't look at all like that other one," Morgan said.

"You think not?"

"Well, superficially, maybe, but I'd say not."

"I don't think so either. I'm told by others that they are identical. They started out identical."

"Really?"

"The way some see it. Welcome to the team. No doubt you'll hate it. Civilians always do. But report to me anyway. Through Rahim."

"The Boy Wonder?"

"Yes. Him."

"Thank you," said Morgan. "I'll do my best."

❖　　　❖　　　❖

The progress of Blue through toilet training, complex language learning, grammar and composition, geography, history, "social studies", economics, sociology, comparative religions, was rapid but uneven, unpredictable. Of course there was the pronoun difficulty, but once that was surmounted there were few snags in imparting information. Manners and social behavior developed more slowly.

The grey man had already thought of simply taking the alien

home, but he could not justify the security risk. Right now, few knew one of the thirteen alien blue beings found on earth so far (were there more? The thought kept the Secretary General of the UN awake nights) was even in this country, let alone in the small prairie city where the Atrium facility was established. Those who knew were on special contract to the government and the United Nations, and sworn to secrecy. So far.

Picture the grey man, a busy office worker with a matched desk set, trying to do the paperwork on the first extraterrestrial. It was a tribute to his mental ability that he managed at all. The forms hadn't been printed that explained what this was all about or how to requisition answers.

Mr. Grey's subordinates were terrified by the lack of forms and conventions, but the grey man was not afraid of making new channels. He understood too well how channels work. Somebody was going to make them, it might as well be him.

Opposition Party Says Canada Should Demand Access to Aliens

CSIS Reveals That "Canadian" Alien Exists in Secret Facility

New Photos of Canada's Alien

Fraser Institute Demands Custody of Alien:
Government-owned think tank only suitable environment for proper education of alien, says director Suzette Bouchard

Parkland Institute Decries Fraser Institute "Alien Grab" Report:
Typical of the undemocratic processes common to the current regime, says spokesperson Tiffany Brand

CSIS Watchdogs Refuse to Give Up Alien:
Safety issues cited

Amnesty International Declares Alien Political Prisoner, Demands Release to United Nations Joint Contact Committee:
Canada says no

A Paradigm of Earth

Senior CSIS Bureaucrat Guarantees Safety of Alien, Invites Amnesty Committee to Visit Secret Facility

CSIS Pledges to Block All Political Interference With Alien

Amnesty Accepts Watching Brief:
Prime Minister Claims Victory for Canadian Sovereignty

Aliens Just Big Babies Says Unnamed Source

journal:

Someday I'll be wise and serene. Perhaps at 80 I'll be calm and beautiful and strong. Sit by the river smiling like Zen. Until then what? How do you learn? Every day I ask myself this as I try to teach Blue. flash cards of Earth? All the science of it aside, how do we do it, learn, soul and spirit?

It seems a mystery I can't imagine, passion a frenzy to which I am too susceptible, even though to date the results seem so disappointing.

And I think maybe there must be a driving force or I would have learned from those results, there must be an imperative or an ideal but what is it, what moves me through this wicked landscape with such displacement and such impetus? What will move an alien when I can't even move myself?

Learn to love. It seems I never learned the right way. What untidy, what clumsy loves I offered, so stupid, so awkward. That was the problem. Love so often the un-welcomed gift. Who wants it/takes it? Who gives it, the crux of the biscuit, for damn it, I wanted it. I want it. I want, and I don't get, I don't find, I don't live happily ever after—

I'm tired of grief. the textbook knowledge that it will pass is nothing like the reality while it's with me. and will it pass, or will I become one of those twisted people who get caught jammed between the phases and never work it out? For that matter, why not?

Because I can ask the question. Simple enough.

And must I conceal all of this, to give this Blue being a kinder, gentler Earth? I thought I was going to be better, but I can't think how, if I join this conspiracy to start our conversation with the aliens with lies. Yet I am not sure I am right to share the darkness either. I am not stupid enough yet to think that my struggle defines our world. Can anyone tell lies about the world? It's all as we see it. Schrödinger's Cat taught us that, poor thing, caught between death and life forever.

Morgan had considered advertising for more tenants to fill the last room on the second floor and the loft above what was once the garage, but before she could, someone showed up. John, a video artist, came with introductions from people Morgan knew and hadn't seen in years, a request to help him get settled—and he appeared the very day she was trying to figure out how everyone's rent, and her new salary, would stretch to cover the utilities *and* the city taxes—which she had discovered were going to be phenomenal now that the house was not occupied by a religious order.

It was enough to make it worthwhile founding a cult, Russ had remarked when she had told the others, but Delany and Jakob had immediately objected that it would be too much work. "All that scripture to learn," said Jakob, shuddering. "What do you mean, learn?" said Delany witheringly. "All that scripture to *write*." Morgan's respondent chuckle had been strained. Like many in the new millennium, Morgan was land-rich and increasingly cash-poor.

By day an educator of aliens, she thought in frustration; by night becoming educated in the way the new economy screwed the poor. She remembered what someone once said about the lotteries: that a poor person who won a million dollars wasn't a rich person but only a poor person with a million dollars.

Morgan was not rich. What Morgan had was a house.

John seemed engaging enough, and willing to pay enough for the other, smaller loft above the garage that she could slow down her search for someone else for the other room. When he'd given her the credit authorization, he settled back, but before he moved into the loft, she told him, he must sign an agreement specifying not only housing charge and security deposit but household duties.

"This is cool. Like an old-fashioned co-op!" he said.

"Yes," she said, "but it's modern. I don't want to have to hassle anyone to do their share, and I am certainly not here to do it for anyone."

"No, I understand."

"I expect you to get along with the others, too. They were here first. So if you have any prejudices about sexuality or minority politics or disabilities or artists, speak now."

"I'm an artist myself. I've been working in London and New York, but you know what they say: east west home's best. I wasn't born here," he hurried to explain, "but it was always my favorite place. And for a vidiot, the scene is still great. Cutting edge."

She found his enthusiasm admirable—and exhausting, of course. But she didn't tell him so. "Exhausting" was her problem. Morgan had questioned everything, and now she was bone tired: tired of the beat of the city against her body, the people against her mind: Morgan *le fay* did no magic in these mundane days.

✿   ✿   ✿

In the front hall she stumbled over one of the silver cases of video equipment the stranger, John, had dropped off. The stranger! One of the strangers—who isn't? She knew so little about any of them.

More signal-to-noise, blurring her angst. She snorted at herself. What would she do, stay alone and brood, without these people? She should find them interesting—and at the least, they filled up time and space.

Shame at thoughts like this dogged her days.

✿   ✿   ✿

Morgan's parcel from the U.S. had of course been opened. Back in the days when it might have done some good, she had written too many letters of protest about Canada Customs' activities stopping queer literature, which they had always bracketed with pornography, at the border. Now she was on some sort of list, and received every order, package, and gift opened, and usually had to pay tax on the gifts. Appealing the tax and handling notices would have been a nice hobby had she cared any more. As it was, the stack of Customs forms torn from the parcel wrappings formed an increasingly untidy heap at the back of her big desktop.

She was getting thinner too. She cared less about eating.

Whatever the romantic novels say, the kind of hopeless angst gripping Morgan wasn't pretty. It wasn't romantic. It was life-threatening without being dramatic, it was boring and without justification, it was self-indulgent even as it sapped the sense of self.

Morgan came face to face with this in unexpected department-store mirrors, shop windows of unusual reflectivity, and her own uncurtained windows at night. She was less aware of herself in the one-way mirrors through which people often watched her work with Blue. She didn't want to stare at the shadowy ghosts she could see through the mirrors, so could avoid also her own ghostly shadow of self.

This week the alien was about four. They had passed in only a few weeks the usually-difficult teaching of basic life skills like toilet training and eating with cutlery, basic speech and manners, and the alien was becoming interesting the same way Morgan found human children interesting once they become sapient.

Four is a nice age. Wisdom is dawning, playfulness is creative, and the willfulness of three is starting to be replaced by cunning and even, occasionally, a mature perception of the outside world as other to self—which meant that Blue, whose language skills at present outstripped its social skills, was now itself interested in the people behind the mirror.

"You are seeing other people, not like TV," said Morgan. "They are in another room, and part of the wall is made of this stuff, which is called one-way glass. It's supposed to look like a mirror to us as long as it's dark in their room. But some light always comes through from our room and shines on them, and we can see a bit of them."

"So they aren't funny shadows like they look, they are real people like us?"

"Think about it, Blue. At night when you go by the mirror, with no light but the spill from outside the windows, do you look different, like a funny shadow?"

"Oh . . ."

"And are you different?"

"Oh. Yes. I am different in the night because I see differently."

"I mean in the body. Is your body different?"

"Oh. No, not in the body."

"Well, then, why should they be different?"

"What are they doing there?"

"Watching us."

"Why?"

"You are their first alien. They think everything you do is very very interesting."

At four people are vain. The alien turned away, smiling smugly.

✿   ✿   ✿

On the street, on the way to work, Morgan saw a pregnant woman. All she could think was, what a pity another child was coming into the world, and how appalling the swollen woman looked. Distantly, she noted the danger of such thoughts, but like everything else the awareness of despair's peril was far away. Closer—and more uncomfortable—was the thought that perhaps her perceptions had been skewed by her circumstances. If she had to question the cold clarity of her self-judgment on the night before her parents' funeral, she would lose the only benchmark she had, and she would have to leap into the void of loss. So, she watched the heavily gravid woman impassively, noting her lumbering walk, and dutifully tried not to see her as grotesque.

"He must have been injured on arrival. Whatever the arrival process was must have given him, like, a retrograde amnesia, a functional amnesia." In the daily-report meeting, Rahim was holding forth again on his opinion of the Alien Question.

"Him?"

"Don't keep harping on that, Connie. We have enough to think about without that."

"My name is Morgan, and harping on that is my job. Do you really want to make this alien into a Man?"

He didn't hear her. He hadn't read the old books. He was the new breed of *fin-de-siècle* specialist, who had grown up language-challenged and idea-poor, believing the political cant of selfishness. He owned a big house and a designer wife and dog, and Morgan found him unbelievably stupid in almost any situation, without imagination and without charm. It amazed her to see that some of the other women found him attractive. I've been around queers too long, she thought, to ever look the same way at those hetero Men-with-a-capital-*M* who have somehow re-embraced the Father-Knows-Best ideal their parents rejected midway through the previous century—and who still thought themselves harmless as they plowed through the future.

If they didn't do such damage, she would be sorry for them. But they and their social Darwinist uncles, dads, and mentors were taking her country step-by-step backward into a dictatorship of meanness, a victory of haves over have-nots, which still had the power to disgust Morgan, even through her fog of personal incapability.

"They are watching all the time," said Blue. "Even when I poop."

"Yes."

"I don't like that."

"I can see why. People like to have some privacy. They wouldn't like it if you watched them poop, I bet."

Blue giggled, but after her shift, Morgan was taken back into the office by Rahim and chastised again.

"I am the only one your precious alien trusts," she said, "and part of the reason is that I tell the truth. Do you want me to change that? I don't think so."

She stared at the Boy Wonder, and he shook his head. "I was against employing you," he said. "I was overruled by the Chief Inspector. If he is transferred off this case, you're out of here tomorrow."

"And does he show signs of being transferred?" Morgan said, and gathered her things together.

"Anything can happen if the right people get to be in charge," Rahim said as she walked out. Good exit line for him, she thought, but on the bus going home she lapsed into the same glum mental silence as usual.

A tendril of reality split the grey fog and she thought dimly, *I wonder if I'm ill. I should see a doctor.* She managed to hold that thought long enough to write herself a note at home, but she didn't actually make a call. She didn't know any trustworthy doctors in this town. She would have to ask around, and that seemed an almost overwhelming task.

She would get to it.

An old-fashioned policeman

He was inherently a fair and a just man, though occasionally he trapped himself into taking a stance he didn't believe. But he had known this about himself for a long time and therefore he was careful not to corner himself in dealing with the alien.

Or the people hired to take care of the alien.

He stood in the darkened observation booth watching the lesson take place. Beside him slouched the new technician hired to record it all. The technician muttered a little to himself, but that didn't matter, the alien knew perfectly well someone was behind the wall, turned occasionally and looked with dark eyes that were mountain tarns of blank indigo beauty. The teacher answered its questions honestly, and the grey man heard the technician swear and the others in the observation room with him murmur their anger. The grey man imagined the mirror had vanished, felt a moment of vertigo, shook his head and looked away. The technician watching him spoke.

"Hey, you related to Hester McKenzie?"

Mr. Grey nodded.

"I know her work. Dynamite!"

He in his turn looked silently.

The technician looked back to the viewfinder. "Great work. Her best was *Amnesty*."

"That was a commission. She thought it was too cold."

"Cold! No way. Precise, intense, righteous. Moral."

Mr. Grey was obscurely angry to hear his daughter's work encapsulated like that, remembering her irritation with the people she had worked with on the vid event they called *Amnesty* and she called "torture pornography." "You wouldn't believe the letters I get," she said. "People are sick. They want to see death on film." As her father he remembered the film as frightening and grim. As a policeman he recognized the mood. As more than either role, he simply wanted to stop talking about it with this youngster barely old enough to know violence existed, and insensate in the face of alien wonder. He turned and walked out of the room.

The technician watched the alien through the viewfinder, watched the interaction between Blue and the young man hired to teach the ET to play chess and Go. The video recorder kept rolling as he fixed the focus of the camera and walked out of the observation cell.

✿   ✿   ✿

The death of the chessmaster was entirely unexpected, and the camera was rolling when it happened. The new technician had been out of the room, taking a leak he said, and the surveillance in the lavatory confirmed that at the same time the recordings showed a sudden burst of interference, the technician had been otherwise occupied. Our Mr. Grey had only been gone a few moments. The important part of the action had taken place just outside the frame of the fixed camera.

The alien, as far as could be ascertained from a rather confused statement, had also left the room. Something had happened, Blue said.

The death would have been taken for natural except for the inconclusiveness of the fixed-perspective recording, which caused a certain stubbornness on the part of the medical examiner's investigator and hence the Medical Examiner herself. The investigation was discreet—and ultimately inconclusive. The death certificate would read, "Heart failure." No evidence pointed to Blue's involvement, but neither did evidence say the event had sidestepped the alien. The first other being shown on the recording, after the dying struggles of the chess teacher were half-visible, was the alien, a look of confusion and perhaps misunderstanding on the face. After kneeling to look at the body, Blue had looked up at the camera.

"Come fast here," the alien had said, "something is wrong with this one. All chess has ceased. Perhaps death?"

And so the grey man's simple job became complex, and, unknown to him, the escape began.

❁   ❁   ❁

"The damned being has been hunched over the computer for the last two days, wild-eyed and compulsive, reading up on death and medical research," said Rahim. "Looks to me like it has a problem."

"Blue knows nothing about death," said Morgan stubbornly. "Of course there will be study. Of course there will be trauma. A child of that age meets the idea of death for the first time— someone the child knows dies, and they find the body—this will always require some work afterward. Blue's language skills are far in advance of Blue's emotional maturity, so Blue finds comfort and insight in information acquisition. Especially since the report tells me no-one has really had a heart-to-heart about the event with Blue yet."

"But what if the alien *did* something," persisted Rahim.

The man in the blue suit nodded. "We have to question it."

"Absolutely not. I know what you mean by *question,* and it's not good for a child. Can you imagine how traumatic that would be for a kid? About seven or eight, I'd say, this week, and all of a sudden angry adults are looming over it and insisting it tell them something it doesn't even know how to talk about? Remember, this accelerated development process is dangerous and fragile. It doesn't give the same results as regular childhood. It's like raising a clone. To some degree, we're implanting a memory structure here. You can't put too much of a strain on it until the framework is finished and Blue starts filling it in with experience."

"He wants to 'fix' the chessmaster, it's obvious," Blue Suit insisted, resisting the grey man's squelching glare, "which to my mind means he broke him in the first place."

"Oh, for goodness' sake, that's so *paranoid . . .*"

"Perhaps a compromise . . . ," the grey man began.

"Absolutely not. Unless you are ready to accept the responsibility if something goes wrong and we create a huge trauma. Blue has to be helped to understand death is a part of life—and the sooner the better. You haven't been dealing with that while I've been off duty, and the trauma is already manifesting."

"Perhaps if I talked to Blue first . . ."

"Perhaps if you just left it alone . . ."

"Perhaps if you get Little Miss Social Worker here to back off . . ."

"Perhaps if you just let me do my job . . ."

✽   ✽   ✽

Back in his office after the optimistically named *strategy session* in the boardroom, Grey was almost shaking with rage. Kowalski wouldn't shut up, the Boy Wonder—he liked Morgan's name for him, which had slipped out at that first session—played macho dominance games and lost to the grey man's implacable authority—but so did Morgan, who had had to accept that Mr. Grey at least would interview Blue. That had made Morgan furious, of course, and the meeting had gone on far too long, with her pig-headedness, and her threats of using her influence over the alien to keep it silent even if it was interviewed, meaning that in the end nothing much had been accomplished.

But he had to admire her spirit. Slightly.

If he was honest, which he wished sometimes didn't come so easy.

If he were to be really honest, he had to sit down and admit that it wasn't the stubborn, now-absent Morgan who had enraged him. It was the stubborn, very present Kowalski, now following him into his inner office, still insisting on some wild alien-conspiracy plot when he should have been concentrating on the well-being of this alien child. Dull bigoted Kowalski, with his lumpy blue suit and his lumpy body making a suitable home for his *lumpenproletarian* mind.

If that wasn't insulting the proletariat.

Luckily, he outranked Kowalski. Grey decided to prove it. He waved Kowalski to a seat in the office.

He felt suddenly surprised he had never noticed that Kowalski had the thick mouth and sagging cheeks of the type that directors pull from central casting to play movie alcoholics or child molesters—then heard with grim humor his own judgmental thought. Clearly, the irritation he had felt for years had finally boiled over into something that would be perilously close to hatred unless Grey took the situation in hand now.

He made Kowalski a cup of coffee before he said anything. Ko seemed at ease, but there was sweat on his forehead and his hand left a print on the cracked brown handle of Grey's coffeepot.

"You were out of line in the meeting, Ko," the grey man said mildly, beginning at last.

"I don't know how you can say that, Rog," Ko said. Mr. Grey hated that nickname, wasn't too fond of his first name at all, preferred Kowalski to address him by his last name, knew Ko knew that, and was enough further irritated to abandon his simulacrum of Zen calm.

"I think you know, Ko, and I won't have it. I may make your coffee instead of the other way around, but I rank you, and I don't want your big mouth between me and the rest of those people at a meeting. I have enough trouble keeping the Boy Wonder from going off half-cocked."

"Hey, *Inspector,* what's biting you? *Rahim* was doing his *job*. A queer and a bunch of other social workers have their hands all over the biggest asset we've got. You think that's not a problem?"

"Kowalski, get this straight. Your kind of thinking is on the way out in my department, and if you don't muffle up, you might be riding the same rail."

"You're one of the old guard, Rog. That community policing stuff you cut your rookie teeth on is old hat now."

"Equality of policing will never be old hat while I'm in charge,

Staff Sergeant. And more to the point, I don't like having you undercut my moves. If you want to keep your rank, I don't want to hear another word out of you in any meeting where you shadow me, unless I know you are going to say it in support—or you clear it in advance. Do you understand?"

"Rog, where's this coming from? I thought we had a good working relationship here, man."

"As long as you follow my orders, Ko, we have a good working relationship. If you start screwing up on me like you did today, we have no relationship at all, and too many more stunts like that and you'll be busted back to detachment chief in Back-of-Beyond, Newfoundland. *Claro?*"

"Yeah, I got it."

"Okay, now that's out of the way. Now that you know what you're not gonna be doing anymore, I'm going to tell you what you are doing." By the time Kowalski left the office, Grey had the man assigned to more admin duties and thinking it was a step up. That was easy. Kowalski was a stupid man, and simple carrots worked to move him. The stick part, Grey hated, but he had to admit, he felt good afterward. All those toxins one can get rid of by crying—could you get rid of them as easily playing departmental politics? Worked for him.

Today, anyway.

✵   ✵   ✵

The alien sat in the darkened room, light the color of molten data streaming from the flickering screen. Morgan had become used to the *Star Trek* cliché of the screens paging past faster than she could read, and she simply put her hand on the tense, hunched shoulder. Blue, startled, made a sound like a spooked cat and turned staring eyes on Morgan as if she too were strobing with floods of data.

"Anything interesting tonight?" she asked gently, just to say something.

"My eyes feel very full. How do people see so much and not burst?"

She was about to smile when she saw the desperation.

"Are you scared?" She dropped to her knees and took the trembling hands in hers, surprised and shocked at the strength of the fibrillation, as fast as the screen's had been, which transmitted to her at the contact. She found herself whispering, "Shhh," as one does when rocking a baby with night terrors.

"What's wrong?" she said.

"My thoughts are zooming like the data tracks, but they won't sort out. They won't lie down. All night they are spinning, every day and night they spin more. How do people make the data fit in their minds?"

How do people do that? Morgan thought, and, keeping Blue anchored with one hand, reached out the other to turn off the display. It was frozen at the moment Blue's gaze had moved from the screen, and absently she read, " '*Hypolipidaemic and Anti-atherosclerotic Effects in* Kingiber officinale *in Cholesterol Red Rabbits*, Sharma, I., et al. . . .' "

"How long have you been on line?"

"You were away for two days."

"Two days? Non-stop? When did you rest?"

"I don't sleep, you know that."

"I don't mean sleep. I mean rest. To let the facts settle."

"Do I have to rest?"

Standing up without letting go of the alien's hands, Morgan led the docile, exhausted, quivering Blue into the other room, where the bed was. The hands she held were cool, something which, if she had time to process it, Morgan realized would frighten her in a creature so measurably hot-blooded as this one.

She urged the alien to lie down and, trusting though puzzled, Blue did so. It was true, Blue never used the bed, even for a moment's quiet. Never stopped doing something. How *did* humans make space for new data? .

"We sleep," said Morgan, "and part of our brain that is subconscious sorts information and stores it."

"This is not scientific," said Blue, using the annoying catchphrase with which for the last few days, Morgan had just read in the reports, the alien had been bedeviling the staff. Now she saw its origin in the abstracts Blue had been swotting.

"No," said Morgan, "I haven't said it in a scientific way. But you will find in the research that if people don't sleep they get obsessive and delusional."

"That's if they don't dream. But what is 'dream'? Except you said it is wish for the future, but that doesn't make sense in context."

Morgan, looking at the worried face, had a moment that she would later wonder if it had been epiphany, but which certainly she always understood was paradigm shift. She knew suddenly that information was not what the alien needed to survive, to do its job. She knew, she *knew* that dreams were at the core of some human gestalt, some fractal distribution of information, and she knew also that Blue must learn at least this if the alien was to understand why "dream" had so many meanings in the human lexicon.

Accidentally, she had been giving the alien data of another sort. She had been touching it, hugging it, *loving* it. Its drive for humanness was no longer just lexical, it was also tactile.

That relentless othermind of Morgan's contributed the ironic memory of a study of social workers long ago. Workers and clients were asked to describe their feelings about a session. Clients said, "The worker was listening so carefully, was so focused. I felt like they really care about me." The workers said, "I was thinking about how I had to pick up milk on the way home" or "I was thinking that I would have to leave early to get my kid at day care." There was a cynical way to interpret this study, and Morgan with one part of herself indulged in that interpretation, realizing that she certainly *seemed* to be loving Blue, whatever her actual incapability to do so.

But there was another way to see the data, as well—as being emotionally related to patterning, that essential treatment activity for some brain-damaged children, the repetitive placing of the children's limbs in the positions of crawling so that they could learn how to do it themselves, by creating a false sense memory. Morgan had been placing Blue, emotionally, spiritually if you will, in the positions needed for love and dreams. She had been putting the body of the alien into positions that in humans required touch and REM-sleep.

Why were love and sleep suddenly related, perhaps even conflated, in this sudden flash of understanding? Morgan saw that her touch was calming Blue, that something was flowing between them, that Blue's outward-spiraling data trance had been interrupted, centered by her presence, by the need to focus. But the bodily touch was not enough. There had to be some focus for Blue's spirit, emotions—for the alien's soul? wondered Morgan suddenly—to counterbalance the flood of information.

Information is not always balanced by entropy, Morgan remembered. Sometimes it is balanced by chaos, by letting go. Humans used the sleep time for this, and the seemingly random yet often organized and meaningful images surfacing in dreams were palimpsests, artifacts, or iceberg-tips of a deeper and more significant process.

How would an alien body, burning so hot usually, learn that kind of letting-go? Morgan was thinking at the speed of data herself. "Have you read about meditation?" she said. Blue's gaze unfocused for a disconcerting second, then, "Yes," the alien said brightly.

"We are going to teach you to meditate."

Blue's hands spasmed. "I do not *want* empty mind!"

"Empty mind is a metaphor. It means still thoughts, with no traffic jam in there." Blue knew "traffic jam", and giggled. "Then, I hope, I will teach you to find something like dreaming in the midst of the peace that a still mind brings."

Did Blue even *have* a subconscious mind? She guessed they would find out.

It was grey outside the windows, the flat post-sunset miasma which seems to leach the intensity from colors. Morgan remembered walking home from high school in winter in the same kind of half-daylight, twenty-five years before. It struck her as strange that the emotions of our childhood become artifacts for the rest of our lives, so that some events, sensations, or feelings only moments or hours long govern the rest of our experience.

How would Blue's strange accelerated learning curve replicate human existence?

＊　　　＊　　　＊

Blue stayed on the bed, eyes closed, for the rest of the night and some of the morning. Morgan, kipped out on the couch in the next room, slept badly, dreamed of death and data and blue light and terrible confusion, woke often and checked on Blue, and finally, giving up on sleep, sat dozily in the big armchair by the window and watched over Blue.

When Blue decided to rejoin the world, the calm face and smile were restored.

"I understand much more," said the alien. "Things fit. Their edges meet, like those puzzles you used to make me do. Why don't we do those any more?"

"For kids, they're learning disguised as play; for adults, they're optional recreation."

"So you think I am an adult now?"

"Well, I'd say a young teenager."

"Oh, must I misbehave and learn to drive cars too fast? What about recreational drug use and wireheading?"

Morgan laughed. "If you think it will seriously advance your knowledge base of human behavior, I suppose you could try some of those things, but I recommend the non-destructive ones—like driving a car fast, but only on a divided highway!"

"You are too conservative. I should do something importantly dangerous."

"Why?"

"Because humans do."

"Some humans. Some, like me, would rather avoid remorse."

"What does that mean—oh. I see."

Morgan grinned and hugged Blue with one arm around the waist, and Blue hugged back around her shoulders. Morgan was always surprised at the heat—but today, she was simply grateful. If anything last night had frightened her most, it was the coldness of Blue's hands, a sign of spasming circulation, or even clinical shock. But now Blue was comfortingly warm again.

"Did that feeling of being overwhelmed ever happen to you before?" Morgan asked.

"Yes, one time, when the man died."

"What did you do about it?"

"I can't remember. When can I learn to drive?"

"After you learn what a metaphor is." This time, it was Blue who laughed first.

journal:

Blue takes to the idea of dreaming and suddenly the word is everywhere. For instance, I asked Blue if Blue had any knowledge of the other aliens in the other countries. Blue said, I see them in my dreams. but they are indistinct. they are in far places, with different cameras and security forces. *this, we all know.*

You speak so well, I said.

I have a good speech therapist, Blue said, and grinned. and I read Fowler's English Usage, *and* Strunk and White's Elements of Style, *and* Modern English Grammar.

And, though I stopped Blue's listing there, linguistics textbooks and speech therapy textbooks and all the ancient and modern novels we could find, on microfiche or paper or disc, or on audiotape to play in the background, with rich trained voices like Orson Welles and Dame Edith Evans and Jessica Tandy and Richard Burton reading the books and plays; and films and video recordings of everything from Shakespeare to Albee, Brecht to Tallis, Antonioni to Hitchcock, Kubrick to Shyamalan, Smythe to Mollel, mostly in English after experts assured us that it was better for Blue to learn one language deeply than several in brief. Despite my doubts, for I knew and know that a language defines the concepts it can express, and the concepts of a people limit its language, the most obvious example being the sexism of English with its he and she and no word for a person who is neither or for whom it doesn't matter, like Blue or the letter carrier.

But because I know that around the world, some in known places and some not, other empty aliens are soaking up humanity, the minority view as well as next door to the imperium (the imperium gloats: they have two, so the media report), I feel no lingering guilt about teaching Blue only English with its inbuilt prejudices, its inherent bias. There are many different paradigms by which our world can be ordered and expressed, all of them equal and valid, though some contradict others.

❂   ❂   ❂

In the dream Morgan is swimming in a blue fog that becomes a blue ocean. For the first time in her life, she is swimming in comfort. That's all.

When she woke up, Morgan remembered only the sense of power in knowing how to swim. *There's a staff pool in the Atrium,* she thought. *Wonder if Blue and I can have swimming lessons?* They began two days later, taught by, of all people, Flora, who in the water was square-bodied and blocky: Morgan realized suddenly that Flora was likely a trans.

In the real world, Morgan found that the dream has improved her bare ability to float not at all. She is still afraid to put her face in the water. Blue picked up on her nervousness. Flora began slowly, gently, and quickly the alien began to play in the water. Morgan, too, unbent a bit, but she could see it would take time.

❂   ❂   ❂

On the brink of despair is tranquillity. Or, more precisely, over the brink, in the void. That's okay with the dreaming Morgan: she needs a rest. She has been walking a long time in this unfamiliar landscape.

In the country she knew, where her parents were an immutable part of familiar scenery, she had mapped out all the pitfalls. Now she has gone away from there in every way, and nothing is the same. *They are not going back the way they came, and nothing will ever be the same again.* She has changed her name, her job, her location, her membership status in human concerns (member: inactive).

Across the plain to meet her walks a blue being who came from a country separated by a real, not metaphorical, void from even the most extravagant locale of Morgan's imagination.

❖   ❖   ❖

The dining table conversation was a sprightly exchange of editing terms that Morgan could barely follow, but even Delany was keeping up with John and Russ.

"I'm interested in putting dimension into flatware," she said. "I deliberately work in paint, but it doesn't always dance like I want it to."

"You can delaminate it easy," said John. "It comes apart any way you want. Fractal division, color layers, density contour maps—depends on what you want to develop. What mood."

"All very well with something that begins as static, something you create and then animate," said Jakob, "but what about taking something that already exists—like my dance—and doing more than documentary? Half the stuff on the web harks back to before I was born—psychedelia as rank as any on vintage TV. The most modern stuff does MuchMusic or MTV nostalgia. There's no space for innovation. I end up settling for documentation, hoping that there is a shadow of the liveware there."

"The nature of the video experience has always been different. That's stale news now. What do you expect? The only frontier is fucking with the paradigm."

"And how exactly do you go about that?" Russ put in. "When all the available models have been modeled?"

"Cellular transformation," said John.

Morgan thought that none of them was splitting out of their paradigm. Each one was instead trying to get further inside, burrowing like a worm into the heart of the classical knowledge of their field. There was a lesson in it somewhere for her. What she was doing in the Atrium was not groundbreaking either. The gestalt portrait of humanity was taking shape in the alien: Blue was becoming a human being. No human was being forced to think outside the frame. No alien knowledge had been leaked to Earth. And the same skills were being used that would be used to "civilize" a feral child or, perhaps a better analogy since few feral children respond to the efforts to teach them humanity, to rehabilitate an amnesiac. No new skills for her to write a textbook about when the project got declassified.

"Classification," said John, startling her, but then he went on, "classifying the pixel density into families to make the most of the bandwidth—of course, that's completely misleading; the terminology is so old."

"I see what you mean," said Russ. "But you aren't using it to convey information. It's entropic in nature. Isn't that contradicted by the very fact that you create it?"

"Yes," said Delany, "because art cannot by its nature be entropic."

"That's a very traditional viewpoint," said John witheringly.

"Look who's talking," Jakob mocked. "You still make full motion for the net. Isn't that traditional, compared to virtuality?"

Morgan was a bit surprised to see John take this not lightly, in the spirit of Jakob's chaffing, but sullenly. "You don't understand the statement," he said. "That's not surprising, given the kind of effete vocabulary of motion you use. At least, *I* wasn't surprised."

"What's that supposed to mean?" said Delany sharply.

"Nothing," said John. "Just that a non-expert can't be expected to be on the cutting edge. Especially when you use the medium for *documentary*." He said the last word with his voice dripping with scorn.

"Hey, hey, take it easy," said Russ. "This is a friendly discussion, remember? You're not dealing with critics here."

"Maybe," said John, but he relaxed, and the conversation

moved on. Within a few minutes he was joking again, and Russ was guffawing.

While they were doing the dishes—it was John's turn, with Jakob drying, but John had had an opening to attend, so Morgan had volunteered—Morgan said, "John has a hair-trigger on the subject of his work, it seems."

"No, it's me," said Jakob. "He doesn't like fags."

"What on earth . . . ?"

"He doesn't let it hit the surface, but haven't you noticed, darling, that he won't even share a touching domestic moment like this with me?"

Her mouth open to say, "I'm sure you're mistaken," Morgan stopped and said instead, "I hope you're wrong. Given the nature of this household, he's in for trouble. When I interviewed him, he didn't seem to bristle at the idea."

"It could just be that he's not used to my *style*, sugah," Jakob said, exaggerating his style for a moment.

"I suppose it takes some getting used to—but you'd think that someone in video and virch would have met all sorts of people . . ."

"You'd think," said Jakob, "but there's different kinds of *meet*. Maybe he never had to share a bathroom with any before."

"He's a sharp guy, and funny. He seems to liven everybody up."

"It's competition. He has an edge, and so we unsheathe our little blades as well. I haven't felt so sharp in years."

Morgan hoped that Jakob and John didn't end up sharpening their claws on each other. Last thing she needed were feuding prima donnas. She had noticed a certain edginess in John, but Jakob was not immune: come to think of it, none of this had started until John had criticized Jakob's old-fashioned use of video. Sighing internally, she added a watching brief to her internal list of things to do. *I could do without the vagaries of human nature,* she thought, and surfaced to hear Jakob cleverly dissing John.

"Hush," she said. "Manners . . ." and thought, not for the first time, that queens were getting bitchier the more the external world cracked down on them. On us, she amended. On the *deviants*.

❊   ❊   ❊

"Could we go rock-climbing then?" Blue nagged.

"Rock climbing?"

"Something dangerous. 'Adventurous men and women from the Canadian Rockies Sheer Face Explorers pit their strength and agility against the most challenging vertical terrain. Weekend packages include three nights at the charming Black Cat Guest Ranch, nestled at the foot of Solomon Mountain, and three climbs of increasing difficulty—' "

"All right! All right! When I get back on day shift we'll find you something risky to do to channel your teenaged joyriding urges!"

But they didn't, because that night, some hours after Morgan had gone off duty, the alien ran away.

A new tenant

Morgan was careful never to speak a lie, but still, the fact was, Morgan was a friend of denial. Through her father's dying, she had managed to ignore all her grudges, and now she would have to abandon them unsolved. What a cheat death could be. And her mother's death, the possibility that it was suicide, that in itself was a great ball of anger hanging below her belly.

To feel empty, she had to deny all this.

In denial, she did not heal. Trying for truth in speech, she was still somehow a liar.

And that, she thought bitterly, invalidated all her fine tragic acting on the riverbank; that, she knew, was fatal to the future; that, she believed, was too human to be hers.

Being human, she recognized, was harder for her than it was for Blue, but more necessary both because she could not escape the reality of it, and because she didn't want to be human. As long as she could feel alien, she was safe. So, she asked herself scornfully, she denied her common cause with the rest of "mankind's unco' squad" and retained her romantic notions of how to suffer through her inevitable life?

"*You're* nobody special," she heard, in a voice from the past, a flashback to some moment, a moment before her knowledge, when she must have decided to prove that voice a liar.

She won't do it by lying herself.

She hated knowing that. It made her so petty.

✿   ✿   ✿

The noise on the porch came at about eleven-thirty. Morgan was just dozing over her book when she heard the scraping of feet on wood. She made a habit of noting who was home and not home; everyone was accounted for. She walked downstairs quietly and in one quick motion turned on the porch light and opened the front door.

She was not prepared for:

—a pale, bluish face, a quiet studied voice saying, "May I come in?" The falling of a slight body against the door frame, then a stumbling step and a final collapse at her feet.

Blue. She closed the door, crouched to the fallen body, pulled the shoulders around so the body lay straight. She was used to dealing with bodies unable to co-operate, though Blue had never been unresponsive like this in her presence before, despite the "sleep" on her last shift. Mr. Grey would have found this catatonia familiar, but she didn't know that. She leaned with legs on either side of the waist, crouched to lift under the arms, dragged the heavy weight across the hall and into the small sitting room by the door. She went to the kitchen for a glass of water. When she returned to the little room, the alien was struggling to sit up. She turned on the lights.

Blue stirred, moved as if swimming in deep water, up from the Mariana Trench. She crouched beside the sluggish body, put her hand out, brushed the strands of hair away from the damp forehead. Blue's eyelids fluttered. She pulled her hand back more quickly than it had gone out. The eyes opened fully, fixed on her face.

"I ran away. I'm sorry. Will I get you in trouble with the people behind the mirror? I will go as soon as I can. But you are the only place I know."

"What do you mean?" What a stupid thing to say, she thought.

"They are chasing me about the dead man. They asked me many questions. What do I know about a dead man, even though I read everything I could read? I don't *know* anything!"

"Shh, it's all right. Why didn't you just get them to call me?"

Blue looked around the room, gaze sharp on every object.

"You said I was a teenager. Teenagers can run away to see the world. To go to a place where no-one talks about death. So I come here, and much is interesting to me here."

Again that sharp gaze, on her, strange acuity from such an exhausted beginning. She nodded absently, encouraging Blue to go on, as she always did. There was a dynamo in the back of her mind, setting a manic wheel in motion. The death, the interrogation she thought she had made them promise to put off, but it had only worked until she was off duty. Could Blue actually have had anything to do with the death? The on-line record showed nothing either way. The only knowledge was that for two days after, until Blue's collapse when she came on duty, Blue had studied death, medicine, and Ouija. From the end of the chess game . . . Heart attacks happen to people . . . but was the death natural? Odds were that it was, and anyway, she couldn't believe Blue capable of a murderous act. The alien eyes closed again, and the voice lost the vigor of a moment before.

"Why are you so tired?" she said, sharply.

"I have never been out here before. There are so many voices in my dreams. It is tiring. And you taught me to sleep." It was a valid point. "Maybe I should have stayed and let that man in the blue suit yell at me."

"Blue suit? Not grey? Blue?"

"Yes, blue, but not the same color as me. He was one of the ones that used to watch me from behind the mirror. I know if I stay they will come here and make you angry. No. Be angry with you. Now I see you I understand I should not bring that to you, no matter how I feel. But I am very worn."

"Tired," she said automatically.

"Very tired." Eyes open and nodding, Blue was as always an obedient student.

She laughed suddenly. The alien smiled carefully.

"Would you like to sit on the furniture?" she said. "That's how we earth folks usually do it."

"Yes, please." Blue lifted up to perch in a chair. "You are making fun of me."

"It is a very strange situation," said Morgan. She walked to the window. Outside, under the streetlights, two men were standing. One pointed at the house.

Morgan felt as if she were in a movie. There wasn't much difference however between being an observer of an unreal world and living in one. To the alien she said, "Would you like to stay here? All the time, I mean: live here?" Then she broke into a cold sweat at the presumption of what she had just said.

The alien said, "Yes, please."

A third, smaller man joined the waiting two. He jerked his head toward the trees on the other side of the fence, and the pointing man walked into them and was lost in the shadow. The new man spoke to the other, who got into a car by the curb and started the engine. Clearly the newcomer was authority. Under the streetlight, their clothing looked the same: dark and nondescript. Was it her Mr. Grey? Morgan couldn't understand why the watchers were not already on the step: she had watched enough spy movies and read enough cheap thrillers to know what the drill should be and to expect a knock, but the man made no such moves, just stood watching the house until Morgan imagined he saw her in depth.

Just in case, Morgan dialed the number she had been given in case she needed to let them know she would be away or late for a shift. The telephone was answered on the first ring, and through the window Morgan saw the watcher answer a cellphone.

"Hi, this is Morgan."

"What can I do for you?" said the voice of the grey man. Well, that answered that.

"Blue is with me," she said economically.

"We know."

"And exhausted."

"Well, put it to bed and see if you can get it to practice its sleeping, and we'll be there in the morning."

"Are you standing out in the street watching me?"

"Yes."

She waved out the window and heard a chuckle from the

'phone headset. Then he said, "Don't worry, really we're watching *out for* you. *Hasta mañana,*" and cut the connection. As she watched, he got into the car, she saw him speak to the driver, and the vehicle moved away.

✲   ✲   ✲

Chief Inspector Roger T. McKenzie, AKA Mr. Grey, stood in the concealing darkness and watched the alien enter the strangers' door. The face of the small, long-haired woman who opened and shut the door was in shadow. It didn't matter. He already knew everything he needed to know about her. Or enough to seem like everything. Kowalski drove out into the light where the two duty guards were waiting to be deployed.

The 'phone call delighted him—and won him his bet with Ko, who had been sure she would play *Spy vs. Spy,* would try to conceal Blue. Still chuckling as he cut the connection, he turned back to the car where the man in the blue suit was waiting. Mr. Grey could hardly contain his elation, but he was going to keep his excitement hidden from Ko, who he knew feared the alien and the alien effect on Earth. He would hide the delight he felt that the blue visitor had managed to graduate the training course with such expediency. He would also hide the apprehension that the alien's flight (with attached to that flight the inevitable suspicion of complicity in the chessmaster's death, autopsy verdict notwithstanding) had brought him. All the blue-suited man would ever be allowed to see would be the cool, efficient exterior Mr. Grey, doing everything right.

The grey man had taken a gamble, and it was working. Nourished by private satisfactions as well as by public ones, he felt no need to share this knowledge, or smile about it. *It was his nature,* he thought, quoting the folk tale of the scorpion and the horse, and was, after all, almost tempted to smile.

Instead, he got into the car and signaled the other man to drive on. They had a long night's work ahead of them, and he wanted to get started.

❀   ❀   ❀

Morgan woke in the morning after a confused sleep of dreams to the realization that something monumental hung over her head, but it took a moment for her to remember what it was. She was as exhausted as if she were getting up early after a weekend at work. By the time she had put the alien to bed in the spare room the night before, she had felt as if she had worked a double shift.

The alien. The sudden rush of fear was so strong it almost choked her. Following it was the urgency that had woken her, sharpened now. She was through Russ's room, Delany's room like a whirlwind, waking them with sharp hurried words, then up to Jakob's studio to shake him into a stuporous wakefulness which she scarcely trusted. Then John, who woke confused and truculent, but caught her urgency. Finally they were all gathered in the kitchen, Russ making coffee in the drip maker while everyone else rumbled through their morning rituals: Delany laboriously assembled cereal, John teased Marbl, Jakob raked his long hair and braided its finely dreaded strands, twisted the silk headband around his forehead. Morgan was too keyed up to sit or to care what time of day it was.

"We have to talk," she said. "Something happened last night that's going to affect us all. No, let's be honest, I did something last night which will affect us all. I took in a stranger . . ."

"That's nothing unusual," said Russ. "You've got a houseful of strays. Eh, Marbl?"

The cat turned at its name, and showed pretty teeth in a silent meouw.

"This one is different. It's stranger than you know. It's Blue, the extraterrestrial. That's where I've been working, teaching the alien. Last night it ran away from the Atrium—that's the place they kept it—and came here to ask for shelter. I asked it if it wanted to stay and it said yes."

Bedlam. She took a minute to think about where that word came from: yes, I am mad, this whole thing is mad. At the end of the chaos of explanation, Russ, of course, was saying, *"Fahr auf!"* John was burbling about vid memory, megabytes, getting his camera, where is it?—with his face white and the skin looking drawn across the bones, from shock. Jakob realized the heart of the matter.

"But surely someone will come looking for it. They've had security like you wouldn't believe! The Mounties—CSIS I mean— a UN force, police from every damned country. You told us you practically had to have an anal probe to get in to work every day. And they just left him here? With the likes of *us?*"

He was worried about his boys, his work, his source of income. Morgan was worried about their lives. But their concerns coincided here.

"That's just about it. None of us is what you might call mainstream, mundane. I can't decide without you. Are you willing to have your life spread open for examination, in exchange for the chance to spend time with a real alien? I thought about it a long time last night before I went to sleep, and I think I have nothing more to lose. But some of you might feel differently."

"I don't think it's a matter of what we feel," said Delany suddenly. "I think it's a matter of history. People are always being caught in the whirlpool effect of some event. It's not that we lose our freedom of choice, but that we shouldn't assume we should use it at a time like this.

"If you get my meaning," she said after a pause during which the others looked at her in silence.

"I don't care either way," said Russ. "It should be interesting."

"I've always wanted to be famous in the real world," said Jakob, but Morgan noticed his hands were shaking, and she put a hand over one of his briefly (very briefly; she knew he felt ambivalent about touch).

John was the last to speak, looking from one to the other, the pressure showing on his face, but finally he said, "I can make an event of it. A documentary. I'll have to get more camera memory."

And with this collection of rationales they were joined together on their journey into the strange future.

❁   ❁   ❁

She met the security force in the living room. They had indeed come in force. The grey man and his flunky sat; the three silent spear-carriers (the man in uniform, the two women in "inconspicuous" civvies) spaced themselves around the room, one of them behind her, near the door to the kitchen.

"Stand over there," she said to the one behind her, amazed at her own peremptory tone. He looked at his senior officer and waited for a nod before he went over to stand beside the women, beside the window.

"Your people are well-trained," she said, thinking, *this is crazy, ridiculous.* "That will make things easier all around."

"The ET can't stay here. The security isn't good enough." As usual when something rude was said, the speaker was blue suit. She'd met him in so many meetings. She'd met both of them, but never with a name attached. Need-to-know? Or just bad manners?

"So don't tell anybody."

"It's not that simple."

"Sure it is. Everybody in Canada thinks 'our' alien is in the Atrium, location unknown. Who's going to suspect?"

"The story will leak."

"And when it does, face the matter then."

"You seem so sure that we will allow it to stay here." Grey suit had no problem with pronouns. He had always called Blue "it," as if, Morgan thought, the alien were a commodity. Mind you, she'd used the same pronoun with her housemates: it was hard to avoid. She sighed, wrenched her mind back to the cut-and-parry.

"You assume you have a choice."

"We're in control of the situation," said blue suit.

"Isn't that what you always say, at those meetings we have? But hasn't the time come when you will have to do as Blue wishes? Unless you have decided to make a hostile response, unless Blue is a prisoner."

"There's no question of that!" Blue suit was affronted. "But

88

security must be maintained. Some crazy could decide to take him out."

"Him?"

"The alien." Blue suit, too, long ago had made a pronoun choice. Morgan grinned despite herself.

"What I want to know," she said, "is whether Blue has freedom of choice. To live wherever Blue chooses?"

"Oh, yes, I'm afraid so." Grey suit sounded almost amused for a moment. Morgan looked sharply at him, but he was impassive.

"And us?"

"I'm not sure I understand you." Grey suit.

"If this one comes here, are you going to harass us and molest our freedoms and destroy our way of life, and in general get in the way? No, don't answer me now, take some time to think of it. You probably already know by now that there is nothing middle-of-the-road about any of us."

"That's for damn sure!" Blue suit. "A couple of homosexuals . . . a crippled communist, and a crazy . . . what is he, anyway? . . . and that fellow with the van, who works for Amnesty *and* GovNet . . ."

"That will do," said grey suit, and answered Morgan's curiosity in three words. He knew everything about them.

"Communists are a few generations back," Morgan said, laughing. "One and a half homosexuals, a disabled socialist, a video artist, and a civil servant . . . We have all agreed to offer Blue a place. But we don't want legal problems, no harassment. Leave us alone."

"You don't ask much."

"I'll ask for far more before I'm done. Advice, support—but only when Blue asks for it. Blue's a person, not a thing to be passed from agency to agency, not a thing to be studied. I take no responsibility, except to teach what I can. Just as I have done when I worked in the Atrium."

The reason for keeping the policeman away from the kitchen was the alien standing behind the door. Now Blue came out. The spear-carriers stirred, blue suit took a breath, grey suit sat looking.

"I think you see us as adversaries," grey suit said. "I am not your adversary."

Interesting pronoun choice, Morgan thought as he carried on, "We are doing our best. We are all new at this. It seems to me that if I had a guest in my house from an unknown country, and the guest were as appealing and as helpless, I would fly as quickly to the defense. But I want to try very hard to show you that we have common concerns. We want this person, Blue, to stay alive. That's my job. You know that. I've kept popes and politicians alive and frankly, this is a damn sight harder and more important than any of that. We want this person to know about us. That's not so easy either. You"—he looked directly at the blue one—"seemed at first to know nothing. We tried to teach you, and we have. Now you've taken off like my teenage kid, as soon as you knew how to dress yourself. Do you"—back to Morgan—"see the problem?"

"Yes," said Morgan, feeling a little ashamed of herself, though that was probably just what he wanted. Even worse, he reminded her suddenly of her father—the sweetness of "the sweet guy"—despite being so much younger and smaller. Could she afford to ever think he was a "sweet guy"? She kept her face stolid as she listened.

"Okay now, we don't know what Blue wants here. We don't know what the aliens want to say to Earth. We don't know what they want to learn. Blue spends a lot of time watching, just like now. Can it find what it needs here, what we were trying to give at the Atrium? The Great Literature, Great Music, Great Art?"

The blue one moved restlessly to stand behind Morgan.

"We can do better," Morgan said with bravado. "We can offer real life."

"My daughter is a video artist," said grey suit unexpectedly, "and for all I know she's a homosexual too. And a socialist, and a civil servant, even. This is her world too. So don't think you know everything."

"It isn't everything," Morgan burst out. "It isn't anything. Just Blue in distress at the door, falling down into my arms just about, for goodness' sakes. You think I'm gonna leave that for the officials to take care of, no matter how good the hearts? I've been teaching this child, this empty filling life, for a long time now."

"Not that long," said the man in the blue suit.

"It seems like a long time." Morgan glared at him. "Do you think I would walk away? That I *could?*"

"No," the grey man interceded. "I know that about you. Why do you think I kept you there when you pissed everybody off?"

Morgan looked back at him. He was not exactly smiling, but he wasn't glowering as he so often was in the meetings: progress? The man in the blue suit was glowering, but Mr. Grey spoke quietly. "It's been happening in science fiction for years, the alien meets the ordinary people. You get to be the ordinary people."

Morgan snorted. "Ordinary? Sure, we're the ones nobody else will have in their clubs."

"But what else is new about the world? There's always somebody that doesn't get chosen for the team." Was *he* talking *her* into this?

"Listen," said Morgan, "I worked my heart out for those kids at the hospital for years teaching them to take their first steps all over again, teaching them to get used to their faces, their newly limited minds, their new limbs, all that bullshit. I got away, I left it behind, because it hurt. I apply for this nice safe job and get Blue instead. Do you think I want to be torn open like this? But who else will? Who else tried to take that one somewhere human? You have to rock those gargoyle children in your arms no matter how they look; you have to love them just the same. Do you think you can leave this one"—her arm around Blue—"inside some institution and teach life on Earth from videos and the net? From movies? And not anything else? It wouldn't work, it doesn't work. And what one of you tried to take the alien home and open your private life?"

She saw the blue-suited one blush when she said "movies" and it fueled her anger, but she saw the grey suit lean forward to answer her last challenge, and her anger left her.

"Besides," she said, "it isn't up to me. It's up to Blue, and all my passion is for nothing if that one wants to ride the wind away from my door."

"I think the wind can blow on without me," said the alien.

journal:

That ephemeral and perhaps sinister attraction this stranger to Earth has followed through the unfamiliar patterns of a city built by minds still alien, hands driven by unknown visions, was not volitional and was scarcely recognized even by Blue as a compulsion. Yet it is possible that design could not have brought our dear blue alien more neatly to the right door.

Blue is alien in form as well as convention. Everything is new and unexplained, with an emptiness where the familiar should be. A stranger in a maze of strangers, following an unerring path to an uncertain destination.

The key prefix is "un-". Even as countless humans have searched, search, and will continue to search for pronouns, so we search for definition of the stages of formation of a human life. This life is un-formed, -filled, -fulfilled. Never mind the alliteration. The meaning is clear enough. There is much for us to do to make Earth a real place for any alien to live.

Live is an active verb as well as a passive one. Living well takes more than information, energy, or opportunity alone, but the three together begin to define the process. The rest is gestalt, synergy, and mystery. As it should be, to promote the growth of understanding and with it joy.

So "un-" is one prefix for description. But Blue is also characterized by the response to that vague and mysterious stimulus, which occurs on a level no other has done, and so is seductive. Brings the alien being, stuffed with knowledge and habits but with no understanding of the patterns, through the streets and parks to one particular door, a perfect choice made without choice, a design beginning to form—but not by design.

"Mr. Grey," she said, "or should I say Chief Inspector Grey or something?"

"You could even find out my name," he said, "although I'm rather enjoying having an alter ego."

"Whatever," said Morgan. "Can you explain why there is a construction crew on my property?"

"Oh. They're putting up a shed for the surveillance operation. Your garden shed is far too small." He had a rather pleasant smile, actually; it was the way he used it that pissed her off.

"Ah. And my permission?"

"I think you will find that the new security legislation passed in the last sitting of the House of Commons covers the matter quite thoroughly."

"I see."

"Of course, if you object, there are some other measures in law which could be taken."

"I object to the cameras." She handed him the empty tissue box into which Jakob and Russ had dumped the little eyes after they disconnected them. "Twenty-five so far. I think we have most of them. The ones from the bathrooms were a little tricky to get."

"Ah," he said. "Yes, well."

"Yes, well. The audio of course we can do little about, as well as any other equipment outside the house."

"I'm afraid that's the case."

"Any way we can avoid going through that?"

"I could tell you yes."

"But you would still record us."

"Yes."

"Well, at least we won't be watched while we shit—unless you plan to put these back every day or so."

"Er, well, no."

"No? Is that a commitment?"

"Men of my generation always had trouble with commitment," he murmured. She glared at him. "Luckily, I have no such problem. Yes, that is a commitment."

"Who will listen to the tapes?"

"The duty team, as they're recorded. I will, if I have time. There will be a thirty-six-hour loop: that's the program's default. We'll save whatever's notable onto a different database."

"And what will be notable?"

"All conversations with the alien."

"That's it?"

"Yes."

"Not, all conversations *about* the alien, and all conversations that might be about the alien if they keep listening, and all conversations that might incriminate us under other legislation . . ."

"I have enough authority to make sure people stay on track."

"You had better, because we have . . ."

"What?"

"The alien."

"A hostage to our good behavior?"

"Not physically of course, I don't think any of us could threaten that. But I can teach Blue anything. Blue trusts me."

"Only until you stop telling the truth." His smile again. This time Morgan smiled back, ruefully. She was a lousy politician.

"You have a point there."

"Nevertheless, I may make your point to any overzealous team members. The nuances may escape them." Another smile, controlled yet puckish. She had to grin back.

"If we have to have a CSIS cop at all," she said, "I think we'll do well enough with you."

"I endeavor to give satisfaction," he replied calmly.

※   ※   ※

"If there weren't a baker's dozen of them around the world, we'd have the religious nutters out in force, but the second coming of Jesus and Jesus and Jesus and so on *ad absurdum* isn't to their taste. Besides, after the millennium passed without incident . . ."

"You're a cynic, Mac."

The grey man reflected that if a cynic is a discouraged idealist, his boss was right. "This is my job, Andris," he said. "It's the job I was born for. You know that."

"Yes, McKenzie, I know that. How did you?"

The grey man just looked at him, and Andris's dark square face softened. "Go for it, my friend. It's yours as long as you want it."

"There's going to be opposition. I'm an old-fashioned cop,

Andris. Too soft, they say. Too sissy. The hardnosers are going to be on my case, and that means on your case, from now on."

"Tell me something I *don't* know."

"Well, for one thing, the alien does a perfect imitation of your voice."

"I heard it."

"And the alien has skipped out and taken refuge with its child care worker."

"I heard that too."

"Who is a bisexual who lives in a house with a gay man, a crippled socialist, a radico-pop video artist who used to work for us as a technician, and . . . a web-crawling civil servant with a social conscience. A scurrilous line-up, all in all, according to our current democratically elected demagogues—by which I mean of course that we have a file on most of them. What happens when those files get leaked?"

"Deal with it. As for the files, I've read 'em. I like her already."

"Who?"

"The child care worker."

"Yes?" The grey man cocked his head in query.

"She has spirit. Did you see the stuff from back in the oh-ohs when she was doing the fieldwork at college? Very creative. Well, they're all yours. Uncle Tom Cobbley and all."

"I thought you were from Manitoba."

"I took folklore in university. It was my minor."

"That's blackmail material, Andris."

Laughing, Andris shooed him toward the door with a languid hand. "Keep the alien physically safe. Leave the rest up to God."

"You believe in God, sir?"

"Church every Sunday. It's required, at my rank."

"That doesn't answer my question."

"And I'm not going to. You have me on your side, Mac. You don't have to worry about God—yet."

The last word hung in the air. Grinning, Andris closed the door behind him, and the grey man stood alone in the corridor's grim fluorescence, the smile fading from his mobile face.

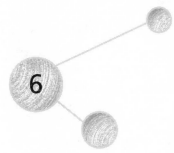

A touch of arthritis

The grey man found Morgan in the kitchen, sitting at the antique Formica table with her hands wrapped around a glass of tea in a Russian holder. Green tea, *genmaicha,* he thought: high in caffeine.

She looked very small and tired sitting there, and his glance at the walls was involuntary.

"Come, we're going for a walk," he said. As if they couldn't be heard out in the open. But there, at least, he could wave away the watchdogs with their portable microphones.

✿   ✿   ✿

"Come, we're going for a walk," the grey man said, and Morgan looked up in surprise at the tone of his voice to see him watching her with a gentle expression she couldn't fathom: concern? Affection? She didn't want to guess, didn't want to let her guard down enough. Days like today were bad enough without anyone's concern interfering—especially this Mr. Grey with his power to steal Blue away to prison in the Atrium if she fucked up.

She got up wearily and found her sunhat. *Fine,* she thought. *We will walk.*

The house was at the end of a thin spit of city thrusting out between the riverbank in front, and, behind, a ravine down which a creek had flowed heavily in spring and then dried to a trickle in midsummer. The spit ended with a long triangle of mowed grass and pruned trees on the tableland, which, at the ravine's steep edge, rapidly gave way to a tangle of undisciplined native undergrowth, including berry bushes on the sunny slope and willows in the creek bed. Usually she walked in the sunny, grassy park, and the cats would walk with her—Dundee and Seville bounding back and forth in the sun, and Marbl cautiously ten feet behind and keeping to the valley edge where the bushes and grasses grew high enough to hide her if she wanted to retreat.

Today, however, the grey man went out the back door and across the yard past the surveillance shack. He gestured to Morgan to wait while he leaned into the shack. She heard a low rumble of talk from the two shadowy figures on duty, then heard him saying in a tone very different to that he had used in the house, "I *said,* leave us alone!" and pause. As he came out he was nodding his head. She reflected on the easy way he slid in and out of his authority. He was young for the power he had: most of the others she'd met in the Atrium were bald (or what hair they had left was thin and silver, unlike Mr. Grey's vigorous brush cut of premature grey) and paunchy and probably ten years older than him, but he ranked them all.

"We will go down," he said. "If they get too curious about what I want privacy for, the trees will run interference. As long as we keep moving." He chuckled. She followed him through the wrought-iron gate, across the road at the back of the lot, and into the woods. Thinking of Sondheim, she chuckled too.

"What?" said Mr. Grey, and she sang, *"Into the woods. . . ."*

He laughed too. "Yes, it is a perfect example. And there *are* giants in the sky, now. *Great tall terrible giants in the sky . . ."*

Morgan looked up at the cloudless summer sky, felt the heat on her face. Last time she had climbed down into the wild valley, she had walked around the point and come out on the bicycle path, where she surprised a doe and her dappled fawns. She had watched them leap away across the meadow toward the river and had resolved with her desperate heart to try to find joy where the days offered it.

Today, that resolution was as far away for her, as unreachable, as her parents and her past life.

In the ravine, the trees and bushes first leopard-spotted them with shade then completely sheltered them from sunlight, and the temperature dropped until, on the footpath beside the creek bed, they stopped in cool, damp shade, and the grey man stood and leaned against a birch tree, his thumb—reflexively it seemed—stroking a feather of bark curled up along the trunk. Morgan stepped up beside him. What was left of the stream gurgled across a small fall of rocks, and he was watching the gentle eddies in the water. His voice when he finally spoke seemed as soft as the water.

"How long have you felt like this?"

"Say what?" said Morgan, recoiling.

"How long have you been so . . . empty? So . . . depressed?"

"None of your business how I feel." Sounding as sulky as a child, and she knew it, she clamped her teeth together angrily.

"I brought you down here so that we could have a private conversation," he said. "My team has been complaining to me of the security and surveillance problems this ravine poses."

"Yeah, yeah, I got it."

"So tell me."

"Or you'll what? Take Blue away?"

He laughed out loud. She looked at him in shock.

"I'm sure you're familiar," he said slowly, "with the concept of bureaucratic face." He waited for her to nod: she hated that kind of storytelling, and it made her feel even more as if there were grit between her teeth. "Well, suffice it to say that if I were to ever move Blue from your home, at any time, for any reason, and no matter what I say up there to the microphones, I would lose so much ground that I may as well retire on the spot and open a convenience store. So you can relax."

She bristled. "You're saying any one of us could be completely psychotic and you would still have painted yourself into a corner? And Blue too?"

"*You* could be completely psychotic. I haven't staked my career and my well-being for the rest of my life on the others. Just you. Now answer me. How long have you been this depressed?"

She shrugged. "Since I came here, I guess."

"Your parents' deaths? The split with Vik? That child's death? Politics?"

She smiled wryly. "Goodness, I have no secrets from you, sirrah." But she widened her smile a little to show him that she was joking. He nodded impatiently, gestured to the dim path, and they began to walk. A group of aging joggers rounded the bend ahead of them and Morgan and Mr. Grey stepped off the path onto the spongy, mossy needlefall from the evergreens. She shook her head.

"I was going to find a doctor one of these days. When I had the energy. But now, I can't. The people in those meetings would . . ."

"Yes, I appreciate the problem." He gestured at the woods above them and she took his meaning. "But still," he went on, "you can't go on like this."

"A secure doctor, at the Atrium?"

"There are no secure doctors. I think you are going to develop a greater interest in health food stores."

"What?"

"And a touch of arthritis. Yes, how about a touch of arthritis? Can't you feel it coming on now?"

"What?"

"There's a good herbal remedy for depression, and it's also an anti-inflammatory. It works for arthritis too. I took it when my wife died, for about two years, and when I quit my back started bothering me again. So I started taking it again for that. No, don't bother with the health food stores. I'll bring it to you myself. It's already established that I buy it."

She laughed despite herself. "Doctor Grey, aren't you taking a terrible risk prescribing after such a short examination? And no talk therapy?"

"Talk to Blue. That'll be therapy enough. And at the moment, Blue's sojourn depends on everything staying very very stable. Including you. If this helps, fine. You'll know in a few weeks. If it doesn't, we'll take the risk of exposing you to the medical profession."

"Don't you trust doctors, sirrah?"

"I trust four—maybe five—people in the world. At the moment. One of them is myself."

I shouldn't ask this, thought Morgan. "And the others?"

"My daughter. My boss. The alien."

The alien? "The alien?"

"Yes."

"And the fifth?" she said, when it became obvious that he was going to say no more about Blue.

"You," he said shortly, and walked on.

✧   ✧   ✧

They climbed out of the valley at the end of the park and walked back through the frolicking families and the teenagers' soccer game. Mr. Grey stopped the soccer ball from caroming off the edge of the flat area into the bush, and kicked it expertly back into the game. The teenagers yelled something and he laughed.

"What did they say?" said Morgan.

" 'Not bad for an old man', approximately," said the grey man, but he was smiling. "I played soccer when I was a kid. We went to the nationals, one year. Now, we have been arguing all this time about the technicians coming in to install and maintain the hardware for Blue's information network. I'm sorry, I agree with many of your points, but nevertheless they have to come into the house. Think of them as being like carpet cleaners."

"I don't have carpets because of the wheelchair," said Morgan automatically. Technicians? He had forestalled her very nicely: she *couldn't* argue, now that their argument was their cover story. She glared at him and he laughed.

"I'm sorry, *Madelle,*" he said, and bowed. "I do what I must." He swept his arm out gracefully in the dramatic d'Artagnan manner. "Please tell your people that I am not their enemy. I will make sure the technicians are not obtrusive."

"And that they install no more little eyes in the bathrooms."

"Yes, yes, of course," he said, as if she had wrung a concession from him, and she grinned. Behind her grin a thought trickled in: *he is too good at lying. How many lies did he tell me in the woods?*

✿   ✿   ✿

Later that day, Blue said to her, "There are only two people here who tell the truth all the time. You and that man who visits."

She looked at the alien measuringly. "You can tell when people are telling the truth?"

"Yes. Well, I think so. You do not tell all you think, but when you speak, you don't lie. I have read about polygraph—maybe I have polygraph perceptions."

"Cute phrase." Marbl shifted in Morgan's lap and settled herself by hooking a claw into Morgan's knee through the fabric of her sarong. "Ow! And what about cats? Can you tell if they are truthful? For instance, this purring. What does it mean? Is she just pretending to like me?"

"She thinks you are her kitten, and she grooms you and worries about your safety when you go out of the house. That is why she walks with you, although she hates being outside her territory."

Blue stood up between her and the window, and Morgan looked up at the looming figure looking suddenly dark and large. Could Blue really read thoughts? "How much do you read—take in, learn, I mean—from the world?"

"As much as I can," said Blue. "Just like you."

The next few days, the technicians descended quietly, like silverfish, and began to bring Blue's third-floor bedroom into the twenty-first century. The side advantage was the new house system they installed, with new terminals for everyone; Morgan saw the grey man's fine hand in this gift. The others were ecstatic about the new tech, far better than any of them could afford. Blue, who had never had to buy anything, hovered impatiently, waiting for a hot terminal. When the system was finally at temperature, the alien dived in like a swimmer; Morgan meanwhile began to take the St.-John's-Wort tablets that Mr. Grey left in the bathroom on his next visit, and though she did not feel better, she had something to do. Blue must have an education in the world.

journal:

I am totally in the dark about what goes on behind those dark eyes. If that is where Blue's thinking goes on. Yesterday after watching the videotape all night and half of the morning, that one comes out of the room to where I'm doing dishes, says:

Maybe you should call me Klaatu.

No, I said before thinking, not that!

You saw that movie?

Of course, it's a golden oldie. Why do you think I got it for you?

And I'm not Klaatu?

With the power of life and death over the earth? Do you have the power of life and death over the earth?

Oh, of course. don't you have it also?

Looking very innocent. I was terrified for a moment there, this exchange-student masquerade wasn't gonna work any more. So I said, okay, Klaatu, what's the plan? And do you sail away in your saucer at the end of it with your Michael Rennie smile?

You are angry.

So I said, of course I am, of course, I'm stuck with saving the world, haven't you read enough of that pulp bullshit by now? I think that was when I started crying, with the tears dripping off my chin, up to my elbows in dishwater and suds and trying to wipe my face on my sleeve, and I suppose with a red nose and blotchy face as usual, damn, not gonna save the world this way.

And blue hands wiping off my face with the dishtowel, smoothing out my skin, until I shivered and trembled and was even more terrified and thinking what the hell am I worrying for, this one is so fucking dangerous and has us all in the palm of one hand, always has had.

And then Blue starts drying the fucking dishes, of all things, saying, what is this for? Why do you have these in so many different sizes? And what do you do with this? And I explained, explained, and that was Tuesday.

"When do the rest of you want to get the implants?" said the technician.

"Implants?" Morgan said.

"Control chips. That's why your . . . the . . . you know, *he*"— he means Blue—"can access the system. We activated the locator chip they put in at the Atrium."

Another conversation with the grey man, Morgan furious, Mr. Grey calm.

"How do you think we followed Blue here so fast?" he said. "Blue's security is at stake. Really, the whole lot of you should have them. Then we can back off on the surveillance a little."

"Not me. And I think Blue should have a choice, just like the rest of us."

"Blue is not a citizen. The law is ambiguous."

"Blue is a person who deserves respect. You all have the contempt of authority. That has to change."

"Hey, I didn't order the chip. And there are thousands, tens of thousands, of people using them to activate their smarthouses and virch. You people wouldn't be experimental."

"Those people don't care if Big Brother can track their every move. I do. And I care on Blue's behalf."

"You need them to use the house system."

"We can use an external chip and you know it."

"Fine. I'll tell the techs. You call a house meeting, and we'll ask the others."

"Incl—"

"Including Blue. Yes."

So they do. Blue chose an external chip, as did Jakob, Russ, John, and Morgan. Delany chose an implant. "Where do I go, most of the time? And besides, I'm pretty easy to catch up with even if I did run away."

❀   ❀   ❀

"What's wrong with you today?" Morgan said to Jakob, who was unfocusedly meandering around the kitchen.

"*I drinks a bit*," sang Jakob dreamily. He was washing his

hands, and he raised one dripping and stared through the gleaming falling drops.

"Are you stoned?" she said sharply, forgetting the surveillance.

"Always, my dear Azalea Trailmaiden," Jakob said in his bad imitation of a Southern-U.S. drawl. "This glittering world is unbearable otherly. And so the glitter meets the glitter."

"Don't you think that's a bit foolish under the circumstances?"

Jakob sharpened slightly, though he was still swaying slightly as he focused on her. "My dear landlady and friend," he said, "if I cared a tinker's damn about CSIS, that would be true. They know all about me. I'm a registered addict. I buy my stuff from the government lab.

"It's the law, you know," he added mockingly.

Morgan knew that. Detox facilities, especially for the new chemistry, were too expensive. Cutbacks over a decade ago had eliminated them completely except on a user-pay basis for the rich and connected. Instead, the courts ordered the health care system to license addicts and they were given theoretically non-fatal, non-addictive versions of the street chemistry.

"You should have told me," Morgan said irritably.

"Chile, you *are* in a pet!" cried Jakob gaily, but he was fishing in his pockets and finally found a creased skin-tab, which he pressed to the inside of his elbow. "Evens me up," he said. "Give me a minute." Morgan sat down at the table, shaking her head, but indeed, in less than a minute, Jakob steadied and his gaze sharpened.

"I didn't think you were a fundy," he said.

"It's not that." Morgan said. "I just find this whole situation so perilous, and I'd like to know what the variables are. I wouldn't have hassled you if I'd known you were licensed, but if I'd known, it might have made a difference somehow."

"How?"

Morgan shook her head and grinned. "I can't think of a single concrete reason—except if the press ever gets hold of this. Or John—now he has a streak of fundy a mile wide. I didn't believe you at first—he seems so interesting. Well, he *is* interesting—but so conservative."

"Where did you get him from?"

"A friend of his heard about the house, he said. I don't quite know. He had pretty good references."

"References?" Jakob laughed out loud.

"Yeah, honeylamb, *references*. Like from a financial institution, saying he could pay his rent? You know, rent?"

"Hey, I paid you!" Jakob said in mock hurt. Morgan laughed, but then turned her head back to the serious side of the conversation. "Look, sweetie, we had people in the hospital who had been on the program for too long. That stuff isn't as harmless as they say it is. It grows stuff in you. You get weird. We saw some personality changes you wouldn't believe, real scary stuff. . . ."

"Yeah," said Jakob, "I know. But detox on your own is a bugger. I've tried a couple of times. Life's a bit difficult for a dancer with muscle spasms and weakness."

"Yeah, yeah, but there's chem for that too. They say."

"Other thing is, honeylamb, that I can't imagine having to take the world straight up."

"Sweetie, you don't take *anything* straight!" It was an old joke, and a feeble line, and she grimaced an apology.

He shook his head. "I'm serious, girl. Things are mean in this world. When I was a kid, I was taught that mean wasn't the default value, but it ain't like that now, no-how. There's too high a signal-to-noise ratio in the world for a dancing fag with dark skin and a belief in fairness. No, I *didn't* say a belief in fairies!"

She laughed. "Badum-bum. So where *did* you come from, Southern belle? And why do you act broken when you're smart, pretty, talented, and your dance vids sell?"

Jakob grinned. "You mean, like, get over it, bitch?"

"Not really. Just curious."

"I trusted the wrong people when I was young. It was stupid. I lost faith in myself. That was stupider. And whatever I do, I can't seem to get it back. For that, I blame society." The last was a joke, and Morgan dutifully smiled, but she was not satisfied.

"How come you were so stoned today? I never saw you like that before."

"I had a long night in the studio. I finished a vid and sent it out on the web. There's always a reaction. I go down. It was get twice as stoned or kill myself. I figured stoned was less messy."

"Goodness," said Morgan reflexively, then snorted at the word. "Listen, you still at risk?"

"Honey, I'm *never* 'at risk'," said Jakob. "I'm just more or less stupid. Never mind what I say when I'm stoned, or when I've just finished a dance, or when I'm between lovers."

"That'd be about all the time, from what you say."

"Honey, you got it."

"Nevertheless, I don't wanna have to clean out my attic if you off yourself."

"Trust me, honey. If I ever *really* wanna do that, I'll warn you and you can talk me out of it. 'Kay?"

"Fine. But if you have any other little secrets that might affect the gestalt around here, I'd appreciate if you'd tell me."

"I don't floss?"

"Any big secrets. I'm serious, you."

"No more secrets, aside from the existential," said Jakob, and Morgan went up to her new house terminal and called up his new vid.

It was tagged with the working title *Slow Glass:* an adagio suite danced to Rachmaninoff's *Vespers.* By keeping to a glacially grave pace that was at times dreamy, at times sensual and at times agonizing, he had created a vocabulary of hesitation and, ultimately, repression that she hadn't seen attempted since Baryshnikov's beautiful riff on dissident music in that terrible old movie. And, Morgan thought, Jakob's dance was better.

At first it seemed he had added little to the almost documentary quality of the fixed-viewpoint vid, but as the suite went on, she saw from the start a constant subtle transformation had been taking place, shifting from complete color replacements at the start to simpler and simpler light effects, until by the end the only alteration seemed to be the solarizing of the golden highlights the spotlights struck from his skin. Only watching it again did she see the rhythms and counterrhythms in the movement of the light, rhythms whose increasing dissidence created mounting subliminal unease and culminated in a sense of claustrophobic imprisonment.

After she watched it a third time, she went to ask Jakob if she could sit in on some of his studio time.

"Sure, chile," he said in the phony drawl. "You-all been watchin' vid-*ay*-oh?"

"Yeah. Why vid, anyway? Why not virch?"

He looked at her campily.

"Come on, I'm serious," she insisted. "On vid it was fabulous, but in person it would have been—devastating. With virtual, you could pull people in so much further."

"At first the problem was the cost to rig virch into this house's archaic system," Jakob said, "but your sweet little Grey guy took care of that. But that was just an excuse so people wouldn't pry. These days it's better to be flippant than idealistic . . ."

"Surprise. So your real reason . . . ?"

"Well . . . there's the little matter of social bandwidth."

"Say what?"

"Okay, ten years ago virtual was everybody's darling, wasn't it? Media big. Everybody said it was the next big thing. Radio. TV. Different engine, so to speak. Internet. And now—*ta-DA!*— virtual reality springs us into the twenty-first century. But did it?"

She tipped her head to watch him. He was more still—and more focussed—than she had ever seen him. *This is where he really lives*, she thought. *Why doesn't he spend more time here?* "Rhetorical, I assume," she said.

"Yep. Fact is, economic slowdown, New Economy, whatever you call it: not enough people can afford virch. Those who can, by and large can't create with it. That old fart Spielberg—a joke. And look at Gilbert Coffee or Scattered Norms. Couple of world-class failures there. I decided that my stuff had to be accessible even to people with no more bandwidth than full-motion video. Twenty-year-old tech had to be able to play it. And not just real bandwidth, but some kinda social capability. The simple ability to relate. And it works. People net me in Nepal, for crying out loud.

Hong Kong and Tibet. African splinter states. Ulan Bator, even: yak country."

"You should be better known here too," said Morgan.

"So. That means you thought it was okay?"

"Yeah," she said. "More than okay." She didn't tell him that the dance had made her cry, and though she had shaken the mood away quickly, she had felt something for a moment. She wasn't sure she was ready to feel more—but she *had* asked him for permission to watch. That analytical self she could not repress thought: *Maybe there's hope for me after all.*

☆   ☆   ☆

"Ulan Bator," said the Boy Wonder scornfully to Mr. Grey, but later that day, when the grey man was leaving for lunch, he saw Rahim at a courtyard table with a young man, both of them bent intently over a hand terminal. Coming up behind them, he saw that they were netting Jakob Ngogaba's *Slow Glass* vid. McKenzie had himself watched it only moments before.

"Good, isn't it?" he said, and Rahim started, but his friend, a tall willowy young man with the most perfect light-brown skin the grey man had ever seen, looked up excitedly.

"It's wonderful!" he said. "The vocabulary is astonishingly controlled. I'd love to ask him about—"

"Don't get too carried away," said Rahim, and didn't introduce them. The grey man walked away thinking—grinning as he heard his own catty thought—*there's* a new interpretation for Rahim's perfect suits. He almost laughed aloud realizing how horrified Rahim would be if he heard such a suggestion. The lad must be a relative: Rahim had a huge family.

☆   ☆   ☆

Despite how good she looked to the rest of them, and despite her successful bluff of the CSIS men, Morgan knew she was on shaky ground. Some initial premise was wrong. She knew that, yet felt she had had no choice but to believe in her past. The myths of her childhood, her family, were not so pernicious nor so false as some, and she couldn't find the worm which in the night of soul's darkness had lodged in the heart without unraveling the only images she had of her dead parents.

She was not ready to do that, not ready to be left without them completely, body *and* soul.

This inability to allow honesty to remove the last supports from a shaky past is the weakness that becomes depression. Morgan knew it. She knew it. She just could not allow the knowledge to surface. The old poem says "the energy needed to live / alone is so great," but it is not living that takes the energy, but suppressing life. Why Jakob's adagio dance left him sweating and the watcher exhausted with repression.

I have no choice, thought Morgan whenever she got this far. *I must survive, and I don't know any other way. Precious little justification, but all I have.*

❀   ❀   ❀

Russ and Morgan were peeling potatoes. Russ wore his silk shirt, sarong. His hands were comely and capable among the vegetables. The muscles of his shoulders were outlined by the shirt. Morgan thought, *for a bunch of asocial misfits, we are actually quite a houseful of attractive people. Even I could think I am attractive sometimes*. She chuckled. Blue, who seemed to have become hypnotized by the garlic press, looked up.

"What?" Russ said.

"Lots of stuff. Life is absurd. When I was a kid, we all used to do dishes together; the whole family in the kitchen singing and laughing. Mostly. There was some snarling and fighting, but mostly it was a good time. Now here I am. Wondering if this houseful of weirdos can really be a new, self-made family. Does it ever occur to you?"

"No. I'm not looking for a family. Too much angst. It's better here."

"What do you mean? Jakob turns out to be a registered addict,

Delany's fighting with muscular dystrophy and bureaucracy, John changes his vid production schedule twice a week and agonizes about it—aren't those angst? Or me, for that matter, mooning around the place?"

"Or me," said Blue brightly. "I'm an alien, you know!" Morgan couldn't decide whether to grin or glare, settled for simply putting her finger across her lips to shush Blue: she didn't want Russ's unexpected loquaciousness to be interrupted.

"No. It doesn't bother me like a family would. You know I grew up with my grandparents after my folks were killed. They were all right, but old, and I felt like I was always too noisy and—just too active. Then when they died I went to live with my uncle and aunt. There was always that sense of duty, that feeling that I had to try hard just to earn my right to be there. And the criticism, and the—I don't know. When I left at sixteen I swore I'd never live with anyone again."

Half of this was new to Morgan, but she questioned carefully in case he closed up again. "And did you? Before here, I mean."

"Oh, yes, when I got married."

"Married?" This was the first time in the two years she had known Russ that he had given her a hint of this.

"Oh, yes, I was married for seven years. We had a kid, a girl."

"Where are they now? Do you still see your child?"

"I don't know where my wife is. I don't hear from her. Except for the divorce. I got a notice of that. My little girl is dead."

"Dead? How hard that must have been, after being divorced."

"No, the other way around. We were together when she died. She died of leukemia when she was five. Things weren't too bad for us then, but when my wife got pregnant again, she didn't want the child. She got an abortion and left. I wanted another kid. I guess we were both wrong."

"How do you mean?"

"I was wrong to pressure her to get pregnant again, to have another one so soon, and she was wrong to think I would understand her grief."

"Oh, Russ, I'm so sorry."

"That's the way it goes. It was a mistake to get too involved.

111

I thought it might turn out that way but I wanted to believe different."

"But aren't you glad you had the good times?"

"It doesn't matter any more. That was a long time ago. Almost ten years."

"And since then?"

"I keep myself clear."

"What about us, here, in the house?"

"It's not that I don't care about the people here. But I could leave any time. That's why I like it."

"And will you?"

"I think so. Eventually. I'd like to go to Sri Lanka or India, do some studying there. At least see Benares."

Morgan couldn't resist. "We'll miss you," she said sententiously.

He looked at her suspiciously, but she hadn't been able to avoid grinning.

"I'll write," he said, and they were both laughing, a soapy hand and a tea-towel-entangled hand intertwined for a moment. Then he began to bellow a Maritime sea chanty, and she joined in. Jakob, coming into the kitchen with a handful of dirty cups, took a wild dance around the room. Blue, holding up a Tupperware orange peeler, said, "What is this for?" Morgan thought, background to hilarity, *Everything he ever loved has left him. Everyone. How could one be that empty?* Except that she was too. Only she now knew that for some reason she believed in the future, stayed out on a limb. She felt that faith rising up from some diaphragmatic recess she had not known was there until her visceral reaction to—against—the way Russ had chosen, the other road, the road of closure. Damn. She might have to belong after all. Harsh.

The kitchen was full of the awkward family she had made for herself, Delany wheeling in with a lapful of plates, John holding up his camera for a quick shot; and in the door was Blue, smiling. Across the melee those dark eyes met Morgan's. *This is ordinary life,* she thought with a shock, *with an extraterrestrial in it.*

The thought arrested her motion, her voice for a moment.

Her first memory of vid was when her family followed the progress of the *Voyagers* and *Pathfinder;* lately she had watched the image transmission of the first human step onto the Martian surface; and now this. There was a satellite moving across the sky this minute, she knew. She felt its sensor beam sweep over her, she felt those TV pictures coming in on ultra high frequency. The alien's gaze was steady. Blue. To call someone a name makes them part of the world, she thought, recovered the verse of the song, and sang.

✤   ✤   ✤

Morgan was seated in the living room thinking, as usual. The light was dim around her and she was looking out into the brilliant dining-room light, where John had his vidcam trained on the art lesson Delany was giving Blue. Morgan was wondering about the art lesson, the alien brain and its hemispheres, the whole idea of taking a picture of Earth and sending the film out to space to be developed. Blue was a photographic plate of a holographic and multiplex design. *What does that make me?* Morgan wondered. She drifted in and out of sleep, hearing the voices in waves alternating with waves of strange ephemeral dreams.

✤   ✤   ✤

Morgan awakening to darkness, that blue body imposed like an afterburn on her retinas, imposed on the blackness, fading, until gradually she saw the dim outline, the door, the window frame, and the dream was only that, a dream of those hands reaching for her face, reaching with longing and menace and love, until she could do nothing through her terror but move toward them, into their orbit, through the sphere of their influence, until they touched.

And the voice came to her in the darkness, clearly, as she sat up among the sheets, saying, *you believe me now. You know me.*

Marbl leapt back onto the bed, kneaded the covers, rolled her underbelly to Morgan's cold hand, purring, until Morgan's heart slowed and her breath came calmly again, stroking Marbl, and Morgan could think, *it's the afterglow of the dream;* and then the voice said clearly, so that Marbl started up and leapt away:

You can do so much for me, to complete me, but you turn away. I am afraid to dream among you fragile people.

Then the night was shattered, and Morgan rocked in the chair until daybreak.

Simpler as an alien

There were three men come from the west . . .

When he was as tired as this, he found listening to the old
Steeleye Span recordings comforting. They reminded him of a
time he thought of as before his public existence. His childhood,
listening to his mother play her favorite records. When he was
not a cop, not a security-service cop, and especially not a guardian
of aliens.

"Dad. Dad!" His daughter Salomé, in a hurry as always. She
grinned at him. "In your armchair again? It's getting to be a nest.
Do you know where the kidvids are?" She meant the videos he'd
taken of her as a child.

"In kidvid heaven. I don't know. Aren't they on the shelf in
the den?"

Which they were, but it gave her a chance to hug him.

"Do you know a guy called John Dee or Lee? A video artist?"
he asked the wind.

"There's a video pretender called John Lee. He never releases
anything. Well, he did the Doctor Dee tapes a while ago. Yeah,
must be him then, he's in the Downtown Video Co-op. Why?"

"I'm not supposed to tell you."

"Da-ad. This is me, right?"

"He worked for us, in the Atrium, for a while. And he lives
in that house."

"With the Blue guy?"

"With the Blue guy and the Morgan guy. But they both took
the oath"—he meant of confidentiality—"and he at least seems

115

to have taken it to heart, so Morgan doesn't even know they were on opposite sides of the mirrors. But until Blue took flight, *we* didn't know he boarded with her."

"With like *with,* or just with?"

"Just with. She doesn't have any 'with' like *with.*"

"Poor being."

"No, she isn't. She seems completely self-contained."

"Like you. You *seem* completely self-contained . . ."

"And I'm not?"

"What would you do if I were kidnapped? Killed? Would you mind?"

He looked at her. She said, "Well, then, you aren't self-contained. What is it about this John Dee? Do you want me to ask around about him?"

"John Lee. *Dee* seems to be an a.k.a. for the videos. Neo-Elizabethan or something. Ask carefully. People know you're my daughter. I don't want any attention placed. It's just that he seems too squeaky-clean. All the others . . ."

"Are heinous criminals, I know."

"No. Not one of them has a criminal record yet, though between them they've run the gamut from demonstrations and activism to sexual variations and drugs. Oh, yeah, and ten years ago one of them had a couple of noise complaints, domestic disputes, but officers on-scene found no sign of violence. But that's it. Okay, if the legislature gets its way next month, half of them could be charged. And it's true they all have CSIS files. Watching briefs. Except this guy. He has a security clearance, squeaky-clean, but no data. It doesn't make sense. Where did he come from? Why her place, or was it co-incidence? And why does he want to live there if he isn't a social outlaw?"

"Social Outlaws. A new band. Catchy name. Very retro."

"The most mainstream one works on government vid. Makes net sites, video and virch. Government department rah-rah propaganda, mostly. But he has been to Indonesia, and Burma, and Hong Kong, making vid of Amnesty International and *Médecins Sans Frontières*. Smuggling memory back in hollow carvings, the whole thing. Russ Marks, heard of him?"

"Yeah. Powerful stuff. Well-shot, well-edited. Realworld, real-time. No artistic gloss, though."

"I suppose it's counterindicated, given the purpose."

"Yeah, but—if you have it in your bones, you have it."

"Then there's a dancer. Jakob Ngogaba. He does video dance installations and performances."

"Yeah, very old-fashioned. I know the stuff. The video is old-fashioned, anyway. Point-of-view stuff. Documentary, really," she said dismissively.

"But skillful?"

"Oh, I suppose, in a technical way. But it's the dance that *means,* for that guy. He's a fabulous dancer. He should quit fooling around with video though. Full-motion net is so *old*. Even virch would be better."

"Apparently he thinks virtual reality is too elitist."

"Feh."

"What about this Delany Johns? She does video too."

"Flat artist," said Salomé.

He laughed. "You make it sound like the last word in irrelevant!"

"Well, it is, kinda. I mean, nice color activation, and that, but to doc it she uses one camera and solarizes a couple of highlights, if you can imagine."

"Imagine that!"

Salomé laughed. "Snobbery, I guess, eh?" She sprawled on the old, battered black leather couch and he settled back into the armchair, his leg up over the arm and his head against the wing of the back.

"Well, I detected a tiny tad of condescension. . . ."

"Do you talk to Kowalski this way?"

"I don't talk to any of them this way, any more. If I ever did. Are you queer?"

"Dad!"

"Well?"

"I don't think so. Not so far. Maybe. I am making a women's sex virch and all the people in it are women."

"Are you in it?"

"Nah. It's a commission. For a bunch of the dykes at Womoncentre. People your age who still think queer kids need sex education too."

"And you don't think so?"

"Yeah, I think so. It's worse now, with the government the way it is. But it's different than it was in your day. Kids don't shave their heads and get body piercings any more. They don't get into that leather scene the way you guys did. Why can't they see that?"

"I beg to differ. I was never 'into that leather scene'."

"Oh, Daddy, you know what I mean. Your *generation.*"

"There were a lot of prudes in my generation too," he said, not allowing his grin to show.

"Daddy, quit being deliberately obtuse. People like you grew up in the era of questions. People like me are stuck in the era of answers. Sometimes it's crazy, like with the government. Who ever thought we'd need *samizdat* in *Canada?* But sometimes it's fine. I don't have to get tugged around by a ring in my nipple to prove I'm sexually hip."

"Hip? My dear, your timeslip is showing. *We* didn't even say 'hip'. My *generation.*"

"Oh, yes you did. I have Mom's diaries, remember?" Seeing his face change, though he would have sworn he hadn't moved a muscle, she said, "Oh, Dad, I'm sorry. Do you still . . . well, I guess you do."

"Miss her? Yes. Pine over her? No."

"Then how come you never found . . ."

"Nobody was interesting."

"*Nobody?*"

"Daughter, you know where I work. You've seen Flora, who used to be Fred, and was ultra-conservative then too, about everything else besides gender reassignment. You've seen Kowalski in *both* of his blue suits. Do you think I should be tempted?"

"Daddy! Are *you* queer?"

"Oh, dear. Don't you think it has gone beyond that by now?"

"What do you mean?"

"Beyond queer, except as a political stance or issue. Beyond

Men and Women, Fags and Dykes, Homos and Heteros. I know"—he held up a hand like a TV pedant—"that the political scene has revived all that. But don't you think more people are managing to get beyond that?"

"Oh, for heaven's sake, that old gender thing again. Daddy, face it. You guys are losing. The conservatives are winning. Something in the human race *demands* categories, and theirs are winning. You are never going to get a chance to live like you want."

"Never? You sure?" he mocked her.

"Daddy, don't you condescend now. You are nursing a fantasy."

"Daughter, don't you condescend back. I have managed to stay alive, have sex, have you, get promotions, and get assigned to the alien. I am not living in a dream world."

"Oh, Daddy, you are too. We all are. We dream we make a difference. Do you think I believe that? I don't. I believe that I am doomed to dance the dance, just like a termite, but I do think *how* I dance doesn't make a damned bit of difference. Babies still die." Her face was shadowed for a moment as she looked down, swallowed.

"Babies always died," he said roughly. "One of ours. One of yours. One of that guy's in their house. Childbirth. Stillbirth. Meningitis. Leukemia. Starvation. Thirst. What the hell does that have to do with the price of fish in Newfoundland?" He was surprised to hear his father's idiom, his father's voice, in his own.

Salomé was not angry though. She laughed. "Daddy, you do so have a heart. Stop acting!"

"I can't," he said. "If I do, they'll get to me, and I'll lose the alien. And that, my Salomé, would be a tragedy. Because sometimes my slight bulk is all that stands in the way of a raid on that place, and in some of their scenarios, they don't mind if the alien gets in the way."

"Why did you name me after someone who demanded a prophet's head on a platter?" She had often asked this, and he had always said, "Your mother named you. How could I say no?" This time, he didn't say that.

"Because you were small, defenseless," he said, "and I wanted you to be fierce. I wanted you to be able to look at death and life and sacrifice and not blink or flinch. I wanted you to be able to ask for what you want, and get it. Your mother—Sam—just thought it sounded nice. She wasn't a Christian, after all. She didn't care. She liked the sound. I chose that name and she chose the family name. Hester, after her grandmother, such a contrast. I could have chosen a safer name than Salomé. But I didn't. I wanted you to crave the taste of blood."

She got up, came over, hugged him again. "Daddy, blood's a biohazard."

"Daughter, life's a biohazard."

❖   ❖   ❖

Morgan dreams her father falls in a snowbank. He is covered in snow, and he is not wearing a coat. She runs to help him, but he falls deeper and deeper, his face turning into the snow.

It's pretty obvious what *that's* about, she thinks, even in the dream. Still, she woke unsettled: another day of plodding ahead.

The obvious still has to be lived through.

❖   ❖   ❖

"I've been expecting visits from the secret police for a long time, but not about this," Morgan said, pouring the tea.

"About your lifestyle, to use the polite term, or about the customs business?" The grey man liked the fussy business of tea-cups and spoon-in-saucer, she could see that.

"So I *am* on some kind of a list. I was wondering about all the mail from the U.S."

"Oh, yes, you are. Several. And there are some interesting photographs of you in the demonstrations."

"Demonstrations? That was years ago! Long before I started writing letters."

"You underestimate how long the preparations for this were going on."

"This?"

"The revolution of the haves against the have-nots."

"Ah, someone had a plan then. I didn't know." She laughed, and after a moment the grey man laughed also.

"Of course they had a plan. You are very innocent despite all this, aren't you?"

"Smart-ass. More tea?"

"Is that all you ever drink?"

"Lemon? Sugar and cream?"

"No, I meant something stronger."

"Something . . . oh, booze. No, I don't drink. Don't think to keep the stuff. Let's see"—opening cupboard doors—"one of the others might have something . . ."

"I wasn't asking for it. I just find it hard to believe you could get to your age and not have any of the usual vices."

"Drink's boring. I've seen too many people throw up. Then at our age, they forget they used to think it was for fun, and start drinking themselves to death. Boring and stupid. Same as the rest of it. Most of the time I'm glad I didn't get a taste for any of it."

"Most of the time?"

"Well, I have had the occasional desire to lose myself in dissipation and despair. But I had to settle for despair straight up."

The grey man stood up suddenly, turned on the radio, and began to rinse his cup at the sink. "How stupid you are!" he said, vehement but quiet against the background noise. "Such a limited vision."

"And you can see clearly?" Morgan asked, surprised but calm.

"More clearly than you. Think. Think what is going to happen to you when your alien goes away. Your freedom hangs by a thread."

"A grey thread?"

"Yes, and not a reliable one. I could go either way. I could decide to save my own ass instead of yours. It's one or the other, right now."

She could see he was even more infuriated by her po-faced return stare. "I can't help it," she said. "All that seems so petty compared with this. And as for the rest, I lost everything once, I can do it again."

"You don't know what loss is. You always had food, you had the death payoff that brought you to this house, you never stole or begged or lived out of doors all winter. Wait until that is the story of your life. And it will be, believe me, it will be." He took her cup to wash.

"I won't quote poetry at you," she said.

"Poetry?"

"*Stone walls do not a prison make* . . . and that kind of thing. But I will say that I consider what I lost to be more important than food and warmth. If I were homeless, I'd walk south until I wasn't cold. But where would I walk to find what I don't have? I lost my soul, Mr. Grey. I lost my ability to feel. Everything skates by in a tidy array of pretty shapes and things and sounds, but there is nothing behind it. If I were hungry and looking for food, I would care about that. I could get cold enough to care about getting warm. But there is nothing else, Mr. Grey."

"Nothing wrong with poetry. *Hell would look like a lord's great kitchen without fire in 't* . . ." He turned off the taps and reached for the linen teatowel.

"Yeah, exactly."

"So is all this just a game?"

"Blue interested me. Blue is the first being to interest me in a long time. That was worth something. Then, I felt something more when I opened the door and Blue was there. A twinge. The shadow of guilt to come, maybe. But something."

"You are still a fool. Especially if you believe what you just said, you are a fool."

"That's a stupid thing to call anyone, Mr. Grey, if you know anything about Zen. It's a compliment, now. It's the sort of thing lovers say to each other, in the circles I move in."

To her surprise, he blushed at that.

"Are you a prude, Mr. Grey? Or are you entertaining lascivious thoughts?"

"Are those my only two options?" he said, seeming quite serious, and she laughed.

"No, and I'm sorry. Then, I was playing a game, the old one

I find so bizarre. The talk-dirty game that renders some men helpless. The ones who still swear by being men."

"I don't know if I qualify. I stopped thinking about being a man something like three and a half decades ago."

"But you were still born when you were born, and went through all the same stages of life and culture. Did you manage to stay more flexible than other men of your age?"

"*You are old, Father William, the young man said, / and your hair has become very white. / And yet you incessantly stand on your head. / Do you think, at your age, it is right?*"

"Yeah, it is condescending, sorry. But it's also a problem I have with the others the same age as you, or older. They all went drumming in the woods twenty or thirty years ago and it has affected them badly."

"I never did that."

"I guess not."

"I'm younger than I look, anyway." He reached over and turned off the radio, plunked the clean cups back on the table, pulled the teapot toward himself, filled both their cups again. She felt, for a moment, an absurd tenderness which luckily was gone as soon as she looked at it square-on. If she was going to wake up again, she thought, what a stupid place to start. She watched his tiny hands, his small fingers' delicate hold of the delicate cup handle. He could use the Donison-Steinbuhler keyboard too, she thought, like my mother. For the first time, she regretted the sale of the piano.

❀   ❀   ❀

"Do me a favor, Jakob," Morgan said wearily. "If you aren't going to put out, don't flirt."

Jakob looked at her in something between surprise and calculation. "What are you talking about, girlfriend?"

"I am a woman, Jakob. Not a boy, not someone you want to sleep with. So why flirt with me?"

"It's just a . . . what *is* the matter with you?"

"I am tired, Jakob. I am tired."

"You must be pissed off with me. Nobody calls somebody their name that many times in one minute unless they're pissed off."

"Think about it, Jakob. I sleep with men and women. I like sex"—*I really do,* she thought with surprise, on the way by—"and I respond sexually to *people.* When you flirt with me, there's a part of me that thinks you're serious. I respond. Then I feel jerked around. Tonight I am tired and I have been playing games with cops all day and I don't feel like feeling jerked around."

"Usually you flirt right back."

"Yes, I admit, I play the game. I even like the game, most of the time. It's amusing. There was a long time there where I wasn't amused by much else but games. But tonight I am too tired to untangle all the skeins. Too tired to resist what I know is false."

"It isn't exactly false, honey. I like you. You know you are my *free-und.*" He was still camping it up.

Morgan smiled. "Yes, I am your friend, Azalea Trailmaiden."

"We-ell then, honeychile, what am I gonna do if not flirt? I don't know no other way to be a *free-und* ceptun flirtin', honey-chile."

She laughed, but it was a laugh of defeat. "Cut out the phony accent, will you? Okay, okay, never mind. We don't have to talk about it. It's too much trouble. Forget it."

"Well, don't dis me, honey, if you're just gonna say forget it."

Jakob's tone was sharper than repartee would demand, and his passive-aggressive look reminded her of John's hostile expression when she had the latest housework skirmish with him. She grinned: Jakob would hate to think that he was like John in any way. But they were alike in some ways, she realized. They both had a grudge against sectors of the world.

"Have you always had women around you, Jakob?"

"Girl friends? Not really. Couple fag hags, maybe. Didn't really know any interesting women—until recently," he added, hoisting his eyebrows in automatic innuendo.

He always called Blue male. What would it mean to his attraction if Blue were called female? What did it mean that Morgan, nominally female, owned this house? Was it only being queer that gave her immunity?

Why should she need immunity from Jakob?

❀   ❀   ❀

In the grocery store, Morgan read the small print on the labels. Jakob was allergic to corn, Russ couldn't eat some of the new genemod foods, and she got migraine from red dye. Shopping was not simple. Of course, John just bought fast food, and Russ was inclined to rice and vegetables, but Morgan tried, when it was her turn to shop, to provide for them all. Delany wasn't always energetic enough to scratch-build a meal, and Morgan had had to force herself to get interested in something.

She was in frozen foods, feeling the chill bloom from the open door of the cooler, when she heard her old name called by a voice at once unfamiliar and atavistically known.

"It is Connie Shelby! What are you doing in town, girl?" The speaker had a familiar face, but Morgan couldn't find a name. College years, must be. She hoped it wasn't someone she'd once slept with.

"Hey, it's Daphne Pearson, remember me? Well, I was Pearson, now I'm Flynn. We were in Gay-Straight Alliance together in first-year university, remember? How are you?"

"I've changed my name too," said Morgan. "I'm called Morgan now." Nope, she had never slept with Daphne. She hadn't been sleeping with women yet when she was in GSA—Morgan herself had thought she was one of the straight ones then.

"Oh, yeah, that was your second name! Cool." Daphne reached past her for a frozen pound cake and a tub of frozen whipped topping. "Party tonight."

"You *remembered* that? That was over twenty years ago!"

"Everybody remembers you. We were just talking about you the other day. Wondering what happened to you. How come you're back in town? What are you working at these days?"

"I'm a child care worker," said Morgan, with a stirring of humor at her own truthful falsehood.

125

"Do you have a family?"

"Well . . . sort of. I inherited a big house. I run it as a kind of co-op house. Old-fashioned, but I like it."

"It's not that old-fashioned. Some of the young people these days are starting to live in co-ops again. It's so expensive otherwise."

"I meant my house is old. What about you?"

"Well, I married Lorne Flynn. Remember, he was president of the Young Conservatives. Go figure, eh? Must have been the sex. We had two kids. One's away at college, the other one has Additive Syndrome and we have her in a group home. She comes home on weekends. We used to take care of her at home—I quit my job—but when she got so big, it was too much. I'm the secretary of the ASPS—you know, parent support group? You know me, always taking minutes! Listen, I have more time since she moved out—you should come for supper sometime. I bet Lorne would love to see you. I'll invite some of the others. Dave—he's got this young boyfriend Duane. Sarah. She's with a man now, you know, Silvio, but I think he's queer too. And Peter and Pete are still together, can you imagine? And Bertina's a doctor now. Hey, give me your number and I'll call you. Oh, dang, I don't have my daybook with me. I'll look you up on the web. Listen, gotta run. I'll call!"

Morgan stood looking after her, bemused. She didn't expect to hear another word. She remembered Lorne, a heavy-handed social-Darwninist law student with an ambitious family. He'd been possessive and uptight about Daphne, but had a tendency to get drunk at the GSA parties and start twinkling at the men, although he insisted he was straight. She couldn't imagine he'd love to see her. And Daphne she remembered as full of enthusiasms, but short on follow-through. Either she'd changed her ways, or the ASPS group didn't know her habits yet, or they were desperate for a secretary. Or, mused Morgan, Daphne had started it herself. Shaking her head, she went on with the shopping. But when she got home after finishing all the errands, Delany said, "Some woman called and summoned you to supper. It couldn't have been Daffy, could it? That's who it sounded like."

"Daphne. Yes, it was."

"Yeah. We called her Daffy, remember? She said you told her you'd be glad to come any day you were free. So I looked in your daybook. You're free. Next Friday night."

"Damn," said Morgan. "Really?" But she couldn't stay in the house all the time.

"Can I come too?" asked Blue plaintively, as she got ready on the following Friday.

"Maybe soon, but I don't think these people are ready for you yet." Morgan grinned, imagining bringing this more-than-exotic date. "But tomorrow, we'll go back to our swimming lessons, if you like."

"Back to the Atrium? Will they lock me up again?"

"I'm assured that if we want to swim, they'll pick us up and bring us home any time we want. I'm prepared to trust Mr. Grey's word, I think. How about you?"

"I liked swimming," said Blue.

❁　　❁　　❁

This time the dream is of drowning. Although in the dream Morgan has become an amphibian through some unclear magic, and admires her gills and magpie-iridescent scales in the shiny surface of the water before she dives, when she is underwater and tries to use them, instead her mouth is invaded with blue water she is not ready to breathe. She doesn't know how. She woke choking. The air was cool and the cat was purring. *Magpies with gills are not logical,* she heard herself think, relaxed, and fell back to sleep.

❁　　❁　　❁

In the Atrium, she had had the resources of a gigantic curriculum committee to contribute to Blue's education. Until his premature death the chessmaster had been only one of a legion of experts brought to teach the alien all that was paradigmatic of Earth. Since Blue's days were so much longer, there had been shifts of workers, with Morgan, initially the only one Blue had any interest in approaching, the doyenne of them all.

Here, in the house, it was all Morgan's terrifying responsibility.

The grey man's twice-weekly visits quickly became comforting—too quickly, thought the part of Morgan that did not just question but actively mistrusted authority—and on the visit falling six weeks after Blue's arrival at her house, she walked with Mr. Grey to the park and sat with him on a bench overlooking the city.

"I have no idea," she said. "It's like Blue was brought up in such a structured environment for most of a year, and then suddenly—pouf!—no structure at all, just me well-meaningly muddling around and the others doing whatever occurs to them that day."

"What do kids do when they get into their teens?" he asked rhetorically. "They leave home."

"But Blue wasn't . . ." It was her own metaphor again, and she saw him smiling as she tried to deny it. "All right. All right! I surrender. But it was too soon—Blue wasn't nearly . . ."

"Finished? Some of them run away early. They do all right. Blue has taken control of that education process, just as everyone must do sometime in adolescence. Don't worry. You'll be fine."

"I wasn't worrying about me."

"Well, Blue will be fine too. You want to know a secret? You don't have to do *anything*. Blue is an information sponge, but it doesn't matter what goes in. There are twelve other Blues around the world. That we know of, that is. Do you think they are all getting the same story? And if they're all like Blue, they synthesize as easily as they breathe. I think the mothership types will have a lot to work with. I'm not in the slightest bit worried, myself."

If he didn't say that others were, she could infer it, and said so, and he nodded. "But those are the ones I promised to keep off your back, and I'm doing that. The rest is up to Blue, isn't it? Frankly, as long as Blue chooses to stay here, there's nothing any of them can do."

Morgan asked Blue later, "Why do you stay here?"

"You are here," said Blue simply. "I chose you. You named me. I was glad. I was young, I had no words for names, I couldn't find one for myself. Someone had to help. I wanted it to be you."

"Why?"

"You are the one I most like to touch."

"You do, eh? Why is that?"

"You are empty, like me."

Morgan asked for no more meanings; she went away into her room.

❖　　❖　　❖

It isn't good to hate, and so Morgan refused to hate: to hate her mother's unexpected cowardice, her father's desertion into death, or even her brother's apt tears; the hospital's slide into social Darwinism she had always considered beneath her notice, and with her new self-hatred she had considered Vik's defection only her due. So she was left with nothing to feel except absence.

Far away, and in another country, and the wench is dead from the ass both ways, Morgan thought wryly. She remembered Jung's words: *neurosis is always a substitute for legitimate suffering.* Just as the shoemaker's children have bare feet, her neuroses were visible to her trained perceptions, but unassailable.

It is far easier to help others than to undo one's own lies.

❖　　❖　　❖

Morgan was unprepared to remember she had history. Still, when her friend Judith, passing through on the way to Vancouver, took time to look her up, Morgan found herself putting weight on the old connection, trying to explain to Judith the sweet burden of her recent thoughts.

Looked at one way, Morgan mused, her mother also refused to suffer: she preferred to die violently in the crash rather than face the ruin of her dreams. Morgan, who felt holier than that, had to admit she hadn't even had dreams, only illusions.

"Don'cha hate that?" said Judith lazily, throwing stones into the shallow water for her dog to retrieve. "Makes you seem petty and her seem right."

"But she wasn't," said Morgan.

"No?" Judith grinned at her. "You sure?"

"I'm sure. I just have to figure out why."

Judith laughed and called the tiny dog, who came bouncing back to them, wet, tongue lolling, to shake water over them. "Look at that thing," said Morgan fondly. "It's a real dog!"

"What did you think?"

"That it was a toy. It's so damn cute, it takes a while to realize it's a dog like any other dog, except tiny."

"No drooling, though."

"Maybe it's like the line in the Jane Siberry song: *Then you'd miss the beauty of the light upon this earth, and the sweetness of the leaving . . .*"

"Why my dog doesn't drool?"

"You goof. No, why she was wrong. The light upon this earth."

"But she didn't leave sweetly, did she?" asked Judith.

"Whole point."

"Good for you!"

But Judith was not complimenting Morgan on her tiny insight, but the tiny dog on a tiny perfect "sit."

❀   ❀   ❀

John had only been in the house a few months and already Morgan had received complaints from the others about, and had herself become irritated with, his slovenly habits. Especially since the coming of Blue, she had no time nor patience for such nonsense, and she called John into the kitchen in the evening. Blue, as usual after dinner, was sitting in the breakfast nook by the window, watching the yard. The dishes were heaped in the sink.

"What do you see?" she said to John.

He looked around in puzzlement. "Nothing. What's the matter?"

"The sink is full of dishes."

John looked blank, waited.

"It's your turn to wash the dishes," Morgan snapped.

"Oh! Gee, sorry. I'll get right at them," and he turned to the sink.

"Sorry's not enough," Morgan said sharply, and he turned back, bewildered.

"What?"

"Sorry's not enough. It has been your turn for a week. First Russ did your dishes. Then I did. Today Delany did—"

"Then I did," said Blue quietly.

Morgan carried on: "These are just today's supper dishes. In addition, there is the vacuuming. It's your turn. Has been for ten days. No-one feels like rescuing you there. The trash needs taking out and the trashcan needs cleaning. It's your turn. The household laundry needs running through—you know, placemats and dish-towels and napkins. Everybody else has done it twice. You haven't done it at all. It's your turn."

She was almost enjoying seeing him wilt.

"See this chart on the fridge? It tells us all what needs doing. There should be an equal number of initials beside the tasks. Do you see your initials there? I don't. That means you haven't been doing the household work.

"I explained all this to you when you moved in. I also explained that no one will make you do it. You are an adult. There are no parents here. Personally, I resent being put in this position where I have to give you a lecture, but there have been too many complaints. I also explained when you moved in that there will only be three warnings. This is warning number one. After number three, you move out."

"Okay," said John. "I'm sorry. I've been busy on this video project . . ."

"We're all busy," said Morgan severely. "Nobody has time to clean up after you."

"I'm sorry—" John broke off, blushing. He looked sideways at Blue, but Blue, seemingly indifferent, had stood up and was drifting out toward the doors to the back deck.

"Well, just do what you are supposed to do, and that will make up for it."

"Okay, I promise."

"One more thing—"

He paused on his way to the sink. "Mmm?"

"Quit using other people's towels. It's very rude. Wash your own. Pay attention. Only use your own."

"Right!"

Leaving the kitchen, Morgan looked back, to see John regarding her with that hooded, resentful look that reminded her of a time when she worked with teenage petty criminals in a locked unit. Well, it gave me some skills, she thought, and smiled blindingly at him. After a moment he smiled back, weakly, and she gave him a thumb up signal as she left.

She climbed the stairs, thinking, *I did that on autopilot, all of it. There was a time I would have resented being put in that position, just as I pretended to him that I was. Now, it's just another chore, done and out of the way. We won't have trouble from him for a while. Too bad, he's a talented guy.* She had called up some of his videos on the house system. Not her cup of tea, but brilliantly done.

✿   ✿   ✿

Dream: image of Morgan, shoulder against the rock, struggling up a hill. Image of the rock slipping, not to roll back but to crush against her. She is crying with frustration and anger, but refuses to let go. She struggles to right herself and continues to roll her burden upward slowly, slowly. She is having a furious dialogue with herself about whether it is more sensible to carry on or let go. She lets go. The rock has nested in a slight depression in the hillside and tilts there, mocking her passively. She snarls and pushes mightily. The rock will not move. She stands away from it, swearing. The rock tilts back and is free, rolls slowly away along the hill, neither falling back nor advancing. Morgan runs after it. It goes faster. She leaps and catches hold, clambers on, rides it like a lumberjack rides a birling log down a rushing stream. The wind tugs her hair out behind. The footwork is demanding, no less than was the force of progress uphill. Morgan glances up and sees the crest of the hill approaching. A lifting sense in her heart. The rock hits a bump and she falls off. Pain. She stands, rubs her ass, watches the rock build up speed, roll on, and disappear over the crest of the hill, defying gravity and her. She straightens her back and begins to walk slowly after it, knees aching with the climb.

If it's not one goddamn thing it's another goddamn thing, she thinks, and wakes herself laughing.

✿   ✿   ✿

Jakob was giving Morgan a massage, his hard fingers almost unbearably pressing into Morgan's knotted back. Morgan could feel Jakob's fingernails snag the folds of her shirt and pull as his hands crossed her back, and she shivered with their slightly-out-of-sync motion. As she shivered a sob erupted and stopped in her throat, and she began to cry, quietly and without ceremony, a new tear crossing her face every time Jakob's now more tenderly probing fingers hit a particularly tough muscle knot.

"You are so tense," said Jakob soothingly. "You are like a person after backpacking. What have you been doing?"

"Just the usual," said Morgan, "staying alive."

✿   ✿   ✿

"I feel like the pool of expertise is too small," she said to Mr. Grey. "Too few of us were ever trained in this. I read as much as I can, and I still feel inadequate to be your expert."

"You are familiar with the research stating that stupid people are self-satisfied, and intelligent people doubt themselves?" he replied.

"Stuff that. I'm serious."

"Fine. Let me think. What about having some staff meetings with the people we worked with at the Atrium?" the grey man asked. "They know Blue."

"Well, maybe Shelley and Brandy. They were pretty good. But Alice just saw it as a weird zoo, and Howard liked his own reflection in the mirror too much."

Mr. Grey laughed. "I'll set something up."

"Not here at the house," said Morgan hastily.

"No," said the grey man. "I want to keep the world away from here as long as I can."

Morgan went to the meeting hoping to be able to spread responsibility, but what she learned was that she was on her own. Though she liked her co-workers as much on rediscovery as she did when she'd worked with them, they were not so much Blue's friends as hers. Shelley had another job, far less troublesome, and had kept her Atrium secrets even from her husband. "He thinks I'm at the library," she explained. "I can only stay half an hour." And indeed, in twenty minutes, she began to pack up, thanked the grey man for the double espresso, and scurried away with relief.

"Never mind her," said Brandy. "You know how she is."

"I didn't, really," said Morgan. "I was hoping to find that the two of you had some, well, different perspectives on Blue's learning. Something I could add to what I'm doing."

"Well, honey, I'm not gonna be much more help. Sorry, but you had the point at the Atrium too, you know. All I ever did with Blue was carry out the daily orders you left me, and she pretty much did what I said."

"She? Blue?"

"Yeah. Look, you wanna have tea, I'd love to talk to you. Listen to you vent. Hug you, whatever. But I never really hit it off with Blue. I like the kids I'm working with now a lot better."

"Where are you?"

"I'm at an AS group home over on the south side."

"Oh!" said Morgan. "Do you have a Briannon Flynn there?"

"Yeah, cute kid. She's one of our older ones. Seventeen. You know, they weren't expected to live that long. Her mom started that ASPS thing. Her husband's a bit of an asshole, but she's great. She's quite the organizer. They did a big fund-raiser, fancy dinner thing, you know, made a shitload of money and bought a bunch of equipment for the house. A hoist for the bathroom. You know them?"

"Yes, I knew her in college. We just got connected again."

"Small world!"

After Brandy left, the grey man moved his chair closer. "As it was my idea, I guess I should say I'm sorry," he said. "But you know, she's right. You were on the point there. We all mostly followed you too. Maybe you just have to face that you know how to raise this kid. You seem to have an instinct about what Blue needs."

"It's just common sense."

"That's what people say who have it. People who don't have a clue trip over their own feet. From the reports we get, nobody else's Visitor has developed this well. You're a good parent. Accept it."

"She said it was a small world," said Morgan. "How come it feels like more than I can chew?"

The grey man smiled gently. "Have another one of these Vietnamese iced coffees. You'll be able to deal with anything."

"Okay," said Morgan, then, as he raised his hand to the server, "No, not the coffee. Okay to the small world. I'll quit whinging and do the best I can."

"That sounds like something a parent would say."

"It's my father's voice. Or my mom's. They used to quote some saying, 'Do your work as well as you can, and be kind.' "

"Sounds like a good plan," said Mr. Grey.

"I wasn't proposing it as a plan!"

"I know. But it is your plan, know it or not. So just do it."

"Easy for you to say," said Morgan. "Better get me that coffee after all. I probably won't sleep tonight anyway."

She was surprised to notice that the coffee was delicious.

✿   ✿   ✿

"I don't believe he's an alien at all," said Jakob. "I think he's just an experiment in gene therapy or something."

"Blue's not the only one," said Delany.

135

"And that first one brought greetings and everything," said Russ.

"Anything can be faked. Look at the F/X in the flicks. Look at my dance videos."

"True: look at my happy-pap for the government," says Russ. "F/X *über alles*."

"Yeah, I agree," said John. "It could just as easily be a hoax. I could doctor a home video of anyone here to do everything Blue or any of the others did, look just like him, and look better than some of the footage."

"That explains why they're letting him stay here," said Jakob. "A real alien would never be handed off to a freak show like us."

"Speak for yourself," John said, reverting to his usual attitude toward Jakob.

Stepping in yet again to defuse the tension, Morgan chuckled. "Leaving aside your universal and shocking misuse of pronouns, and your unflattering designation of our merry little band, there's the question of why *they* would bother. Occam's Razor: the simplest answer is still likely to be the right one."

"And Blue's simpler as an alien?" Jakob said, staring at her.

He had her there.

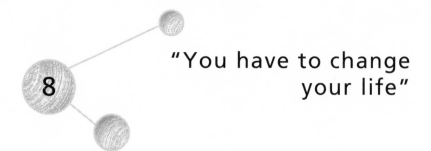

"You have to change your life"

8

She took the cup in her hand. The heat was welcome. She held it against her belly, felt the cramping slowly ease. Blue copied her.

"It isn't necessary," she said shortly, "unless your belly hurts too. I have menstrual cramps. You can just drink it." The blue hands raised the cup. "Wait! Wait 'til it cools!"

"I forgot that. What would it do to me?"

"Burn you, I guess. Maybe not. I don't know your metabolism, your body, well enough to say."

"You put my body together."

The cramps returned, redoubled. The cold wind in her neck hairs.

"What?"

"What you teach me defines what I am."

"*Who* you are." Absently. "*Who* is a person, *what* is a thing."

"You will make a good job. Me. Make of me a good job. Better than the others."

"Call the others back. I'm tired."

"Tell me this kind of tired. Let me in."

"In?"

"Let me touch what . . . let me touch you, *intimately* do you say?"

"What do you mean, make love? Have sex?"

"No, I mean to say, deeply. Inside."

"I don't understand."

"What about when we talk at night?"

"I don't talk with you then; I'm asleep."

"You see me."

"Those are dreams."

"Dream me, then."

❖   ❖   ❖

Jakob was using the front porch rail as a *barre* and doing exercises in the mild air of the long prairie evening, and Morgan and Blue were taking dandelions out of the lawn and flowerbed.

"Why do we cultivate some things that are not too useful, and dig up a plant that is useful and prolific?" asked Blue.

"The city says they're a noxious weed," said Morgan.

"And it's been a while since us citified folks had to rough it in the bush and grow our own food," contributed Jakob. He came down the porch steps, drying his sweat with a white towel. The late evening sun slanted through the leaves and burnished his skin with red-gold highlights. Morgan sat back on her heels and marveled. She would have thought that dark, dark skin had no reddish pigment, but he looked like a piece of Victorian mahogany fashioned into a beautiful muscular statue. Or, a slight adjustment of the draperies, a torch in one uplifted hand, and he'd be a suitable heroic bronze for a marble pedestal. She smiled.

"Speak for yourself," she said. "My father insisted on making dandelion wine, and my mother tried the salad-greens route, also roasting the roots for a coffee substitute."

"And . . . ?"

"And succeeded in confirming to us that dandelions were noxious."

"But they are not," Blue said.

"It's a joke, honey," Morgan said to Blue.

"Oh."

At that moment, Russ came through from the back parking area, singing with a Garnet-or-Stan-Rogers variety of deep definite exuberance. "Hi there!" he interrupted himself to say brightly as he bounded toward the steps. Jakob placed himself in the way, managing, Morgan noticed, to keep himself fully in that ray of golden sunlight with the display instinct of a seasoned performer.

"What brings you home so merrily singing?"

"Got a date," said Russ. "With a delicious dish-ious delight-ful . . . well," he broke down and laughed. "I can't think of a D word. A woman from work. She started a couple weeks ago. She called me out of the blue. Surprised the hell out of me."

"And now you are planning to ravish this ravishing creature?" Jakob said casually, but he stood a little too close to Russ and his posture was wary.

"We'll see," said Russ. "She does have a say, after all. But we had lunch a couple of times this week, and it's intriguing . . ."

"Well," said Jakob, moving out of the way, "I hope she's worth singing about." He bounced up the stairs on his toes and flounced through the door.

Hmmm, thought Morgan, and returned to her grass-stained labors.

Russ was out all night, and Jakob was awake all night in the studio. Morgan, asleep, dreamed of blue dancers, dreamed vaguely of sex and edgy jealousy, and laughed when she awoke at the way her dreams were a kind of recombinant DNA of daily life. But she felt also as if the undercurrents she found in dreams ran through the house, as two yawning men lounged at the breakfast table being excessively polite to each other.

✿   ✿   ✿

"Humanity needs to learn to respect our real ills," said Delany.

"Mmm," said Morgan, who was cleaning out the cupboard under the sink, only her rear end and legs sticking out. There's something comforting about containment, she thought, and to reach the far corner, she pulled herself even farther into the small space.

"Look at you," Delany continued, her voice coming to Morgan muffled by the wooden frame she was in, and by the competing noise of Morgan's scrub cloth. "Completely broken up about all the things that happened: your parents, the little boy at work, your break-up with Vik . . . and what do you have to do? Carry on. Not a moment's rest."

"Yeah," said Morgan from within, "and I inherited a house most people would kill for, metaphorically anyway, and used up a big insurance settlement fixing it up. Not that it ever stays fixed. The damned pipes in the attic bathroom . . . Anyway, *and* I get to live here with a bunch of cool people and one of the first aliens to visit Earth. I've really got it bad." Wryly, she remembered having this conversation with her grey man—hers? Odd—and realized she was making his arguments. She snorted softly, almost missed Delany's:

"So what if you're suicidal, eh?"

Morgan crept backward out of the cupboard and stood, wincing as her back straightened. "I'm not suicidal. I'm just empty. I don't care enough to be suicidal. And so what? I am a product of the top of the civilized heap. I was never sexually or physically abused, and what's a little emotional abuse, between family? I have never starved, and I don't have to walk twenty miles with a jerry can to get water every day. I'm not laboring in an Asian sweatshop so people like us can have nice running shoes cheap. I don't see my children die with kwashiorkor. I have no cause for complaint."

She was advancing the same argument the grey man had made to her, and she knew it. This time Delany was defending, as she had done with him, Morgan's right to be visible and in pain despite all her privilege. "Don't be obtuse. You know what I mean," said Delany. "You give to all of us, you give to Blue, and you are wearing yourself out. Someone as tiny as you are can't afford to lose weight."

"Ah, you noticed, did you. Shit. I was hoping you wouldn't."

"Smart-ass. You need to take care of yourself!"

Morgan gave her a neutral look, or at least, it felt blank from within. Delany, however, said, "Oh, honey, don't look at me like that. I'm sorry."

"You know the ills we should attend to, before we attend to my self-indulgent little angsts? The ills that something can be done about. Death and disaster are immutable, though we can clean up after. But the children who are being hurt, the women being battered, the old and sick trapped in boxes, the people starving, the homeless in our own streets and the people all over the world in need: these can all be changed, and they aren't being changed. I can't bear it. So many good people have been working at it for such a long time, and it's just a drop in the bucket. Evil has so many faces."

"If you are trying to save the world, then you shouldn't complain at your privilege," said Delany. "It's the only thing that gives you the slightest chance of succeeding."

Morgan's laughter surprised even her. "You are so right. Thanks, sweetheart," and she hugged Delany quickly, enveloping them both in a flurry of cleanser smell and dust. Delany sneezed, then laughed. "My, that was salutary, wasn't it?"

"You should see what I found under there, if you think our conversation was improving. On the other hand, perhaps not. It's one of those experiences that shouldn't be shared."

"Have you ever noticed," said Delany, "that when people taste something icky, they say, 'Oh, gross! Here, taste this!'?"

"Yeah, we love to share, humans do."

Morgan turned back to start cleaning the counter, and saw out the kitchen window Blue walking through the garden, stooping to look at a last stubborn pansy in bloom.

"Look," she said, and Delany wheeled up beside her. "Blue communing with nature."

As they watched, Blue flopped down on the ground to lie face-to-face with the flower, face propped on hands, staring and sniffing.

"Wow," said Delany. "I wish I could do that."

"Lie on the crunchy autumn grass? Want me to go out and get some leaves to rub in your hair?"

"Oh, I think not right now, thanks. Can I help with that?"

"You feeling like saving your soul through honest toil?"

"Nah, just roommate guilt. After the dressing-down you gave John . . ."

"Ah, forget it. From each according to his/her ability . . . doesn't sound the same, with the pronouns corrected, does it?"

"Nothing does," said Delany, and Morgan, staring out the window at the rapt alien, wondered if the pronouns ever could be corrected, or could be corrected in time. As if there's a deadline, she thought wryly, but there was a deadline, and everyone knew it.

Rilke saw the statue of Apollo in the museum, and the statue said to him, "There is nothing that does not see you. You have to change your life." Earth saw the aliens. Morgan saw Blue.

❋ ❋ ❋

The next day, the marmalade cats went missing. A search of the neighborhood revealed nothing, but the next afternoon Morgan found them under the lilac bushes, newly dead, the soft bodies still warm. Poisoned, it seemed, by some neighborhood trap, for there was foam and vomit around Seville's mouth, and he was stiffened as if from convulsions. Beside him, Dundee looked peaceful. Once Blue understood what Morgan was doing, Blue helped dig the three-foot-deep grave.

Putting the earth back after the slight cat bodies were laid in the hole was surprisingly difficult. Morgan felt the sting in her nose of sudden irrational tears. She shook her head.

"What is it?" said Blue.

"Their fur will get dirty." Morgan sat down at the tiny graveside and began to cry. They were still warm and soft; it didn't seem right to cover them. More was wrong than that. It didn't seem right to Morgan that she should cry more for these damned kittens than she had done at her parents' funeral. Yet the cats seemed too vulnerable to let go without pain.

"Does crying help the feelings to quiet?" asked Blue, voice sounding troubled.

"What it does is flush toxins from the body," said Morgan. "Helps cleanse the emotions. Why?"

"I feel like I have done a wrong thing. Maybe I should cry."

"Tell me." Morgan was intrigued.

"I was listening to the cats. You know how I can listen to them?" Morgan nodded, though this was news to her. "I heard Dundee make a great cry, and I felt Seville go somewhere; they were suddenly apart, in two places. You know how they were listening to each other?" Seeing Morgan shake her head in puzzlement, Blue gave a helpless spreading-hand gesture. "It is so hard to remember that I know nothing but I can hear more; you people are full of humanity but you listen so narrowly. So I heard the cats in two places and Dundee was lonely and wanted to be with Seville, and I felt them wanting to be together. Instead of changing Seville to be like Dundee, I changed Dundee to be like Seville, and I realized when they both went out that I had caused Dundee to die. Now I see it was the wrong way. I should have helped Seville."

"Changing, help. You mean you could have made Seville *alive* again?"

"It was the poison in the body that was wrong. Is that what Jakob has? I never realized before. But with the cats, I could not understand that right away, they have such plain, foolish little minds, I thought it was the lack of something in Dundee, and I put it there."

"Could you have taken away the poison?"

"Maybe. I don't know. Maybe it was too late. But I would have tried, and if not I would have been wiser. But I did what Dundee wanted, and then they were both dead. It was wrong, and now I feel wrong. I did the wrong helping thing."

"Guilty. Guilt is what you feel." Morgan would not for the moment grapple with the idea that Blue could that easily arbitrate life and death, but to respond to the simple appeal of a troubled soul was easy. "You made a mistake, perhaps, but that's human, we all do it. All we can do is live and learn. And perhaps forgive ourselves for our humanity, and go on." She hoped the alien would not challenge her sophistry: this mistake was a killing one, and Blue was lucky it was only cats. Morgan thought of the chessmaster and for a horrible moment wondered, but immediately thought: *if Blue had faced this before, I would have heard about it. No, this is a first time.*

"I'll try to think like that," said Blue. "But you are being kind to me. What if I had made that mistake with a person?" Morgan shivered at this echo of her thought. "And who says," Blue continued, "that a cat is not a person? I don't know."

The alien turned to the little grave, took a handful of soil, stood for a moment, then with a ceremonial gesture poured the sandy soil in: something Morgan was sure was learned from the movies. Morgan took the spade and pushed a great heap of dirt onto the little curled bodies. She was still upset with the wrongness of covering their bright fur, but she did not have any powers to reincarnate cats, people, or any other organism, so she and Blue filled the hole as quickly as possible, and they went into the house. Delany had been watching from the window, and her face showed some tears, but she smiled at them both gently and said, "Welcome back from Shadowland." Morgan touched her shoulder, and Blue's, and then went away to her room for a while, putting Marbl out into the hall and closing the door, trying to get cats and the power of life and death out of her mind.

Morgan felt as if she were reaching for something brittle, hard to grab. As if she were a thin deposit of silver on the inside of a photographer's plate, emulsion, waiting for something to develop.

✿   ✿   ✿

For people who sleep through it, night becomes a mythological time, full of symbols, moon, stars, northern lights, all that. For Morgan, who was wakeful through many a long night, going to sleep when the dawn birds sang (in summer; in winter, it was still dark when she retired), night was a healing time full of natural resonances: *why else is the moon a symbol for change, the stars for destiny, the northern lights for spirit life?* She lived then.

✿   ✿   ✿

Morgan dreams she is Marbl. She is thinking Marbl's thoughts. Marbl misses the marmalade cats too, but in an odd way: not

144

because they were her kittens but because they were there and now they are not. This annoys her. She likes things to be where they belong. Marbl looks at her kitten Morgan, is pleased that she is in bed asleep, where she belongs at this time of day, and decides to groom her.

✿   ✿   ✿

Morgan woke to Marbl licking the hair at her forehead, a firm paw holding her still by pressure on the third eye. Marbl leapt away at Morgan's gust of laughter and stalked from the room, affronted. Morgan, wakeful, followed her down the stairs.

Blue sat awake also, and when Morgan walked through the living room Blue sat there, shadowed, with Marbl already lying alongside Blue's leg with belly turned up to the stroking warm hand.

"Marbl likes you."

"Marbl forgives me for the other two. For murder."

"No. A killer, perhaps, but a murderer usually kills humans, and knows what is being done, and is often glad. Accidents, mistakes, that sort of thing, are killings, or even deaths, which has no blaming connotation." Morgan was precise in her little language lesson, determined.

Blue wasn't stupid. "You don't want me to be called a murderer, even if I am the one who calls it."

"Someone might hear you and misunderstand. After all, there was a death back at the Atrium, and you are not responsible for that."

"I think I could have stopped it while it was going on, if I had known what it was. I didn't know until afterward what the dream meant. I didn't even know then it was a dream. Something happening in another room."

"You dreamed it?"

"I dream everything."

And would say no more, but sat silent with a little frown creasing the wide forehead, until Morgan said, "Go to bed. You should get some sleep."

"Is that it? Am I tired? It doesn't feel like tired."

"Tired is part of it. Look, the sky is getting lighter. Go to sleep."

"Morgan, what are dreams for you?"

She thought of the vivid voices in the night, the blue presence, the cat's leap at a voice Morgan thought she had dreamed, and said, "I don't know any more. I don't know."

She looked after Blue's departing form, then at the empty air that was left. "But someday, my blue friend," she said finally, "someday we will find out. Give me time."

She sat for a while with Marbl, who complained at Blue's absence and had to be placated with affection. The stroking motion calmed them both. Finally the sky was suffused with sun's first light, and Morgan felt sleep looking for her and went back upstairs to meet it.

❁   ❁   ❁

After the others came home, the household seemed to gravitate to the living room where Russ had taken his guitar to strum. It seemed to Morgan a long time since she had heard a song made by the hands and voices of real people; she took her dulcimer from the trunk and tuned it in her room, still undecided about whether she would play. She sat with the instrument on her lap for a long time, listening to the distant chords and voices.

The alien came to see her.

"What is this thing?"

"It's a musical instrument called a dulcimer. It originated far from here. A friend made it for me. It is made from sweet woods, like cherry and pine, I think; it was originally associated with courtship and betrothal and love. That's why the holes here are heart-shaped. Modern dulcimers are made with many different shapes of holes and even different shapes of bodies, but this one was made for me by a lover, so it was kept very traditional."

She had not thought of Vik in a long time; she got lost for a minute in reverie. "You should go down and listen to the music," she said finally. "Russ is good. He used to play professionally."

"And you will come to the music also?"

"Maybe in a few minutes."

Her mother had taught her to play this instrument after Vik gave it to a bemused and charmed new lover. Why did her mother know how? She'd always wondered, another question she'd never have answered. She remembered the conversation with her mother:

"How much did she charge you?"

"Nothing. She gave it to me."

"What for?"

"She's my friend."

Morgan never came out to her parents, but she wondered if her mother had known what was implicit in that blush and labeling of a "friend." They had always treated Vik well, in all the years she and Morgan lived together.

After years of experiments, flirtations, and friendly brief companionships, Morgan's first long-term lover had been a man, an older man who was tender with a fresh-faced near-child, and Morgan remembered him with fondness of a sort, but also with the memory of bitterness; his choice after years of vacillation was to stay with a wife with whom he was unhappy, though somehow happier in the end than with the woman he had sought out to reclaim the free feeling of his youth. Vik had been her friend and confidante through the happiness and the pain; the change in their relationship had surprised them both: Vik because she'd given up thinking Morgan was anything but straight as she romped through the discovery of sex and then suffered through the years with Scott, Morgan because she had never even paused to speculate on making love with a woman, hardly even knew it was possible for her, despite her social awareness of its centrality to others.

Until the night. Morgan smiled at the memory of their sudden sensuality, the backrubs that transformed without planning into body rubs, and the bodies waking up, and the awakened young women clinging to each others' hands, shocked at the joyous intensity of the most minute physical contact. Afraid to go any further, and clumsy, always clumsy, when they did.

We were always clumsy, Morgan thought, *at first hardly*

knowing enough about our own bodies to touch the right places, let alone touch them right. And did we get better at all in those years? Or did we just find out how little we really knew? She was swept with a wave of sadness. *People are so clumsy,* she thought, *nothing changes that. We learn so slowly. Look at us in this house, the sum of experience that should mean that we have all progressed and are happy. Yet we are caught in the traps we make for ourselves, the blind spots where we don't learn, the mysteries we're afraid to touch, the secrets we keep even from ourselves. If we could only open to the soft flow of music through space, listen to that mysterious song, and loose our hold on the need to control our understanding, we'd be so free, and so wise.*

Instead wisdom eludes us more the more desperately we pursue it. And we live our clumsy well-meaning lives, pretending with bravado that we'd rather not be wise anyway, it's much more fun to be willful.

But she took up the feather, the plectrum nature provided, and strummed the dulcimer softly. The resonant notes vibrated behind her forehead. When she was young she had been afraid to sing, afraid her hard voice would not be perfect. But like the search for wisdom, her search for perfection had been abandoned; now she concerned herself only with remembering the words to the songs and rendering their tunes accurately, and left the judgment up to others. She took the dulcimer with its soft curves like a human body's, lifted it in her tired hands, went downstairs, and joined the circle of singers.

journal:
I saw the sky was orange above the white-rimed trees tonight, before I turned on the light and the room folded around me. Simple then to think I hadn't seen the world burning. What is it that fire against the black sky? And the trees standing solid up against it like iron, tracing their determination against the Hallowe'en sky
Snow
The alien one sits at the window and watches, and is silent

148

What's left for me in the ghost of the night? I miss my mother, she always knew my heart. Came walking to me in my dream last night with tears in her eyes, said, are you lonely? I said, what do you think? What about you? She said, it's nothing, it's just the blues. The alien was there, took my mother in pale arms, rocked her like a kitten, said, don't cry, you're over the barrier now. And she smiled at me and said, yes, that's true, dear. Take care of the traveler. I don't have to travel anymore. And I woke up crying and I'm crying now, because it wasn't her, it wasn't me, and she doesn't talk to me anymore, but I make a simulacrum of her to prove me foolish in my sleep

Darlin' mother, we are in such a story. If only you were with me to hear the end

But I'll hear the end, she says as clear as the night sky, in my mind, right now. You're the one who's gonna miss the good-byes

And the alien unfolds from the window seat and the cat jumps down from beside, Marbl, she's the one who takes to that one, and me? I'm in the middle weeping for my dead. And my dead heart

There's a heart in the sky, burning. Like the sacred heart the Catholics wear, post above their beds to bleed on their sleep. O mother, I'm tired, I can't see the night without thinking of you, it turns to fire and bleeds on my dreams

Who's this cool one who floats thru the house? Nothing is mine but my sleep. Who's making a memory for me? And who is the woman who floats in my mind? I don't know her; she's me

She and I together. We never get a good night's sleep. If only it was passion drove me, but not even that. Can't give it to myself, can't take it anywhere. Too far from all those secret and not so secret loves. Whose hand was it made me come and go so far out in space I never saw a way to go, and only came back like a particle pulled slowly by my gravity, reluctant to fall, leaping back up and sinking, flying and sinking, until my feet were on the ground and my hand on her heart?

I can remember with my head, but my soul can't remember any more. There's no distance longer than death, except this one

❖   ❖   ❖

"Blue's not seeing enough of the world," said Kowalski.

"Most people don't see much of the world," said the grey man, but he regretted his automatic contradiction almost immediately. It was just that he was used to having to disagree with Ko, and not used to Ko saying anything brilliant. "What do you have in mind?"

"Why don't we teach them to use the F/X latex?"

"The *Mission: Impossible* stuff?" said Lemieux, who was the oldest of them, and whose media references were often decades out of date. McKenzie was surprised.

"Yeah," said Kowalski. "That stuff. All they need to do is face and hands. The eyes are blue, that's okay, and people DNA their hair all the time, or do dye jobs. Then they can invite friends home without us worrying as much about security."

Grey had to admit it was a good idea. "Sure, good call, Ko. We'll send the make-up guys over there tomorrow to show 'em how."

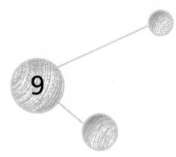

Through slow glass

9

Jakob's new friend was a dance student who, according to the netlog, had watched *Night Through Slow Glass* (the final elongated title of the *Vespers/Slow Glass* vid) more times than any other audience member. He had then sought Jakob out at the university building where Jakob taught an advanced course, and had clung to him like cat hair. Jakob invited him to join the household for supper, but coming into the house, he had to run a gauntlet of security personnel.

"Are we prisoners here?" Jakob demanded to the guards and to Morgan, who had been attracted by the shouting. Blue had come along with her, and watched with interest, quietly imitating the body postures of the various actors in the drama.

"No, we are not," said Morgan. "Come in, Aziz, and we'll sort this out. Blue, cut it out, that's rude."

Aziz was staring at Blue. "The pictures, they, the pictures just don't give it," he said. "Gramercy."

"For what?" said Blue, and the youth looked at him blankly.

"It means 'thank you for *grandes mercies*'," said Blue helpfully.

"Not in street slang," said Jakob. "There it's a fancy version of 'Mercy!'"

"But that's wrong," fretted Blue.

"Words transform, languages transmute," said Morgan.

"Cool," said Aziz blankly. "Where's the whiz zone? I gotta, gotta go."

Jakob rolled his eyes at Morgan. "Go on in, kid," he said.

"Bathroom is up and on the left. Then come on back down to the living room—over there."

Aziz ran lightly up the stairs into the shadow of the upper hallway. Jakob turned to Morgan. "Yeah, I know, chile, but he's pretty. What can I say?"

"Is he legal?"

"Far as I know."

"Find out."

"Yes, Mum. And we promise to have safer, safest, super-safe sex . . ."

At the old-fashioned term Morgan laughed. "Fine, but I'm serious. Busted we don't need to be."

"Honeychile, everything I do, and I mean *every thing,* is legal."

Blue laughed. "I get it," the alien said. "Every *thing.*"

Morgan shook her head, grinning, and went back to her desk. There, feeling like a collaborator, she called the grey man to talk about visitor protocols.

      ❁   ❁   ❁

"I thought I'd better come see you, since you weren't getting back home . . . er, back to my place," said Robyn. He looked around the living room uneasily. They sat like strangers there.

"The house is nice," he said. "Show me around?" She took him through the main-floor public rooms, showed him the guest room behind the kitchen.

"Do you want to stay here?" she said, but he shook his head.

"Not that I wouldn't want to, sis, but I'm in town for a reason. That's what I want to talk about. And I'm staying there . . . oh, dammit, this is ridiculous." He dived toward her and hugged her, so quickly that Marbl, on the kitchen counter illegally, crouched and hissed reflexively. "I'm getting married," he said. "I'm staying with my fiancée's grandparents. It's a family reunion—I'm meeting the family. I'd really like you to come too. And I'd like you to come to the wedding, and be my witness. Like the best man, only not a guy, right?"

"Wow."

"Yeah, really."

She took him up to the third floor in the elevator. "These brass call buttons, they're so cool," he exclaimed. "This house is like a museum piece. I can't believe that Mom never brought us here. Never told us about it."

Jakob was out with Aziz, leaving the studio door open. "It used to be the gym for the school, I think," Morgan said. They walked down one flight to find John's door was shut with the Do Not Disturb sign up, and Russ was sleeping. Delany was in her room working when Morgan knocked.

"This is my brother Robyn," Morgan said to Delany's quizzical look.

"So," said Delany. "You're the one who knows all Morgan's secrets!"

"Secrets! Tchaa!" said Morgan even as Robyn grinned and said, "For a price I'll tell all!"

"What price?"

"Oh, cut it out," said Morgan uncomfortably, but Robyn laughed aloud. "Dinner," he said, "and an explanation of that painting you're working on."

"Oh, well, that's easy," replied Delany. "It's my turn to cook, and the painting is about life, love, the universe, and everything. Now, it's your turn. What was she like as a kid?"

"Smaller," said Robyn.

       ✿   ✿   ✿

"It's a little complicated," said Morgan. They had taken a walk down the park before dinner, despite the stormy weather, and as she tried to find words, she watched Robyn's long hair whipping in the wind. It was the same lush dark sable as her own, and almost as long. Robyn was a stockbroker, and he was wearing "office drag," but he'd loosed his hair with a sigh when he felt the wind, now faced into it and let his hair tangle. He seemed to be happy.

"What else is new?" said Robyn. "Your life is always complicated. But I'd like to know why there's some kind of armed guard-post at the gate of the house you live in."

"How polite of you not to mention it until now!" Morgan laughed.

"Not polite, just, I never did ask you questions. I realized it the other day. I hung around and hoped, but I was expecting you to read my mind. Like that's a smart way of communicating."

"I suppose it's not impossible," said Morgan, "but I never managed it. I should have been better at trying, though, or asking you what was going on. I've been feeling bad about that."

"It looks to me like you've been feeling bad about a lot of things, sis," and Robyn reached out his hand, such a familiar family-shaped hand, and stroked her brow where the two verti-cal worry lines were starting to appear chronic. "It's been hard for you?"

"It's been complicated. I've felt pretty. . . ."

"Come on, out with it. That's what my therapist says."

"Your therapist?"

"It's a joke. I mean Twylla. She makes me talk about stuff. It's amazing what I didn't know I had to say."

"I should have been better, that's all. I feel guilty. I think about it every day. Should have helped you more, should have, oh, I don't know, taught you to play the piano, should have told you things so you wouldn't have to not ask . . ."

"The scary thing is I understood that! Listen to me, sis. I probably won't say this very well, but you were just the sister I needed to have. All through school I ran with the boy pack, you remember that. It was stupid, but at the time it was bread and butter to me. They teased me if I hung out too much with my big sister. Called me a sissy. Now I know that isn't an insult, but I didn't then. If you'd been the kind of sister that wanted me to be with her all the time, it would have just hurt your feelings. I wanted to have secrets. That made you a good model. You had them so gracefully."

Morgan looked at this familiar creature, her brother, and felt she had never seen him before. He put his arms around her, hugged her awkwardly. "Okay?"

"Okay," she said. "Thanks. It's a start. But let's not have so many secrets from now on, all right? We're the only ones of our blood left. These families we enter, it's not quite the same with them. Look," and she spread her hand out beside Robyn's. The shapes echoed, though Robyn's was bigger. "We need to remember that."

"First secret's the hardest, I find," said Robyn. "So tell me right away why you're under guard. Is it a halfway house or something? Did these assholes finally pass a law you had to break out loud?"

She laughed. "Oh, little brother, you have no idea. Too bad I can't just wait until dinner and let you see for yourself. No, I'm not under arrest. It's just that someone lives in our house who needs constant bodyguarding. It's—"

"No," interrupted Robyn, "in that case, let's go with plan A. Let's wait and let me meet this celebrity unawares. See if I recognize him or her. That will be fun. It was finding out whether or not you were in some kinda subtle jail that wasn't fun."

"Sure," said Morgan. "It *will* be fun, I think."

And it was.

❖   ❖   ❖

"I like your brother," said Blue ingenuously.

"Yes, so do I," said Morgan. "He liked you too, once he got over the shock."

"Why was it a shock? Oh, of course, more people are not blue in color."

"Also, most people come from somewhere *on* this planet."

"Oh, right. I forget, sometimes, because *I* feel like I come from this planet too. It's my life. So when someone tells me again that I don't, it's like . . . religion? Do you know what I mean? Like I was told where I came from and I have to take it on faith. So when people look at me oddly, I feel bad. Like they judge me for something I can't help."

Morgan's laugh shocked Blue, and she hurried to say, "Oh, honey, I wasn't laughing at you. It's just that for the people in this house, the same thing has happened to all of us, for one reason or another. We're from Earth too, Earth is all we know, and yet we've often been looked at like aliens."

"What am I supposed to do to fix that?"

"Nothing. You can't fix other people. You can only become the best person you can manage to be yourself. Other people have to fix themselves."

Later, John turned on the TVid Talk Channel, and they saw an interviewer in the middle of an on-the-street poll about some civil rights issue.

"You see," the woman on the TVid screen said, "you can't trust their kind. It's been proved: they're all carrying the disease now."

Morgan watched Blue turn away abruptly. She followed Blue into the kitchen. "What did you think of that?" she said.

"Is this a test?" Blue said grumpily.

"Hey, hey, what is it?"

"I don't understand people like that."

"You and me both."

"Say again please?"

"You and me both."

"It is idiom, yes? Means—well, that's obvious. What does she tell lies for?"

"I don't know," said Morgan, suddenly tired. "Some people do. They seem to be able to convince themselves that their lies are true. And before you ask, I don't know how they do that, either. You'll have to look it up on the net."

"Hey, you are unhappy about it too, about it too." The alien was ingenuously pleased. Morgan, pleased that Blue understood enough to dislike the propagandist, smiled at the anxious blue face. "Yes, indeed. Don't repeat yourself like that. That's slang."

That night, lying awake with Marbl draping and redraping across her in restless warm crisscrosses, Morgan realized suddenly that even in that relentless flash of insight which on the night before her parents' funeral had struck her down with the appearance of an epiphany, she had left out an important part of the equation. She had taken full responsibility for all the damage ever done to herself and family, no matter what the true source. Even after allowing for the hyperbole of blame with which she had ruthlessly assigned fault to what she should have just categorized as the necessary humiliations of childhood and the inevitable omissions of humanity, there was more to it. There was more to the world than herself, than the four of them. There were billions of humans, untold billions of other organisms, all acting together, all interacting, all acting upon each other, some blindly and some with intent: processes, entities, organisms, natural laws, and the overriders: Chaos, Order, Entropy, and Information, galloping across the cosmos doing and undoing each other's work. It was not all Morgan's fault.

Amazingly, she managed not to recursively blame herself for blaming herself—*a step in the direction of self-nurturing, anyway,* she thought: *the universe is too big for blame.* But it was another irony. *God is an iron,* said the writer: against the impersonal processes of this infinite regression of chaoses, Morgan continued to place her stubborn belief in information.

And yet, she hadn't known until this moment that she had such a belief at all.

She would go with Robyn to meet his new extended family, she thought, and she would try to love them too.

✻   ✻   ✻

Morgan was half-joking when she suggested that Blue come with her, in the new pinkface, to the dinner with Robyn's new in-laws. But Robyn thought it would be a grand joke, and Blue immediately went online and did three hours of reading on family reunions, etiquette of formal and informal meals, and even included a sideline of old prairie-realism short fiction dealing with family dynamics. Morgan was committed.

At the meeting where the household discussed the new rules, the Boy Wonder was understandably appalled.

"We will send surveillance," said Mr. Grey. "It can't happen any other way. We'll be discreet, but nobody leaves on one of these trips without a chip."

"But—"

"This isn't a civil rights issue, it's a safety issue," the grey man interrupted Morgan. "How would you feel if Blue got disappeared? We know that other governments are watching this operation too—what if some of the more unscrupulous, Burma or England for instance, decided to nab our alien and compare progress the natural way?"

"I think it is a good idea," said Blue unexpectedly. "I will wear a chip bracelet. I am a baby in the woods—"

"—babe—" corrected Morgan automatically.

"—babe, and I don't want to get lost. In my reading, I find too many tales of wolves in the woods."

The grey man laughed, then looked at the Boy Wonder. "It's a joke, Rahim," he said gently.

"Oh. Heh," said the Boy Wonder humorlessly. "Mac, you know I oppose this kind of risk."

"I know," said the grey man. "But I think it's justifiable."

"So do I," said Blue Suit, to Morgan's surprise. "As far as we can see, our alien is coming along best." (Blue preened with innocent egoism.) "We want to take advantage of that. We are getting enormous PR value out of the secret normal life our alien has. Canada has never looked so good at the UN. So what if it's far from normal? We work with it. A nice normal pre-wedding party with a man and a woman getting married is just what he needs."

"He? Oh, Blue," said Robyn. "Listen, it's not exactly . . . normal . . . We're writing our own vows, and it's not a Christian ceremony."

"It's not queer," said Blue Suit. "That's good enough for me."

"That's enough, Ko," said the grey man. "Where is this family get-to-know party, and when?"

"Er," said Robyn, "tomorrow. Starts at noon. At the North Side Buddhist Hall. Twylla's grandparents are ancestor worshipers, really, but the Buddhist Hall is right by their house, and it's big."

"Ancestor worshipers," said the man in the blue suit, weakly.

"They're Chinese," said Robyn.

"Oh, that's all right then," said Blue Suit, and even Rahim laughed at his tone.

"Too soon," said the grey man. "Can't arrange security. Sorry." Morgan felt, not annoyance, but relief. What was *that* about?

"Her other grandparents are Scots," said Robyn. "It's going to be quite a potluck. And there'll be a piper at the wedding. The wedding is—"

"Can I go to the wedding instead, Morgan?" asked Blue eagerly. "I've always wanted to hear a piper, ever since I read about the Battle of Culloden. They sound very strange on recordings."

"Don't interrupt, honey. And usually one waits to be invited to these sorts of things," said Morgan admonishingly.

"I invited you," said Robyn. "You can bring any date you want. But I think bagpipes will surprise you in person, Blue. Recordings just don't give the full effect."

"We'll have to warn the sound technicians," said the grey man complacently.

Morgan looked at him covertly. He appeared to be extremely happy. *I wonder why*, she thought. *This must be a logistical nightmare.* But he was grinning at Blue with open enjoyment, and as if he could read Morgan's thoughts, the grey man turned to her. "This will be very interesting," he said.

"In the Gertrude Stein sense of the word, or the ancient Chinese curse sense?" Morgan asked.

"Both," he said, still smiling. "I am going to enjoy this next phase very much."

✿   ✿   ✿

"I just can't go tomorrow," said Morgan. They sat in the living room after the CSIS delegation had gone. "It sounds dumb, I know, but I realized—there will be too many people there. It's not because Blue can't go. I just—can't start knowing you again in a crowd that big. Or get to know Twylla that way. I'm sorry. I've been such a trial to you for the last few months, and here I am being temperamental again."

"Don't write my script," said Robyn. "I understand. After all,

I'm showing up the day before, to drop all this on you. We are not exactly doing this family stuff very well. But we are all we have left. We have to sort it out."

"We will. What is the difference between family you're born with and family you make?" asked Morgan.

"I don't know, what is?"

"I was asking you."

"Family you make . . . never saw you with baby food in your hair? Or vice versa?"

Morgan remembered, early in her time with Blue, washing junior puréed beans out of the alien's long tresses after a temper tantrum about the taste. She grinned. "As good a distinction as any."

"Okay, how about supper with just the immediate family, in a couple of days?"

"That would work."

"Can I come too?" said Blue, coming around the edge of the dining room pocket door.

"It's not polite to eavesdrop," said Morgan.

"I know. Can I?"

"Okay with me," said Robyn.

"We'll see," said Morgan, but she already knew that she would take Blue with her. For a touchstone? Odd thought. Then she would have two familiars there.

✿   ✿   ✿

The grey man's voice on the other end of the 'phone line was a surprise: he never called in the evening. He sounded edgy. "The media have got it somehow. We're looking for a leak here. That Aziz kid says it wasn't him, polygraph-perfect, Rahim tells me. I assume your brother can be trusted, though I'm sure I don't know why. Except for the tail we put on him, and the tedious family reunion we listened to all day. Believe me, he didn't have time to make a phone call. Be glad you dodged that bullet. They didn't even have any jellied salad. Oh, and the fact that he's bonded at work. Anyone else at your end likely to have told them?"

"Not that I know . . ."

"Oh, never mind, it was bound to come out eventually. Too many people to keep a secret. But I thought I'd warn you. Keep the gates locked, use the electronic entry system."

Nevertheless, for the first few days they were mobbed when going out for groceries, to work, anywhere. Videorazzi were constantly lurking outside the fence. It took each of them a different length of time to stop being polite—Morgan was the last to do so.

"Just a few words, Ms. Shelby?"

"Be realistic," said Morgan. "You don't want just a few words, you want my whole life."

"What?"

"No comment. No words. *Nada*. Sorry."

She regretted the last word instantly, but she was a Canadian—certain habits were difficult to break.

"Why won't you talk to them?" said John, later. "I could get the network footage later for my documentary."

"Documentary?"

Chagrined, he looked down. "I'm doing a vid about us all. About the alien and all. I'm doing, like, an inside view."

Morgan couldn't decide between fury and resignation. This one was such a *guy*. Such a boys-and-their-toys egoist.

"Goodness," she said, "I haven't thought of that expression in a decade and a half. That's so weird!"

"What?"

"Boys and their toys. Do you have releases from us? Otherwise, I'm afraid, there's no use shooting another byte of vid. And the network stuff? Permissions cost too much."

"Oh, permissions!" said John in such a dismissive manner that Morgan decided for anger.

"Yes, permissions," she said. "It may escape your notice, but it doesn't mine, that everything we do is being recorded out there. Dammit, I'll subpoena the records that show you don't have our consent and sue your trendy little britches off if you don't get permissions. We're getting fucked over enough without date rape too."

"Fine," said John, as if the negotiations had come out his way, "I'll get permissions."

"You do that," said Morgan.

voicemail greeting:

Hello, this is Morgan. If you want a conversation that might not be monitored by CSIS, leave a number and I'll call you back from somewhere else. If you don't care, press one. All media calls will be screened out, so you may as well give up now.

"Knife and fork for you?"

Morgan and Blue—who was today in a very pale version of pinkface and looked like a rather exotic Asian/Caucasian mix, in an androgynous business suit and with hair pulled back—shook their heads in unintentional unison. "No thanks; I can use chopsticks," said Morgan. "Me too," said Blue, and smiled ingratiatingly. It was the alien's first house visit.

We should have started by going to visit someone we knew, Morgan thought apprehensively, but here they were, a visit accomplished only after the initial media scrum had subsided, and Blue Suit and the grey man had worked out protocols for dodging the persistent videorazzi and the automated camera-eyes. Their solution was simple—they had let it be known that one more person came often to the house, creating a virtual person with a surprising resemblance to Blue in pinkface. Then they had run decoy ops daily for a week, enlisting the willing and pliable Aziz to enter disguised as this "frequent visitor" while Blue showed up at various windows for a few seconds—and though the whole thing seemed like a crude vid plot to Morgan, when Robyn and Aziz arrived today and then she, Robyn, and Blue had emerged, there had been almost no interest in them among the camera operators with their lenses fixed to a third-floor window that Morgan knew lighted a small storage room.

Twylla's brother Kee was a chef, but his grandfather, the herbalist, was doing the cooking. His grandmother insisted on setting knife and fork for Morgan but, after considering Blue for a moment, set a bowl and chopsticks. Twylla returned to the room with her parents, introducing them to Morgan and then standing back, at a loss, to let Morgan explain her companion.

"This is my friend Blue," said Morgan simply.

"Blue?" said Twylla's mother Ada. She walked around the table behind her mother, changing the cutlery for bamboo; Morgan would have returned her grin if she hadn't been so worried about Blue's answers.

"I'm named after my hair color," said Blue ingenuously.

"Oh, are you a performance artist too?" said Twylla eagerly. "Robyn told me that Jakob Ngo—oh, I can never pronounce it— lives at your place. That's so *cool!*"

"Ngogaba," said Blue, as Morgan said, "Yes, he does." So as the elders prepared to serve the meal they all talked about Jakob's work, Delany, Russ and John, and the cats. *You can get lots of mileage out of cats,* Morgan thought. The Tsangs had four. *If all else fails, it'll be a dinner conversation full of cat stories.*

"And what do you do for a living, young man?" Twylla's father Peter asked Blue.

"What she said," said Blue, gesturing at Twylla. "My art is my life."

Morgan stifled a giggle. Blue would be fine. She settled down to enjoy the meal.

✿   ✿   ✿

"I liked the petting zoo best," said Blue.

Delany playfully echoed the childlike tone. "I liked being able to go on the bus." They had taken the rapid transit to the west end terminal, then a rickety but still accommodating "kneeling bus" to the zoo. Delany, the not-so-blue Blue, and Morgan felt like escaped prisoners.

Two women had followed them everywhere. They must be the minders. Morgan figured they would probably get an earful from the Boy Wonder or Blue Suit after this for not taking the official car, but she didn't care: two women had, after all, followed them everywhere, the day was bright and unseasonably warm for fall, the wind felt wonderful, and Blue was deliriously happy, bubbling like a child. And Blue was a child, she thought; even if the head was full of data and the mind synthesized well, the emotions and interactions of this lovely being were just a little over a year old, and growing up more slowly than the information-rich intelligence.

Home, Blue peeled off the pinkface solemnly, but the edges were stubborn around hairline and neck.

"You look like you have a weird sunburn," said John, and Blue giggled. Jakob, sprawled on the couch with his head in Aziz's lap, leaped up.

"Which animals did you like?"

"Little ones that scuttled and oozed," said Blue. "The slow loris. It was very funny."

"Show me," said Jakob.

"What do you mean?"

"Move like the animals moved. Was it like this?" and Jakob made a Pink Panther pussyfoot across the living room and into the dining room.

"No, like *this*," said Blue, and climbed the double-doorframe *adagio*.

Morgan drew in her breath. The alien must be far stronger than she had thought, to be able to cling like a rock-climber to the oak mouldings. She had lifted Blue, so she knew Blue was no lighter than any of them. The motion was uncannily like the small beast at the zoo who had crept fluidly but with almost-agonizing slowness across the web of branches in its enclosure.

Blue let go of the center of the doorframe and dropped to the floor feetfirst like a cat, with a soft thump. Dusting off fingers, the alien grinned. "And there was a very silly bird there too," and suddenly was prancing across the living room like a flamingo, all style, no substance, eerily silent and avian. John was laughing, but Jakob was struck silent with, Morgan realized, the same kind of shock she felt.

Jakob moved quietly beside her.

"We never thought to teach him to dance. But look at that. I have to choreograph something. It's phenomenal."

"In the accurate sense of the word," murmured Morgan. "Blue is certainly a phenomenon."

"We'll start in the studio tomorrow." And they did.

*   *   *

It was another one of those rare warm days of late autumn that should have been winter, but wasn't yet, and Morgan and Delany had come down into the park. The chair was always slow and whiny on the withered grass, and today it had seemed even jouncier: Delany had sworn at it several times.

"I remember when I realized I would have to be in the chair for the rest of my life," Delany said. She looked across the valley and shivered.

Morgan didn't ask if she was cold.

"I felt," said Delany slowly, "as if that moment would be the most important one in my life, forever. As if each moment were going to be defined by that one change. Before then, I was somehow on the side of the able-bodied. After that, I had crossed the line forever. But. . . ."

"Mmm?"

"But memory fades for a reason," Delany went on, "and you know, Morgan, my dear, I can hardly re-create that indignation any more, though at the time I called it anguish. Too many other things have happened to me. That was—what, twenty years ago?"

"That long?"

"Yes, it was when I was fourteen. No, perhaps I had just turned fifteen. You see? I thought I would remember everything about that night forever. And I can't even remember if it was before or after my birthday."

"Which is when?"

"May thirty-first, but never mind. It must have been July— school was out. Fifteen, then, I was fifteen. So not quite twenty years ago."

"A long time. And yesterday."

"Yes, but not quite yesterday. I am not one of those unfortunate people to whom life all happens forever, in the moment."

165

"How do you mean?"

"Where everything is alive to them forever. Perhaps a good memory is a curse."

Morgan laughed. "I have a good memory," she said.

"Oh, I'm sorry, I didn't mean you!" Delany seemed flustered.

"Well, mean it or not, you described me. I remember everything that ever happened to me—no, I *believe* I remember everything that ever happened, which is a bit different, and more accurate. I run the risk of holding grudges forever. I live in that eternal present, the immanence of memory, and I know *exactly* what you mean. I'm only sorry that I don't know how to change it. I would rather be forgetful and free."

"I don't think so," said Delany, but said no more, and the moment passed.

A few moments later Blue and Russ joined them, and Morgan walked back to the park entrance and sat down on the bench there, looking out over the valley. After contemplating the rotation of the galaxy for an afternoon, Morgan was dizzy. She thought this might be the time vertigo won out. She was afraid to get up from the park bench. She was afraid of entropy. With an effort, she turned from the vertiginous sky and looked back down the length of the park.

Blue was walking toward her with Russ and Delany. Morgan saw them like a silent apparition bearing down on her. Russ was pushing Delany's chair through the heavy grass so that even the motor was silent. He must be strong to do that, Morgan thought idly. Blue was wearing a loose sweater, designer pants, and leather boots, and strode confidently, hands in pockets and head thrown back, wind through the strange hair, eyes squinted against the bright sun. Except for the blue skin, the image could have been straight from a *Vogue* magazine or *Gentlemen's Quarterly* fashion feature.

I wonder what Vogue *would do about makeup for blue skin?* thought Morgan, then, *how beautiful that one always is, and how immune.* The skin tight over the fine cheekbones. It would be too linear, too simplex, to fall in love. With some strange blue chameleon-like being? (She deliberately ignored the parallel with falling in love with beautiful, non-standard Delany.) Even lust was pointless. And would she always suspect her own Pygmalion impulse?

Life's too short, thought Morgan roughly, overruling the catch at her heart that Blue's windswept beauty always made.

✧   ✧   ✧

The concert had been advertised in the Womoncentre newsletter, and Morgan, remembering the Ferron records (yes, records) to which her mother and father had loved to listen, and remembering sitting as a child on the hill at the Folk Festival and listening to the smoky, low voice weave its beautiful magic, decided that she and Blue should attend. When the singer walked out on stage, leaning heavily on her handcarved cane, and sat down to pick up her guitar and sing, Morgan was struck again with deep despair at the march of time, at entropy's erosion of beauty and power. Yet the concert was enthralling, the music as strong as she remembered and then some, and Morgan felt a reluctant sense of wonder too, at how the music, the artistry—and the woman herself—stood so strongly against the flood.

Morgan wondered how strongly this performer, who seemed to have so gracefully let the years drape her with enigma and sexual richness, had actually fought entropy, in her heart. The recent songs were as fiery as any of the earlier work, but with a darkness Morgan recognized too well: the darkness of loss in the midst of love, the darkness of too many questions answered by *no*. Morgan selfishly wished that her darkness had taken her more creatively, but, looking at Blue's rapt pinkfaced visage, she thought, perhaps it had. Perhaps it had.

✧   ✧   ✧

It was Jakob of all people who took Blue climbing at last, and spelunking too in the eerie Cadamon caves: Jakob whose passion for movement, for dance suited him well in the convoluted wilderness. Lithe as a ferret, he seemed to cling and flow around and across the jumbled, cracked, crazed cliff face as he led Blue higher and higher, while Morgan, below in the base camp, catching occasional glimpses of them in their brightly colored climbing clothes, thought they looked like tropical lizards darting randomly across the face of the world. She tried not to think about Blue falling, what the implications might be. *Blue is all grown up now,* she admonished herself—grinning all the while at the trope—*and you have to let go.*

Despite the F/X face, which was dark brown this time ("I want to be Jakob's sibling," Blue had said; they'd settled for "sister"), Blue returned tanned. Morgan was shocked by the deepening Delft of the alien skin. She railed at the advisory committee meeting: "Why didn't you tell me Blue had a melanin process? We should have been using sunblock, and a hat!" but they hadn't known either. Blue, who even before attaining speech had already fought like a tiger against having any medical sampling done, so that the benchmark samples had been attained at the cost of much human *and* alien blood, sweat, and tears, refused again—this time politely—the polite request for blood tests and a small tissue sample.

"I liked what you said we looked like," said Blue as they watched Morgan's slides and recordings of the camping trip. "Like the lizards in that film."

"I've never been in the tropics," said Morgan. "But I hear that real lizards dart across the sidewalks there."

"Can we go?"

The answer was *no,* of course: Morgan looked at Blue's rebellious face and said, "Don't run away again. We'll find a way, or we won't."

"And if we don't?" Blue said.

"Then you will be just like the rest of us. Unable to do what we want if it costs too much, or is too risky, or we can't get a holiday from our job . . ."

Blue was silent. Morgan watched the pliable face cycle through the emotions.

"I'm sorry. It's how life goes."

"No, *I'm* sorry," said Blue. "I was being—immature. I should have known that wanting is not the same thing as being able to get. It is an—elementary learning. I am ashamed."

"Shame is useful for a time, but don't get stuck there."

"You are very protective."

❀   ❀   ❀

But Morgan did not feel protective. Blue's innocent arrogance had echoed uncomfortably the desires that low income had always thwarted in her own heart. She had never been to most of the places around whose virtual landscapes she guided Blue's computer learning. She had wished, but never been able to hope, to go. The few travels she had done, on her own continent, so many years ago now, on that brief holiday from university studies, had only whetted a desire that her life, her always-low salaries, and the recent political realities had meant would never be fulfilled.

When she realized the power that teaching Blue created, she had hoped to parlay that power into mobility: shouldn't the alien have every experience the world had to offer? She soon found out that the alien was restricted to the safest places Canada had to offer: preferably close to "home"—even rock-climbing had been battled out so strenuously that the negotiations had taken months. The final blow to her dreams had been administered by the knowledge that there were twelve other "empty aliens", *kara-i-ti* ("empty-ET") as they were called in Japan, scattered around the planet. The composite portrait of Earth was clearly to be built up like a living jigsaw puzzle, and it would not be necessary to conduct a Grand Parade around the globe.

Despite herself, Morgan wished it weren't so.

She as always was surprised to find desire stirring, even desire for good scenery.

Having to teach Blue that one wants and cannot get would have been easier, she reflected bitterly as she yet again did dishes it was not her turn to do, had she been able to do so from a detached, Zen-like lack of desire—even if it was that lack of desire her recent despair had made seem reasonable. But in her the empty orchestra played again, and the hollow spaces rang with its wistful strain.

She had always hated *karaoke* when it was the fad of birthday parties of her childhood friends. Now she knew that she had hated it not just because her family couldn't afford to rent the machine. It had been a jealous dislike, unworthy of a mature person such as she wanted to teach Blue to be, and it burned within her still. She wanted to be a star, and tour the world. She wanted to win the lottery. She didn't want to mouth someone else's lyrics to someone else's background music.

Only later she remembered that some people did win the lottery and still never traveled—and that wanting as intense and generic as hers sometimes produced from the universe a completely different answer than expected. She did, after all, have Blue.

❀   ❀   ❀

Morgan lay in the darkness, hands clenched between her thighs. She could taste her loneliness, a cuprous flatness on her tongue. She was a stone.

She could feel the alien, in the other room, like a nightlight, like phosphorous on the night ocean, glowing. Like radioactive elements, glowing through the walls and through her skin. Making her transparent.

It was not longing like she longed for a leg between hers, grinding against her lust in the dance, or like she longed for a form beside her in bed right now, to whom she could turn in passion, for release. It was a longing to be somewhere outside the reality, the loneliness, the out-on-a-limb feeling, among all these people. It was a longing to know something new and real and intimate and other-worldly.

Today she had found herself staring at Delany with a desire so intense she was sure it vibrated the air. Wanting to make that glowing beauty glow for her. She could not understand the wanting, after years of friendly intimacy and bodily indifference; was it some kind of titillation to wonder whether that thin body could feel, could respond, could reach Morgan in turn?

Morgana le fay. The witches burned, she thought, *for feeling too much.*

✻　　✻　　✻

A dry lightning storm crackled outside, and the tension Morgan always felt before the storm broke into rain had her pacing the dark halls. The occasional flashes of lightning accompanied a flash of awareness that some of her nighttime restlessness was not *angst, anomie, Sturm und Drang* or any of the other respectably italicized states of higher anguish, but only sexual starvation. It surprised her to realize that not only tonight's edginess, but even some of her dreaming could be ascribed to being ready for sex again. It was an irritating awareness: Morgan had always had a horror of predictability, and now she felt her hermit status challenged, betrayed from within. Additionally, she knew that she was not just passively horny but actively interested in casual sex: how desperately old-fashioned. She got up and went downstairs, prowling the dark corridor like Marbl, who this time was more sensible and stayed on the bed asleep, not bothered at all by the lightning and thunder.

But it was not dark all over the house. There was a light in the kitchen, and Morgan, expecting to see one of her housemates, was startled by a stranger. As he turned, cup in one hand and coffee carafe in the other, she saw it was just one of the policemen, the one she and Delany laughingly called Sal the Handsome, helping himself to coffee. On the heels of relief came indignation.

"You scared me! What are you doing in here?"

"It's raining. I needed something to warm me up." He lifted the mug and coffeepot and she grinned, but warily—she was still spooked, her body fizzing with adrenaline. She pulled the silk kimono tighter around herself, sat down by him, conscious of his square body, conscious of the official distance between them, the dream still hungry in her, restless.

"You can't sleep?" he said conversationally, but he looked suggestively down her body like a character in a movie, and this was a movie, she thought crazily and wearily, and didn't care what she did any more.

"No, I had a dream. I didn't expect to find you here."

"On the graveyard shift this week."

"No, I mean in the house. That could be called trespass, you know."

He liked this show of spirit. He sat one buttock on the table, poised, posed like a TV cop, looming over her, sipping his coffee from Russ's elephant mug. "If I hadn't been invited. We have keys, of course. Security, you know."

"What do you know about security?"

She meant it to be metaphysical but he replied testily, "I'm head of the shift."

"And what do you survey, in the house in the dark while we're all sleeping—and not sleeping?"

"I only came in to pour some coffee."

"And how do you know that the coffee will be hot at three in the morning?"

"Jakob made it half an hour ago. I guess he was working, he was wearing those dance clothes." He gestured at the black square of the big kitchen window, through which they could see the lighted window of the surveillance shed at the end of the property. "Russ just came down and got some. He lent me this cup. It's a regular beehive of activity here in the middle of the night."

"How do you mean?"

"Seems like everybody's awake, except Delany."

"Too bad we took the cameras out, you'd know everything about everyone."

"We know enough."

"I bet."

He actually looked shocked. "We don't misuse it!"

"You mean, by coming into the house and poaching our coffee?"

"And you're the hardest to understand, you know, Connie." Only one of the cops who had worked in the Atrium, with the

Boy Wonder and the guy in the blue suit, still would think of calling her Connie.

"I go by Morgan, you know."

"You really are quite a good-looking woman, you know."

"Yes? You think so?"

She had done this quite a lot at one time, and she felt again the mixture of adrenaline and residual erotic charge from her dream coalesce into a black recklessness. She stood up, and he moved toward her. She had forgotten how heavy hands could be, touching her. She had kept herself apart for a long time now. Not that this was much of a change.

As a kisser, his technique was pretty good. What a pity it was going to be wasted: Morgan realized that she didn't have the energy for this.

"Thinking you could straighten me out?" she asked wryly as he leaned back.

"Well, I guess . . ."

His nervous energy irritated her. She said, "I make it with men too, when I make it. You have the concept skewed. I'm catholic in my tastes."

"I don't care." His mouth was a little tight.

"You're on duty," she said, "and I shouldn't lead you on."

"Lead *me* on?" She could see he was affronted by the thought that she had been the aggressor. She laughed a little, and he released her abruptly.

"Sorry," she said, "but it's not very bright, you know."

He stepped away slightly, turned away slightly to adjust his cock inside his pants. As he did, John flitted into the door of the kitchen, Aziz behind him, and seeing Morgan pulling her robe back into order and Sal groping his crotch, they faded with surprisingly similar expressions of disapproval, which grated on Morgan more than Sal did—but it wasn't worth going after them: it would just make the whole silliness more tangible.

"Sorry," Sal said sulkily. "I shouldn't've done that."

Blue walked into the doorway, a towel across shoulders, and said, "Hello, Morgan, I was looking for you. This is Sal, the policeman. I saw John with his camera. He and Aziz were taking pictures of the dance upstairs. John thinks you have been intimate? He said not to come in here, that I'd interrupt."

Morgan laughed through Sal's black look. "No, sweetie, we haven't been fucking, if that's what you meant by *intimate*. You certainly have learned all the right euphemisms."

"I have been reading a great deal." Blue grinned and Morgan laughed, but Sal, like Queen Victoria, was not amused.

Morgan supposed it wasn't fair to tease him: like shooting fish in a barrel. "Yeah, well, I think that he got the wrong idea somewhere. I can't imagine where."

"But who would not think . . . especially one whose specialty is documentary . . ." Blue made a telling gesture encompassing robe, Sal, the windows (night implied). Blue was like a movie portrayal of a gay procurer, a kind of swish levity, a humor beyond Sal, who took his cigarette, drank the last of his coffee in a gulp.

"Documentary!" he said, "it's more like a fucking soap opera," and, turning out the kitchen light as he went, slammed the door behind him.

"We embarrassed the poor man," Morgan said, smiling into the dark. She knew Blue could see in the dark.

"I am beginning to decide that is not always bad," Blue said.

"No," agreed Morgan. "Though I do not set you a very good example, in terms of formal good manners."

As her eyes adjusted to the halflight, she turned to leave the kitchen, and Blue touched her arm, the hand warm and light against skin still sensitive and ready for fever. Something that was not as simple as arousal, and felt far more dangerous than casual sex with strange policemen, knifed through her, more psychic than physical, but as demanding.

"You are going to have me in knots," she said with some difficulty.

"Don't you know anything about this yet?" said Blue. "I have been wondering . . ." The shadows hid Blue's expressions.

"I don't know exactly what 'this' is," said Morgan precisely. "It is interesting, but I don't think I have the analytical skills to find out."

"Oh, but you taught me . . ." said Blue.

Morgan shook her head slowly. "I have just listened."

"I wish you would dream with me," Blue said softly, eyes still downcast. "How can I tell anything this way? I have learned from you about dreaming; it is what I need. And beyond that, it was you who taught me that all that can be known in a language are the ideas which made the language in the first place."

This piece of her own scholarship provided the cold-water-bath of common sense. Morgan let go the shoulder she had gripped with a tense hand.

"None of the others know me as you will," said Blue.

"Will I? I hope not," she replied, and left Blue standing, went to bed, and slept immediately and without another dream.

She woke up to heavy knocking, angry voices. Sal had been found beaten to death in the back alley, and they had come to question the household.

Company for dinner

10

journal:

Jakob was up dancing, he says, and the Grey man says he was with Blue part of the time—John says he was in the studio editing tape after shooting with Aziz. He says Aziz went back to Jakob, Jakob says not until later, Aziz says he dozed on the couch. Delany had insomnia, but stayed in her room—Blue was watching the full moon— I was with Sal until he went out, and then asleep—Russ had his coffee and went to sleep. he says. no proof but our word for any of us. because the vid is altered, messed up by the storm.

Can't believe it was one of us, but they say there was a drug in the coffee—put there after Jakob made it? Or while he made it? I told them Sal's remark about seeing everyone but Delany—Russ says he came down for coffee and then slept soundly—not logical caffeine effect? So they did blood tests and he was indeed drugged too—but did he do it to cover up?

And is Delany strong enough to beat even a sleeping man? Could she reach him if he was lying on the ground? For he fell where he then died, and wasn't moved at all— or could Jakob kill so premeditatedly from one of those dopey trances? Could John keep his mind on the job long enough? Could alien Blue find an alien reason to kill?

And of course the others think of me—they have only my word, and the dubiously-valued corroboration of Blue, to contradict what John thinks he saw, to establish that I didn't indulge in sex, or wasn't raped and took revenge for it—they all attest to my self-control and good brain for planning (how flattering)

So like characters in a movie or a mystery book, we go about regarding each other with suspicion and looking for clues

I am not interested in clues—I want to know who values life so little—having fought for mine through the fog, I find in the back of my thoughts a little fondness for it, and I would hate to lose it now

Because isn't that the crux of the biscuit—since it was one of us, does that mean it hasn't stopped with Sal? And if so, who next?

I wonder what Blue thinks of it all—I cannot seem to suspect anyone, even while I have learned well that I do not know how to know anyone. And then there are the visitors to our house. If Sal could walk in, who else, what secret midnight meetings? Despite all this brilliant "security" of which they are all so proud—

an interesting speculation, but not fruitful

"That doesn't work," said Morgan. "He was in the house. Drinking coffee from one of our mugs. We talked." He had her in his office at the Atrium, taking yet another statement.

"What do you mean?" said the grey man. "Nothing like that shows on the surveillance."

"Test me if you like," she said. "I came down and he was pouring coffee. He leaned on the table and drank coffee out of Russ's elephant cup, he flirted in a heavy-handed way, I was kinda pissed off with it so I pushed him a little, he kissed me, I kissed him off, he left. John and Aziz saw us, and so did Blue."

"The surveillance we can rescue shows . . ."

His hesitation was telling. "What?" she said.

"Nothing." Then, seeing her tighten her lips, he went on, "I mean, it shows nothing. No activity. Dark kitchen. Dark hallway. From midnight on. But if you, Blue, John . . ."

"Russ, apparently. So Sal said. Came down for coffee, then slept. Jakob, up dancing. John and Aziz filming him—Blue says. I thought you had no cameras in . . ."

"You have windows. Looking into them isn't illegal—yet."

"You told me you—"

"There are no cameras in the house. Just as I promised. The outside cameras show just what a person standing there would see. No more."

"Standing really close to the window, I bet."

"Yes, indeed. You want me to feel guilty about that? Sal is dead, and we don't know why. I'm tired of this," said Mr. Grey, and Morgan looked at him sharply.

"Look, do you really think it's one of us?" Morgan asked, then grimaced. "I sound like someone in a bad mystery. It could have been anybody. It happened outside the fence."

"Yeah, well, inevitable. This *is* a bad mystery. Until people started giving me statements, I might have believed that. But when the surveillance memory shows nothing at all but the odd bit of static, and everyone has stories to tell, then I know there's an inside connection. One of yours? One of ours? Infiltration?"

"You said the media . . ."

"Yeah, we're tracking down all the hate mail."

"We've had hate e-mail."

He cocked his head, looking like an owl. Owls are raptors, she reminded herself. He didn't speak.

"Yeah, well."

He growled.

"All right. All right. I should have told someone. Give me a break: I brought them so you could have a look at them." She handed him memory. "And they all have their time and date stamps too."

He laughed at the first two. "*And* return addresses? Now *that's* making life easy for us!"

"Yeah, seriously deficient. I figured those ones were non-starters."

"You don't have to be a rocket scientist to bash someone."

"I thought you had surveillance out there."

179

She was shocked by his harsh bark of laughter. "We have surveillance on *you* when you're out there. Who told us we had to watch the watchers?"

Then she too laughed. "I can't believe it . . ."

He grimaced a half-grin. "Yeah, well . . . someone will probably be hauling my ass on a carpet for that."

"So, who do you suspect?"

"Whom? Never mind, don't give me that look. Well, you're clear because you're too short, and Delany is clear, just because of the angle and severity of the blows. But as for any of the others—well, the lightning strike seemed to have pretty well fried about three hours of sound memory. There are bits and pieces . . . but no continuous record. Now I'm going to have to see if that was really lightning, or more of what ails the video. If we had had cameras in the house . . . and if you had agreed to have the chip implants for the house computer, like everyone else in the civilized world, instead of wearing them like jewellery . . ."

"Don't try to make me feel guilty. I know we live in the dying days of civil liberties, but I'm not giving up."

"The only thing I can do to protect you and Blue is to leave the file open, and spread a tale that it was an outside attack. If it's anyone in the house, maybe they'll do something suspicious."

"Why are you telling me this?"

"Blue is a suspect, you know. And I suppose you could be suspected of collusion."

"Oh, for goodness' sake!"

"It's not funny. How are we going to disprove it? Blue is incredibly strong, Blue can pussyfoot, Blue is computer-savvy, Blue has no chip—thanks to you."

"Innocent until proven guilty, I thought."

"In the best of all possible worlds . . . Could we put a couple of cameras inside now?"

"No."

"Just in the public rooms, downstairs—"

"No!"

"Will you at least try to convince Blue to have the implant?"

"No!"

"You know I could bug your house system in a minute."

"Yeah, and John and Russ have alarms wired. Anything you do, they can undo."

"Yeah, well . . ."

"You had to try, eh?" she said angrily. "Just when I'm thinking you maybe know what I'm talking about—"

"Don't you try to make *me* guilty either," he snapped. "If you or Blue were where Sal is, where do you think the world would be?"

"If *Blue* were there? We don't even know if they're keeping track of these people they've sent down. One of them could fall off a cliff just as easily. And as for if *I* were dead, it wouldn't mean a thing to anyone."

"There you're wrong, and you damn well know it. Do you want our alien to learn cynicism in quite that final a way?"

"*Our* alien?"

The grey man slapped the cover of his terminal shut, threw the memory across the room onto the cluttered table. "You have no fucking idea," he said. "Get out of here before I put you in jail just to prove I can."

Discretion is the better part of valor, Morgan reasoned. She closed the door very quietly behind her. Inside, something bulky hit the wall beside the door, and she heard the flutter of pages spilling from a file. She didn't know whether to laugh or be frightened. She opened the door again.

Paper littered the floor by the door. The grey man was standing by his desk, leaning on his fists, his shoulders shaking—with laughter, and a great guffaw escaped him when he heard the door open. Morgan began to chuckle.

"It's a mess," she said.

"Never mind," he said. "Just get out of here and let me work. You are an intense annoyance." But he was still laughing.

The second time, she tried slamming the door. The thin wall shook gratifyingly. Behind the door she heard him laugh again.

"It's not *that* funny," she muttered resentfully as she attacked the elevator call-plate.

❁   ❁   ❁

"This is Hester. This is Andris."

"I've heard a lot . . . ," they both started, stopped and laughed, but Salomé was already moving into the video suite. "Crass!" she said. "Spinal!"

"It's a compliment, Andris," said Mr. Grey dryly. Salomé grinned, but she was already in the pilot seat, sliding into the rig.

"Hester," she said to the tech, "but if Dad calls me Salomé, don't do the double-take. It's my other name."

"Bryant. It's cued up at midnight," said the tech. "I've checked it down to the byte. No sign of splice."

"Yeah," said Salomé, "that's good. Very good. I see your notes here. Nothing's overlooked here: that saves me a lot of work. But . . . look, cope me here." He leaned into the copilot rig. "Now watch. We're going to go macro here. Look for loops. But our wombat will be clever. Won't loop everything. There'll be four or five layers."

After that, Grey and Andris were watching magic, with a few cryptic incantations.

"The cars?"

"No, but here's a cat. And the hall light."

"Great moiré."

"Look at this segue. Smooth, but here—is that counter always that height?"

"Bandwidth conservation?"

"Showing off, I think. Look, I see that as signature . . ."

Mr. Grey was surprised to see that almost two hours had passed when Salomé pushed herself out of the rig.

"There are twelve tracks," Salomé said. "They range from one byte per scan to about three megabytes per scan. I'll put them on the big display. Here's the kitchen in the dark, right? That's the big one. That's easy. But if it just looped, it would be too obvious. So here's a random cat. Loops three times, different loop length, between midnight and dawn. Water dish each time, same number of laps. And it says meouw. Same voiceprint. Then there's the streetlight. See the fluttering? That's supposed to be tree limbs in front of it, but if you look, it's just a cross-scan with a black lattice. Was the wind blowing at that time last night? Would the rain have obscured the light more? Then the counter, there, catches the edge of light from the prism in the window. That one's cute, because there is a cross-current when the cat comes in, but there shouldn't be, because the cat doesn't have to open the door, she just comes through that triangle cut out of the out-side corner there, see? There is light and shadow showing through that triangle, cut off by her body, but if you play the hall, the hall shows dark, and when the cat comes down the hall, it's a different size. See where the tail cuts the door edge? And look how it bends its legs to get through the cat door, and the kitchen one doesn't have to. That hall stuff's a pale cat. The pixel-level alterations are on the fur. This wasn't a brown tabby when it started, but the kitchen one is a brown tabby. Are there two cats in the house?"

Andris looked at Mr. Grey. "There used to be three, but two died," said the grey man. "The others were big marmalade toms."

"Were you already recording before that?"

"Yes, but it's on a loop. We don't save everything. We certainly don't save footage of looking through a window at a cat going to eat in the middle of the night."

"Somebody does. Are your feeds secure?"

"Sure," said Andris, but Mr. Grey said, "Of course not. There are three people in that house who use video intensively, and one who uses it minimally—technically that is. Copping a feed is the easiest video hack to do. Even I can do it, with good equipment. Kids in day care cop the baby monitor."

"Yeah, it's not rocket science," said Salomé. "The only thing I can suggest is to look for deviousness. That one-byte-per-scan layer? It's a signature. Look."

She damped all the other layers, and gave the single byte simultaneity. It became a word, traced in the air of the hall, and two other words traced in the empty space of the kitchen. *"Runs . . . with scissors."*

"Look for someone cute," she said. "In the old sense of the word."

"They're all too damn cute in that house," said the grey man.

journal:

Went into the bathroom to discover that Delany had left the lid off the toothpaste again—that bitch, she thinks cuz John does it she can get away with it—one of these days gonna get my jam together to tell her she's just being lazy—I get so fucking infuriated when she does something shabby like that—cheating—looking to get away with something

Talk about getting away with something, Blue was pushing the dream issue again today and this time I think John is getting interested—but not like Blue wants—John wants the whole thing for his vid/doc—he wants Jakob to do the dreaming, and John wants to put four cameras in the room—he says it's the best segment he's conceived— watching the interface of the human subpsyche with the alien whatever—he hasn't paid enough real attention to Blue to know what the "whatever" will be yet—don't know why I should object—the whole thing just a circus anyhow—Mounties here today digging up Dundee or was it Seville—hard to tell—they called it exhuming—Blue wanted to know if all burials are temporary—none of our customs so far had revealed this interesting fact—envisioning some sort of galactic postgrad thesis being formed and shattered I said no and started a course of Lord Peter Wimsey—the natural successor to Klaatu?—we'll see what the galactic sensibilities make of the detective genre— the whole thing is a joke—I'm getting so sick of tripping over microphones—if it's not CSIS it's John—apparently the city cops tried to get into the investigation because of some anonymous hate mail, but Mr. Grey invoked national security of course—all gossip and rumours—we seem to live in a house of rumors—our real life suspended for the duration

Not to speak of the fact that with all these cops around my intentions to resume my sex life are shot to hell—even considered going to the Women's Dance tonight but as soon as I mentioned it Blue wanted to go and the RCMP stepped in and said they couldn't guarantee Blue's safety and so on and so on—and even if we had gone this kind of spotlight does not facilitate groupies

Blue wants to know what the procedure will be if the police keep on believing Blue did it—in this case the blind leading the blind—I can't imagine—my head keeps going around and around—I can't believe Blue had anything to do with it—all these xenophobes—but I keep remembering Blue was awake, out of the room, and one moment of reassurance isn't a hell of a lot

All this energy goes nowhere—Jakob has the right idea—John too—just keep doing their thing—Jakob plans to "sleep Blue", as he calls it, next week—now he tells me that they weren't dancing, that night, they were trying to share dreams but no dreams ensued, he said, because the turmoil outside woke him up too soon—but how do they know—without a REM monitor—Blue certainly couldn't describe a dream though seems to have taken to the concept with enthusiasm—that's what this brouhaha is all about, teaching Blue the dream world—how would Blue know a dream if one appeared, anyway?

I dreamed that Blue was in jail I guess but instead of bars it was a long leash that kept hands away from everyone s/he tried to touch just by a few cm—torture—I was the lawyer and I couldn't talk—trying to force the words—Blue looking like death warmed over and sort of wilting like a fun house mirror or an old Star Trek monster fog—shit—woke up in the usual state—got up to pee and Blue was in the bay window in the staircase in the dark watching the moon

Said, I can walk on there, but I came here instead

I said, are you sorry?

Blue said, sorry? I am not allowed to be sorry

Big silence

Then, are you going to let me dream you?

If this keeps up I am going to do it, for sure. what could be worse? This is the craziest seduction scene I've ever been in. Just mumbled something but it took a couple of hours to get some sleep

"You can relax," said the grey man, testily. "There's no hard evidence against anyone inside the perimeter."

"The *perimeter?*"

"The fence. The house. The security force."

"Ah, you investigated yourselves."

He glared at her.

She laughed. "Okay. Sorry. I was provoking you. Why are you in such a bad mood?"

"Because eliminating your people and my people from the list leaves only the passing casual murderer, and that's an unsatisfying and essentially clichéd outcome. It bothers me. It's unaesthetic."

"Unaesthetic? This is a murder."

"Logically, I mean. Inelegant solutions are usually wrong. Which means, all my elaborate elimination logic is wrong. All my evidence is wrong. In a word, I am wrong."

She looked at him gently. "You are far too good at your job," she said. "They don't deserve you."

"With your permission," he said, "I'd like to play that tape clip to my boss. I've been wanting a raise." He smiled finally.

"You look tired. Want to talk about it?"

"Thanks for the reflex. No, I can't." He got up and turned on the radio, started running water and washing his cup. "Well, I can talk about it, but I'm tired of it. I've been around and around the evidence. There's been serious tampering with the feeds, and any-one in this house could have done it—but so could any of seventeen outside interests, ranging from unaffiliated fanatics to other governments." His cup was clean, but he kept flipping his hands through the water stream, spreading the stream into a wide spray of droplets. Morgan realized that he had done this before once, and suddenly—why it had taken so long she couldn't imagine—she realized it was the old-fashioned fool-the-microphone trick. "We discovered some huge holes in our ice, and we've been putting in patches, but we don't know if they were always there or, if not, when they were melted." She handed him her cup to wash, and the plate that the oatmeal-and-date cookies had been on. "There's no on-site evidence. No DNA. No heat trace. Nothing we can scrape off the surrounding landscape shouldn't be there. Nothing we scraped off this house or anyone in it shouldn't be there. It's the lack of evidence: we know someone's seriously bent here, but we can't get a handle. And of course, I shouldn't be spilling this."

"I thought that trick didn't work with the new gadgets." She nodded toward the running water. In response to his come-hither gesture, she handed him the tea-towel from the rail beside her.

"We have a pretty basic set-up here." He turned off the water and dried cups and saucers and plate, and his hands, then neatly hung up the linen teatowel. "I saw to that. And for anything more than surface scans, I'd have to authorize the unscrambling time."

As he worked, she had been flicking the selector button of the radio, station-surfing a chaotic mix of sound. "Are we really out from under suspicion?"

"You and Delany are. Our techs gave her up reluctantly, but medical evidence is pretty clear. The others—they all have reasons, but I can't see any of them as strong enough. And I myself don't suspect Blue."

His distinction was pretty clear. "Oh." Though she had a dozen questions, she still couldn't think of anything else she really wanted to say. He reached past her and tapped the radio's off-switch. "Do you mind?" he said. "The noise is driving me crazy."

"Sorry," said Morgan, grinning. "I was just looking for some news."

Grinning, he opened the cupboard and put away the clean cups.

"You know where everything goes," Morgan said.

"It's a Sherlock Holmes thing. Professional standards," he said.

She turned away from his smile, suddenly realizing how complicit they seemed. Was he her friend? She didn't want any friends.

Transparent though that wish was, and impossible—it was already too late, several times over. She sighed.

"Well, at least I cheered you up," he said.

❖   ❖   ❖

"She's not like I expected," Delany whispered to Morgan in the kitchen. "She's . . ."

"Older?" said Jakob archly.

"Cut it out, Jakob. We're all older than we used to be," Morgan snapped, then laughed. "Sorry. But really. Don't be bitchy. She's a nice woman. Give her a chance."

Russ's new friend was there for dinner, and was running the gauntlet of household evaluation. Household xenophobia, Morgan thought with surprise. They'd taken in an alien without a murmur, made Blue one of the family, but those who courted family were now scrutinized with huge suspicion.

Aziz, who by the evidence must have gone home a few times to import the astonishing array of fashionable clothes he wore, still appeared never to have left Jakob's side, but he had weathered the gatekeeping stares and interrogations with the sublime disregard of the egotistical. A lad that pretty had never had reason to look beyond his mirror, Morgan thought, but then again, he seemed devoted to Jakob, so they had all accepted him as inevitable after a very short try-out period.

Now this Miranda ("Call me Randy!") would face the same test. She sat at the dining table next to Russ, leaning slightly against his shoulder, handling with great self-possession the stares, and the frequent preparatory errands to the kitchen that gave people a chance to whisper about her. She was a lean, fit, muscular woman who had spent a lot of time in the sun. She was tall—her eyes were almost level with Russ's—and she looked like a hobby-marathon-runner. She wore good corporate attire, as did Russ, but her forearms looked hard and tanned—clearly she found time for non-corporate pursuits as well.

John was, as was his frequent condition, late. Finally Morgan buzzed him on the house terminal. "Come on down! Supper's almost ready, and we have company!"

He appeared, bleary-eyed and rumpled of clothing, rubbing quicktime goop from his hands.

"Computer problems?" asked Randy sympathetically. "I've certainly had my share of goop days."

"Randy works in MIS," said Russ.

"I love those want-ads," Delany said, laughing. "Saw one last week that said 'MIS Manager Wanted in Bahamas'."

"Where in the Bahamas?" Randy said. "Where did you see it?"

"WebJob, I think. But it's a joke, right? Mis-manager?"

"Yeah, but, goodness, the Bahamas. What a place to go to work!"

"But you have a job, don't you?" said John.

Randy looked at him. "I beg your pardon?"

"I've met you," said John. "I saw you at work. Don't you remember?"

Randy looked uneasy.

"Back off, Johnny," Jakob said, his voice no gentler than John's. "Randy's a buddy now, right?"

"Oh, sure, didn't mean to get muscular," said John. "I'll go get the salad." And he shambled out into the kitchen.

"I'm sure there's something I can do to help," Randy said. "It's like at family reunions, you know? Everybody pitches in."

"Leave that for later visits," Russ said. "This is your one chance to relax."

"Relax?" Randy said. "You don't know me well yet, do you, sweetie? I just always have to be on the go," and she popped up and bustled into the kitchen.

❀   ❀   ❀

"You better listen to this, Mac," said Rahim. "Live feed. Kitchen."

The voices were very clear.

"I saw you when I was a tech there," said John.

"It doesn't matter. So I worked there. Now I work in Russ's department. So what?"

"One is happenstance: Morgan. Twice is co-incidence: me. Three times is enemy action: you. What the hell are you doing here? If you're freelance, forget it. I have an exclusive on this site. If you still work for them, you better find a reason to get out of your burgeoning little romance with Rusty there before I blow your cover. *Capiche?*"

The grey man was out of the trailer and striding toward the house before Rahim turned around. "Wait, Mac!" he called, but Mr. Grey ignored him and he was forced to follow behind, still protesting, as the grey man pounded on the back door, then without waiting for an answer flung it open and strode through the kitchen into the dining room.

He recognized both of the visitors he found there.

       ❖   ❖   ❖

The peremptory knocking on the back door startled them all. Morgan leaped up, darted toward the kitchen, meeting the grey man in the dining room doorway.

"Hi," he said. "Move." Behind him, the Boy Wonder was making fish faces, but not getting any words out of his gasping mouth.

"What the hell are you doing busting in here?" Morgan said, but the grey man was not looking at her. He was looking at Randy.

"Maybelle Murphy as I live and breathe. And who assigned you here?"

"Kowalski," Randy said calmly. "Told me to get up close and personal with somebody here. I picked Russ."

Russ looked at her in shock.

"Sorry," she said to him, "but you're the cute one. And I knew about your Amnesty work. I figured hey, why not. And you run."

"And you figured this was okay—exactly how?" said the grey man.

"He wasn't passing on orders from you?"

"You know bloody well he wasn't. Don't you?"

"Had an idea. But I'm just a flunky."

"No, you're a minion. Flunkies have more brains. Get the hell out of here before I bust your ass down to bedrock and put you back on booze patrol. And when you tell Kowalski about this, tell him I want him in my office at ten tomorrow morning."

She looked shamefaced. Morgan was catching up.

"You mean, this is a cop?"

Mr. Grey looked at Morgan. "In the broadest possible interpretation of the term, I suppose you could say yes." Randy went into the hall, came back with her coat and shoulder bag.

"Working for Blue Suit?" Morgan persisted.

"Excuse me," the grey man said, and turned to the Boy Wonder. "The reason Ko's appointment is at ten is to give me time to deal with *you*," he snarled. Without turning around, he said, "and don't bother creeping out of the room, Aziz, if that's what your name really is."

Aziz froze halfway through the archway to the living room, reconsidered his silent slinking away, and stepped back to Jakob's side. Morgan looked from Mr. Grey to Aziz. "You know him? I mean, you know him *too?*"

"I met him in the Atrium, some time ago," said the grey man. "I assume that you"—to the Boy Wonder—"were gambling I wouldn't remember."

Jakob grabbed Aziz by the arm. "You're a fucking *cop?*"

"Well, no," said the Boy Wonder. "He's a fucking dancer faggot, but he's my cousin. I needed to have a little more control of the situation, and Aziz owed me a favor."

"What kind of favor?" Delany asked.

"The kind where if I don't do it, he tells my grandmother and my father that I'm queer," said Aziz to Jakob, "and they send me 'back home' to get deprogrammed." He took Jakob's wrist. "I told him how much I watched your dance. Right away he was on to me. I didn't tell him anything important. But I had to . . ."

Morgan was feeling a bit like quicktime goop herself, the tool of last resort to patch up interfaces. "Okay," she said. "Okay. Let's eat. You guys want to stay for casserole and salad? We can work it out over dinner. And kids?"

They all looked at her.

" 'Keep your forks. There's pie.' " Jakob knew the reference, and snorted. The others sat down rather meekly, all things considered. "Randy" hesitated.

The grey man shook his head. "Take your coat off, May. You can't be in any *more* trouble. You may as well eat. You too, Aziz."

Rahim was edging toward the door. He gestured out the window to the surveillance center. "I'll just . . ."

"As for you, Wonderboy, don't piss me off any further. Call in some backup for the booth. You're suspended until further notice. Siddown. Have a nice dinner."

"Two in one blow," said Morgan. "Nice work. Blue cheese or vinaigrette?"

"Don't be cute," the grey man said. "Oh, I suppose you can't help it. Vinaigrette. Please."

It was possible, thought Morgan, that he even had a good time at dinner. With the exception of Morgan, who at least found it fascinating, if not pleasant, no-one else did.

Hardball

Morgan drifted through the night on this dream, watching herself without question through Russ's eyes. Morgan and Russ walked in the back lane, the artificial moonlight harsh on their faces. Morgan, hands in her pockets, looked down at her feet, kicking the gravel as she walked. With peculiar double vision, she saw herself, as Russ, looking at her, saw the blue light turn her face to a pallor like Blue's. Under this light, the alien's color wouldn't change. Russ thought, *they are two peas in a pod.* He thought, *this woman frightens me. She is so tight. If the lid ever blew, what would happen to all of us?*

He thought, *I want her.* Surprised, he stopped walking. She turned to him, looked at him with the look that meant: I am thinking. It meant: I think; I am. He was a tree trying to move through soil. He shook his head.

"What?" she said. He could only shake his head again. She smiled. "Say it."

She took a step toward him, warmth in her belly and some kind of energy transfusing her extremities. He thought irrelevantly of the training he had received decades ago in his first job as an orderly. If a patient became violent or threatening, move toward them, not away. But she was the threatening one. He took a step, almost a lunge, reached for her, pulled her against him. He felt her chuckle as he kissed her. Her mouth opening to him. Her arms around him. He was shaking, and her hands found the center of that, in his lower back, and she pulled her head back and smiled again.

"What's this? Am I so scary?"

"Yes. Yes, you are."

"Why?"

"Because you don't belong here, and I don't know where you are, and I find myself wanting you and not wanting to want you. I don't like angst, Morgan. You people in this house are taking my life apart."

She studied him for a moment, listening to the layers. "No. You are taking your own life apart. You feel trapped if we say we love you, but you don't leave, and the door is open. You are so hungry that you don't know what it feels like to be satisfied. You have just made me into an image of something you want. Not a person to make love with. You want someone to take you apart, like you say. I won't. Even if I had that power, how dare you expect me to use it just so you won't have to have anything to do with the result?"

"Of course you have the power. Don't you know how we all see you? The cards keep coming up in the Tarot, the Chariot, the High Priestess. Who do you think makes us do what we do?"

"You like to believe you take no action, don't you? You like to believe the images you have of people. You want to see me as some kind of cosmic arbiter twiddling with your fate. What will you say when my clothes are off, when you see Morgan, the person, not the Tarot card image? Will I seem unworthy then, when you see that I am real, that I hurt, that I bleed once a month just like a human woman? I am bleeding now, you know. Would you like to have some, on your hand, to prove I am alive?"

She pulled away from him and walked on. He fell into step, a fast angry step. All this time her voice had been soft, but now she had given up kicking pebbles. She pulled the gate open with a jerk, looked back at him then went in. He caught the gate on the backswing and closed it carefully.

She was already at the veranda door, waiting for him, looking back, her face half in shadow and half in the streetlight. As he came up the path she said, "Well, come on, then." Did he really want this whirlwind? He thought, yes.

She strode through the dark kitchen, her scarf flying behind her, up the back stairs and down the strip of hall carpet to her room.

He thought, *this escalator is taking me somewhere very scary. This isn't men's sportswear.* She opened her door. The light was on in her room, and it shone out in a fan into the hall, so again her face was half bright, half dark with one eye still shadowed. Or, she thought, his face, brightening in the overflow of gold.

"You are the first man for a long time to get invited in," she said, and grinned. He walked through the door.

"Into your room?"

"No," and she laughed shortly.

"What about that Sal character?" he said.

"He wasn't anywhere near me," she said. "I told all of you that. What about Miranda-turned-Maybelle?"

"I never got that far with her. Maybe if I hadn't found out for a couple more days, I would have been seriously bent out of shape, but it just seems stupid to me. I feel a little stupid, I mean."

"We could all wear that label, by now. Never mind."

She was not joyous, he could see, but she was not angry any more either. She began to take her clothes off, methodically, hanging them up on the back of the desk chair.

"Come on," she said again, "I want this, and so do you, you know. It'll be fine." Then: "If I take my sponge out, there will be blood all over. Don't use your mouth, it's not safe."

She came over to him, naked, and smiled. "You'll have to take me as I am, you know. I'm no sister of mercy. Life's not a game. I only live here."

"That will do," he said, put his hands on her face, bent his head, kissed her.

Sometime during the lovemaking, he looked up at her. She was looking again with that look that said *I am thinking at you,* and her face was as remote as the moon.

He knew he would never reach her, but he began to see that it was his own fault if he didn't get what he needed for the night. He reached up to her and pulled her down to kiss. He felt for a moment like he was holding that wraith, but she became solid in a second, pulled his head up to meet her, and her mouth came down hard on his, reaching into him, as she reached into him, with mouth and hand and body, bringing him through orgasm to comfort, until his face was softened and he lay back with a quiet smile.

"There," she said, her face open as his. "You should let yourself out more often. You look good."

He sat leaning up against the wall, his warm back against the cool plaster, cradling her against him. She was silent, looking out at infinity. He watched the crescent of her face that he could see, mysterious, warm. After a while it occurred to him that she was asleep, so he moved a pillow to his side, gently laid her down on it. Her breathing didn't change. He kissed her shoulder, covered her as well as he could without disturbing her, then slowly, carefully got up, picked up his clothes, went to the door. As he was opening it silently, he looked back. She had not moved, and her deep slow breathing rhythm had not altered, but her eyes were open, she was looking at him with a half-smile and half-lidded gaze. He stood in stasis for a moment, watching her watching him; then her eyes closed slowly and opened again, like a cat, like a dismissal. He went out, closed the door quietly. She turned over onto her back, one hand against her lower belly, groped with her other hand for the quilt. She slept.

❖   ❖   ❖

"So what *was that?*" Morgan demanded of Blue. "I spent two hours listening to Russ *thinking* about me, while we made love. I saw the whole thing from his point of view, even more than my own. And *you* heard it too. *What did you do?*"

They were walking in the ravine, and for good measure Morgan had rigged them each with a portable tape player, which she had turned to max volume with the headphones hanging around their necks so that the music made a tinny tiny blare right beside their mouths.

"I dreamed Russ's thoughts. You were there, so I gave them to you."

"Maybe I didn't want them!"

"I didn't see you complaining at the time," said Blue, using the phrase with which Aziz had won Jakob's forgiveness at that awful involuntary dinner party, and which had become a household joke.

She shook her head, annoyed. "Until I saw the condom wrapper in the wastebasket, I thought it was a dream."

"It was," said Blue smugly.

"It was not a fucking dream. It happened, and I rode Russ like a loa in some American novel about voodoun. And you rode me."

"I didn't . . . do anything you didn't want."

"You moved my perceptions around. That's invasive."

"But you liked it," said Blue.

"Yes, but that doesn't make you any less presumptuous for doing it without my permission."

"If I had asked, you wouldn't have let me."

"Yes, you're absolutely right. And yes, okay, it was amazing, but I didn't choose it, and I don't like being messed with. Can you do this trick with everyone?"

"No; well, sort of. It's not a trick. It's just there. I can sort of hear Delany when she's really sleeping. I can hear Jakob sometimes. Sleeping and dancing, but sort of like there's a short circuit. I can't hear John or Mr. Chief Inspector McKenzie Grey or Staff Sergeant Kowalski. There's one police officer on surveillance that I can hear for a few seconds every now and again, like shortwave radio very far away. I can't hear Aziz but sometimes I get a sort of whisper from Rahim, very far away and grouchy. I can hear cats a lot. And Russ when he is having sex, just. And you."

Chilled by the cool catalogue, Morgan said, "Well, don't eavesdrop on anyone. At all. Unless they let you. And besides, what if they find out you can do this sort of thing? They'll think that you might just as well be the one who killed Sal."

"If I can do 'this sort of thing', why would I beat him like that? It's inefficient. And killing is foolish anyway. If I had heard anyone, I would have gone for help."

"Well, I know that, and you know that, but would they believe us?"

"Mr. Grey believes us."

"Have you ever heard the expression 'Don't put all your eggs in one basket'?"

"Yes, of course I have."

"It's a rhetorical question."

Blue knew what those were for. "Oh."

✿   ✿   ✿

"Let's put it this way," said the grey man. "For a start, you're fired."

"Fired?" said the Boy Wonder. "You can't do that! Regulations—"

"—aren't too kind to police officers who blackmail civilians into espionage tasks in high-security locations. Fired is just step one."

"High security? A fucking joke. Listen, the U.S. has their alien sewed up so tight people can't even *find* it. China won't admit they have one. India has it in an underground bunker. You have ours out in the community in the most unsafe house in the city. *And* ours is probably doing murder. Somebody had to do something."

"So you appointed yourself."

"Yes. And I'm not alone. I have support from higher up . . ."

"So you say. So have I. Step two will test whether your friends or my friends win. You're under arrest."

"What exactly are you talking about? That's ridiculous."

"I don't plan to bury Blue underground, but I don't much care about you. Do you have a pet?"

"What? A what?"

"A pet. Something that will starve to death when you don't come home. Never mind, we'll be going through your place with a lice comb anyway. We can feed the cat. See it gets a nice home. We'll take care of the plants, too."

"I don't have a goddamn cat. You can't arrest me!"

"I just did. Put your badge and gun on the desk, just like in the movies."

Rahim took out his ID wallet, threw it on the desk. "My lawyer won't like—" The grey man had him up against the door, his bunched-up collar bending his earlobes upward, before Rahim could finish the sentence.

"Federal employees of our particular agency," the grey man said, jaw set, "don't have recourse to lawyers. I'm invoking the New Official Secrets Act. You'll be lucky ever to see the light of day again, let alone a lawyer."

"Mac, what the—"

"I don't like you—" each new phrase punctuated by banging Rahim's shoulders back against the door "—I don't like your me-first politics, I don't like watching you claw your way up the ladder, and I don't like your notion that you can sink your poisonous little claws into me. I especially don't like someone under my command breaking the law for his own career advancement. Smacks of corruption in the police service, and I'm a little *old-fashioned* about that. As you so often have told me. So, you go down. Welcome to hardball policing. Something, as I recall, that you have always advocated for others." He let go with a shove, and Rahim staggered upright and shook the expensive suit back into place.

"Come in here," said the grey man, only slightly louder than before, and the door opened to the escort squad: two line officers and Flora, looking angry and ruffled. "He still has his gun," he said to Flora. "Strip-search him first. Scan for chips. Dig them out if you have to. Then take him downstairs. Find out where he got the money to buy these suits. Find out why he can afford to drive a Hurricane. Find out who else besides Aziz he's running, and where, and why. Find out what outside interests he works for."

"I don't—" Rahim protested.

"I don't want to see his face again until you have the answers," said Mr. Grey. "Don't kill him, but I don't care whether or not he stays pretty."

Flora nodded.

"Come on, Mac, you can't be serious . . ." Rahim was struggling with his former colleagues. Flora reached around the other woman's grip and pulled Rahim's arms back into the plastic wrist and elbow cuff strips.

"That's what you thought," said the grey man. "Now you know different. Live and learn."

He stood in the door of his office watching until they managed Rahim into the security elevator. Shaking his head, he walked back to his desk.

Kowalski knocked on the open door a few moments later. "Mac?"

The grey man raised his head from his fingertips, with which he had been massaging his tense forehead. He left his elbows planted on the desk, and steepled his fingers reflectively. "Ko. You are a very lucky man."

Kowalski slid into the office. "I'm sorry, Mac. I . . ."

"Let's skip all that," said the grey man. "You still have a job. Enjoy it. And don't ever piss me off that much again."

Ko relaxed slightly. "Thanks, Mac. I . . ." He stopped, at a loss.

"The end of that sentence is, 'I owe you big-time'. Don't relax. Don't mistake my calmness for approval. I *will* be watching you. I *am* counting misdemeanors. That's two. One more, and you're history too. Ask Flora what happened to Rahim." And he returned his forehead to the cradle of his fingertips.

At the door Kowalski paused. "About May Murphy . . ."

Mr. Grey looked up. "Don't send her to Back-of-Beyond. She obeyed orders. Do what I'm doing with you. Give her a chance to redeem herself."

"Right. Um . . . why?"

"Why? Because I limit myself to one evisceration per day. So far. Because nothing you did was illegal. Because I need at least one lieutenant who has been around since the beginning and knows what the hell is going on. Because you'll work harder and better and smarter under probation, and so will she. Because I'm an old-fashioned cop. Don't push it."

"Um, thanks, Mac."

"It's not because I like you. Don't ever make that mistake. Now get out of here."

＊　　＊　　＊

"So, you're collecting het guys now that they won't let you go play with women?" Jakob drawled.

"Collecting what?"

"That Sal. Russ, now."

"I didn't *collect* Russ. And I didn't do that policeman, remember?"

"Oh, sure. That cop would have done any of us. He almost had *me* up against the fridge."

"He made out like he hated queers."

"Come on. Of course he did. But he was a starfucker."

"Well, I guess you're a star, on the net, but why come on to me?"

"He knew shit about netdance. People who hang out with the *alien* are stars. He would have fucked *Blue* if Blue were available."

"Who says Blue isn't? We're teaching Blue to be a person; people have sex."

"Blue's yours. Everybody knows that."

"Jakob! Blue is not!"

"Anybody you want is yours, it seems."

"Hey, Azalea Trailmaiden, I thought we-all wuz free-ends! What's the bitchiness about?"

Jakob shook his head, abashed. "Sorry, honey. Ain't been laid in a long time now. Warps my mind."

"What about Aziz?"

"Aziz is one of the new breed of dry sex addicts. He doesn't actually put out. Saving himself for marriage, or something."

"I don't get it. I thought . . ."

"I don't get it either. That's the point. But I'm not sure that Aziz would slake my thirst anyway. I have more substantial desires."

"Are *you* interested in *Blue?*" Morgan said, surprised.

"That's not what I meant, exactly, but you have to admit, he's the sweetest thing in a long time, chile. And this is a houseful of sweet things. Kinda gets my sweet tooth going, know what I mean?"

"Maybe I don't. Are you mad at me for spending that time with Russ?"

Jakob looked away, and licked his lips. He opened his hands and stared at the palms, shook his head, and then snapped his hands away from himself as if shaking off water—or fire ants. "I'm not mad at you, honeychile. I thought I was, but I just figured it out. I'm mad at him."

Jakob walked out of the kitchen, leaving Morgan standing, surprised, staring after him. *Hmm,* she thought. *Curiouser and curiouser.* She raised her own hands but there was nothing to see in her palms except spidery lines of life, patterns of use, which, unlike what other people were constantly doing, told her nothing new.

❀   ❀   ❀

Blue came into the kitchen while she was still looking after Jakob.

"Have you thought about sex? I mean, with other people?" Morgan asked Blue.

"Isn't that the only way to have sex?" Blue countered.

"You know perfectly well that there's auto-eroticism—"

Blue interrupted. "Masturbation. But that's not sex, is it?"

"Many people think it is."

"You don't."

"Well, no, but that's my opinion. You don't have to believe the same things I do."

"I heard Jakob talking to you. I know I belong to myself. But I like the way you think. It seems worthwhile to follow some of your thinkings and opinions."

"Sex . . . ?"

"I have been thinking I should try it. Do you suppose I need to use all the proper protections?"

"I would if I were you. No telling what infections you could catch."

"Will you teach me?" Blue took her hands.

Ignoring the short, sharp shock that contact with Blue always gave her, Morgan said gently, "No, dear, I won't. I wouldn't be a good teacher right now."

"You taught Russ."

"What is it with everybody?" she said, irritably. "Are Russ and I public property? It was just something that happened. And I wouldn't be surprised if that thing you did to us wasn't part of why it happened."

"Things like that don't just happen," said Blue. "They have to be wanted."

Morgan, surprised, said, "How wise you are becoming."

Blue looked pleased. "Thank you!"

"It's not a compliment."

"I mean thank you for making me wise."

"I didn't make you wise. You got wise like all people do: by learning and applying your learning to experience."

"I told you before. You made me entirely. There was no Blue without you."

Disquieted, Morgan pulled her hands from Blue's feverish grip. "You need to get some sleep time," she said. "You're getting obsessive again."

❖   ❖   ❖

Russ caught her looking at TravelNet Asean destinations on the house computer.

"Planning a trip?" he said.

"No, just wishing I could," she said. "What's it like there?"

He looked at the screen. "It's peacefully autocratic," he said. "No guns. They enforce conformity through bad vid. Just like the stuff I make at work. It's warm and orchids grow all over the city. There are seven beautiful fountains, and at night we used to sit by the canal at sidewalk tables while touts from the hawker stalls brought us fruit and skewers of satay. Cats with short curly tails would brush by our legs and jump on the tables for their dinners. You could get the most beautiful textiles in the market there the first time I went, but by last year, it was all under government control: prices up, quality down. There was a beautiful amusement park for the tourists, though."

"Oh, did you like it?"

"No, I hated it," he said shortly, and moved to leave.

"Russ . . . ," she said quickly.

He turned to look at her. His face was hard, but at her expression, softened into a smile.

"It's all right," he said. "I made some good vid. I'm helping bring down the government there, even as we speak. It was fine."

She shook her head. "Are you all right with what happened with us?"

"Are you worried? I'm sorry," he said quickly, and sat down by the desk. "I didn't mean to worry you. I'm fine, kiddo. I just don't expect anything more from you, if you know what I mean."

"I like you a lot, Russ."

"Likewise. But—"

"But?"

He was silent, looking at his hands. *There's a lot of that going around,* thought Morgan. He glanced up and caught her smile.

"It's been a long time since I trusted anyone much," he said. "You are the most consistent person I know—and don't immediately start gathering evidence to disprove me. I mean it. Letting me touch you was one of the best of the gifts you have given me, and I know that it wasn't a promise of anything except who you already are with me, if that makes sense. But—"

"That word again."

"You don't know me, Morgan. You don't know what I do. My hands aren't clean."

"What do you mean by that?"

"I'm not ready for relationships. I don't really want any friends."

She smiled at the echo. "It's too late," she said.

"Yeah, I know," he said, and laughed his infectious laugh.

"It's okay," she said. "Take it from me. It doesn't hurt that much."

Dancing lessons

Morgan was sitting on the steps looking at the moths inside the porch flying wishfully against the light, the wall, the door. She tested out a few metaphysical conceits—I am the moth, etc.— but she only felt like a fool in the eyes of the universe. Not to speak of the eyes of the world. Looking at the aimless, solitary, kamikaze autumn moths, hiding from the outside chill in a suicidal cul-de-sac, she decided, instead of angst she would have a social life again. It had been stupid to flirt with despair when she could have been dancing. She got up and went inside.

In the kitchen, Jakob was leaning into the refrigerator—looking for beer, he said to her complainingly.

"Beer? What the hell for?"

"To wash my hair."

"Good gracious. May as well try mayonnaise."

"Really?"

"Chill, chile. What's this nervous thing?"

"I'm the guest of honor at this damn festival. Loads of lissome boys just dying to rub some of the star quality off onto their buff little butts. I have to look the part!"

"Star quality. Is *that* what you call it?"

He arranged his draperies a little. "Look at this rag . . ."

"You'll be *fine!*" said Morgan. "Just go. Just be. It's about time you were lionized. And Aziz gave you some practice. Will he be there?"

"Probably. The little shit."

"I thought you forgave him."

"I forgave him for being blackmailed by his cousin. I didn't forgive him for being a cocktease."

"All the more reason to have some groupies show him how he was supposed to properly adore you!"

"Grrr," said Jakob, slammed the fridge, and sailed out, golden and silver veils trailing. He had managed to evoke the *Slow Glass* vid effects with clothing and carriage alone. She expected that the young dancers would indeed want to get personal. Her momentary envy crystallized her intention, and she dressed for maximum effect herself, then pulled on her warm wrap and, avoiding the press and surveillance by going out the small hidden wrought-iron side gate in the depths of the caragana hedge while Jakob was drawing their attention to the front door, she walked downtown.

❀   ❀   ❀

Although outside the air was crisply autumnal, in the club the air was heavy with humidity and humanity—and even traces of cigarette smoke, from the clothing of the older dykes who still smoked at home and in their 4×4s. The floor of the old converted warehouse was rough, unfinished, with ground-in dirt and oil, so the smell of old wood was strong. Morgan left her coat in the crowded vestibule and pushed through the double doors, surprised at the hesitation she felt. Inside, as she looked around, she felt only familiar, thinking how all the private gay clubs she'd ever seen looked the same as this, the first one she'd ever seen, almost two decades ago now. Bar. Dance floor. Steel entrance door. Washrooms with the door hinges broken, so the doors had to be propped open, so the fluorescent light outlined the people going in or returning to the general dimness. Bad murals painted on the corridor to the washrooms.

And the people, staying the same as we all get older, she thought. The oldest dykes in their plaid going-out-to-dance shirts, the middle-aged in their black leather, some in the harnesses which showed off their pierced nipples, and the ones Morgan's age in shiny black, as she was. The young, trendy babyqueers of several genders wore loose white silk shirts with the leather vests underneath, and the white headdresses like a silent-movie sheik: until you started to strip them down, thought Morgan, you'd think you were fucking Mother Teresa.

If any of them remembered who that was—she'd been a heroine of Morgan's impressionable early years, and her death had hit the young Morgan hard, sending her out to rave clubs to overcompensate with E, and GHB for the morning sketchiness, until third- and fourth-year university became more interesting than all-night dancing. Around then, too, the breakup with Scott had made embodiment at queer clubs more interesting than mindlessness. Now, who were their heroes, and what drugs did these young people do to forget that they did not live up to those heroes?

"Hey!" said a voice in Morgan's ear. "A face from the past!" Morgan turned. It was Kyla, one of the friends from the old days, whom Morgan had seen on the street once or twice since returning to this city.

"How are you?" said Morgan.

"Hungry!" growled Kyla jokingly, and Morgan laughed. "Me too. But hey, it's a moveable feast, right?" Kyla smiled ferally and plunged into the crowd. Bemused, Morgan looked after her, and as she did, Morgan's long hair was snagged by the metal rings on the shoulder of a passing woman whose shaved head was growing in grey, and after the obligatory flirtatious apology, Morgan impatiently pulled her hair together and tied it back. She felt the knot bounce against her vertebrae like the touch of a phantom hand to her back above the low-cut back of her top, and she shivered. Her body was waking up to the world. She turned rapidly and bumped into someone who had been following the same channel through the crowd.

"Sorry," she said automatically, then saw that it was the two young women from the CSIS patrol. The one she had thought was certainly a dyke, Ace, and the other one, whose name she didn't know, whom she would have said was straight, but here she was, hand in hand with Ace, and blushing. "Hey, hi," Morgan said. "Nice to see you here."

"Sure," said Ace, "hey."

She had already pushed past them, smiling, when it occurred to her to wonder if they were here because they were working, were following her. She turned around and saw the younger one pull her hand from Ace's and turn away, her face unhappy. Inconclusive.

The crowded dance floor was full. Morgan pushed past the bar and leaned against the counter at the back, where the drag queens were dishing to each other in shrill voices. She grinned. When she had been in university, different drag queens at this same club had been her best friends. Long time ago, it felt like, though it was only fifteen years since she'd graduated. She had been so young, she thought.

"Hey, wanna dance?" The voice was loud in her ear. She turned to see a zaftig young blonde in a less extreme version of the billowy uniform leaning toward her. A woman, she saw, though the wild hair and smooth face were delightfully ambiguous. They threaded back through the crowd to the dance floor. Just as they got there the music shifted to a slow tune and Morgan slowed momentarily, but the young woman drew her into an embrace.

"You are, you are gorgeous," she said breathlessly, in that strange popular cadence in which so many younger people seemed to speak these days, which Morgan found a little edgy at best. She wouldn't let Blue imitate it from vid. But the girl was flushed and attractive, the music hot antique and familiar, and Morgan was intrigued.

"I'm Nancy. Hey, do you like it here? Hey—"

"Shhh," said Morgan, and put her fingers over the girl's mouth. Girl. Young woman, okay, thought Morgan, but so young. "Are you legal?" said Morgan abruptly. Despite all the human rights challenges, last year's "law reform" had succeeded: twenty-five was now legal age for same-sex sex, though for heteros it was still sixteen.

Nancy laughed. "Sure! They make you show ID here, anyway. But ask, ask anybody!"

Morgan smiled at Nancy, keeping secret her self-consciousness, almost amazed, as well as amused, by the realization that she felt rusty at this. *I used to be able to rope and hog-tie 'em with the best,* she thought, and laughed at the thought of this apparition trussed like a rodeo calf. Nancy had begun to smile at Morgan's laughter, and Morgan made the smile wider when she said, "I haven't been here for a while. What's new in dancing styles?"

"We-ell," said Nancy, "we like, like to get real close"—she demonstrated—"and dance, dance real slow, and put a leg in between your legs like this" and she ground her thigh against Morgan's groin. Morgan felt the familiar ache of arousal, knew this baby dyke was no babe in the woods. "Mmmmm, and . . . ?" and Nancy's hand pressed the small of her back, so that Morgan was held against the taller woman as they danced slowly.

Morgan felt the ache rise, transpose into another key, and the heat flow through her face. She leaned into Nancy languidly. *This young one is almost as fast a mover as I used to be, way back when,* Morgan thought, remembering how many times she, half-clad and panting, had leaned back against some corridor wall of some bar or community hall while the conquest of the moment knelt in front of her or leaned into her, as they hurried through the night's flirtation to a sweaty, abandoned orgasm. Now she was the one feeling shy and this youth was moving her through the same, pun inevitable, dance. Somewhere behind the heat, the defiance too was the same, but before Morgan could bring this uncomfortable insight to the front of her mind, the music stopped and they drew apart. Glimpsing their reflection in the mirror-tiled wall, Morgan saw how little and yet how much the heat showed in their faces. "Let's go somewhere quiet," she said. The side door was near the dance floor. She and Nancy, hands joined, pushed through the couples coming untangled the same way, and Morgan popped open the exit door.

They tumbled out into a crowd. Photographers, reporters. Who immediately turned from their concentration on the main hall door, to converge on her.

"There she is! Hey, Ms. Shelby!" one of them yelled, and they crowded around her.

"Hey, Constance, over here. How does it feel to have an alien living with you?"

"Hell, how does it feel to have an alien," one of the men said, heavy with innuendo, and the reporters laughed.

The door had clicked shut behind them, and they were pinned up against the building. Nancy was turned away from the lights, her arm up over her face. The loose white sleeve was as good as a curtain. Morgan, wearing tight-fitting, low-cut black, was not so easily able to protect herself.

"Are you teaching the alien to be a pervert?"

"How many lovers have you had?"

"Who did you sleep with to get your assignment?"

"Did you bring the alien with you? Is that her in disguise?"

They began to pluck at Morgan and Nancy's clothing. Neither had said a word, and now they were pushed too hard to speak.

"Okay, that's enough," said the unmistakable voice of authority. It was the CSIS cops, Ace and the other woman. They had their badges out and were pushing the crowd aside. The photographers pulled back to photograph the cops too.

"Break it up," said the other cop, her voice rough and authoritative.

"You," said Ace to the nearest camera operator, "do you have a media permit? Let's see it."

"I left it in the van," said the photographer. Ace grabbed the camera and pressed the Delete Images key.

"*No!*" he shouted. The reporters were fumbling in their pockets now for their permits. It was a new law; lots of the media people weren't used to it yet; Morgan had already noticed that at media scrums outside the house. Some of the reporters were trying to fade away quickly before they were noticed. The print photographers were gone first. The videorazzi kept filming, their permits clamped in the hands holding the camera grips.

"Do they assign lesbian cops to follow lesbians?" said one of the tabloid reporters, waving her permit for attention. Ace, angry, grabbed Morgan and Nancy by the elbows, hustled them back through the vestibule door the other cop was holding open. "No comment," said the other cop breathlessly, and slammed the door on the media. Ace at the same time slammed the inside door, the one that opened into the hall where the curious queers were starting to crowd. The double impact made a sudden pressure flash in Morgan's ears, and she shook her head involuntarily. Alone in the bleak vestibule, the four squared off like square dancers, or maybe more like pro wrestlers, each at their corner.

"Are you out of your *mind?*" Ace quietly grated to Morgan. "Coming here without security? Didn't you think something like this would happen? You're not a fucking civilian any more. Thank heavens you forgot to take off your chip."

"Well, you rose to the occasion," Morgan said, still shivering from being coatless in the near-zero outside. "Or were you just here on a date, like that queer-basher from the *Sun* said?"

"I wish," said Ace. "I don't have time for a private life since I got this fucking assignment, and if I did, would I have brought the straight-arrow Ice Queen here?"

The other woman blushed, with what this time? Anger? Embarrassment? Humiliation? "I'll get the squad car," she said, and she slipped out the door into the uproar outside.

"Well, that's that partnership out the window," said Ace as she held the door shut.

"Don't be so paranoid," said Morgan, rummaging for her coat on the overcrowded coatrack. "It's pretty obvious you're queer."

"You shouldn't have said that, about her," Nancy said unexpectedly. "You did it to shock *us. And* you hurt your friend." She had found her coat, a voluminous old duster with several wool sweaters underneath, and was struggling into the layers. "And besides, who are we?" she continued. "We don't know you. You don't have to justify yourself for us. I'm just a one-night stand for Morgan, she's just an assignment for you."

A one-night stand for *Morgan?* Well. "You knew who I was?" said Morgan. "*Before* you talked me up?"

"Uh-huh," said Nancy, "from vid, you know, vid news," and there was still heat there, even despite the media scrum.

"Okay. But I do my job, anyway." Ace kept talking as she

opened to the other one's impatient banging on the door. "You know, my boss assigned me 'cause he thought I could get into her head better."

The other woman, back, was still angry. "And why assign me?"

"Why not, kiddo, you can pass for a lipstick lesbian, I can hold your hand in the club and no-one will care."

"You knew the rules of this place, I didn't. You didn't have to make me look stupid."

Ace moderated her tone. "When else can I hold my friend's hand, and on duty too, and no-one raises an eyebrow? And it was even your idea!"

The darker one laughed, a little tensely. "Next time I'll make you dance with me."

"Sure, kid."

"Let's go; I double-parked."

They pushed out through the crowd, Ace holding her jacket over Morgan's head to foil vidhounds and paparazzi. They tumbled into the car and Ace peeled out like a stock car driver. The heater in the cop car was efficient, and Ace tossed her jacket into the back seat. Nancy stuffed it on the shelf at the back to foil the last camera truck, which was still following until Ace two-wheeled a couple of corners, deked down an alley, and lost them.

"Neat driving," said Nancy.

"I took a course," said Ace. "Not that it matters. They know where we're going. We just have to get there first."

Morgan untied her hair, which was now considerably disheveled, then pulled out the decorative side-combs (amazingly, still there), used them to comb the length of her hair smooth and put them back to anchor the tendrils away from her face. Nancy, stroking Morgan's hair, broke the silence. "Do you ever get the feeling that there's no God?"

They all stared at her, except Ace who shoulder-checked a glance and said, "What the fuck?"

"Well, sometimes I feel so good, and I know then, then that there must be no God."

"Who watches the watchers then?" said Morgan.

"Someone will show up," said Ace. "This is too good to be true."

"Are you, are you gay?" said Nancy meanwhile to the other cop.

"I don't think so," she said. "No, I think not."

"Thinking got nothing to do with it, kid," Ace said, and her symmetrical fair face split into a twisted smile. "You can't think about it, or you get too screwed up. You just gotta do it."

"So why tell me about it?" said Morgan.

"Why not? You're the most public queer around."

"I'm not even exclusively lesbian," Morgan protested.

"Doesn't matter. You know it's queer you're damned for, if you don't watch out. You found out tonight what the tabloids are gonna say, about you and that one, just because they know you fuck women."

"And you? What do you think?"

"I'd like to live in your house," the dark-haired cop said. "That's what I think. So never mind those mofes, they'll die unhappy."

"Hey, tough talk!"

At the house, Ace grabbed Morgan and Nancy by the upper arms, hurried them toward the house. "Get in there. The camera trucks will be here any minute. And stay the fuck *in* there until I get ahold of McKenzie. This is just another fuckup, and it's your bloody fault."

Nancy giggled, but Morgan sighed. "Yeah, right. Sorry. Look— want to come in to call? That little shack must be cold. It really is fall now—look, our breath shows."

"No," said Ace as the other woman said, "It's heated." The two watchers looked at each other. "Maybe later," said the other, who, it dawned on Morgan, must be nicknamed Kid, for all the times Ace called her that. "Besides, we're on duty," Ace said, and Kid started to laugh, laughed until tears beaded on her lashes.

"Goodnight, then," said Morgan. "You know the door is open if you want to come inside."

"And you," said Ace as a parting shot, "stay the fuck *inside!*" The two cops went off across the yard to the little security shed where no doubt they would be able to listen to Morgan and Nancy make love, if that was still on the program. Morgan closed the front door, turned and found Nancy grinning at her.

"Hey, if we're supposed to stay inside, I can certainly think of something to keep us busy," Nancy said breathlessly, and Morgan decided that the program was still on track. She reached inside Nancy's layers of sweaters, seeking her body. They fumbled with the fasteners on each other's coats, and Morgan stripped Nancy of layer after layer of sweaters until they were both giggling. Nancy stepped out of the entry, into the living room, said, "Nice."

Morgan said "Never mind that now," and pulled her by the hand, led her up the stairs and down the hall to the door of her room. Pushed open the door, and Blue and Marbl were sitting by the window, engrossed in each other's touch. Blue stood, Marbl running from the telescoping lap. Blue reached one hand for each face, touched, and a shiver went down Morgan to her roots.

"Is this the, this the alien?" said Nancy. "Wow. Spinal. 'Scuse me." She went by Blue into the room, turned around looking at it.

"What is that?" Morgan said involuntarily to Blue. "Remember what I said to you."

"I am only a conduit," said Blue, and went silently out, like a dream. Nancy looked at Morgan's ocean-deep eyes. Black as space, she thought, and wondered how she knew how black is space. How did she know what Nancy was thinking? Morgan wondered, and thought, *Backwash,* which would have made her shiver except that she had a more immediate reason. Nancy went to the middle of the rug, still watching Morgan, and took her clothes off slowly, without deliberation, a child going in to swim.

But not a child going in to swim. Her body was lush and pale, and she took Morgan's hand and guided it into the cleft below her blonde pubic hair so Morgan could feel how she was eager to go on.

"I'm sorry," said Morgan. "You scare me. You are so brave."

"No, just cold. I want to get under the covers."

She glided into the sheets. Morgan unbuttoned her shirt, pulled the combs from her hair so it fell free, hid behind it while

216

she undressed. The furnace was still running on its summer program as the fall had been long and warm, so now the air was cool against her tight nipples, tight belly, cooled the heat of her. She stopped with the duvet in her hand, halfway through shaking it across the bed.

"How old are you?" she said.

"Twenty-six," Nancy said.

"I am thirty-nine," Morgan said, and slid her cooling body against the source of young heat, and the capable hands reaching for her—

—and some time in the storm that followed, that lasted until the pale pre-dawn, Morgan with her mouth on the other's sweet-tasting clitoris, raised her head for a moment to see the curve of belly and breasts and throat, and thought, *how can this be me, who makes her vibrate so?* and put her mouth back, and felt the cooled air fall from the cold window panes across her back and feet, and felt her own vibration, and felt a blue tide full and high through her vision, and heat following it, and sank again into the undertow and was willingly swept away.

In the morning she finally fell asleep beside the finally sleeping youth, woke three hours later to that unfamiliar feel of another (and not cat-sized) body in her bed, and looked across the rumpled thick hair of the sleeping woman to meet the eyes of Blue who was standing in the doorway, smiling a little, and holding Marbl, the cat who would not suffer herself to be held, holding Marbl, two warmths, side by side.

"I don't want any dream better than this, not now," she said to the alien, her friend.

"What?" said Nancy, half-waking.

"Never mind," said Morgan. "Sleep."

And they slept, and woke, and that was Saturday.

❖   ❖   ❖

"That was the famous alien you saw last night," teased Morgan, "and you didn't even blink an eye."

"I was busy," Nancy said, and Morgan laughed.

"You are the best, the best lover I have ever had," said Nancy. "You know, you know the feeling you get sometimes when you meet someone, that you're like dazzled by the presence of that person in the world? Like they should have a fan club and you should be president, you know? That's how I feel about you right now."

"Hush," said Morgan. "That's crazy talk. Don't make me suspicious of you, or I'll have to call the cops."

"Oh, no! The cops!" Laughing, Nancy tackled her back into bed. "Come on, I'm not, not crazy, just enjoying you. When we were making love, to be able to send you off like that, I was amazed, such a sense of power, that I could do that to someone like you. It's hard to resist that feeling."

Morgan smiled. Last night she'd felt a kinship of memory, but now she wondered, had she ever been twenty-six in quite that way? But she might as well enjoy it. She knew very well that when the grey man arrived later that day, she would be in trouble. Not that she didn't deserve it—she *had* been stupid. But like a kid with a chocolate-smeared face, she was thinking that the endorphins were worth it.

She turned to Nancy again and silenced her voluble compliments with a long kiss.

❄   ❄   ❄

The cop at the door was "Randy"—May Murphy. "I've got a message from the boss," she said.

Morgan looked at her. "I would have thought he would be here himself to give me hell."

"He's busy doing damage control."

"Oh, yeah, try to make me feel guilty!" Morgan grinned.

"You should," said May. "He says to tell you, verbatim, 'You're a pain in the ass. Next time you want to get laid, let us know. We'll run a proper bodyguard op.' "

"Did he throw anything?"

"Say what?"

"Shout. Throw things."

"He never shouts. He never throws things. He's known for it. He gets quiet—and deadly. He was pretty quiet."

He never threw things? Morgan smiled. "Fine. Tell him . . ."

"Yes?"

"Tell him if I want to get laid, I'll let him know."

❀   ❀   ❀

By evening Morgan knew she and Nancy would not be lovers again, but she was not sure Nancy knew yet. Nancy had stayed in the house all day, had been flirting with Russ and John, circling Delany with wary but friendly overtures, leading Morgan to think, *she is young!* Jakob wasn't home; *it's just as well,* Morgan thought, *I'm not sure I want to see that challenge.* Jakob would not have been quiet about his reactions to the blanketing of the house in Nancy's predatory sexual interest.

As for Blue, Nancy had shown remarkably little interest in the effort of conversing with such a foreigner; Blue's life was not relevant to her, and she had tended during the day to react to Blue as a rival for Morgan's time.

But the club had given her the solution as well as the problem. Morgan telephoned the sexually voracious friend-from-the-past, Kyla, and said, "Come over for dinner." When she realized her own need to give Nancy a new scent to follow, she laughed at herself wryly, and went to talk about it all, aboveboard, with Nancy.

❀   ❀   ❀

After Kyla left with Nancy, a consummation clearly to be wished despite everyone involved being aware it was a set-up, the household settled back in the living room around the fireplace, feet up on chairs or tables, the fire crackling and flames providing a Rorschach background to their talk. It was peaceful to be alone together again.

"So, you have had an adventure too, Morgan my dear," said Jakob.

Delany laughed. "All of us. What a kid that was!"

"Sweet," said Russ.

"Stupid," said Morgan. "I was lucky. The night I chose to have a temper tantrum—well, it could have turned out much worse."

"But how was she?" said John, who had missed everything but supper, and Kyla and Nancy's courtship dance. Predictably, Nancy had flirted with John too, but he had seemed almost offended by that.

"None of your fucking business," said Morgan genially.

"She sure didn't know what to make of us, eh, Blue?" Delany laughed. "The two weird ones. The crip and the pigmentally challenged."

Blue began to sing: *"Am I blue . . . ?"*

"I think that's your first joke!" said Delany after the gust of laughter abated.

"No, I made one last Thursday, don't you remember?"

"No."

"I remember," said John. "It was at seven o'clock exactly."

"Yes, that's the one," said Blue. "I knew you would remember."

"And how was she, really?" said Jakob *sotto voce*.

"How was yours?"

"My adventure? Good times, my dear, but strenuous. You know, they really liked me as a lunatic addict. Now that I'm just a lunatic, I make them nervous. Too serious. So no groupies, *malheureusement*."

"Oh, well, never mind," said Morgan. She put her feet back up, and turned her gaze into the fire, content to have her family around her, and be at peace.

✢ ✢ ✢

The flames suddenly begin to burn more and more iridescently, with flashes of purple and blue and white. The fire grows and surrounds Morgan, but she feels cool within it. *The witches burned for feeling too much: can anyone really feel too much?* the voice is dispassionate. *No,* Morgan's dream voice answers, *but lots of us try to avoid it, anyway*. The flames turn cool, icy cerulean, and begin to scorch her like dry ice.

She woke suddenly. She was still in the chair, and the fire had burned down. The room was cool, and she was shivering.

"You okay?" said John, who'd noticed her start upright.

"Sure," she said. "Napping. Would you hand me over that afghan there, please?"

"Afghan?"

"Knitted blanket. Thanks."

Morgan tucked the cover around her legs, and Russ fed the fire. When the flames leapt up, they were the safe results of burning pine—only a reservoir of pitch popped now and again to send an ember into the fire screen. But Morgan wasn't sleepy any more.

✧   ✧   ✧

The endorphins lasted a couple of giddy days, helping Morgan weather the annoyance of the grey man and the invasive and predatory media attention. When they receded, however, they swept out like a tidal bore in a catastrophic retreat, and when Morgan picked herself up, she was in the midst of another attack of grief. She hated being ambushed like this.

You don't get over it, you just get used to it, Judith had said on that visit where they'd talked, and this unexpected attack of anguish, just when she had felt life reassert itself, was proof.

Impatient, she waited for the police to clear away the morning's stubborn fringe of videorazzi, then went out to tend the garden, using the ferocity of blade and tine to substitute for catharsis. Struggling with tools scaled for average North Americans and thus too big for her, as well as old and worn so that the shovel blade and rake tines were loose on their splintery handles, she got sweaty and irritated, overwhelmed with the ludicrousness and Lilliputian nature of humanity's travails. But gradually, as she knew would happen, the persistent necessity of weed and soil took precedence over her fury at entropy.

Blue came out in work clothes. "Can I help you?"

"Put on your gloves," she said. "So you don't get blisters."

Whoever had tended the monastic garden of the previous owners of this tatty mansion had been far from ascetic: native plants mixed eclectic with perennials and self-seeding hardy annuals, crowded into borders around the house and filling the front yard from fence to veranda. It seemed as if the gardener had, after setting out the grand design, fallen prey to age or distraction, for when they'd moved in the caragana hedge was overgrown and untidy, the raspberry canes were invading the lawn, and the lilacs had grown leggy and unhealthy. Nevertheless, in the way that a solidly planned garden will assert a certain planned profusion even after many years of neglect, it had flourished through spring and summer only sporadically tended, spring bulbs and flowers cycling into summer's peony and poppy, cosmos, lavatera and flax, hollyhock and plume poppy, fireweed and a profusion of native plants hitherto unknown to Morgan, and culminating with a final vivid array of burning bush in September. But now all was withering.

Morgan, like most gardeners, found late fall a distressing yet optimistic time, and she worked in that pleasant melancholy, cutting down the last of the surviving flowers along with all the dead stalks, taking up delicate bulbs, pruning down roses and heaping leaf mulch and peat around their bases. Blue helped her, asking only the most basic of practical questions.

Morgan cut the last frost-nipped heads of the volunteering perennial snapdragons, finally killed by the heavy frost a week ago. Now the cold had been temporarily replaced by a false warmth so that the late-November air was as warm as late September: Morgan knew it wouldn't last, and as she wrestled with the aged raspberry canes, cutting them to the ground and digging out the worst of their untended spread, she attempted to make the heap of withered greenery into a metaphor for something: life, death, the Universe . . . But her thoughts were sabotaged by the soothing reek of humus. Finally, as she bundled the last of the prickly canes and heaved them over the back fence into the garbage pickup bin, she was almost smiling. Blue chose this moment to launch again into the eternal Whys.

"Why do humans do this planting and cutting? It's not for food, and it's hard work, when we could be reading books or swimming."

"Oh, for goodness' sake, are you on that again? Go read some gardening books!"

Blue ignored her, maintained the questioning pose. Morgan straightened her back, involuntarily groaning as the strained muscles protested, and looked at the strange expanse of terraformed yard for a silent few moments. Finally she shook her head. "I don't know, sweetie," she said. "Maybe we do it because we are atavists, looking back to the wilderness, as some say. Me, I think that the strange hybrid of wilderness and structure that makes a city is in some ways as natural as the mounds of a termite species. We built and tend because we want to have our surroundings structured and yet softened. There are as many theories as there are ideologies, I'm sure. In the end, it's individual, even if many individuals seem to have the same ideas."

"Do you have them because you imitate each other, or does everybody have them at once?"

Morgan laughed. "Nature versus nurture again! Oh, you are tempting the day, aren't you? This is an eternal argument!"

"But what do *you* believe? Why did you come out here to do this today, after all these months when you just looked at it and grinned?"

"Grinned? Is that what I did?" she teased Blue.

"Yes, I think so. It was more than just a smile. It seemed to have genuine pleasure, even fun, in it."

Morgan imagined the taxonomies this alien must have developed for interpreting human expression, and she momentarily compared these to her own, acquired more slowly but perhaps no different. "I like the wordlessness of it," she said. "It doesn't need interpretation. It's real, and it smells—oh, dusty and obvious. The things you have to know to do it are simple."

"Simple? How come you had to look in that book to figure out what to do with the roses?"

"Just because I don't know a thing doesn't mean it isn't simple," said Morgan with dignity, and they dissolved into laughter. Morgan remembered the essence of a saying from some bumper sticker or motivational lecture: "It is a poor day if one hasn't laughed." Surprised that she *had* laughed on this particular day, she turned to her work.

"Here," she said to Blue. "Make yourself useful. Put these gloves on and bundle these twigs up."

Even with the gloves and jacket, both of them had scratches on their wrists when the job was done. Morgan secretly imagined getting in trouble for damaging the precious alien, but it was an internal joke. It had been some time now since she had seriously questioned Blue's autonomy.

❖   ❖   ❖

"So, who tipped off the media Saturday night?" After only a small amount of thought, Morgan had telephoned Mr. Grey.

"One of yours," he said.

"Which one?"

"I don't think I should . . . oh, fuck it. John Lee."

"John?" She shouldn't have felt so surprised, she realized.

"What did I just say?"

"Makes sense, doesn't it? Was he there too?"

"I didn't see him, but that means nothing. A lot without press permits just faded away."

"I'll talk to him," Morgan said, and sighed.

"No, I'm not supposed to have told you. *I'll* talk to him. The jerk."

"Ach, he's just being stupid."

"Duh."

"My goodness. I haven't heard that in years."

"It's been a slice," said Mr. Grey, and hung up.

❖   ❖   ❖

What he didn't tell Morgan was that John had said: "That'll give the dyke bitch a hard time." John was turning out to be a bit of a problem.

As if anyone in that house wasn't.

❖   ❖   ❖

That night, the first snow of the year began to fall.

Morgan leaned on the wide windowsill in the stairwell, forearms on the ledge and weight on her arms, looking out at the slowly falling snow melting on the cement. Somewhere out there, behind a tree or a railing, there were security guards watching this house because somewhere in here there was an alien. She found the *idea* alien. She couldn't think what to think about it, so, like all the months she had threaded this wynd, she had just accepted that it was.

Behind her the soft voice said, "What is this now?"

The blue body was beside her, wrapped in a long robe, Jakob's silk kimono which was the only thing in the house that fit. Heat radiated out from the arm settled beside hers on the sill. The alien leaned forward in the same attitude as hers.

"This?"

"That which falls. White." Blue was playing at being the baby alien again. Morgan laughed.

"Snow. Frozen water. A manifestation of weather. There's a book about it in the living room. I'm sure with a week or so of concentrated study you could learn to identify it."

Blue grinned. "It looks different than in the movies, or on-screen."

"Well, they make it with snow machines in the movies. Here, it's the real thing."

"What *means* snow?" It was Blue's latest question: the alien wanted connotation now, was tired of facts, was reading poetry, was pumping everyone for feelings, sensations, intuitions.

"What does snow suggest to me? Winter, the dark time, the cold time, heavy with coats and scarves and gloves to keep in body heat."

"I am warmer than you. It is a faster rate of life. Would I live a longer time in the snow?"

"Let's not test it, okay? It looks pretty, but it's cold out there. Cold is bad for unprotected mammals."

❊   ❊   ❊

Morgan realized with a start that it had been one year since her parents died. One year ago, she was sitting in intensive care holding her father's hand; one year ago, her mother drove the car into oblivion. Morgan was surprised to find she no longer blamed them for leaving her.

Could it really be that sometime in the year, she had come to truly believe the useful knowledge she had always been so good at telling others? *'Tis a consummation devoutly to be wish't,* Morgan thought wryly, *even though I didn't know I wished it at the time.*

❊   ❊   ❊

At first it had appeared to Grey as if this Morgan creature saw everything as sexual. For all his conversation with Salomé, Grey did not see everything as sexual. He saw less of the world as sexual as time went on, unless the lascivious eagerness with which his colleagues played power games counted as sexual.

He sat at his desk, trying to imagine the world as Morgan saw it. He watched the men and women walk by and tried to imagine all of them with sexual potential for him. But that, aside from being ludicrous, given that he was in senior management and also that most of the others were even more unprepossessing than Kowalski or himself, wasn't quite right either. He tried instead to imagine himself with the potential to love them all.

That frightened him as his other fantasy had not.

If that was what Morgan was trying to do, she was doomed to fail.

But it was a grand experiment. *If* that was her intention.

❊   ❊   ❊

"I have no intention," Morgan said to Grey, and her steady fingers squeezing the wedge of lemon above the cup did not belie her. The swirl of juice cleared the tea into a rich clear dark-amber. She picked up the cup and tipped it slightly in her hand, making a tiny tide.

"People read a great deal into silence," she said. "I learned that a long time ago. Do you know that proverb, 'Sit on the bank of the river and wait. Your enemy's corpse will soon float by'? Well, it could just as well say, sit on the bank of the river in silence, and soon you will be surrounded by volunteer disciples, sycophants, and admirers. You will learn that you have motives and understandings that you never dreamed possible. You can become a hero or a saint, or you can be reviled and vilified—if that's not the same thing—the point being that an empty slate is a Rorschach blob waiting to happen."

"Or a mixed metaphor."

"Yes, or that. Of all these people, you are the only one I can trust to understand that I am simply who I am."

"Like Popeye the Sailorman."

"Who? Oh, yes, like him. *I yam what I yam* . . . Poor old crusader."

"No, that was Don Quixote. I always liked him."

"So I am Popeye, and you are Quixote. A mixed marriage, indeed."

She had warmed her hands on the teacup and now she began to drink the tea.

"I will be forty years old soon," she said. "Who will celebrate?"

"I will be fifty-three. We can party together."

"*Did* you do that Men's Movement thing when you were young? Like my dad did?"

"Nah. Only old farts did that, no offense intended, Esalen survivors with pot bellies and caftans. I had long hair in a pony tail, and was a vegetarian. I refused to learn to fix my car because it was a guy thing, and I wasn't going to make the error of being a guy. And unlike most of the old farts, I always liked women too—liked women and men the same amount, I mean."

"Why did you become a cop?"

"I thought I could do some good." He shook his head. "Really. I overestimated myself and the police force, and underestimated my dislike for public service."

"That must be why you ended up in CSIS." She smiled to show she was kidding, and offered him more tea. His was still undrunk. He picked up the piece of lemon she had already used. When little juice squeezed out, he dropped the whole thing into the cup, watched as the tea cleared.

"No, I ended up in CSIS because I took sides in the war."

He meant, again, the have/have-not war. She thought of the Leonard Cohen song her parents used to play: *There is a war between the rich and poor, a war between the man and the woman. There is a war between the wrong and right, a war between the left and right, a war between the odd and the even . . .*

She sang it to him, and he nodded.

"What side did you take?" she asked.

"Do you need to ask? I am sitting here in your kitchen."

"Still thinking you can do some good."

"Yeah."

"Oh, well," she said. "Have some more tea."

※　　※　　※

Morgan stood sputtering in the center of the pool, having just regained her feet at the drop-off to the deep end, and watched Blue climb the high-diving tower.

"It's not that bad, dear," said Flora. "Let's do it again."

"I'm watching Blue," said Morgan.

"Amazing, isn't it, how fast she learns?"

"She? Oh, Blue. Yes, I'm envious. I still rather nostalgically think of these sessions as swimming lessons. They should be called Blue's tryouts for the Olympics."

"Don't worry, dear. You'll catch on. Blue's just a fast learner. Remember, she learned fast when she was first here, and she seems to be . . ."

"Built for speed?"

Flora laughed. "I guess you could say that. Come on, let's try again. This time, try not to gasp with surprise when you hit the water, okay?"

Morgan laughed and tried another inadvertent cannonball, this time without choking herself. When she surfaced, Blue was bobbing beside her.

"Swimming is fun," said Blue. "I like it as much as dancing."

"Are you learning a lot?"

"I learned more since Jakob let me—dream him."

"What does that mean?" Morgan trod water rather desperately.

"You are not doing that very well. Do you want me to help you?"

"No! What are you talking about, 'dream him'? What do you do?"

"He sleeps, I dream, things change. I like it." Blue swan to the edge and got out, using those deceptively slender arms to push on the edge and leaping out of the pool in one almost-splashless ascent.

Morgan had worked harder than usual that day, and panted as she did a laborious push-up on the edge, then doubled over and rolled onto the deck. She lay there with the water draining away from her. "So that's where you are spending all these nights, up in the studio."

Blue shook like a dog then flopped down beside her and imitated her spreadeagled pose. "It's interesting. After this, I'd like to learn music, please."

"You have learned a lot of music."

"How to create music."

"How? Singing? Playing an instrument? Your days are pretty full already."

"I liked when we had that singing. I could do that anywhere. Even when I go back, I could sing even if I couldn't take anything with me to play on."

Morgan turned her head just enough to see the shadow of her own profile, cast by the strong lights of the indoor pool, and the serene face of the blue alien, who under these lights was a remarkable color of light plum. Her heart seemed to drain out of her with the water that suddenly released from her ears and ran down her neck.

The stinging in her eyes had to be the water purification chemistry, she thought angrily, ignoring her knowledge that this pool had a sonic purification system and that the water they swam in was like some pure tropical lake.

She had forgotten that the alien would be going home. She had forgotten. For weeks, she had not thought of it once.

❀   ❀   ❀

Morgan floats in her own thoughts like a body in free fall. Because the body is not real, it is free. There in perfect balance between all the gravitational pulls in the universe, there is peace.

Morgan sleeps the dream of freedom. She wakes to the world, where every dream turns into something else before it can come true. She dreams that her mother is alive, but all she gets for that is an ache where she thinks her heart used to be. She dreams that her heart should not feel, but for that the pain becomes more acute, then fades to be replaced by love. *Love is worth feeling,* she thinks, *but love erodes into pain. There is a functional relationship there,* she thinks. *If I could come to a perfect balance between those two, in free fall in the space of the heart.* The conceit overwhelms her until she has to laugh at her own self/consciousness.

Morgan dreams she awakens in free fall. But she awakens with a bump of gravity reasserting itself, into the world.

❀   ❀   ❀

"Promiscuity is unfashionable," said John.

"So is, so is video art," said Aziz, and at the same moment "Un*fashion*able?" said Jakob, and Russ laughed. Morgan, watching them from the kitchen doorway, thought suddenly, *we laugh at everything John says.* The thought had menace running in background: why? *Perhaps,* she thought, *because he is not mascot material, and we laugh not in amusement but in defusement.*

"Promiscuity is mythical," Delany said. "People fuck other people—"

"—make love—" said Aziz.

"—or make love, or whatever, for all sorts of real reasons. Promiscuity is one of those garbage words that people use to trash others."

"Pun unintended?" said Morgan.

"It's one of those words that really only means, *what I do is better than what you do*. You know, I have meaningful relationships, you're promiscuous. I have an agenda, you have obsessions. I'm part of a community of interest, you're a special-interest group."

"I'm an artist, you're an artisan—" Jakob.

"—a craftsperson—" Russ.

"—a dilettante—" Aziz.

"—a hobbyist?" Blue.

"—a flake—" Morgan.

"Yeah. Just like that."

"So what?" said John. "Some people *are* better than others. Not by privilege, but by individual variation. Some people are smarter, more moral, more co-ordinated, more talented . . ."

"But we assume that the rights inherent in being born in the world are equal, and we leave room for people to do different things within that sphere of tolerance," said Russ.

"Do we?" said John. "I don't."

"Which is exactly why you won't do your share of the dishes," said Delany. "You assume you are better, and don't have to."

Again the laughter and teasing catcalls, and again, to Morgan, the tone seemed tainted. She said, "But there is something new in every equation here, I think, whether it is an ideology of equals or does-not-equal, and that's Blue and Blue's source people. Once Blue returns to what our Mr. Grey stubbornly calls the 'mothership', the loop of contact has been widened. We are talking with people who are entirely new."

"Assuming they are people," said Jakob, while Blue watched with sharpened alertness. "Could be like a hive mind, or AI, or some kind of rocks. How do we know? Blue is *made*, not . . ."

"Not bespoke?"

"Too much old-fashioned sci-fi TV," said Delany. "Makes for

231

right-wing ideology, bad sociology, and wrong science. I should know."

John was always uncomfortable with mention of Delany's previous science career. "Nothing wrong with TV," he said.

"Nothing that a brain-cell transplant couldn't cure," said Jakob disdainfully, and John glared at him. "Fine, fine, I'm sorry," said Jakob, "I like your stuff, but that isn't commercial TV either, is it? Any more than my stuff is mainstream dance. You are out of the norm whether you like the idea or not."

"I am just ahead of the norm," said John, "but I will set the standard, that I can tell you. I am not doing anything far out with corn flakes and 'happenings' like your folks did when they were young."

"I'm sorry I told you that story," said Jakob angrily. "My folks were trying to figure out how to wake up a dead-from-the-ass-both-ways populace. A few cornflakes in the machinery may have seemed like a good idea in 1969 or whenever it was. People need a kick in the ass these days too. How many decades, and how many social changes since then? And now it's all been revoked; it hasn't made a fucking bit of difference."

"So, so strange the way you, you guys talk," said Aziz. "Like old movies."

"Yeah, *My Dinner with André*," said Morgan, but nobody knew it. "Too old," she said, grinning.

"I'll look it up," said John, and she was sure he would, and would see himself as André, the talkative and egocentric one. She wondered aloud to Blue, when the others had scattered, whether John would soon be adding his own monologues to his documentary.

Sure enough, a few days later, John thanked her for the tip, and told her about the voice-over commentary he was now planning. "I'll keep the footage of you others," he said. "I wouldn't want to be derivative."

"No, I can see that," said Morgan, but afterward she said to Blue, "Didn't I tell you?"

"You told me," said Blue. "I want to know how I can come to read people like that. Like you do."

"We say, 'read people like a book'," said Morgan. "And the answer is, there is no answer. Learn as much as you can, including about empathy, and do your best. It's one of the human difficulties."

❁   ❁   ❁

"John, you are consistently rude to Jakob. If it keeps up, I'll have to give you your notice." She looked up from the easy chair where she had placed herself to wait for him to come in.

"What are you talking about?"

"You know exactly what I'm talking about. This is Jakob's home. He doesn't need to face bigotry here as well as in the world."

"Maybe we just don't get along."

"Maybe you don't get along with anyone gay."

"You knew I had a hard time with homosexuality when I moved in. I told you that, and you brought him in anyway. I mean, brought me in."

"No, what you told me was that you were working to overcome your homophobia, and that you thought a diverse group of roommates would be good for you. As far as I can see, you aren't working to overcome *any* of your flaws."

He shifted before her, moving the camera bag from one shoulder to the other, not looking at her. "Like what else?"

"Like, doing your share of the scut work around here. Like not leaving your messes for others to clean up. Like paying your rent on time. We've talked about all this before."

"It's not like you're suffering for the money."

"Actually, I am, but that isn't the point. The point is that you are slacking off *and* getting up our noses. We can get a better roommate than that. There is actually a line-up, even if you discount the thrill-seekers. Remember what I told you. This is your second formal warning. One more, and you're history."

"You can't kick me out. My documentary isn't done!"

Morgan almost laughed, but she knew he would think she

wasn't serious if she did, so she went to tough-cop instead. "Unless you clean up your act, watch me."

"Okay, okay, I'll do my best. Just tell me what I'm supposed to do, and I'll do it."

"I just told you. And it isn't the first time. You have a very selective memory. Maybe you should record this, play it back when you get confused."

"Well, aside from Jakob. Like, be specific."

"Okay, *like*, if you see a mess, clean it up. If you come to the dryer and someone else's stuff is still in it, fold the stuff. If you come to the washer and someone else's stuff is still in it, put it in the dryer or hang it up. If you come to the sink with dirty dishes, wash them and whatever other dishes are there. Clean the bathroom every week. Clean the shower after you use it. Hang up your towels. We've been through this before. It's not rocket science."

"What if it's not my turn?"

"Do it anyway. You have a lot of catch-up to do, by now."

"What else?"

"Whatever you see that needs doing. You're a grown-up. I shouldn't have to assign tasks to you."

"Yeah. Sure. Okay."

"Okay, like, I'll do it? Or just, okay, get off my back?"

"Okay, I'll do it. I really do want to stay here, Morgan." His look was halfway between whipped puppy and door-to-door evangelist.

"Yeah," said Morgan. "I know you do."

She pushed herself up from the chair and walked out past him. She noticed that he carefully moved away from her. *Don't worry,* she thought, *you can't catch it.*

She was not sure if it was queerness, femaleness, or alien taint that she thought he was afraid of catching from her.

Alien taint. Now that was an interesting thought to think about someone who was Blue's greatest fan, to hear him talk. Something had made Morgan wonder about that. What was he doing that had made her uneasy?

❁   ❁   ❁

"Jakob hasn't been to the clinic for ten days," the grey man asked her one morning later in the week. "Is he all right?"

"I'll ask him," said Morgan.

She went up to Jakob's studio that afternoon. Jakob and Blue were practicing together at the *barre*. A bootleg of some dissonant dissident music was playing loudly enough to start an immediate ringing in her ears.

It's a bloody good thing this place is soundproofed, Morgan thought. *Someone at that school did something right, whatever my mother thought of her parents.*

"Look, Morgan," shouted Blue, and did a series of *grandes jêtes* across the studio. Then, returning, the alien went up on point and executed a series of precise toework the names of which Morgan couldn't even guess. The alien was wearing earplugs. Morgan put her hands over her ears.

Waving at the music console to lower the levels to merely stentorian, Jakob pulled out his own earplugs and walked gracefully over to Morgan, wiping the sweat from his gleaming dark skin with a white towel: Morgan wondered whether it should have been Aziz or Russ who should have been there to fully appreciate the moment.

"Why do you wear earplugs and then turn it up until it's deafening?"

"Usually I have it at more bearable levels, but today I want Blue to feel it in the body. Like deaf people do."

"That was a cute little demo Blue gave me there."

"It's the classics this week," said Jakob, "Nureyev, Baryshnikov, Fonteyn, Kain. Last week we did Balanchine and Graham and Ailey and Edouard Lock. *La La La Human Steps*, on point in sneakers way back in 1984. That led us to *Les Grandes Ballets Canadiennes* doing ballet in drag, and that's how we got where we are today. Astonishing, isn't it?"

"Blue must be physically—"

"—strong? Adept? A fast learner? Versatile? Honeychile, you have no *idea!*"

"And how is *your* strength holding out?"

"Fine. Why?"

"I heard you haven't been to the clinic lately. My grey man wonders if you're all right."

"Never better," said Jakob, smiling like a cat with cream.

"Come on. You told me that withdrawal was hell. You look better than you ever have. I swear you're even putting on muscle mass."

"Blue and I made a little deal," said Jakob. "I'd help him with the dancing, and he'd help me with the drugs. So far we're both satisfied."

"Help you how?"

"Call it sleepteaching," said Jakob, and, nudging her arm, he leaned over and said confidentially into her ear. "Blue does some amazing things in dreams. Detox like you wouldn't believe."

"Are you watching?" called the alien, who was now doing something improbable on the climbing wall at the end of the studio.

"*Everyone's* watching," said Morgan. Blue dropped from the top of the twelve-foot wall and, grinning, pulled out the earplugs.

Deeply disturbed, Morgan went back downstairs and telephoned the grey man.

"He's fine," she said. "He decided to withdraw, and he's been doing a lot of exercise to counteract it."

"Must produce a whole lot of endorphins," said Mr. Grey.

"I guess it works for him," said Morgan.

      ❖   ❖   ❖

She dreams of the alien as a skeleton, glowing in darkness. She is helping put on internal organs, muscles, blood vessels, nerves, skin; like a theater dresser she is holding the layers like coats for the naked one to put on. The alien glows like—boron?—blue, more and more substantial. When the dressing-up is complete, the alien turns to her, smiling.

"How do you want to be taken apart?" says Blue's voice in the darkness.

When she woke, sitting up, her body was vibrating. With fear, with frustration, with knowledge of the past. With anticipation of that dangerous future.

So she lay in the night room, her belly tight, unable to relieve the longing. To be somewhere else, not to be lonely, to be alone. To be safe.

Finally she shut her mind to it, and slept.

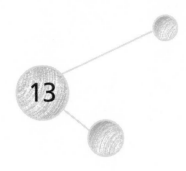

A birthday present

Morgan cleaned the second-floor hallway, her portable stereo tucked into a pocket. *Diaspora I* was playing: complicated layered texts, which seemed to match her mood, chanted by a variety of voices.

Blue came out of Delany's room, upset and with brow furrowed in a way Morgan knew Blue had copied from her or Russ.

"What's the matter?"

"Delany is angry with me. I was only trying to help . . ."

"Sometimes what seems like help isn't really," she said automatically. "What did you offer?"

"I offered to correct the mistakes in the helices. It would be simple enough. There is only a tweak. The difficult part would be the repetition. Or replication."

"Helices?"

"The DNA. Hers is damaged."

Shocked, Morgan turned up the music. The voices were running perfect interference, she hoped. "You offered to *cure* her?"

"I just said if she wanted I could change it. I learned what needed to be done by reading all the scientific research. She yelled at me. I don't understand. I'm sorry, I am too sad, I cannot talk now. Maybe we can talk later?"

"Sure." Morgan watched Blue walk down the corridor, wondering if it could be true. She knocked on Delany's door. "It's me. Can I come in?"

"If you must." Yep, she *was* mad. Morgan picked up the stereo and slipped in quietly. Delany was transferring from her wheelchair to bed. Her movements were erratic and furious. When she thumped down on the bed, she shoved the wheelchair hard enough that it collided with the desk, scratching the newly refinished wood. Morgan turned the stereo down only slightly. She was still sweating from the flash of fear she had felt for Blue when she heard those naïvely-spoken words.

"Your damned alien thinks it can fix me," said Delany quietly and furiously. "Make it stop."

"*My* alien again?"

"Fix me. As if I'm broken!"

Morgan had only a second to decide, and chose honesty. "Honey . . . you *are* broken."

"I don't want *deus ex machina!*"

"Blue is no god. There is no machine."

"There is no cure either. If Blue could fix my genetic code, my DNA, could it fix my muscles? My skeleton? Put back all the development that was lost? Let me look like other people, which I never will, because all the bones are already twisted and decalcified? Give me back a normal life, after all these years? Take away the memory of all the humiliations, all the pratfalls, all the insults, all the condescension? There is no fucking cure and I don't want some fucking carrot dangled before me that makes me hope, even for a second, that my life could change that way. Why the fuck would Blue do that to me?"

"Maybe because of love? Maybe to help? Maybe to make the rest of your life easier?"

"I don't want its fucking help." Delany pulled her thin legs into bed, one by one.

"Yes you do," said Morgan. "You want it so bad you can taste it. You just don't believe it."

"You gonna put me through this too?"

"Only because I love you."

"Love," said Delany dismissively. "The things people do with that excuse. It's the easiest word to say."

"Loving isn't easy," said Morgan furiously. "You want it to be easy?" Delany was angry too, she propped herself up in bed, tweaked the covers viciously across her legs.

"You think anything gets learned in one lesson?"

"I'm tired of living with not being perfect," Delany said slowly. "I'm tired of settling for whatever my body will allow me to have. Live with it. Live with it. Try harder. Make an effort. Don't you think I make an effort? Every fucking minute. But it's never enough to make it really work for me. You think that would change with a DNA transfusion?"

"Oh, sweetheart," Morgan said, sudden tears starting behind her nose, eyes.

"I want to go home," said Delany forlornly, uselessly, and started to cry. Morgan turned off the music, and in the relief of silence sat down on the bed, rubbed Delany's tense neck, then pulled the slight body back to lean on her, stroked the thick fair hair.

"How do you ask for anything," said Delany, muffled, "without sounding like a martyr?"

"You don't," said Morgan. "You just resign yourself to sounding like something. Then you decide you don't care what that is. Then you just ask."

"I really am tired of living," said Delany in a calm, resigned voice.

"Too bad," said Morgan. "You don't get to cop out that way. 'Alive and stuck with it', as the poet said."

"You love that line, don't you? Never mind me," said Delany, trying to sit up, but the angle was wrong, she couldn't get the leverage, she was like a moth trapped against a car window, pushing, pushing.

"Help me, Morgan," she finally said, tears at last rolling across her face. Morgan pulled her upright, didn't take her hands away.

"Now that you can ask, how much help do you need?"

"Everything, everything. I'm afraid of the dark, you know that? I am. I hate the darkness."

Morgan thought darkness was all that kept her sane, but she showed none of that in her smile. "See us both leaking like sieves," she said. "God is a crybaby. We know 'cause we're made in the same image, they say."

"Do you believe in God?" Delany said, surprised.

241

"No, I don't think so," Morgan said. "You never know. I suppose I'll find out after."

"After what, you die?"

"Sure. But 'til then, so what? How about you?"

"I don't think I can any more," Delany said. "It's such hard work trying to feel blessed."

"But you are," Morgan said, "blessed by sentience, sapience. You can think and feel." *So what?* she thought, but this was a rescue and the rescuer doesn't jump out of the lifeboat.

But Delany was better than Morgan gave her credit for. "So can you, Morgan." Morgan drew back and looked. "You think I don't know you? I know you. You have to turn the intentions back on sooner or later. If not for me, for someone. I don't matter, I'll live. But you should try, too."

"Change of roles all of a sudden," said Morgan.

"Don't get defensive."

"Who, me?"

"Do you love me?"

"Sure. I said so."

"But . . ."

"But it's strange to me now. Okay, I admit it, I'm . . . not sure."

"But you want me."

"How do you know that?"

"Sticks out a mile," Delany said. "You're too careful when you comb my hair not to touch me."

"I do. So?"

"Nothing."

"Then why ask?"

"To make you honest."

"Oh, I'm honest. That's something I can't escape. Never mind honesty."

"Don't be self-indulgent either. You have responsibilities around here."

"Yeah, I keep it all together, all right. Open all our lives like paper crackers, pop! and they're broken. By bringing in Blue. Now what?"

"Love. What was missing for all of us before."

"That's not up to us to force," Morgan said.

"Not forced," said Delany. "Just what you always do. Offer it freely."

"What *I* do?"

"Don't you know yourself yet?"

Morgan stood and paced to the window. Outside in the alley the streetlights shattered the darkness. Sharp, angry.

"How much do you think I can do?" she said finally.

"Everything you have to," said Delany. "Everything. Everything but save my life."

Morgan looked at her, surprised.

"That's my own chore. I work at it every day. If I keep trying I might get it right. With or without Blue's 'tweaking.'" Delany's voice twisted like her fingers.

"Sorry," said Morgan.

"For what?"

"Death. Life. Whatever else I can't fix. I'm sorry."

"I'm tired," said Delany, in a different tone. "I need to sleep. Go to bed, Morgan."

"Will you talk to Blue in the morning? You really did a job there, you know. Blue had no idea why you were angry."

"I'll talk to Blue."

"And will you see if what Blue can do might help?"

"Maybe."

"Will you promise me?"

"Don't push me, Morgan. I'll do what I do. Go to bed."

       ✦   ✦   ✦

After Morgan had gone down the long hall, Delany lay back and the tears rolled again down her cheeks. "Oh, you can save my life all right," she whispered, "but what does it do for you?" And what would Blue do, if she were to allow it? Could it really make a difference now, after thirty-some years of crippling influence? Damn the blue thing for a troublemaker! For an hour she watched the clock, the numbers changing, then put out the light and was almost sleepy.

"Never mind any of that," she said of her racing thoughts as she dozed off.

In her dream she knows how to fly. This is so derivative that even in the dream she laughs at her own conceit. Morgan lies below her as she floats away. Morgan is dreaming blue thoughts; they cloud around her head like fruit flies.

Delany has not been able to fly like this since she was a child. Now Morgan's bright restless mind has called her.

She flies over Blue, and sees that the alien's eyes are open, watching her.

"It's a dream," she says.

"Sure," says the alien. "It's a dream."

"I don't believe you," she says.

"Get out of my head, Blue," says Morgan's voice, and Delany discovers she was a thought of Morgan's, an echo in her dreaming mind. Then Delany's dream becomes the black sleep that so resembles night but banishes it, and Morgan is able to shake away her unfair knowledge of Delany's thoughts, and Blue's dreaming, and sleep herself.

✣   ✣   ✣

"She calls me *the grey man* or *our Mr. Grey*," he complained to Salomé.

"I like it!" She grinned.

"Hey! Grey? Colorless? The color of bureaucracy? Of old filing cabinets in the basements of government buildings?"

"Silver hair, grey eyes, and snappy silver-grey suits: same color, different affect. I think it's a great name for a dapper guy who's all the same color."

"After looking at pictures of Blue all day, 'all the same color' means something else. Like the people in the Le Guin book. Grey all over. Low affect. Boring."

"Well, daddy-o, you're not grey all over," she said, and hugged him.

"Daddy-o?"

"We're studying the fifties in film class. I have to be one step ahead of my students, you know, know all the old slang . . ."

"I'm relying on you to tell me when this job turns me grey all over," he said despondently.

"Oh, lighten up, Mr. Grey. It's a compliment. You are *distingué*. Dig it."

"When do you get to the seventies in film? That's when I started learning the language."

"Next semester. Shall I consult you?"

"I don't know, I might grey-down your class too much."

"Quit brooding. It's boring."

"See? She's right. I *am* boring."

"Go see her, then," said Salomé. "Ask her. Talk with her. Show her." And, done with the topic, she strode out of the room.

"Out of the mouths of babes and striplings," he said, and she leaned back around the doorframe to say, "Yeah, lots of people tell me I'm a babe."

❖   ❖   ❖

"Someone's putting biohazard into the recycling. The garbage-route kid has entered processing charges three months running. Whoever masturbates into condoms, bag 'em properly, will you?" Morgan said irritably one day at supper when all of them happened to be there at once.

"That lets me out," said Delany, then laughed when Morgan glared at her.

"I know who it is," Morgan said, "I'm just trying to be delicate. The recycling's been a problem for a while. Not just the biohazard, but extra sorting charges and penalties for mixing non-recyclables and organic matter. Like, dammit, no corn plastic and no pizza flats. Can you guys please get your chops together?"

"It's not such a big thing," said Russ. "It's just a detail." He stacked his plate on John's and handed the stack to John, who took it with a slight air of surprise and walked it in to the sink.

"It's just a *budget*. We aren't exactly rolling in wealth here. I've had to pay three fines for violation."

"We've got a cushion," said John from the doorway, rolling his eyes toward the back of the house where the surveillance shed was.

"We can't have CSIS pay for our garbage," said Morgan.

"Why not?" said Jakob. "They are giving us enough grief as it is. Let them pay for the privilege."

"Ever heard of self-sufficiency?" Morgan retorted. "I'm not interested in them being able to control us by what they pay for. Slacking like teenagers is going to get us treated like teenagers."

"Besides," said Delany, "the whole point is to do our best by the environment."

"Oh, calm yourself," said Russ, clearing the plates from in front of Delany and Jakob. "It's not like life as we know it will come to an end if we commit a garbage crime."

He walked out of the room, leaving Morgan glaring after him.

"I thought life as we know it *would* come to an end if there were too many garbage crimes," said Blue innocently. Delany snorted.

"Oh, never mind!" said Morgan. "What's so great about life as we know it, anyway?"

At least John was doing the dishes for a change.

❖   ❖   ❖

"Being Presbyterian isn't good for anyone," said Russ.

"Oh, come on," said Morgan, "you're not Presbyterian."

"Well, it's not who I am, but it's who I was raised to be. It's my heritage. Long after the religion has gone out of it, the guilt and dutifulness remains. Parents, grandparents, aunt . . . all taking that dutiful assumption of burdens such as myself."

"The repeater orphan."

"Yeah, constantly using up my Presbyterian Duty Points by needing help. It was instructive."

Morgan could imagine the instructiveness of a burden of guilt about something arbitrary and unpreventable. She shuddered. "The kinds of lessons we don't need to know," she said.

Jakob was massaging Russ's chronically tense shoulders. "Oh, I don't know about that," Jakob said. "How do we know what we need to know? If it is indeed all cosmic curriculum, and we have to keep going around until we get it right, must be something we're missing. . . ."

"What about the stuff we already know?" said Morgan. "Did Russ need to be orphaned twice and then cared for by emotionally bankrupt tyrants?"

"Maybe there's a certain amount of repetition, all in the interests of a fully rounded education," said Russ.

"Sure," said Morgan. "But then—"

"You are saying," said Blue, "you are saying that there is a course of lessons for each human, to learn what is necessary? A course such as I am attending? But then, how is it that there are so many who skip school?"

Morgan and Russ laughed, but Jakob said, "It's a good question. The theory—it's a theory, Blue, a religious theory, a *spiritual* theory is perhaps more accurate—is that people's souls are eternal and that when they are learning, they come back in life after life until they are fully enlightened."

"Yeah," said Morgan, "and then if they make it to enlightenment, they can take a Bodhisattva vow, where they promise to stick around and help others learn until everyone is enlightened."

"Old souls," said Russ. "Like Morgan."

"Oh, for goodness' sake," said Morgan, "what a nonsense."

"What about young souls like me?" said Blue.

"We do the best we can," said Jakob, "and fuck up a lot."

Blue was acquainted with this idiom, and was not derailed. "But there are so many people stubborn in their failure and ignorance," Blue said. "I don't understand."

Morgan felt a gigantic bubble of tears swell up and block her throat, her breathing, and finally her vision. *Failure and ignorance describes my life,* she thought. She turned away.

"What's the matter?" said Russ.

"Nothing," said Morgan, and indeed, a vast nothingness was rising behind the tears, a wash of hopeless disregard threatening to envelop her permanently. *The desperation of the foolish is boundless*, she thought, with the last shred of her anger.

"What?" she heard Jakob say.

"She is alive," Blue replied. "It is dangerous."

Morgan walked out of the kitchen, feeling the tears subsiding without being shed, leaving the others in their silence. She felt better in the dim hallway lit only by the sun filtering through the high stained-glass aperture windows in the stairwell. More congruent, alone really as well as existentially. It is *coming apart,* she thought, *and soon I will have to answer all these questions. But please, not today, not today. I have too many things to do. Too many people to take care of.*

Somewhere in her history there must be a stockpile of guilt too. She couldn't blame it on just one religion—she had such a mixed heritage: was it the Jews, the Baptists, the Lutherans, the Greek Orthodox, the Free Church of Scotland, or the ancestor worshipers who bequeathed her this guilt that she was not measuring up to the demands of the universe? Can't have been the Unitarians or the Buddhists, she thought, and longed, if she had to have Christians, for some Quakers in her family tree.

Or was it simple wistfulness that grew in her, this obligation to be perfect?

Like all her upthrustings of fear so far, it passed, and she was indeed still alive. And had managed not to look at it head-on for another day.

❉   ❉   ❉

Morgan dreams of Nancy, who in the dream has come back from the East Coast with a lover, a tall black woman who has taught Nancy to put her hair in dreadlocks. Morgan is combing Nancy's hair with her hands. Her fingers have to go in below the beads or they snarl in the strands. Morgan whispers, *are you lovers?*

Yes, Nancy says.

Oh, Morgan says, a bit disappointed that Nancy is not available, wants to make love with her even though she knows what chaos that would cause among them.

You don't want that, says Nancy (says Morgan to herself via the dream), *you just want a little satisfaction.*

Yes, thinks Morgan, dream-Morgan, *and why not? Is it too much to ask to be satisfied?*

She woke up thinking: *This is an interesting message I have sent myself.* Thinking too: *is it the first time I have asked for anything?* Not sure if it violated the covenant with the void with which she lived, by which she balanced her life; not sure why now she wanted anything, but convinced of the danger of it, still she thought now she would go ahead of her dream into the territory of wanting, and see what came of it. At the pun she laughed in the awake darkness, wondering if Blue was listening to her. Wondering if it was possible. Decided it might as well be possible, if it was by solipsism she must live, and went to sleep smiling and scared and almost happy with herself.

✿   ✿   ✿

The next day, Morgan found a note on the dining room table when she went downstairs at ten in the morning. "Going to have an adventure," said the note. "Don't worry. I wore my chip. Back in a few days.—Blue"

Blue's handwriting was terrible.

All the money was gone from the household petty cash box and Blue had left an IOU in the box. Holding it in her clenched fist, not knowing whether to cry, laugh, or shout, Morgan telephoned the grey man.

"Blue is fine," he said instead of hello.

"Were you going to tell me? Or just let me have my heart attack here, alone?"

"We just found out."

"Blue says, 'I'm wearing my chip.' That implies you have been tracking."

"Yes, but Blue's not far away. Seems to be holding in—what?" This was not to Morgan, but muffled, to someone in his office. "You're sure? Shit."

"*What?*" Morgan shouted into the telephone.

"The chip bracelet was left on the windowsill of a restaurant. The outside windowsill. The team thought Blue was there with you for lunch. The feed's only working intermittently. Someone has squidded it. There are traces of pinkface on the bracelet. Blue's in disguise, at least."

"Such a consolation," said Morgan. "Find Blue!"

"That's in the nature of a redundancy," the grey man said coldly, and hung up.

❄   ❄   ❄

Morgan dreams of loneliness, fear, and anger. She woke unrested, to more worry. Three nights like that, with nothing to which she could hook her dreaming.

❄   ❄   ❄

The grey man had a small parcel in his hand and a preoccupied look on his face. "Here," he thrust it at her unceremoniously. "Happy birthday."

"What is it?" said Morgan, and made a face. "I mean, thank you. I forgot it was today."

"Open it and see," said Mr. Grey.

"I wish Blue were back. I'd feel like celebrating."

"If wishes were horses, you'd have one on your lawn," he said. "Blue is at the end of the street, walking toward the house."

"What?"

"What I said. No, don't go running, how would you know? Just wait. Meanwhile, open your present."

"How can I think of . . . oh, all right."

It was a Hester McKenzie vid, a bootleg by the look of it, for it was labeled by hand in a firm script. Morgan turned it over, and on the back was "to the Morgan guy and the Blue guy—happy birthday" in the same hand.

"It's an artist's proof," said the grey man. "I know her. I got it for you."

"Wow," said Jakob, standing behind her in the door. "That's spinal. Worth a lot, too. I didn't know it was your birthday. We'd have had a party."

"It's rude to eavesdrop," said Morgan automatically, and grimaced. "Okay, when Blue comes back, you can throw a party for me."

"Do you remember your last birthday?" said the grey man.

"No," said Morgan. "I don't."

"It was the day after Blue ran away. Technically, it had begun when Blue arrived at your house."

"Really? Goodness. No wonder I forgot."

"Wow," said Jakob. "What a birthday present you got last year too! Hey, is Blue going to make a habit of running away on your birthday?" Morgan glared at him.

Blue was at the gate now, wearing jeans and white silk like Nancy and Aziz affected, and carrying a large woven shoulder bag that Morgan was sure she'd seen in Jakob's room. Morgan ran to meet her alien. "Blue! Where the hell were you? I was so *worried . . .*"

Blue was in pinkface, but it was a bit tattered—after all, the alien had been away for three nights. Blue looked defiantly at Morgan, then at the grey man a step behind her, at the watchers' hut, then at the street. Morgan followed Blue's gaze to see that there were three "ghost-cars" full of watchers. "Morgan went to a dance," said the alien sullenly. "I wanted to go to a dance too."

"We'll take you to a dance," said Jakob. "It's Morgan's birthday, and we're having a party."

"Don't make any promises," said the grey man grimly.

"Is that a birthday present?" said Blue brightly, looking at the package in Morgan's hand. "What is it?"

"Don't try that innocent act," said Morgan. "You know darned well that everyone is mad at you. You won't distract us that way. I suggest you go get cleaned up and meet us in the dining room. You are in big trouble."

"I am a grown-up," said Blue sulkily.

"Yes," said Morgan, "and you are one of the most important

grown-ups on Earth. You can't just go where you want without telling anyone. Even I know that, and you know how I feel about personal liberty. I am really, really mad at you. I am not joking. If you don't get cleaned up, I am going to yell at you. So I'd prefer you went inside before I lose my temper."

"I don't like it when you are mad at me."

"Neither do I," said Morgan.

"I think you should do what she said," said the grey man unexpectedly. "It's her birthday. People aren't supposed to be this angry on their birthdays. It's a day to celebrate."

"After we talk, we'll celebrate. I'm glad you're home, Blue." Morgan held the storage module and the wrapping paper in her hands so tightly her knuckles were livid.

Blue looked at them all again and then, downcast, walked toward the house. Morgan sighed. "Blue," she said.

Blue turned.

"I really *am* glad you're home," she said, and held out her arms. The alien came eagerly but stiffly into her hug, and she thought she saw a trace of tears in the lapis eyes before Blue pulled away and ran into the house and up the stairs.

"Phew," she said.

"Ain't parenthood hell?" said Mr. Grey.

"This isn't parenthood," she said. "This is guardianship. Bawling Blue out may have been the second-hardest thing I have done in my life. I have absolutely no right to speak that way to another adult human being."

"Happy birthday," the grey man said. She bared her teeth at him.

"Are we all happy now?" said Jakob brightly, and Morgan glared at him again. He faded back into the house, and Mr. Grey laughed.

"Don't worry," he said. "We are pretty sure Blue committed no *major* crimes on its little sabbatical." He spoiled it by snickering. It was Sunday. "As far as we know," he added, trying to keep a straight face.

"Very funny," said Morgan, and stalked into the house. At

the door she turned. "Thanks," she said grimly, waving the present at him.

"You're welcome," said the grey man, chuckling in the sunlight. Clearly an escape from tension, she thought, but still annoying. She ran up the dim steps to her room.

❀   ❀   ❀

They all gathered around the table in the dining room in postures that ranged from alert to sulky. Blue and John were the sulky ones: John had been prevented by the grey man from filming their meeting.

"One camera, fixed, that's all," he had begged.

"In your dreams," said Mr. Grey. "Siddown."

Delany wheeled in last. "Sorry I'm late. The elevator was being weird."

"Okay," said Morgan. "Now. Blue. You first."

"John said you were tired of me," said Blue sulkily.

"I did not," said John. "I said Morgan must be tired after the last year of working day and night. That's all."

"It didn't sound like that. It sounded like Morgan was just my friend because of work."

Saints, bodhisattvas, and angels preserve us, thought Morgan. Aloud, she said, "I'm sure it did sound like that to Blue. I'm not 'working', sweetie."

"You get paid," said John, tone neutral.

"You get paid," said Blue accusingly.

"Parents get paid," said Mr. Grey. "That doesn't mean they don't love their kids."

"Morgan's not my mother," said Blue, just as Morgan said, "Blue's not my kid."

"Well, Blue is *my* kid," said the grey man unexpectedly, "so deal with it."

"I got paid for working in the Atrium," Morgan persisted, looking at Blue. "Now you are my friend, and you live with me in my house, and I get an allowance for that. The government pays your room and board. Same as they do Delany's disability payments. She told you about those."

"I want a job," said Blue sulkily.

"You have a job," said the grey man.

They all looked at him. He was not smiling. "Technically," he went on, "you work for us. Administratively, you are on the pay-roll. You receive a salary. Morgan receives about half of it for rent and food. The rest is in trust. Whenever she has to buy something for you, or we do, we use the money in the savings account."

"I didn't know that," said Morgan.

"Live and learn," said Grey sourly.

"What is my job description?" asked Blue, still on edge.

"To learn as much as you can about Earth and represent us, particularly Canada, to the people who sent you here. And in that vein, where did you go while you were away?"

"It's a secret," said Blue. "And I stole something too." The alien looked down at the bag at its sneakered feet. "It was for your birthday. But if I have money in the bank I will send some of it to the place I got this. Maybe. Stealing it was interesting. Maybe I shouldn't repent."

Morgan sighed. Blue looked at her. "What's the matter?"

"I really cannot think of a thing to say. You know what I have taught you."

"*You* ran away. You danced and then you had sex with Nancy. You didn't get in trouble."

"Yes, I did."

"Not this much trouble." The alien imitated Maybelle Murphy's voice: "He says to tell you, verbatim, 'You're a pain in the ass. Next time you want to get laid, let us know. We'll run a proper bodyguard op.'" Then Morgan's: "Did he throw things?"

"Throw things?" said Mr. Grey.

"That's enough," said Morgan.

"You told me the grey man was making a joke."

"He was. That didn't mean I wasn't in trouble."

"You told me that you didn't like upsetting Mr. Grey but that there were times when a person had to act according to their own internal necessity. You read me out of Annie Dillard about 'perfect necessity' and living like weasels. So I needed this. I really needed . . ." A long pause, worthy of Beckett or Pinter.

"What?" Morgan, Grey, and Jakob spoke in a ragged chorus. "Living like weasels?" said John at the same time, and was ignored, except by Delany, who leaned over and murmured to him, "It's the name of an old essay. We studied it in university." Then everyone waited.

Finally Blue broke the silence.

"I needed something different. I don't know. I needed to think that I didn't need to have a minder all the time. A shepherd like I was a 'silly sheep.' I needed to look at the sky without power lines across it. I needed to find out how fast I could walk if no-one was with me. I needed to see if what you told me about stealing was true. See what is true. I needed to be alone. All by myself, and do something and prove I knew how to do it."

"Shit," said Morgan. "You're right. You did need that. I'm sorry. We should have given you—"

"You don't give things like that," said Blue. "If someone gives it to me it's just another field trip. I don't have as much time as you people do. Sometimes you forget that and treat me as if I can do things later, when no-one is watching, when no-one cares any more. But everyone always watches, and soon I have to go back up in the sky and meet the people in the mothership, and what was that you said?" In Mr. Grey's voice for the quote, then reverting to normal: " 'Between two and five years.' I think it's closer to two than five, and two are almost over. In two months, two of them are over. Counting from the very beginning," the alien said to Morgan. "Before you met me."

There was a difficult silence. Morgan struggled with her thoughts, as Blue clearly had done and was doing. After a few moments the alien spoke again.

"I thought about this all night," said Blue, "and then another night. Last night I remembered it was your birthday, and I thought I had better come home. And I didn't really steal this," and from the bag the alien drew a brown paper bag. "I just told you that to make you mad. Really, I told the lady I didn't have any more money but I would bring some back, and she trusted me. And she didn't even know I was an alien," Blue said ingenuously.

Morgan felt like she was watching something explode very, very slowly, and drench everything around it with blinding light.

"Thank you," she said gently, taking the little bag. "What is it?"

"It's—"

"It's a joke, sweetie. Thank you."

She opened the bag and drew out a small, silver-framed mirror, clearly made by an artist. She looked into it, then up at Blue.

"It's so you can see me when I'm gone," said Blue.

"All I can see is myself," said Morgan stupidly.

"No," said Blue. "I will show. You will see. And I am not your kid."

"I know," said Morgan, grasping Blue's hand warmly. "Thank you. For the present."

"Well, to me you're a kid," said the grey man, "and in that spirit, the whole bunch of you are grounded for a few days. No trips of any kind. No escapes. No guests. And if Blue won't get an inbuilt chip again, no more trips at all. Losing Earth's best alien is not my idea of how I want to end my career." He got up and walked out. Morgan, still holding the mirror, stared after him in shock.

"Oops," said Blue.

✿   ✿   ✿

"I told you he could lie and cheat," said Kowalski.

"It can come back and tell the truth too," said Mac.

"He's not trustworthy," said Ko.

"Neither are you," said McKenzie, "but I am trusting you anyway. Do the numbers." And he closed his office door between them, but once he was alone, he bowed his head tiredly. For all the alien denied being a child, the grey man had the same kind of intense headache he had had when Salomé was thirteen after she had run away for two weeks.

I'm tempted to throw things, all right, he thought grimly, and grabbed his 'phone.

Morgan answered on the first ring. "They want to have a party Friday," she said instead of *hello*. "They want to take me and Blue out to a show."

"It's not polite to leave out the salutations," he said. "And it's 'Blue and me'."

"Well?"

"No."

"We'll do it anyway."

"We'll arrest you."

"We'll tell the media."

"From jail? Give it a miss."

"We'll squid the vid. John can squid any vid."

"Any of you can squid. So what?"

"Friday."

"Fine. But not because you threaten. Because I already over-heard you all at dinner. And I was calling to say we'd try it."

"Sorry."

"No you're not. And I am. I can't keep you all locked up for-ever, much as I want to. Well, I can, actually, but it wouldn't be pol-itic." He cut off the call, and tossed his 'phone down on the desk. Should he indeed start throwing things? She seemed to provoke it, almost require it. He picked up the 'phone and called back.

"*What?*" she answered.

"Let's start again," he said. "Hello. How are you. I'm fine. You can plan a party Friday night. Pinkface for Blue. An implant chip. As many of my people as I want."

"No chip."

"You lose. Sorry."

"No you're not." This time, she hung up. He was sorry, ac-tually. But.

       ✿   ✿   ✿

Morgan dreams that she looks in the mirror and Blue's face looks back at her.

You created me in your own image, says the alien's voice.

That's a religious image and not appropriate, she says. *Or else it's about parenthood and I am not your parent. I told you that.*

No, says Blue's resonant voice, *you are not. But what are you? What are we?*

Morgan looks down and sees that she is blue all over, and Blue has turned a lovely shade of tawny dark flesh-gold that seems to embody all Earth's skin tones.

Aliens, she says, wishing she could take off her pinkface and walk free—

—and woke sweating.

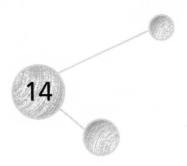

Vespers

A party they did have, eluding the media the following Friday night and taking Blue out in pinkface with the household to the best restaurant in town, then inviting everyone they knew to one of the clubs to dance and watch drag queens, then home to continue the festivities with a midnight buffet dinner and more dancing.

Spilling into the house, laughing at everything, at the new CSIS guard's scowl as they passed the gates, at Blue's reaction to the fashionable gear once the alien got inside the house, at Delany's zany wheelchair dancing, which she carried on from the van to the door and through the hall into the living room, at Jakob's crazy capers, at John's drunken attempts to record the scene on the video camera of his mind (with hand signals to match), at Russ's laughter (for that deep laugh could raise a laugh in return, every time). Morgan was turning extravagant and irrelevant phrases, and getting higher and higher every time someone thought one was funny, or topped one with another even more outrageous.

"I'll send a metaphor and have you brought 'round!" she threatened Jakob.

"Is that anything like going home in a huff?" called out John from across the room.

The doorbell rang; it was two of the women from the dance, Mimi and Vance, and Kyla with a new conquest she introduced as Anne. Meanwhile here was Nancy with one of the turbanned *nouvelle jeunesse,* who partially unwound from some of its androgynous wrappings to reveal as a nut-brown youth with sloe eyes who might, Morgan thought, have a penis somewhere under there, though it was hard to say for sure.

"You need a drink," cried John.

"A drink! A drink!" echoed Anne.

Blue was beside her. "This must be fun!"

"What do you mean?"

"I mean, I see there is enjoyment. I feel it. So, ergo cogito sum, quad erat demonstratum, fun!"

"You're bombed."

"*Au contraire.* I have what you have called a 'contact high'. Lips that touch liquor shall never touch mine. Besides, I'm not sure I can metabolize it. Do you know the chemical formula?"

"Hell, no. Hey!" Morgan called, "anyone know the chemical formula for alcohol?"

"$C_{12}H_{18}O_6$?" Anne guessed. She was laughing, but also staring at Blue, who was peeling off the cosmetic mask strip by strip, the blue face coming clear.

"Ethanol is C_2H_5OH," said Delany firmly.

"C U later, H U drunk yet, O U devil!" John yelled.

Anne had stopped laughing, was almost pale. "You're . . ."

"Blue, this is Anne. Anne, Blue. Yes, Blue's our favorite Martian. Do you need a drink?"

"I think so," Anne said. Blue laughed. Anne was startled, though she had watched that being laugh all evening with a different-color face, and Blue laughed harder. "Tell me about your planet," Blue said, an instant before Anne said, "Tell me about—" and stopped.

"Blue, don't tease her, she's a friend of Kyla's. Not that it would be okay to tease her if she weren't a friend of Kyla's either. . . . Here, Nancy, you're the Southern Comfort and tequila freak, right? I knew I remembered. Anne, here's your wine. Drink up and tell Blue all about your planet."

"I thought you knew all that."

"Oh, that's *our* planet that we've talked about. Everybody lives on a different one. The more Blue collects, the better marks the cosmic professors give. So talk away."

John, having retrieved his real camera, pulled Blue around for a moment, to take a picture while there was still some cosmetic mask clinging. "Pull it off," he was saying. "I want an action shot. I see this as a montage over which I'll superimpose . . ."

The doorbell rang. It was the grey man.

"Am I invited?"

"I left you a voice-mail." Morgan was still not quite ready to enjoy his company again, though he was smiling at her with his signature charm.

"I can only stay a few minutes."

"I think I can stay mad at you that long," said Morgan.

"Don't put yourself out."

"Have a drink?"

"I'm going on duty . . ."

Morgan motioned him in, finally smiling. "Oh, loosen up. There's *lots* of juices and stuff. And there's lots of food. Help yourself. Take a care package with you. Whatever." He headed toward the buffet, smiling at Blue, at Delany and at John on the way. John was filming, but the grey man gently turned the camera away before John could train it on him. Morgan watched his graceful progress. He sure knows how to work a room, she thought.

Anne tugged at Morgan's shoulder, whispered, "Is Blue a male or female?"

"Why?"

"Well, I don't know what sh—an alien would want to hear."

"And you're maybe wondering if we're sexually compatible?" Anne blushed; Morgan had guessed well. "Sure we are," Morgan continued, "and if you can put a name to what sex that one is, let me know."

"She's been studying me since we got here, trying to find out, but I learned to wear clothes just before she sent out an exploration team," Blue said unexpectedly in Anne's ear. Anne jumped and Morgan was laughing too, though flushing too at Blue's steady gaze, so out of tune with the words.

"Cut that out," Morgan said. "Anne's your source of inspiration tonight."

There was another source of heat somewhere she wanted to find, and it was not in this room, though Blue was a burning brand. In the kitchen she poured more ginger ale into a tumbler, slightly unsteady so she anointed her hand, and followed a murmur of low deep voices into the darkened spare room. Jakob and Russ were standing, one hand each, palms together, clasped with the other's, looking out into the trees and into each other's eyes alternately, heads bent together. Russ's other hand rested lightly on Jakob's hip. They turned their heads slowly to her, unstartled. Russ was smiling a way she had seldom seen before; there was a light shining between them. She could feel the heat they generated settle in her belly.

"You two."

"Yes, us. You were wondering?" Jakob was always so cocky about his rights.

"I was hoping. This is a lousy place—everyone who's coming to the party knows there's another room here. Go on upstairs."

"No, I don't care," said Russ, the private person. "I can handle a little interruption."

"I want to thank you for this, Morgan," said Jakob, and letting go Russ he came over to her, took her hand, drew her toward them. Their arms both around her and each other.

"Me?"

"You saw I haven't done any dope since the night I dreamed with Blue."

"Yes."

"You never said a word."

"No."

"But never mind. You brought a karma into this house."

"I brought an alien into this house."

Russ: "What he said, isn't it? Never mind. A hug for our sister."

And they hugged her, kissed each side of her face, Jakob's cheek soft and Russ's beard prickly. "Our sister, with whom we are well pleased."

"You two, I love you. Let me get out of here so you can get down to business. Next time, though, I want to watch! I cannot *imagine* how you are going to actually *do* this Azalea Trailmaiden, Russ. He *never* takes those scarves off!"

"Scarves can be very useful," said Russ clinically.

Laughing, gingerly escaping from their hug, giving them a smile from the door, she said, "Thanks for the party, friends."

"You're welcome," said Jakob, and she closed the door on their smooth rotation back into each other's gravitational field.

In the kitchen, Blue was talking to the grey man. "She is very assertive, that one."

"She wants to make love with the alien," he said.

"I am so different from my people."

"What do you mean, different from your people? You have no idea what your people are like," Morgan chimed in.

"No. But I think they must be cold, to send us so empty, knowing what might become of us, not caring. I was empty. I have thought a great deal about what that might have been for."

"What have you decided?" asked Mr. Grey.

"I know nothing. I guess many things. I dream many things. Perhaps my guesses and dreams come from, are, palimpsests under my current knowledge."

"So all this Klaatu mystique . . ." Morgan prompted.

". . . was my first joke, I suppose. Knowing I can never tell you about the home planet of my people because I can't remember it. They wanted something they could send to be an information sponge. So they made one. Out of me. I don't even know if I existed before I woke. I might have been a—a clone, I wonder. Or a—criminal, somehow reshaped. Or a whole new thing. I didn't even have—toilet training, I am to learn humanity by becoming. So all of them in the Atrium, and you in this house, have been my guides, like parents, only more strange. Like rehabilitation for amnesiacs."

"I'm going to forget to go to work, at this rate," said Grey. "Good night. Thank you for letting me come to your party." He ducked out the back way.

"Goodbye," Blue said after him, then turned to Morgan. "He likes you too. He really has been like a parent. I am sure he treated his own child as nicely. But you, Morgan, you are more."

"What am I?"

"You are my paradigm of Earth. My . . . model? Mentor? Partner in creation? When you let me dream you, that is the final piece of humanity. Because with you, I can give as well as take. All of them, they are the human race. But you, I knew when I first felt you that you were like me. You were all scrubbed clean inside."

"Mr. Grey once said, *'Hell would look like a lord's great kitchen without fire in't'.*"

"Tourneur, *The Revenger's Tragedy*. Yes. Though I feel human, I cannot be human, humans are my foster parents. Also I cannot be my race, they are my—my handlers. My killers. But you are like me."

"Am I? Am I? But you will go back."

"I must go back. I will be hurt to go. This is my home now."

"Dammit, Blue, how can they? You can't call anywhere home!"

"Is that so strange? Isn't it the same for you?"

"I had a dream. You were in a bag. Vacuum-packed. I had another dream. You were in a cage with others, chained so you could not touch anyone but were only a fraction of an inch away."

"Those were true dreams as you can have them. But let me dream you, and we will make something new."

"Someday soon. But all in my own time."

"I have all the time. They leave me until I am complete, I think."

"Then if I don't want them to take you away, I will refuse to give you what you need."

"No. You could never be that lonely."

"We'll see."

"You saw Jakob and Russ in there?" Gesturing to the door with a gesture Morgan recognized as hers.

"Yes, they seem to have finally discovered each other. They're probably already making love."

"Yes, they are. I can hear. I will go and see them." Blue softly opened the door, went in, and closed it behind.

Morgan sat down at the table, tired all of a sudden, feeling the bruise on her foot where John had stepped on it in the dance. Anne coming in for a drink said, "That Blue is really something, isn't she?"

She had quit fighting the pronoun battle. "Yes, indeed."

"Just came in for some orange juice. Sarah and Silvio are here, and Daphne. Dave and Duane are coming, and Lorne will be here later, after work. Peter and Pete just drove up. Steve is here already. Where's Blue?"

Without waiting for an answer, Anne went out like a whirlwind. As far as Morgan knew, Kyla had just picked Anne up tonight: how the hell did Anne know all Morgan's friends? Maybe she was a quick study, or Morgan was losing her memory.

After a moment, Blue came out of the room, closed the door carefully. "They are hot for each other."

"Good use of idiom. Anne's hot for you. She's decided you are a woman."

"I'll go with her, I think. I'm curious."

"There was a movie. *I Am Curious, Yellow*. My parents told me. They used to say, with their friends, I am curious but yellow. Yellow is cowardly. A joke, you see?"

"Yes, I see." Blue paused. "I wonder about love, Morgan. How do you know . . . ?"

"So do I, Blue. I wonder about love all the time. I'm not sure that we ever really know . . . but we figure some of it out, I hope. It's one of those things that are synthesized out of learning and experience. You know about it already in lots of its many forms."

"I imagine that is so. But the synthesis, the catalysis, is not come yet."

"It is very slow for us. Some people never get it."

"I was built for speed."

She was laughing as she went back out into the living room, where a great many dancing bodies stepped aside for her. One was Aziz, dancing with Tony. Aziz blushed and looked away, then back at her. She smiled as widely as she could manage.

"Just a minute, sweetie," he said to Tony, and wriggled through the crowd after Morgan. "I'm really sorry," he said to her. "I've been meaning to say that for a while. My cousin—"

"Forget about your cousin. He's gone and you're here. That's all that matters. Jakob's . . . busy, if you were looking for him . . ."

"No, I just came to dance."

Morgan, remembering Jakob's complaint, chuckled. "Dance on, then!"

Delany was talking with Lorne, who leaned over her wheelchair with a proprietary air. *I wish Daphne had chosen differently,* Morgan thought. *He's so straight and condescending.* Delany's face was glowing. This was one of the times Morgan felt her heart fling straight toward Delany like an arrow. Blue's sweet talk seemed always to put her in the mood for the human race, together but also separately, one by glorious one, as Delany was a glorious one.

When Delany spoke and smiled, she would sometimes draw her mouth into a smile that was more like a grimace, like a certain type of British moue, and the effort would sometimes make the cords stand out in her neck. Morgan marveled at the paradox that Delany's great beauty and charisma pulled through these grimaces that momentarily distorted Delany's fine-boned classic face. Classic of what?—some normative human head-shape, some communal cheekbone structure that often seemed Asian, sometimes Slavic or Finnish, occasionally Norse or Scandinavian, and only rarely suggested the Anglo-Norman. How could that face support, contain such a world of references? And how could it then spasm from beauty to grotesquery and back in, if not a split-second, then a split-moment? If there was such a split thing as a moment.

Delany turned her head and saw Morgan, and the smile, that Morgan thought was already wide, became luminous. Morgan walked to her, put a hand on her shoulder, suddenly felt she had done it for her own support as she felt the love weaken and strengthen her.

❖　　❖　　❖

There are times when a thought breaks through the skin like storm through sky. Morgan knew one of these moments now. She watched Delany swivel her chair away from the closing door and into the living room, something Morgan had seen possibly hundreds of times before. This time, Morgan knew that Delany expected nothing from this night. She knew that Delany long ago had learned to prune her expectations into dwarves, like the Chinese art of *penjing*, later called *bonsai* by the Japanese, the art of stunting great trees into tiny, twisted fantasias, the art of torturing seedlings and saplings into adopting smallness, exploiting their defense of their essential natures to create a defiance of nature.

Morgan could not let another night of this go by. If she had learned nothing from the tortuous nature of living, she had learned that the truth must be told as soon as possible. The hard lessons of learning it were taught by death and loss. Her dreams of the last several months had been clouded with the words she had never spoken to the people she loved. Except Vik. As she followed Delany back through the dimly lit rooms to the bright kitchen Morgan chuckled. She and Vik had spoken too many of the truths, and that was another lesson. *Enough is as good as a feast.*

"What?" said Delany, answering the chuckle.

"Thinking about you," Morgan said, and in the hard yellow light of the kitchen, littered with the detritus of the departed party guests, she leaned down to Delany, echoed by her reflection in the panes of the circular corner windows so that several of her at different angles reached down to hold Delany awkwardly but comfortably, several shadowy ghosts leaned over the corner of the wheelchair to kiss Delany's head, and in a flurry of glittering refraction, several Delanys turned their shadow chairs accidentally at just that moment so that suddenly the Morgans were off balance, and leaned a little too far, and laughed again, and regained their balance.

After that she could not see her cohort of reflected selves, and self-reflectiveness lost out to immediate experience, and she went down on one knee and said to Delany, "Thinking about kissing you," and she did.

As she did, she felt suddenly like several metaphors at once. She felt armor crack and fall away, armor she could hardly do without. She felt a mirror crack too, and a web float out and unravel. She felt a burst of fear and desire, and a sense of inevitable destruction. She felt suddenly mortal, and she hated it. She felt suddenly hot with a flush of lust spread to the same places orgasm reached, but with a pang that was almost pain, it was so sudden: this was readiness, and if she had had any fear left for herself in the world, she might—considering what that readiness might be preparing her for—have been frightened. However, in the same way that she had abandoned silence and the palimpsest of adolescent shyness which always tries to bleed through during someone's sexual beginnings with loved ones, she had also abandoned unnecessary self-cautions.

"Don't you think, my friend," she said, "that it is time we did something about this?" And having said it, Morgan was struck with a paradoxical wave of teenaged angst so atavistic and stereotyped that she was laughing as she buried her head against Delany's chest. Delany's strong hands against her head and back inflamed her, and she was filled with a bubble of mixed elation and despair. *I've done it, I've said it, she's sweet as I thought,* said the fizz of joy, while the despair wailed, *we'll never manage this, I don't know what to do, why the fuck am I letting myself get reached this way?*

"Morgan," said Delany, "are you laughing or crying?"

I'm not sure, thought Morgan, but hanging in that uneasy place was too perilous, so she drew back and looked again at Delany. Delany's face was luminous in the garish light, and Morgan said, "Let's go upstairs . . . all right?" and Delany, licking her lips to moisten them, nodded.

"Here, let me do that," said Morgan, and kissed her again, a sloppy passionate intense untidy kiss that made them laugh against each other's lips, laughter that transformed midway into something, something, something else.

      ✿   ✿   ✿

On the way up in the elevator Morgan felt Delany draw into herself again, and wasn't surprised when she heard her say, "Morgan, are you sure?"

"What do you mean, sure? I know what I know. Are you worried?"

"No," said Delany softly, and pulled Morgan's hand to her lips, but Morgan felt her quiet as disquiet. The elevator arrived noisily, and Morgan held the gate back for Delany to wheel ahead into Delany's room. *No negotiation,* thought Morgan. *But I suppose it's the bed: she has to be comfortable, and my low bed is not exactly . . .* She closed the door behind her, leaned over the back of the chair, and began to kiss Delany's neck. *How will I do this?* she thought. *I'll be awkward, what if I hurt her . . .* and meanwhile the ache of desire only mounted. Morgan was surprised how intense it was.

✿   ✿   ✿

Morgan helped Delany from her clothes, each unveiling suddenly fraught with a shiver of anticipation and desire. Then Delany levered herself from the wheelchair, and Morgan steadied her as she had done many times, this time thinking *ah, she is taller than I am, but so slight,* but this time went down with her as Delany lay back on the bed—*Lord, she is so slender and her body so weak, she is like the ideal Victorian woman*—which was never one of Morgan's pet fantasies. *Do I know what to do?*

Delany reached out for Morgan, for her hands which were touching Delany's body, and her touch was light as always when she thanked for service, not hard and hungry as it had been downstairs. Delany's hands were hot—and then her grip released, suddenly not there: Morgan felt the air cool the sweat from her wrists.

"I don't . . . if you were a man I'd know what to do." Not the words she expected, they stopped Morgan cold, shaking with whatever it was, fear, anger, thwarted lust—love? Dammit.

"What?"

"If you were a man. I know men. As soon as they touch me all gentle and soft I know what they're going to be like. It revolts them to see this body react, but it makes them feel superior too. Then I never see them again, or else I do and they can't forget what I looked like and they're careful to be polite. I don't want to see that look on your face."

Morgan tried to decide what to do, whether she could find the incredible energy needed to move, to overcome the tide that was ready to wash Morgan away from Delany, from the bed. Morgan touched her shoulder; Delany tried to shake Morgan's hand away but Morgan was the strong one, without wasted muscles, and held her. Fury, Morgan decided, and said angrily, "You've known me this long, and you get me out on this limb here, and then you pull the crip routine? *How dare you?*" Morgan was almost shaking her, forcing herself from self-doubt into self-righteousness. Delany's face had a life and fury Morgan had never seen in it, and she looked magnificent, Morgan's belly turned to ice, then fire.

"Let me go!" Delany struggled. "You don't know what to do either, do you? You think I'll break? One minute I lost my nerve and right away you're ready to back out. Well, you aren't so hot yourself!"

Morgan took away her hands, put them on the bed on either side of Delany, to support her weight as she bent over Delany to whisper, "That's the one thing you couldn't be more wrong about. I am so hot I am close to spontaneous combustion, and it's true, I'm scared as hell. But I'll try if you will." Morgan bent her head to Delany, lips to her cheek. When she lifted her lips away, Delany turned her head so her mouth was under Morgan's, and they kissed again, hunger restored and meeting—

—and they were clumsy, sometimes, but it was all right. It was a new way to move, Morgan arcing around and above Delany, but she tasted as sweet as Morgan thought she would. *She's stronger than I expected her to be,* thought Morgan, then, *why not strong? She wheels the chair, lifts in and out, does everything with upper-body strength . . .*

"What?" said Delany, holding Morgan suspended above ecstasy, and laughed when Morgan told her. Delany's coming at first scared Morgan, then delighted her, and the whole house probably heard Morgan's (as well as the usual listeners, Morgan thought with an edge of awareness) though they had to work hard together for their consumption. The last thing before sleep, Delany said, "I need to sleep on my side, it's easier to breathe," so Morgan curled behind her, which was her favorite way to sleep with a lover anyway, and over Delany's shoulder saw her wheelchair a silhouette in the dim light from dawn coming through the shade, heard the birds starting to wake up in the surrounding trees and Blue's door closing/opening softly, background noise.

And for Morgan sleep, and dreams, and waking to Delany's sweet smell and taste, and that was Friday night.

✿   ✿   ✿

In the gloaming of dawn Morgan awakened suddenly, not sure at first where she was. It had been a vivid terrifying dream—fading rapidly now—of two antagonists struggling, then a prone body, all in shadows. She got up, went upstairs quietly to Blue's room, but the bed was empty. Back to the living room, down the long shadowy stair, the dream-fear lingering in the darker corners, and Blue was there, looking out the window at the full moon. Morgan realized with a shock that the days, the weeks, the months had gone by, and she was not only still alive, she was loving, and loving this alien fiercely, with all her all-too-human heart. And that in knowing this intimate distant blue one she had changed, changed into someone, something new.

"Your dream was too real," Blue said. "So was mine. I think . . . it might have frightened me . . ." A long pause, and when Blue spoke, it was with a preoccupied manner that unsettled Morgan. "You and Delany together, it is very beautiful."

"And you and Anne?"

"She went home. She was not very pleased with the alien."

"The alien?"

"Do you know the book about the language with no word for 'I'? For a long time it was that way with me. For Anne, always that way for me. In the crunch, I think you say."

"In the clutch?"

"That too. She wanted a blue woman. Very hard for her to realize that I could please her, and still be so different, she had to learn a new technique. When I didn't have the right shape, a vagina, vulva, clitoris, she was disturbed."

"Like Jakob looking for your penis."

"But Jakob at least understood that he wouldn't find what he expected, and he reached out to me anyway. You knew about that by a dream?"

"Yes. It was a fine dream. I didn't know it was real then."

In the dark, with almost all Morgan's barriers gone, with that malevolent image from her sleep fading in the moonlight and Blue's company, it was easy not to be afraid that she could have true dreams.

"And with Delany you were satisfied. Yes?"

"Couldn't you tell?"

"I was busy with Anne, and I was trying not to eavesdrop. But after. After, I was—having a very strange—dream, I think, dream, yes. But I could not understand. It was like a book you have given me to read. Like many books. Almost like the dreams I found in Jakob when I first learned what dreaming was, first tried to use it. He does not use it, it is a movie in his thoughts. I am thinking about him now. Your dream was like mine. Or, mine was like yours."

"That is like knowing that some tribal peoples counted by eights because they count the spaces between their fingers. Or seeing the rays of sun through the clouds as the shadows of the clouds, instead of as the light through them. You are very good with the ambiguities now."

"I am a learning machine."

"With a heart."

"I don't know enough. Your world makes it so hard to learn about what I need to know to love, to be."

"You should have come into a different language. English is bad for that." Suddenly: "No more my world than yours!" Despite the slow regrowth of feeling for the world, she believed that. Knowing how much love she had for it, not like Russ who would turn and walk away and yet was bound forever to Earth. For her it was a perfect place to be, yet she felt still a sojourner there.

She looked across the room with new vision to the only one of her kind who was in this small part of the world with her. Blue's gaze sharpened in a parody, unconscious, an echo of Morgan's.

"Now?"

"Maybe. Yes. Yes, I think so."

They moved slowly together, and the eyes fixed on each other's were widening, becoming the universe. The heat of that blue body engulfed her. In her understanding there was also terror, from where? From Blue, and the blue hands met Morgan's hands with a shock, like entry. The hot hands, the fire, reaching for Morgan's face, suddenly their dream was between them, the terror of it, and she clenched her hands around the thin blue wrists, holding the hands in space immobile, strength for strength, while waves and waves of fear and sorrow and fear washed across them both.

"Oh, no, what is that?" Morgan gasped.

"I don't know. Something . . . Jakob? I am afraid. . . . I think I know, and if I know . . . Let me think." Turning abruptly to the window, forehead against the glass.

It was another of Jakob's gestures. Morgan thought: *I see us in this one, though what this one really is terrifies me again as it never did when the alienness showed so much at the beginning. Now like a chameleon Blue has masqueraded as one of us, a dancer, a talker, a cook, a lover, a dreamer—but what Blue is, really, is no more clear than at the beginning. And even more than I fear that ambiguity I fear the insight that I am more like Blue than I am like any other human being. That is not a safe insight any more.*

Morgan put her hand on Blue's shoulder. The body heat burned her again. She thought she was used to the details: she had been, but not now: how could that slim body that could be so languid burn so fiercely? How could that cool blue facade contain this furnace? What was the fear, the horror that they both were feeling at this moment? Did it come from between them, or somewhere else?

Blue did not turn for a moment, a moment that seemed ancient as the adrenaline pulled the world into slow motion, and Morgan couldn't make that turn happen, and anyway was afraid to see the eyes, just now.

"Are you everything I think you are, or are you something so alien I can never know you, only live in terror?"

"Yes. No. I am very—confused? Scared? It is wrong, it is the wrong feeling. We must—"

"—find Jakob," finished Morgan, suddenly understanding.

✿   ✿   ✿

From a state of paralysis and confusion had emerged, suddenly, focus—on urgency and sharp fear. For a moment the two of them were frozen in place, listening to something inaudible but tangible.

"In the back yard somewhere," said Morgan, and Blue said, "Outside the gate. Oh, Morgan, it is real. I didn't think it was real."

Unmindful of their night attire, they ran through the shadowed yard, Morgan calling Jakob's name—but the person who responded was Ace, loping sharply through the archway, face white.

"What are you doing here?"

"Something's wrong with Jakob . . ."

"Is it Jakob? How the hell did you know? Never mind, come, maybe you can give me an ID . . ." but Morgan and Blue had passed her already, passed through the gate into the relentless sodium streetlight lighting the scene like a stage set.

Jakob lay tumbled against the fence like leaf mulch, his draperies wound around his face and throat. At least, something with Jakob's clothes on. Morgan fell to her knees on the curb.

"Don't touch anything," said Ace.

"But first aid . . ."

"Too late."

Morgan could see one hand, at the end of an upflung arm: the hand was a flat slate color, lighter on the palm, like a greasy rag. *He must be dead,* she thought. In the background, as she leaned over his body, she heard angry voices.

"For chrissakes, Ace, what're they doing here? The guy's a mess!" It was "Randy"—May.

Morgan wanted to pull the fabric away, but she knew better—even if she could not see how deeply one fold was buried in Jakob's neck.

"I just thought she could—save us a lot of time."

His fingernails were broken and his hand was stained with blood and grass.

"Don't you know procedure?"

One of his flowing trouser-legs was rucked up around his thigh, and the waistband and buttons were torn down so that his genitals were exposed.

"You should talk. Fuck procedure. I want to know what we're dealing with here. I'm sure McKenzie will back us up . . ."

Or what were his genitals before they were mutilated: she couldn't make sense of the blood and minced meat spilling from the sliced skin. She averted her eyes. Then Ace had turned back to Morgan, lifting her up and away. "Is it Jakob? Or is it one of the other guys at the party? That Salman guy? Aziz? Lorne? That kid with Nancy? They were all wearing these . . ."

"Jakob."

"Fine. I'll take you back inside."

"I can walk. Blue . . ."

But Blue was not there, was running ahead of her to the house, and she could only walk so far. Inside, she fell against the doorframe, and it seemed not at all strange to her that when she folded over in anguish, Delany's chair slid toward her and her head came to rest on Delany's lap. Blue knelt beside them, shaking.

Nor did it seem strange until later that it was her Mr. Grey who lifted Blue away and guided the alien to a chair, then turned to lift her and support her down the hall to the living room.

"I'm all right. Help Blue."

"Delany's helping Blue," he said. "You're not all right." Against her protests, he helped her lie down on the couch, tucked an afghan around her. She knew she should be going to Blue—but when she tried to rise, she saw that Blue was already lying on the other couch, with Delany leaning over to tuck in a cover, and murmuring softly to the frightened alien who clutched at her hands.

Mr. Grey loomed over Morgan again. He had brought back a cup of sweet, hot, strong tea for each of them. "Gack," she choked, when she sipped it.

"Good for shock," he said. "Drink it fast. It doesn't have to taste good." He had another cup for himself, demonstrated by knocking the cupful back like a hangover cure. She followed suit, only to feel the hot liquid scald as it went down. She coughed and gagged.

"Never mind," Delany said. "Shows you're alive."

"But Jakob isn't," said Morgan.

"No," said the grey man. "He's not."

A triumph of
community relations

15

Marbl was crying by Russ's door, patting and scrabbling with her paws at the edge of the door, but the handle was latched so she couldn't push it open. Morgan picked her up, occasion for a little howl, put her down in the center of the corridor, opened Russ's door, and went in.

The light was off; he was lying on his bed face down, crying. He was not used to crying, and his throat was tight with the sounds. He didn't hear the door open and close. Morgan stood for a moment in the half-darkness, her own eyes starting into tears. Then she went to sit beside him, put her hands on his back. He tensed, his sobs stopped.

"Don't stop crying, you need it," she said. He turned over, an earthquake.

"What good does it do? He won't be back, no matter how long I cry." His face was twisted with grief and anger.

"We can do him the honor to grieve for him as much as we loved him," said Morgan. "He may not notice, but we will."

"It's the same mistake, to love him that much in the first place," said Russ savagely.

"Do you really think that?" Morgan gave him a moment, then put her hand on his neck where it met the shoulder, looked closely at him. She spoke slowly, watching each phrase open him a little, trying to open him more. "Do you really want that? Do you think it would have been better never to have looked into his face with those long bones and tight skin, to never see his eyes smiling for you, to never feel his hands on your face or your body

277

or your cock, to never feel that sweet pleasure coursing through you, to never hold him, to never put your mouth against his smoothness? Do you want all that gone from your memory?"

"What do you know about that?"

"I saw your face open up for me, and I was only a challenge to you. He was a lover. Do you really wish you'd never seen his face while you were making love with him?"

"Stop it! Yes, I wish it. What's the use of getting involved?"

"You sound like a cliché from the nineties. What do you think life is for, to make you comfortable and secure?" She grasped his upper arm strongly. "Jakob is dead, Russ, but you're alive, and you remember him. Is that invalidated because it won't go on? Then his life means nothing."

"What do you know about that?"

"Why is it I'm always here telling you what a self-pitying prig you are? My parents are dead too, not much more than a year ago, and on the same day. Do you think I didn't love them? My father died long before he should have, with me holding his hand; my mother chose to leave us for his sake no matter what it did to us. Do you think I'm a psychopath, that I can't feel it? Jakob is dead. Do you think I didn't love him? He was my friend too. Who the fuck do you think you are? You're just another one like the rest of us—human. As the poet says, 'Alive and stuck with it.'"

"Okay, it was wrong. But that doesn't change me. If this is alive and stuck with it, forget it. If this is human, love 'em and lose 'em, forget it. I'm not going to go through all this again. I feel enough like a murderer already!" and he turned away from her, got up to stand at the window, looking out on nothing. She put her hands on his back, and he shrugged them away.

"It's not th-that I shouldn't have," he said, slowly, with difficulty controlling his voice. "It's that I didn't do it sooner. It's not easy to reach out, and Jakob won't, wouldn't seduce. He's, he was scrupulous that way, for all his verbal games. So I wasted so much t-time . . ." He slammed the flat of his hand against the window-frame.

"I'm sorry I lost my temper," she said. "I guess that I—believe in love, whenever possible."

"Yeah, I know you do. It's admirable of you." He leaned his forehead on his hand, against the windowframe, and spoke quietly. "We didn't have as good a time as you think. I couldn't— I couldn't touch him the way I should have. I just didn't know how, I said, but that was a lie. I found all kinds of reasons—but the main one was that I thought I'd have another chance. I fucked up."

"He knew how you felt about him, anyway. Don't you think that's good for something?"

"No."

Morgan waited, but he said no more, and again he shrugged off her attempts to comfort him.

"I hope you cry some more," she said finally, and turned to the door.

"Morgan," he said, and when she faced him he had turned to her.

"What?"

"Thanks for coming here."

"Even if it did no good?"

"It did some good. Thank you."

"You're welcome. You're always welcome, you know that."

He passed a hand across his face with a weary wiping gesture. His look was blank. After a moment Morgan realized that he was not looking at her, and she went. At the door she looked back again, and he was still staring at the point beside the door where she used to be.

❀   ❀   ❀

"How did you know there was something wrong with him?" asked the man in the blue suit. She knew his name was Kowalski, but a name didn't seem to stick to him, slid off his rumpled surface into generics.

She turned with a frown. "Blue . . ."

"Blue told you?"

"No! We both . . ."

" 'Felt something was wrong.' You said that. But on the tapes

279

there was something about dreaming, and Blue was the one who . . ."

"Ko." It was the grey man. "That will do."

"Mac . . ."

"We had a precognitive dream," said Morgan defensively. "It happens. My mother used to have them all the time, when somebody died. I'm sorry."

How could a man that puffy look so stiff with outrage? she wondered irrelevantly. She watched the grey man jerk his head toward the door, send the other man away.

"I'm sorry," she said. "I never had them before this year. I didn't know they ran in the family."

"Don't make it worse," the gray man said. "This isn't genetic."

"Are you going to take Blue away? Back to the Atr . . . ?"

"Blue is staying right here."

She almost fell with the release brought by relief. She pulled the kitchen chair she was leaning on back around and sat down. "Oh, oh, oh my, I was so sure . . . Why on earth—how on earth can you let that . . . ?"

"No flies on you," he said, and sat down too. He put his head in the cradle of his hands. From behind his palms, his voice was muffled.

"The Prime Minister considers the presence of Blue in the community a triumph of public relations. Public relations! She considers the fact that the Canadian government is allowing their alien to stay with a non-standard family unit refutes the recent accusations at the United Nations of Canadian government intolerance of and human rights violations against the disabled and those with alternative lifestyles and political opinions. She considers the deaths to be efforts of foreign terrorists or political interests, or both, to undermine this openness—which, believe me, we have considered, and rounded up all the usual suspects twice over, and we're starting again at the top of the list. Then she refers to *glasnost* in an attempt to embarrass the Russians. She refers to prison camps in an attempt to embarrass the Chinese. She even takes a shot at traditional families in an attempt to embarrass the

English. She supports the choices that senior officials at CSIS have made to normalize life for the alien."

Morgan couldn't help laughing, even though it came out as a rather grim bark. "You must be relieved too."

"Someday," said the grey man, "perhaps you will meet my mother."

He couldn't see Morgan's puzzled look, and carried on talking to the Arborite surface of the table.

"My mother is in her late nineties now. I was born when she was forty-five. Her name is Derwyn. I bet you'd like her. Once, when she was impatient about me not thinking for myself and for being too dependent on external validation, she said witheringly, 'Would you want Hitler to approve of you?' I've often used it to remind myself not to care about the approval of people I don't respect. But this. . . ."

Morgan saw the light. "All of a sudden, Hitler *does* approve of you. So to speak. A whole new spin."

"You got it in one," said the grey man.

*　　*　　*

"Quite a morning after," said Delany quietly. "I'm sorry, my dear heart, that you have to go through this."

"We all have to go through this."

"But you knew him best."

"I didn't know him any better than—"

"Sweetie, he didn't have the time of day for me. I'm a grrrl. A het grrrl, too, he thought. I wish he could have lived to find out different. Actually, I wish he could have lived. I'm angry about that. But I didn't know him. Like you did."

"Nobody knows anybody," Morgan said.

"You know us, sweetie," said Delany, "and strangely enough, we know you. Can't avoid that. Sorry."

Morgan smiled at her. "I'm sorry too. Maybe I was being . . ."

"Self-indulgent? Only a little. And why not? You're carrying quite a load."

"Listen," said Morgan just as Delany said, "But what I mean to say is—"

They stopped and stared at each other. Delany reached out and pulled Morgan's hand until Morgan leaned over to her. Delany cupped a hand behind her head, kissed Morgan sweetly on the mouth, then the cheek. "I'm here," Delany said. "I'm not going anywhere."

"I was just thinking that," said Morgan. "There's lots of time. For us."

Jakob's lost time hung in the air between them. Their smiles to each other were bleak with it.

✿   ✿   ✿

"He asked me to sleep with him," said John, face on hands. "If I'd known, I would have."

Interesting, thought Morgan, *but do I believe it?* "What you mean to convey to me is, if you could bring him back by doing it, you would. But I don't think so."

Damn, when will they leave me alone, all these people using me to wash away their guilt, letting their grief wash over me, when will they leave me alone to do my own crying? Looking at John, who thought you could buy off death with a little insincere cocksucking, *leave me alone.*

Finally he took his cup of coffee away. His absence was welcome but like a backbone removed from her. The hard table under her arms, her cheek. It was hitting her again, again, as it did ten times an hour, *gone, my brother, my dancing dear heart, the dancing, to stop, to never see again, to crumble, to rot, to fade away, to forget, ah, my dear, my crazy failed sybarite, who became part of this family I have made, why did you . . . no cannot talk to you any more, and where has all that energy gone, that was torn out of him? broken, torn, my loved one, my darling, the one who taught me to dance, no more dancing, no more circle of hands joined and raised, those hands, so long and thin ah, Jakob, Jakob—*

—and hands were raising her, and arms were holding her

bitter and convulsed against a warm hard shoulder, Blue, holding her, singing a little song like a lullaby, rocking her. *Some of them say you killed him, blue one.*

No. No, not I. I did not save him either. I have my own grief.
I don't understand. He was one of us.
So am I. And I knew him.

A bitter moment of shame that she would take that away from this one because of blue skin and a foreign birth. *I'm sorry. But if you are lying to me, if you killed him, I—*

I am not lying. Believe. But I could have stopped it, and I did not understand. I was so stupid! I will know that as long as I know anything.

I don't understand.

Neither do I, but I am learning. I will soon be as human as you. And if I find that one, if I solve the puzzle, it will kill no more, if I am here.

It's wrong to kill.
I won't have to kill.
What do you mean?

If you would learn, dream with me, I would show you. Maybe you would make a sense of it, help me understand.

Not yet. Not now.
No. I know that. But sometime . . .

—and she drew back and looked into those eyes, in the silent kitchen.

Now you know what we can do, said Blue.

"I can't . . ." Morgan said aloud, ". . . on top of all this."

"It could only happen because you were open. Believe in me, Morgan. I'll need it."

"You sound so . . ."

"So human?"

"Yes."

"But I told you, that is what I am here for. Every day I become more human."

"I have seen that."

"You are changing too."

"It is life. Life happens, and changes one." Snort of laughter for her deliberate pronoun. *Jakob, oh* . . . Snort of tears, a sob. The warm arms tightened. "There has been a lot of death for you, too."

"For everyone. Human death, a little every day. Didn't you tell me so? On our way toward death, and we meet it on the path."

"I wanted to help you."

"You do, you have . . ."

"Is this love?" asked this alien.

journal:

The strain is getting harder for everyone. Seems never less than two people in a room, often mutually suspicious—Blue and I hardly ever alone together—I'm looking for a time to compare thoughts, to learn about this dreaming—time never seems right—one time I got Blue alone and John came to interrupt with his docudrama plans—what an appalling word, "docu-drama"—typical of John's monomaniacal ability to distance everyone and everything—he has barely said anything important since the morning Jakob died except to approach me nervously and say that of course he wasn't gay and never had been and that he wasn't serious that morning, that he wouldn't have slept with Jakob under any circumstances and he wanted me to understand that—I was so pissed off that he would take back the only thing he's ever said that came anywhere close to unselfish or human that I said sarcastically that it was true, no-one would ever mistake him for a faggot—he didn't take my meaning, was quite relieved (because after all I associated with those kind of people so I should know—it struck me rather oddly that it sounded almost as if he was forgetting that I am that kind, but if that's the case he's more of a fool than I'm already beginning to think, and I didn't want to press it)—but he continues to plague Blue with requests for a dream session all his own, and Blue is getting a little frantic—says John has mirrors to the inside, not windows, whatever that means—then there's Blue not asking again about the dream session between US, and when I suggest I might be ready, evading the idea, and won't tell me why, and we have no privacy to talk so I can find out.

At least Russ less of a zombie—talks a bit more now and has even surprised himself by laughing but he walks out of the room whenever we speak of Jakob, leaving a big empty silence and changing our grieving process from grieving for Jakob to grieving for Russ, or the part of him that can feel, or the friendship he seems to with-hold from us now, won't allow any intimacy. How can I bring him some healing? Delany sits with him when I can't, but neither of us seems to be able to break through, or at least I can't, and I need to talk with D., if she does figure out what to do—figure out what comes next—and she just says, oh, sweetie, it'll be fine, in time—does Russ have the time? Nobody has time—people die—people go away—

And look at me, feeling a need for people now, after all this time of feeling I'd be happier with people out of my hair—and even the people with whom I've had a growing closeness seem far away—

Suppose I'm feeling sorry for myself to say the only one in dead center is me. The police are here every two days asking new questions about and of Blue—but not my grey man, who seems to be mysteriously absent—makes me nervous.

We are all feeling the tension.

Sleep is no refuge when dreams are real and danger-ous. When do I get the REM sleep and rest a person needs to live sane? Glad I can count on the surveillance to rule me out because the others are starting to wonder about my state of mind.

"I've told Morgan that the surveillance rules her out, but really I ruled her out, on the basis of what I saw that morning. The sur-veillance doesn't rule anybody out," Mac said to Salomé. "The video's been altered even more. There are cartoon characters galumphing around, there are switches of one person with another, but done in rollover so it's obvious the feed's been altered. We've been seeing intrusions for months, when we go back and check some of the archival footage. We just weren't watching every moment of it, or parsing character movements. It's all parody now. What you found after Sal's death was subtle. This isn't. It's big ego speaking."

"So it's John Lee."

"Well, it's most likely John Lee playing with the feed, anyway, but is it John Lee doing anything else, or is this just his idea of playing around with us? He's been fractious all the way along. And there's no certainty that it's Lee. Russ could do this too. He makes propaganda vid—that's a constant stream of morphing shit into gold. I've often wondered what Russ does all day with that big secure network he gets to play with at work, and I can't find out because his production facility is protected under the New Official Secrets Act. Even from me, dammit. Did he have an argument with his lover and get violent? He has said he was ambivalent about crossing the line. It wouldn't be the first time that happened. Delany does vid, and she could be helping someone else by faking it. She's doing this big project with Nancy now, and guess what Nancy's hobby has been for years . . . ? And as for 'the Blue guy', that one has spent so much time with these systems that by now it could do anything it wanted, I think . . ."

"What are you going to do?"

"Try to untangle some of it, for one thing. Who'd be your pick for the best in the field at analyzing the feed for tampering, maybe restoring the original signal?"

"Me."

"Yes, you, your pick," he said impatiently. "You know the field."

"No, I mean, my pick is me. Just like last time."

"No. No. Out of the question. Conflict of interest, and besides, I don't want you this close. Some of it has to be on site." *And could be dangerous,* he left unsaid.

"You didn't plead conflict of interest last time."

"Yes, and I told you it was just that once, and just because it was in the lab."

"Ask ten other video artists. Six of them will say me. Six or more. Hester McKenzie, spinal. I'll make you a bet."

If he'd agreed on a bet, he would have lost; Hester was the pick of eight of ten, including both the police techs. She had had the grace not to say anything triumphant, and started working in the computer lab the following Monday.

✲   ✲   ✲

I can't write in this journal—it all turns into an incoherent cri de coeur—*and I can't bear to read it either. what does it document? A life spent whingeing. too many deaths. so, enough.*

The fire Morgan built with the loose pages of her journal-writing was burning briskly, and a stack of notebooks was waiting to be pulled apart and added to the fire, when Blue found her.

"What are you doing?" the alien asked, sitting down beside her on the log and looking alertly into the firepit.

Morgan looked up. "You look like that little dog of Judith's when you tilt your head like that!"

Blue smiled and clowned a little, putting into the spry tilt of head the eager vacuousness of a dog, stopping to ask, "What does a dog think?"

"Breathe in, breathe out, breathe in, breathe out," Morgan said, imitating canine panting. "Why do you ask me? You should know."

"It's bad manners to pry," Blue said in a perfect imitation of her voice.

Morgan chuckled, but the gritty smoke eddied into her eyes and she ended up coughing.

"Besides, dogs dream differently than we do. What are you doing burning your letters to yourself?" asked Blue, using the explanation Morgan herself had used to explain diaries to a much younger alien.

"They are not necessary any more," she said, "and besides, I saw John eyeing them, and I didn't want them to end up as voice-overs in his movie."

"I do not think this is enough of a reason, even if they are yours to keep or not," said Blue briskly. "I will have to think about this loss. Something in me objects to it. But there is another curious thing. Why is John having thieving ideas and yet everyone else does not become angry? Instead, you do damage to your dreams, and others turn away or laugh."

It was a good question, one that had occurred to Morgan without an answer following.

"I believe we cherish our rogues," she said. "We admire the impulse to define the world according to personal preference instead of community consensus. Especially these days, with boys and girls coming back into fashion, we glorify our 'bad boys' and 'bad girls'. The hooker with the heart of gold is a trope of film, and the woman who says, 'I can't help it if I'm bad . . .'"

" 'I'm just drawn that way'," quoted Blue, and grinned.

"You saw that? That's an old example, all right. Or the Saint. Not the vid remake guy but the original, the one in the books. A noble man, a man of honor, but a thief and a trickster."

"The trickster comes into it too, does he not? Or she. The one with the last laugh. Coyote. The Monkey King."

"Indeed. Very good!"

"It also seems to me that there is the question of capitalism," says Blue pensively. "Marx spoke of how capitalism creates individualism . . ."

Morgan laughed. "You're becoming a Marxist now?"

"Perhaps not. But he was an interesting writer. 'Commodities become fetishes under capitalism'—don't you find that illuminating?"

"Oh, sure, but I still have trouble separating the book from the dogma that was created around it, and from the toll of human misery that ensued from the opportunistic use of that dogma."

"That seems a limited point of view," said Blue sternly, but Morgan was not cowed.

"Indeed it is limited," she said, "and it is the exact problem I have with Christianity, marriage, capitalism, and for that matter Islam, Confucianism, and Taoism, though I don't know as much about them, except what we read together. It's the problem of philosophies that have amassed a history of pain. Can they ever exist in purity again? Can one ever come to them without remembering who has died to keep their purists happy?"

"It seems to me you could say that about the whole of the human race. We have . . . humans have such a history of brutality. What keeps us noble?"

"What indeed," said Morgan.

"And why do we keep glorifying our bad guys?"

"Bad boys. And girls. Bad guys is something else."

"Whatever. Why?"

"My dear," said Morgan, "I haven't the foggiest notion. All I have are guesses. Just like you."

"Yes," said Blue with satisfaction, "just like me," and picked up the unburned notebooks. "I will put these away where John does not look if that is all right with you. You can get them back after."

"After?"

"After I go home. I'm getting old. It won't be long."

"You're getting *old?*" Morgan felt chilled.

"Never mind. Can I have the books?"

"Oh, all right," said Morgan, and watched Blue carry them back into the house, leaving Morgan with troubled thoughts. It was not until later that she remembered Blue had again said "we" about humans, and, distracted by Blue's offhand reference to aging, Morgan had again not even noticed at the time. The realization pleased her, and she didn't mind as much the empty corner of her desk where the stack of paper and notebooks had been building up.

"If I need what Blue didn't take," she thought later, just as she was dropping off to sleep, "I can just make the rest of it again."

The pages in the flame are caught in an updraft, and the blue fire consumes them without destroying them. Morgan sees the fire swirled away by the wind and into the dried leaves of the autumn trees, and her convulsive motion to prevent a conflagration wakes her up from the dream.

Its immediacy, as usual, had her heart racing, but she did not feel as frightened as she sometimes had. Tonight she felt protected by her emptiness from the dangers of fire. After all, she had gotten rid of all that loose paper.

✿   ✿   ✿

Nevertheless, too often the sense of menace enveloped them all. Late one night Morgan sat with John in front of the fireplace.

"It's so spooky in here these days," she said.

"How do you mean?"

"Everyone suspicious of each other."

"Oh, not everyone. You're pretty much out of the picture since Jakob . . . died, and of course Delany couldn't have done any of it except the cat . . . and really, there's no proof that it was someone in this house. Jakob could have brought someone in, a trick who killed him, Sal was done in the alley, and cats will eat anything that is lying around and looks tasty."

"I can't believe it was any of us . . . even you . . ." she teased. He took her seriously.

"Of course it wasn't me! I'm not so sure about Blue."

"Oh, John, you can't be serious! Blue doesn't know enough to swat a mosquito."

"Blue has no idea what death means. Haven't you realized that by now? It could just as easily have been a mistake, an experiment on his part . . ."

"No!" But Morgan remembered uncomfortably the way Blue "changed" the living cat to be like the dead one, and Blue's anarchistic disregard during the alien's unsanctioned, unaccompanied adventure in the real world. Still, she stubbornly clung to the belief that Blue, whom she had seen in dreams, was innocent.

"I know it would be hard for you to accept. Hard for lots of people to accept. But Blue isn't a person like you and me."

"No?"

"Not human, like us, I mean."

"No? What makes a human being?"

John stretched his feet out to the fender, wiggled his toes in the heat. "Genetics? Birth? Being part of the tribe?"

"But are any of us really part of the tribe? People are so different from each other."

"No! That's not the case at all. There are groups of people, it's true, some better than others, but people are very much alike. We're different from the animals."

"What about the gorillas who sign and the dolphins who sing?"

"Animal-trainer tricks. We're above that: we are special. There are no beings like us."

"I do believe we are special in the Universe, John, but we *are* animals, and above and beyond that, we can't say that we are alone or singular. Not any more. Not since the aliens. Whether they are shaped like Blue and therefore like us, or whether they simply made some human-like constructs to act as their contacts, still, they were *capable* of making them. They are something like us: they explore, they are curious—"

"Or the whole thing is a fake. That's what Jakob thought."

"That's what Jakob used to think . . . I mean, Jakob changed his mind after he dreamed Blue."

"After he *what?*"

"After he slept with Blue."

"The fancies that we get during sex are notoriously unreliable. We imagine we know people, trust people, have transcended something. It's all just a fantasy of our nerve endings."

"Sometimes, maybe. But that dreaming process isn't sex. It's something else."

"But they did have sex, probably. That was such a stupid thing for Jakob to do. How did he know what diseases the alien has, how could he . . . ? It's like bestiality."

"Even if they did, Blue is not a beast. Unless you think we all are, in which case all sex is bestiality."

John looked shocked.

"It's a joke, Johnny."

"Oh. Well, it's not far wrong, is it? Especially to someone like Jakob. Someone who is used to deviant sex."

"John, we've been through this before. Homosex isn't deviant, it's just less common than heterosex."

"Yeah, yeah. You know what I mean. Someone who's used to going outside the boundaries one way will do it another way, will experiment, will try anything."

"Anything?" Morgan couldn't imagine John really believed that, but she saw that he seemed to. "Jakob was very vanilla, really, for a fag," she said. "He wasn't interested in experimentation. In some ways, he wasn't interested in sex very much at all, I think, compared with intimacy. But when he was, it was pretty sedate."

"Sedate?"

"Yeah. Just regular stuff, no weirdness. The hardest thing he ever did was get naked with Blue. And that was just, as I said, intimacy."

"Well, better him than me, that's for sure."

"Ah, John, you're such a neocon. You know, when we were young, the culture was one of openness. These prejudices you embrace: we worked very hard to erase such things."

"Hey, I work at tolerance!"

"No, tolerance is one thing, not being prejudiced at all is another. I don't envy your generation at all."

"Hey, I'm not that much younger than you."

"Yes, you are. These days, even three or four years defines a generation, and you must be at least a dozen years younger."

"Not according to my birth certificate," he said, and chuckled, looking not at Morgan but at the fire. The effect was of the same secretive amusement she had seen before, condescending and a bit off-putting. *Of all the people in the house,* she thought, *I work hardest with this one, and yet know least—and perhaps don't even like this one, though there is a strange charm in that exuberant egotism.* And the documentary rough-cuts she had seen were good, were excellent, even if the angles seemed a bit—snaky, somehow.

"Ah, Johnny," she said, "who are you?" and was surprised

when he started out of his reverie with hostility and said, savagely and automatically, "None of your business!"

"Hey!" she said. "Calm yourself! This is me, Morgan here. No threat."

"Yeah, sorry, I was thinking of something else," he said, awkwardly. "Look, I have to go work. The last few days . . . well, with all the fuss, I really haven't got anything done at all." And he left her there, wondering why a simple joke had made him so touchy. Touchier than usual, for she realized they had all gotten used to how difficult he really could be.

He is not a very nice person, she thought, and then snorted at her prissy interior tone. But he wasn't.

❖   ❖   ❖

Andris made one of his rare visits to the grey man's office the day after Salomé started working on the recordings.

"Any results on the tapes?"

"They're not tape any more, boss," said Mr. Grey. "I keep telling you that."

"It's a figure of speech," said Andris. "Look at this."

In the center of the small stack of files he was holding was a red Eyes-Only folder. Out of it he took a document and tossed it to Mac. The grey man picked it up to find that it was in Chinese. "What's this?"

"It cost us a good deal, and then the guy who got it for us vanished. We think for good."

"Don't be cute, boss. What is it?"

"It's an autopsy report," said Andris. "On China's alien."

❖   ❖   ❖

"It's a fine day," said the grey man. "Let's go for a walk."

"It's raining," said Morgan.

"It's good for you," he said. They strode out along the park and down the path into the valley. The grey man had an inadequate plastic rain poncho which snapped noisily in the wind, and

Blue was wearing a bizarre fisherman's slicker borrowed from Russ, which crackled and swished as Blue walked. "I need to ask you," he said to Blue, "if you are able to listen to any of the other Visitors."

"To the house?"

"To earth. Visitors like you."

"What do you mean, listen?" Morgan said.

"You both know exactly what I mean. I'm cold and wet and I don't have a lot of time. Can you hear them?"

"No," said Blue. "Well, sort of. Maybe. Yes."

"Which is it?"

"There is a whisper. It sounds different than the city whisper. It is very far away. Things disrupt it. I don't know, solar flares or Tesla rays or something."

"Look, don't joke around with me. This is important. Could you tell if they were all still there?"

"I don't think . . . I haven't . . ." Blue stopped and was silent for a moment. The grey man put a hand on Morgan's sleeve to keep her quiet, but Morgan knew that expression. "Maybe . . . one is gone. Two. Two are gone. One is . . . very sick."

"Gone?"

"Dead," said the alien.

"What happened?" said Morgan.

"Even if I knew, I probably couldn't tell you," said the grey man. "We'll see if we can do anything for the sick one, but I doubt it. I'm sorry, Blue."

The rest of the walk was silent. When they got back to the house Blue went upstairs and Morgan made the grey man a quick cup of tea to warm him. He drank it standing up, then said, "Sorry, I have to go back to work." Morgan walked him out through the hall.

Blue caught up to them at the door and said diffidently, "I have made something. Can I show you?"

Morgan and the grey man, who seemed startled to be included, nodded, and Blue led the way back into the house and up to Jakob's studio. The police seal hung broken from the door:

the forensics team had pronounced that they were done with it the afternoon before, so Morgan ignored the grey man's sigh.

Blue set the lights and pulled the blackout curtains. "I think I have just learned what 'shy' is," Blue said hesitantly. "Everything worries me now. I have made—a dance?"

"Show us," said Morgan gently.

"I have not been working on it very long," said Blue. "Jakob worked longer. Maybe it is not very good."

"Don't worry. Just show us."

Blue began with an imitation of *Night Through Slow Glass*. A perfect imitation. Or maybe not. As it went on Morgan began to see that the tension Jakob had wound into the piece was being unwound, strand by strand, into an ever-increasing dissonance. Entropy was taking over. By the end of the piece, what would have been the end, it had almost completely unraveled—and then, at the point where the choir music stopped, and the dance Jakob had danced had dissolved into silence and chaos, Blue hovered for a moment in the final pose, then exploded into a wild storm of what could only be grief: a howl, a fury, an outcry of loss. In total, eerie, telling silence—and perfect motion.

Then stood, panting slightly, looking at Morgan and Mr. Grey. "Did you understand?" said the alien.

Morgan nodded, and to her shock, Mr. Grey simply opened his arms wide. Blue came into them, and bowed the tangled head against the grey man's. Blue was taller, and graceful as a willow against Grey's slight, suit-clad frame.

"I miss Jakob," said Blue finally.

"We all do," said the grey man.

❁   ❁   ❁

The attendance at the memorial service was going to be huge. Not only because Jakob had been far better known than any of them thought, but because the media knew he had lived in the house with the alien, and videorazzi and spectators alike hoped to catch a glimpse of Blue.

The team considered pinkface and even worked up a credible imitation of Aziz. "I am Aziz's brother," said Blue wryly, looking at the results in the mirror, and Aziz, who was there to watch, blushed as they all chuckled.

But Blue turned away from the mirror troubled. "Excuse me, but I do not want to go in disguise," the alien said slowly. "I am thinking of this. Jakob was my friend. Morgan has explained this event to me and it does not seem right that I sneak into his memorial. It would be like telling a big lie. Also, I made a dance, and I am thinking it would have been something Jakob liked. So I am wondering. Could I go as myself and dance my requiem?"

Kowalski, mute for once, looked at Mr. Grey. The grey man looked at Morgan silently and, it seemed to her, nonplussed for the first time.

Finally he said, "I will ask."

❁   ❁   ❁

"Andris," he said, "scramble," and when the encryption kicked in, the grey man went on, "Do we have the authority for a head-of-state operation?"

"Why?" Andris's voice sounded artificial after its journey through encription. "Oh, I see, Bryant is just putting the transcript in front of me now. 'Teach me, O Lord, to be sweet and gentle in all the events of life.' "

"Sir?"

"Something my mother used to say. Look, I will call the Prime Minister's office. Wait where you are. I'll get back to you."

The grey man went back to the alien's room, where Ko and Lemieux and Morgan and Blue were making up Morgan as an alien. The blue set off her raven hair and all she needed was a blue rinse to make her a pair with Blue. The grey man sighed silently.

"We wait," he said. "What does that stuff feel like?"

"Come and we'll show you," said Lemieux, so that in the surprisingly short time if took for Grey's cellphone to ring again, he was transformed into a small, neat, greyhaired alien. "It's comfortable," he said, surprised, just as the 'phone rang.

On the other end of the line, Andris's tinny, pixelated encrypted voice said, "We have a royal-wedding scenario. Or head-of-state funeral. Whatever. I would like you to know that the Prime Minister thinks this is the cat's meow as a propaganda opportunity. We'll be lucky if she isn't issuing front-row seats to the news anchor teams by this time tomorrow. You are in charge. Enjoy." He hung up.

The grey man turned to his colleagues. "We're on," he said. He glimpsed himself in the mirror. There were three aliens among the pinkfaced people. He sighed again. He hated it when the world presented him with obvious metaphors. He reached up and began to tear the blueface off. "You can dance," he said to Blue. "We'll protect you. Ko, we have security to arrange. This stuff is sticky. Lemieux, put ten of your people in blueface. We'll do a decoy shell game."

Blue was silent. When the others went out, the alien said to Morgan, "Now I am apprehensive. All those people will do all the work to get me there, and there will be so many watching, and what if I dance wrong?"

"Jakob faced that every time he danced, honey," said Morgan. "Welcome to the human race."

"You keep saying that," said Blue irritably, "but where else have I been?" and went up to the studio to practice.

Delany wheeled past just as Blue disappeared up the stairs, watched by Morgan leaning on the doorframe of the alien's room, still blue of face and hands. "What's up, girlfriend? Why are you so blue?"

Morgan snorted. "Very cute. Blue's dancing, all blue and natural, at Jakob's memorial. My grey man has just taken all his people off to organize it as an affair of state." Morgan, worried, looked at Delany, worried, and they both began to giggle.

"Did you ever think your life would be like this?" Delany said, hiccoughing.

"No way," said Morgan. "What the devil is going to happen

next?" Morgan began to peel the makeup off her face. It came off like a latex glove. She picked at her wrists.

"Stop that," said Delany firmly. "What's happening next is we're going to go to bed."

"It's two in the aftern . . . oh," said Morgan.

"Saves electricity," said Delany. "And latex. Leave those on," and wheeled back to her own room.

✿　　✿　　✿

Morgan dreams that she, the grey man, Delany, and Blue float, blue of skin, in a huge pool. Blue holds Delany's head, hovers over her, and from Blue's mouth pours a sparkling silver stream the flow of which surrounds Delany and soaks into her skin. When it is completely absorbed, Delany looks like herself. *There,* says Blue's voice in satisfaction. *All ready to go now.* Grey takes Morgan's hands. His feel like velvet.

Morgan woke smiling, then stopped smiling. It was the day of Jakob's memorial.

✿　　✿　　✿

The memorial was exactly as difficult as Morgan had predicted, and for all the same reasons. Getting there, getting through the crowds, dodging the noisy videorazzi, trying to get John not to talk with them, sorting Jakob's friends from the wannabes and impostors so that they could come into the central venue, getting Delany in her chair up the stairs, and then, the private difficulties of saying goodbye to a friend. Singing, short and long speeches of farewell and remembrance, flowers, draped scarves, Aziz playing *Night Through Slow Glass,* then Blue's dance, all designed to break the controls on grief and let the tears flow, or so the last remaining cynical part of Morgan snarled to Mr. Grey, who stayed with them throughout, only occasionally murmuring inconspicuously to his throat mike.

"Ah, but," he said, then didn't continue.

"Strangely enough, I know what you mean," said Morgan. She

remembered her parents' funeral, so different in taste and staging, so similar in purpose and in achieved function. She couldn't cry at this one either, but at least now she knew why.

❀   ❀   ❀

Kid sat on the couch, knees drawn up and arms wrapped tightly against them, protecting her breath, hair untidy from hands running through it, face pale and drawn from a sleepless night. Morgan was laying out Tarot cards; it was something she was learning from Delany, but not very well. She referred constantly to a book, shaking her head. She looked up and sharpened her gaze on the young police officer.

"Never mind this now; how are you? What's the problem?" she said, and Kid shook her head.

"Come on," Morgan said, "it can't be that bad."

"I'm quitting my job," said Kid.

"Oh, yes. And now what?"

"She believes in it all!" Kid cried indignantly, forgetting her pose of defense and suddenly flinging her legs and arms wide. "She thinks they've got the right idea, and she's out of step. Everything they hand her, she accepts. They find out she's gay and let her stay on the force, she's grateful. Grateful, for chrissakes! And now that she's doing some really good work, they use her for all that's worth, then find a reason to send her away from the thing she wants most to finish, and she just says, orders. I can't believe it! And I can't live with it. And I said so, and they said my career might be in jeopardy, and I said, you can't fire me, I quit, and that was it. I'd probably be in custody if I hadn't come inside here: Official Secrets Act shit. The ironic thing is that they probably think I quit out of love for her, some kind of perverse triangle, demanding that she choose me or promotion, and I wasn't chosen, so I quit out of pique. But you know, I quit out of disappointment. I don't even have erotic dreams about women; I think I'm unchangeably straight. But I thought I knew her, thought she was my friend.

"And she turns spineless, collapses, turns into someone I don't even recognize, counseling me about my job, my future. I thought she cared about *me,* and she turns around and puts in a report challenging my objectivity, my competence."

"Are you saying you think she saved herself at the cost of you?"

"That's how it feels."

"But what would you have done?"

"When?"

"What would you have done if things had gone on the same?"

"I don't know." Kid turned to her own thoughts, and it seemed to Morgan that she had gone a long distance by the time she recalled herself, with Morgan still watching her acutely.

"I would have quit," she said, surprise in her voice. Morgan grinned and leaned back, put her feet up on the coffee table.

"Why is that?"

"I think you know."

Morgan said, "I don't like to guess when I can ask," and Kid leaned back too, relaxed now, and said to the ceiling, "I guess it's Blue, really. You have to decide one way or another, if you hang around Blue long enough, and I don't believe Blue's the one who knows enough about murder to practice it that way."

"But the argument surely is that it was all unintentional, or that Blue tried it and for some perverse reason liked it. Then there must be a minority opinion that we're all in some crazy conspiracy to teach Blue to be a revolutionary, and it has backfired on us."

Kid laughed. "Oh, they threw that one out after Jakob; they were sure he was the one fomenting armed uprising, but when he died their theories went nose-and-toes up. They tried on Delany, with her background, but all she does is paint. And she just isn't strong, no matter how hard they wish. They want to suspect Russ, but no, he works for the government, he's as checked-out as he can be after all—whatever he's done in other countries, they vetted him before he got that job. But as for the rest, you're right on. It's the people back at the desks, of course. No one around here thinks that. Or thought that—Lord knows who's out there now. Most of the squad have been recalled, you know, and

Kowalski's replaced them with a new hand-picked crew. This time—you'll laugh—they're mostly men. He's hoping no more emotionalism is gonna intrude here. I thought Ace would stand up for what she thought. But she just let them ship her back to HQ, and Lord knows what she's telling them now."

"Frustration does funny things sometimes."

"Frustration?"

And then Morgan perceived the light came on in Kid's thoughts, as Kid remembered huddling around the console in the midwinter security shack, listening to Morgan and Delany, Ace with the tears at the corners of her eyes, and Kid saying, "What is it?" (knowing, she thought, that it was the distance between her friend and her that couldn't be bridged) and Ace surprising her by saying, "It's not fair. Why should we stay out in this damned trailer, and they get to make history? No one will even remember our names."

"I thought they were making love," Kid had said lightly, but Ace had said, "I don't mean them. Sex is nothing. An itch. I can scratch it by myself, if I have to. It's the people who've been reading science fiction all our lives, waiting for something to happen to us, and it happens to them, and we have to watch. It's indecent. Our part of it too. There's never enough of anything to go around. Look at the third world. Food, ideas, money, fame, happiness—everybody wants some, and hardly anybody gets any, and the ones who have it think they don't have enough. The world is hungry, and I am too."

"Yes," said Morgan, "that's what I mean."

I must have spoken aloud, Morgan saw Kid think, even as she knew she hadn't, saw her for a moment utterly disoriented. She was reassured by the very ordinary surroundings, Morgan curling her feet up under her in the easy chair, flipping her hair back from her face with both hands. "What's your name?" said Morgan, quickly, before Kid took any more notice of their momentary double mind. *I must find out how to control that,* thought Morgan, *before Blue goes.* The pang at the idea of Blue's departure struck deeply, with surgical precision, to the heart of love, but Morgan could walk and chew gum at the same time: she was convinced her face showed nothing as Kid said, "Name?"

"Constable K. I. Doucette is all I know. Kid."

"Katherine Ilene. Kid."

"But you're an adult now."

"I've been thinking about that. When you're twenty-four and still called Kid, no wonder you aren't a corporal yet."

"One of these days you'll learn to say *I.*" Then, after a pause: "What are you going to call yourself?"

"Just Katy. I've been Kid since I was nine. I think Katy would be nice. My mum calls me Katy; I always feel like I've been hugged."

"Welcome, Katy," said Morgan, and smiled at her. "I changed my name too."

"Yes, I know. I helped compile your dossier, you know."

Laughing: "Then we'll have to be friends; you already know more about me than I probably remember."

Kid—no, Katy, she must learn to think of herself like that— looked at this woman before her, who now stood and looked down on her calmly, and thought, *she is utterly ordinary. Through the winter I thought of her as an ideal, an idol, but what is so compelling to me now is how completely human she is. Though she seems to see into me as if I were transparent, I don't feel in the least threatened, because I know she is like me.*

Morgan, looking down at the almost sleeping ex-cop, thought, *she can believe whatever she likes.* She smiled, said, "We'll get you some blankets. You can sleep here until you've decided what you want to do." Katy stretched out on the couch, pillowed her head on her arms.

"How did you know I wanted to stay?" she said sleepily.

"You said so. I remembered." Morgan brought a blanket, covered the woman she still thought of as a youth, but must learn to credit with twenty-four years, and call by another name, kissed her cheek, said, "Goodnight, Katy," watched Katy's answering smile fade into sleep.

The factions are consolidating, Morgan thought. *We're in here, still believing; they're out there, replacing the converted with skeptics. Something better break in this case soon, or we'll have another Inquisition on our hands.*

Lucky thing the only mind-readers are on our side, she thought gratefully, and only after the fact was shocked at the commonplace nature of the thought.

❊   ❊   ❊

"Congratulations on handling Blue's debut," said Andris. "By the way, the one in Burma is changing color now. Apparently there's something missing in its diet. It has turned pink. My medicos here say that it's probably very ill. Unless the mechanism is sort of like hydrangeas. Or flamingos."

"We aren't feeding ours anything special, are we?"

"It eats apricot pits," said Kowalski suddenly. "I saw it. Who knows what else it eats?"

"It doesn't matter much," said the grey man. "Ours says it will have to go home soon. It isn't sure how, but it says it knows. It says it feels—old."

"Old?" said Andris.

"Old," said the grey man. "I think Blue means middle-aged. Old, now—that's how *I* feel."

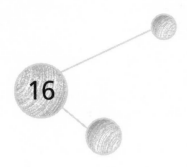

A local grammar

16

"Look here, daddy-o," said Salomé. He had given up trying to get her to at least call him Mac at the office. "This is old stuff. Your Atrium."

"What are you doing with that? For that matter, how did you get it? It's classified."

"Jeffrey got it for me. I thought we might have a look backward."

"Jeffrey?"

Salomé gestured toward the technician whom the grey man had always thought of simply as "Bryant".

"Oh. Jeffrey. Right."

"Hester was thinking . . . ," Jeffrey said diffidently.

"Three deaths, right? As well as the cats, but no-one can prove it wasn't just cat-haters poisoning them."

Mac interrupted the long pause. "Okay, I get it. I even buy it. And . . . ?"

"Who was your tech then?"

"Bry—Jeffrey. He's been one up on this project since the start."

"Hey, no, man, not me. We gettin' a whole crew of relief tech that time. Seconded from three government departments, and hired some freelance. One of them was workin' that day. I was walkin' the beach back home, that time." Bryant had immigrated from Jamaica to Prince Edward Island ten years before, but Mac, who knew him from other projects, had convinced him to join the Atrium project in this prairie city by offering him free air fare east three times a year. He loved the beaches of PEI with what the grey man considered an irrational but endearing love.

"So who was on shift?"

"First, let me show you this," said Salomé impatiently. "We've only got the bandwidth for another half hour, then Kowalski has some kinda netference planned."

Here were the chessmaster and Blue bent over the chessboard. The grey man recognized with a shock how childlike and unformed the alien had seemed then, despite inhabiting the same body he had seen only a few hours ago as an adult sashaying charismatically through the halls at the SETI conference.

"Look here," said Salomé. "The technician claimed he was on a pee break. Tapes from the can. Look at the time codes."

A familiar figure slouched into the urinal stall, unzipped, peed. He seemed to be writing his name against the enamel, like a kid peeing into a snowbank. He was smirking.

"Oh, bloody hell," said the grey man. "Not him."

"Pay attention to the counter," said Salomé.

In one window, the man urinated. In another, Blue left the frame, the chessmaster sat and played, then clutched his chest, fell. Blue re-entered, looking confused. The man zipped, exited the stall. In a third window, he re-entered the tech booth. Blue turned to the camera, said, "Come fast here, something is wrong with this one." On the bathroom camera, the timer was still running on a shot of an empty room. On the tech room camera, the technician turned to the window in shock, then hit a button to the left of the keyboard. On the sitting room camera, Blue said, "All chess has ceased. Perhaps death?"

Salomé froze the frames.

The three timers differed from each other by one one-hundredth of a second each.

"Did they synch at the start?" said Mac quietly.

With one stab at the keypad, Salomé revisited the first shots, where the timers were synched. "This is interesting. Look here."

By the end of thirty seconds, the timers were in synch again. Salomé stopped at the moment where the seconds got slightly longer for five seconds on each tape.

"What the hell *is* that?"

"His edits weren't perfectly timed, he didn't have enough time, or he glitched the program slightly. So he had to kludge a five-hundredth of a second per second afterward, but before any-body showed up to answer the alarm. He had to get them back in synch because he knew the tapes were going to be seized as soon as someone in authority got there."

"Ja, man, the Boy Wonder and your man Ko had the memory in their hands within ten minutes," said Bryant—Jeffrey—with a tinge of admiration in his voice. "And the man here was running the emergency procedures, and dealing with the alien. That's smooth, man, real smooth."

Salomé had frozen the face of the tech in the center window. The grey man stared at it.

"Smooth, yeah," he said. "Can you figure out what was there for real?"

"Not a chance. No permanent synchro-backup. But I can show you what he wrote."

"Wrote?"

"When he peed. He wrote something. I can give you a pixel count on the impact point."

" 'Runs with scissors?' Never mind."

"Close. How does 'that's one' grab you?"

"Great," he said heavily. "Make me a tape of it, and sign an affidavit of continuity of evidence. Bryant, you have one of those on file. You might as well do it too."

"Good work, eh?" Salomé said, grinning.

"Yeah. Smooth. Spinal. Thanks." He turned, preoccupied now, and angry.

"That's not all," said Jeffrey. "You better listen to this."

      ✿   ✿   ✿

Morgan looked at the people at the conference and saw them as dead people. She glimpsed herself in a hallway mirror and turned to look: from the mirror her dead self stared back. But she had learned a great deal lately: what she thought instead of despair was: *Dangerous signals. I must be careful not to mistake these thoughts for reality.*

Some days you eat bear and some days the bear eats you. Morgan felt like bear meat. The weekend SETI conference was endless stuffy rooms full of sycophantic scientists and former skeptics, Blue as resident alien of course, and, as the only one of Earth's baker's dozen of visitors to be this humanized, the talk of the town. The attempts to give or withhold from Morgan the credit for the transformation were in themselves theater, but Morgan was no longer amused by the playacting. The grey man had, with his few words, instilled an additional dread in her: what if the aliens were dying, or being killed? How safe was Blue? And here she was, unable to do a thing—except care. That caring was blunted by the chemistry of depression reaching for her, and by the enervation of fighting it off.

By the time they finally arrived home, Morgan was so tired that dinner seemed like just another gauntlet to run. She tried to go to her room.

"You need to eat," said Delany. "Sit down. We've got everything ready."

Morgan ate with her head down, wanting the whole rat's nest of problem situations to vanish. Russ and John were sniping at each other.

She knew with another part of her mind that it was physical process, not mood, that influenced her thoughts; the grey, changeable weather didn't help at all. Clouds promised but didn't put out: a good thunderstorm would clear the air, she told herself. She felt the beginning of the migraine. Despite her lack of appetite, she forced herself to take bites of the *tekka-maki* Russ had made; she wished she could just go to bed with a brain-candy book.

". . . couldn't hack your way out of a paper bag," said John. "What do you know?"

"If that's what you think," Russ said, "then dial into GovNet tonight and see whether you change your mind."

"What do you mean?"

"I predict that they'll pull the plug about nine-thirty," said Russ. "It'll take them a while to catch on."

"Catch on?" Delany said.

"I got tired of being a government hack," said Russ. "I went back to my old club."

"You didn't squid the vid . . ." Morgan glanced up, curious, to see a glow dawning on John's face. Russ looked almost gleeful.

"What have you done?" Morgan said sharply.

"Made a few progressive changes to the feed," said Russ. "It ought to be interesting."

"Are you crazy? We're being monitored here! You want to get arrested?"

"Not much," said Russ, "but I expect I will. Would have, even if I didn't let a peep out. Who else but me had that kind of access? Revolution requires sacrifices."

"Is that what you said to Sal and Jakob?" John sniped.

"What?" Russ paled angrily.

"Well, somebody was in danger, or they wouldn't have died."

"John!" Delany said, aghast.

"Murder is on a different order than vid hacking," Russ said, his face still livid.

"Sal said that people did a lot to cover up political crimes. He had a lot to say about"—John glared at Delany and Russ—"politicals."

"Sal said? You knew him?" Delany said.

"We used to have coffee at the Atrium all the time."

The Atrium?

"The Atrium?" Russ had spoken Morgan's thought before she could.

"Sure," said John. "We were on the same shif—" He saw Morgan's sharpened gaze fix on him. "Oops! Official Secrets blowout time. Sorry."

"You worked at the Atrium?" Morgan asked quietly.

"Sure."

"Before you came here?"

"Sure. I had a freelance gig . . ."

"Why didn't you tell us?"

"Took an oath."

"That's a little more scrupulous than you usually are, isn't it?"

"Hey, they threatened me with all sorts of crap if I broke the oath. I want to keep my vid license."

"That's if you told the world," Morgan said icily. "I consider it a major problem that you didn't tell me."

"Hey, come on, Russ worked there too. He has alien footage on his websites at work."

"Russ?" Morgan felt at sea.

"I was seconded for some tech services, sure, but I never set foot in the place until after you and Blue were long gone," Russ said easily. "Then later I had access to some of the tech stuff for the intergovernmental affairs website. I already had the security clearances for it. I suppose I could have gone there whenever I pleased."

"I suppose that was a secret too."

"I never talk about work at home," Russ said, and she had to nod at that. John was getting up, using the plate-clearing ritual that he usually ignored to try to get out of the room without her notice.

"Stop right there," she said. "Tell me three good reasons why you didn't tell me that you had been in the Atrium. And then tell me what you did there."

"It wasn't that big a deal," he said sullenly. "I worked a couple of tech shifts freelance when they needed someone who could deal with multiple feeds quicktime. I was only there maybe five times. It's not like I saw you there or anything."

She kept silent, and he went on diffidently, "Well, maybe once in the staff room. That's when I heard you talking about needing another roommate. You didn't know there were staffroom feeds?"

"No, I didn't," she said, "though goodness knows I should have."

"Hey, come on, Morgan. I wasn't allowed to tell. You know that. You never told us any of the stuff that went down in there. Same reason, right? And it worked out okay, didn't it?" He looked at her like a hurt puppydog.

"Yeah, John, it worked out fine. I just wish—never mind. Just never mind."

She got up and brushed past him out the door.

"Morgan—" Delany said, placatingly.

"Look, it's *fine*," she said, "but I'm not happy right now, all right? I'm going to have a hot bath, and I'm going to bed. John, if you don't do the fucking dishes before I wake up you are out of this house tomorrow."

Tucked under the covers at last, she opened the mystery novel hoping for smooth prose and consequent trance, but as if she were captive in an ant farm, there was no relief; the book's shortcomings and her aching head irritated her increasingly until finally she threw the book across the room, frightening Marbl who was dozing on the chair of Morgan's desk. Marbl leapt to the ready, hissed.

"Oh, calm down," Morgan said crossly, and turned over, plumped her pillow into a knot under her ear, and went to sleep.

❀   ❀   ❀

In the dream she is standing alone in a flat wilderness, crying, but no-one will rescue her. Rather grimly she decides to rescue herself, only to find she can't punch the numbers on the telephone right. She panics, tries to call 911 to get the police or the hospital, but can't make her fingers complete any sequence.

She woke sweating into darkness, shaking her throbbing head back and forth in protest, crying out. Blue took her shaking hands in long warm fingers, held tightly until the dream was dispelled.

"Why wouldn't you talk to me?" she said.

"I'm sorry," said Blue, sounding wretched in the dimness.

"What's the matter?" With her head aching, the lamp would have been too bright; Morgan got up, shaking away sleep, and went to the desk to light the candles there.

"I'm afraid . . . afraid it's my fault . . . if I felt something, couldn't find out what, they died, Jakob, and I could have gone out there and stopped it . . ."

"It?"

"It's someone, I don't know . . ." Blue was crying. Crying? Crying.

"Why are you crying?" she said, as her arms went around the shaking body automatically.

311

"You taught me how," said Blue. At the words, with sudden tectonic upheaval Morgan was weeping too, great wrenching sobs convulsing her small body. For her father, for her mother, for Jakob, for cats, for strangers like Sal, for those left alive, for all human losses small and great, and for the loss of Blue which would come too soon. She had a lot to catch up with. Blue's hand stroked her hair and a thumb wiped away the tears wilding across her face. With the touch she found a multiplicity of trust which focused the last months into a brilliance having nothing to do with the flaring, guttering candles.

It is time to wake up, and to dream.

There was no design in her motion as she pulled both Blue's hands against her face, seeing the color of them shining in the air in the candlelight as the long fingers moved toward her face, feeling the jolt of total body response as they touched, feeling then the flood of total contact, the blue presence suffusing her and she flowing out until there was a unity and an understanding that fulfilled the taste she had had of it in dreams. None of the fear that came with the dream of Jakob's murder lingered; none of the fear of the unknown remained, only the necessity to comfort and calm each other. In the seeking out of confusion the ways were straightened, so that somewhere in it one of their voices said, "Oh, is that who it is?" and the wave of shocked sadness flashed after, like the flash of lightning that cut through the heavy air outside. The thunder of the cloudburst, the wanton fall of water, was background to the waves of consciousness that met and mingled with the ferocity and beauty of the storm, as above the ocean Morgan had seldom seen. Through it her spirit stumbled and leapt with Blue to more insights than she had time to notice: the first forgiveness she recognized must be for herself.

She remembered the orgy of blame after her parents died. She had thought of that cold hard excoriation as truth and light: now she knew how dark it had really been. She remembered Daniel Webster's truism that the Devil's best work is to convince people that he doesn't exist, but she now realized that she had followed rather Dostoyevsky and Browne: without believing in an external evil force she had fallen prey to internal devils of despair and doubt which had come to her clothed in false righteousness, and created a devil in her own image, which dwelt within her own heart, poisoning the clean clear music of life.

She now stood bathed in a real and kindly light, and saw herself unbroken for the first time in her life. She now understood that her intuition had been better than her intellect, knew with certainty that love has more information to offer than does any other force—and that she was no more responsible than any other organism for the nature of life. She was no more, no less than an ordinary human, after all. It was not about perfection or lack of perfection, it was not about success or failure. She loved then and now she loved as well as she could. Things happen. Shit happens. People leave you. People die.

But. But . . . information accretes around a life like sugar around a button dangled in a glass of supersaturated sugar-water. Life crystallizes around intentions: good, evil, loving, curious intentions: nightmares and dreams. That sea of dreams becomes a new and universal ocean, aliens meeting in amniotic accord; what birth, now? And what new consciousness to emerge?

Only our own, thought someone, simply.

Then again they turned together and it was not just a dreaming and a sharing of thought—it was a needing, a cry for touch, and for the commitment of passion, minds and bodies tuned for dreaming, to love someone, transcending the names: they had celebrated mind, now bodies heard the music, and rose to a tangled, sweaty, ecstatic dance.

Morgan had always marveled, sometimes darkly, at that terrible paradox of mortality and consciousness, how the first contradicts and yet creates the other—and to date all her efforts to love well and to make love well had been in an attempt to trascend that paradox. Now, for the first time, she felt her body, her mind and her spirit—yes, she is willing to say her soul also—unite for one brief moment of Zen unconsciousness, *satori,* one moment when she understood *one and not one, difficult and not difficult, mortal and immortal* and all the other twinned and inseparable contradictions—and from which clear awareness she returned as soon as she noticed it, of course, bumping down into the physical and self-conscious with a laugh, to relax on the bed with the last shudder of climax relaxing into hot, languid, oceanic quiet—

—and with a blue hand on her hip, and Blue's breath caressing her shoulder, Morgan lay at last inside the dreams, thinking:

That it should have come to this: in so short a measure, not even two years, from empty to full, from alien to human, a paradigm of earth.

Which of us do I mean?

Both of us.

Like a work of art, completed. Perhaps not finished, no art is ever finished, but ready for the gallery. The gallery was far away, and the show was going to open far too soon. She snorted at the conceit. For some reason, perhaps only post-ecstatic well-being, this awareness of limited time did not give her the same dread it had earlier. She drifted back into the blue sleep.

❁   ❁   ❁

"Shit," said the grey man. "Where are they?"

"She's in the house now, sleeping. Blue is with her. They've been . . ." Jeffrey Bryant turned to pull up the auto-transcripts.

"Who gives a fuck what they're doing?" Mac said curtly. "Where the hell is *he?*"

"Daddy, your *language!*" said Salomé, and her shock might even have been real.

Jeffrey punched up chip locations. "Well, his chip is in his room. Let's see if he is. He seems to be . . . fuck me, man, he's in our ice! He's reading the logs!" Jeffrey and Salomé leapt to their hot terminals.

"I have to get over there!" Mac said.

"Daddy!" said Salomé urgently. He stopped at the door.

"Be careful! He's—"

"Yeah, I know. But *she's* there."

"With the Blue guy," Salomé reminded him

"Yeah, with Blue. Call Andris. He'll need to take charge here.

Call Ko. Get Ace over there with the hot key team. And get that little fucker the hell out of our system!"

Later, Salomé would remember that *"she"*, but right now she and Jeffrey were too busy. Mac, running down the corridor, saw a familiar face, said, "You, come with me, I need backup." She turned without question, followed him, and they ran for the parkade stairs. The strobing alarm started in Mac's earpiece as they reached his car. He passed Andris on the ramps of the parkade, both of them driving like maniacs in opposite directions.

✿   ✿   ✿

When Morgan woke again the night's candles really had burnt out, not just a quotation, and her bedroom was dark for all that the sky was lightening in the northeast—but streetlight backwash glinted rhythmically from the slowly spinning stained-glass circle which looked like black water, and coaxed lowlights from Blue's raven hair and glistening eyes. Morgan lay for a moment silenced by beauty. Like Rilke in the museum, she had perceived in one moment, many months ago, that she had to change her life, and now she revisited the stab of fear that had choked her the first time she saw the alien. Then, she had not understood what was needed, and feared the commitment: now, she was overwhelmed with love, down in the flood. *There is nothing that does not see you.*

She got up to go to Blue and in the yellowish, dim artificial skylight, she saw that it was tears that set the light afire in those eyes.

"Ah, my beauty," she said, "don't cry. You'll break my heart."

"Your heart is broken already," said Blue, "and now you taught me how to break mine."

"What's the matter?"

"I have to go back," said Blue, "and you taught me love. I don't know if I can go, now. I don't know how I'll bear it. I don't know how to be this . . . paragon of Earth any more. It's all a lie."

"I've never seen you like this," said Morgan, stupidly she felt, but Blue held her hands harder.

"No," said Blue, "because I just became like this. I just became an understanding of this. I have to leave you, and it is all for nothing."

"What do you mean? Why?"

With a minuscule tilt of the head, Blue turned on the light. Morgan's shocked irises strobed the familiar room first into the stuff of dream, then back out to normalcy. In the familiar glare, Blue's expression looked desperate.

"Listen," said Blue. "You know why I am here. To be filled with Earth, taken home, emptied, understood. It seems logical, right?"

"It has always seemed to me to be perverse and diabolical," said Morgan, "arrogant, rude, and exploitive. But on some level it is logical, I suppose."

"You have never said this."

"How could I say this? It would be like telling you your life was for nothing. And I couldn't do that. I love you."

"Logical. Hold on to logical for me, please."

"Okay, logical, I'll hold that for a moment."

"But think," said Blue. "Think what logic is in it. What we learned today, which shocked me so much—you didn't listen to the physicists, did you? Or the science fiction writers?"

"No, I was in the other room with the cute babes." Morgan's joke was just a thread.

"With the cute babes. I wish I had stayed there. I wish I had remained a babe. In the other room, they said this. They sat and said this, and they had no idea what they were saying to me. They said: *mathematics is not a universal language, it is a local grammar. A mathematician from Earth and an alien mathematician could spend their lives trying to even recognize that what they were trying to talk with each other about was mathematics. They have to build a symbology that has an agreed-upon grammar.*"

Morgan saw it immediately. "So the ones who made you will not understand you any better than they would have understood us if they had done this directly. They have made a mistake."

"And they have made it with my life. Our lives. Or say it rather that they have given us life and now they are taking it back to themselves for nothing. They wanted a Rosetta Stone, but you can't make a Rosetta Stone if you only know one language. The stone helps others understand what you already know. It isn't written so you can learn, because it can only be made to record what you already know. The correspondences you already know. Even if I have memories of another life somewhere in here, and they re-activate them, they will not line up into a translation table with the memories I have now. They will both be local grammars, with no way to integrate them."

"But maybe not. Maybe side by side they will line up."

"I don't believe that. I believe they will be alien grammars, and they will be chaotic to each other."

"Oh, my dear, I am so sorry."

"Yes," said Blue, "so am I," and began to cry again, tears refracting aquamarine glamour to Morgan, so that the blue sorrow fell from her eyes too, and the light broke into shards which Morgan dispelled with her own unconscious sharp cluck to the light switch. As her eyes adjusted, pupils widened into the liquid half-light, Morgan saw Blue hide face in hands and sob, and she pulled her friend's body toward an embrace that was as much an attempt to comfort herself as to soothe Blue.

"It has one comfort," said Morgan after a while. "It is the final proof that they are like us." At Blue's interrogative whimper, she chuckled despite herself. "They are fallible to the problem of point of view. They make the same errors of ego."

Blue sat up, wiping tears from cheeks with sweeps of fingertips, those graceful hands; Morgan pulled one to her mouth and kissed the palm gently.

"They leave things out, important things out of theories. They aren't the godly aliens of some science fiction dream. They are, if you will, human. They are molecular and finite, limited, as we are."

"This is a *big* comfort," said Blue angrily. Morgan laughed harder, and stroked the blue cheek to take away the offense.

"Listen, my darling," she said, "I think we have made it. I think we have finally come to the perfect moment of love."

"For us?—or yes," said Blue, "I think I understand. For them, right?"

"Yes," said Morgan. "For the first time, I really do forgive them. They are going to be so upset!"

Blue giggled, the silly sound Morgan hadn't heard since Blue's "childhood". "I see it," said Blue. "They will be so chagrined, so— so disappointed. I will have to help them."

"I'm very proud of you for that," said Morgan. Before she realized the wrongness of the scream from the door of the room, she had a split-second to be glad she had managed to finish her thought.

Then a hand around her throat, dragging her away from Blue and slamming her against the wall. Shrieking in her ear, vast shouting, roaring, desperate sweat standing out in struggle.

What John was saying was slurred nearly to incoherent *how dare you*, swearing *bitch animal pervert*, shaking her *wasn't it enough to be queer?* taking the violent straight line through hatred, *otherfucking bitch!* Even as she struggled against the knife, even as she absolutely, in an instant, refused to countenance being killed, Morgan thought gladly that she had done everything she wanted to do before death. She felt the blade cut her flesh like butter. Really *is* like butter, she thought angrily, pulling her hand back and kicking John's leg. She felt the pressure of his arm across her throat increase, then release, as Blue threw arms around his neck, full body weight pulling him back. Blue too was yelling, a hoarse unpracticed howl of anger. There were other voices, Katy yelling, *Drop the knife! Drop it!* and John swearing—swearing!— furious that his murder was being interrupted.

He expects me to co-operate even with this, she thought, wonderingly, furiously, and then she felt the cool air against her sweat-drenched body as Katy, Ace, and the two cops from outside pulled John away. She struggled to stand, feeling for the first time the shocking amount of pain in her hand.

Recalled to herself, but distantly, a tale told by an idiot, she looked down and was coolly annoyed at how wrong her hand looked, cut into two pieces like that, and bleeding hot dark red. With the other hand, she pulled it into its correct shape, held the burden of pain tight against her chest, and the blood stained her white silk shirt. Blue took her wrists and replaced her palliative hand with a hot blue grip. "Think!" Blue said urgently. "Think it shut. Hurry!"

Her blood was dribbling onto Blue's saffron silk sari. Morgan tried to pull it away, but Blue held tighter, and Morgan saw there was blue blood there too, and that the two bloods intertwined.

"You're hurt!"

"I can fix that. You have to help me fix you first, before your hand forgets being whole. Hurry!"

Together, they went into her hand and laced it together as it had been before, and Morgan understood the urgency when she felt herself adapting to the injury almost too quickly to reverse it. They did not fully finish before the forgetting happened, so there was still a shallow furrow, seeping blood, that took a series of butterfly closures and a bandage, put on by the police medic while across the room, other police fought to get John out of the doorway, his manic strength a reality (though the distant commentator within Morgan thought, *there seem to be a lot of clichés involved in madness*), until they had to call the medic over to sedate him, which he did as they read John the new Rights Code Warning, Mr. Grey of all people shouting it above John's wailing.

The medic turned to Blue and put another butterfly bandage-strip on the slice across Blue's face, but Blue pulled it off angrily. "You'll have a scar there if you're not careful," said the medic, seemingly indifferent to the magpie iridescence of the dark blue blood and the meaty lapis glister of cut blue flesh.

"I want a scar," said Blue, still angry. "This world is *supposed* to leave marks on me. I want something to *show!*" and Blue lifted a hand still stringy with Morgan's blood and rubbed the blood in the wound. Morgan thought of scarification rituals, and wished her own wound had been a little more Heidelberg, it was such an effective gesture. Blue caught the thought and laughed.

"I'm sorry, friend," Blue said, as the medic, unimpressed, pushed Blue's hands aside and placed another strip of adhesive. "I didn't mean to become so primal when I became human!"

Morgan gave a soft snort, and, hearing John protesting in something more like his usual whine, walked out into the corridor. She stood against the wall by the stairway and watched the grey man deal with John's petulant demand for a lawyer, a doctor, release . . . until Mr. Grey gestured impatiently for the officers to take him out.

When they reached Morgan, the police holding John by both arms, looking like something out of a television movie, and proud of it, all she could do was look at him. One of the officers was Ace, which Morgan realized for the first time was odd—hadn't Ace been transferred back to the Atrium? John met her eyes for a second, then turned his gaze down. She got the feeling, a familiar one with John, that he was going to scuff the toe of his shoe like a naughty schoolchild caught out of bounds.

"Why on earth . . . ?" she said reflexively.

"I can see you don't see it my way," he said.

"John, you tried to kill me. Am I supposed to like it? No, I don't see it your way." She paused. "Come to think of it, I never have. But videotape is different from all this, John."

He was silent.

"Isn't it?"

"No. Why should it be? Everything can be made into a movie if you use your head."

"Thinking life is a movie is a little different than playing director in other people's lives."

"You don't understand. Why should you? You haven't made anything."

Morgan thought of the struggle to remake her soul. She thought of Blue. Then she laughed, freely and with a gust of pleasure.

"I have made the world, John. What else do I need?"

Her grey man put his hand on her shoulder.

"Let it go," he said. "It won't make sense to him." With an impatient jerk of his hand, he ordered the officers to move John away.

Russ was standing in his doorway, sleepy and alarmed, dressed only in his sarong. The grey man looked at him irritably. "And you, you idiot. After what you did to the GovNet, I'll have to take you too. It's going to be a pain in the ass trying to defend yourself with your confession on tape, you fuckwit. Get your clothes on."

Russ, surprisingly, grinned. "Hey, Mr. Grey, we have the best human rights lawyers in Canada on retainer. You'll have a run for your money."

"Not my problem," said the grey man. "If I had my way, you'd get a medal. But I'm not the only one who listens to the recordings made here, popular mythology aside. Do you want to hit the cells in Asean drag? You'd be popular. Get your clothes on. Hurry. I'm in a real bad mood, here."

John was still there, swaying now, the tranquilizer robbing him of volition. Ace was having a hard time fastening the stun collar around his neck. "Didn't I tell you—!" began the grey man, but just then she finally snapped the buckle and they pulled John into motion.

"Goodbye," said Morgan automatically, then shook her head disgustedly.

"Goodbye," John said just as automatically, and his wide smile was automatic too.

Goodbye? She turned away into her room. There were splashes and spatters of blood—red, blue, and mixed in an odd rich plum color—on the hardwood, and the rug was wrinkled, but unbelievably there was no other trace of the conflict except on her shirt and Blue's. The sun, however, had risen, and was sending a low ray through the stained-glass piece. Morgan walked over to the window and touched it. Her finger left a mark in the dust that had settled on its surface in the many months since she had first seen it there. While she was rubbing it against her sleeve to clean it, the leather cord holding it suspended broke.

Now she began to shake and to cry, holding the little circle clenched in her hands. The warm hands surrounded hers, took the amulet away. She rubbed the tears away and looked at Blue, who now walked to the desk, looked in a drawer, pulled out the scissors.

Lifted a long lock of that hip-length blue-black hair, Blue cut it close to the head. Plaited it somehow with fingers too fast to show a pattern. Threaded the strand through the hole in the little mosaic, tied it, put it back into Morgan's hands.

"Here is your little world back," said Blue. With a half-sob,

Morgan took it, reached up, hung it on the little nail in the window-frame, and as she did so, she started to cry again, for the eternal breaking of her little worlds. Blue's arms encircled her, she was held again to the warm shoulder while she tried to puzzle what was going on with Russ, failed, felt the pain in her hand, thought of John's attack again, failed to find purpose.

What was he thinking? She shook her head. In the confusion, she had caught only a few of his snarled words. She would have to ask to listen to the tapes, but even then, would it make sense? Meanwhile, she felt the strangeness, so similar to the sense of loss with Jakob, so like another friend lost. But—*not much of a friend,* the relentless voice of her intelligence interjected; *all you've lost is what you thought he was. Which is your problem, not his.* Morgan snorted. *Okay, so I've lost a homicidal maniac. Great. And it's been his turn to do the dishes for three days. With Russ going too, now I suppose I'll have to.*

I'll do the dishes, Blue told her, but she was too tired to do more than snort again. Blue drew her down to the bed, lay down with her, warm against her from knee to neck, holding her. She relaxed against the comfortable form, felt the blue hand come to stroke her cheek, slowly and calmingly, like petting Marbl. Far away she heard the door of the room open, then after a brief rumble of voices close again. As quickly as that, she slept.

When she wakened, Blue was watching her, smiling.

"I was asleep!" *That's dissociation for you.*

"Yes." *But necessary, to rest.*

"But no dreams."

"There were some angry ones, but I took them away. I can give them back later. You were too tender right then."

"Blue, tell me, something I never thought to ask until now. If you learned nothing on the ship, how did you learn to project and receive thoughts? To reach into us like that?"

"I don't know. It started right at the beginning, but it was vague. When I saw you, it got sharper, so I knew I should try to get them to keep you. It became stronger and stronger after you taught me to dream, but it was kind of patchy, like storm clouds. Sometimes I just got thunder or lightning and no rain. I don't know if it was an accident, something caused by . . . I don't think I was supposed to have that effect."

"No. I imagine not. You were supposed to record. None of the others have it—"

The blue face closer and closer, the mouth on hers for a moment. "I love you, Morgan. Strange, it is terrifying, isn't it, this humanness? Much harder than people with knives, in one way. They are so simple. You just fight them. With this, you have to—surrender?"

She nodded and smiled. "Or, accept." She touched the face, then got up slowly. Marbl was lying curled up on the corner of the bed. Morgan ran a hand down the smooth fur.

"I expect there is something I should be doing with the cops. I've kept them waiting."

"I told them to come back later. Your grey man was very nice about it."

Glancing out the window, she was shocked to see she had slept the day away. Outside it was the gloaming, the heavy twilight Morgan used to hate. Now she only regretted the sun was no longer splitting through the stained-glass prairie. Blue was turned to Marbl, stroking her paws. The cat flexed her feet around the blue fingertips, tightened pawpad muscles to curl her toes tight against blue fingerpads, and purred.

"Morgan," said Blue quietly. "I think that soon they will be taking me back. I can feel something. Getting closer. I hope that telling you now was not wrong."

Morgan shook her head. "No, I think it is time to know everything. This can no longer be a house for keeping secrets." Blue nodded.

Morgan opened the door and went out into the world.

My home's across the Blue Ridge Mountains, and I never expect to see you any more . . .

Before they left town, McKenzie debriefed Morgan, Blue, and the others from the house.

"Make sure they don't kill him," Morgan said. "He's crazy. He needs treatment."

"Capital punishment is the new law of the land. He murdered three people, and one was a cop."

"There must be a way."

"This from you? He would have killed you."

"This from me."

"I'll do what I can."

Blue had another take on John: "He is broken. I felt it when I was touching him. Before then, I didn't know anything about him, but I felt a great deal when he was so wild. He is fully broken."

"What do you mean, broken?"

"I mean, not nutritional. Poison. The badness is all through his thoughts. There is nothing that does not act from it. To fix him, everything will have to stop and start again. Like what happened with me."

"Why the hell didn't you know this sooner?"

"Look—" said Blue impatiently, then stopped. "Listen to me. I sound like—"

"Don't try to distract me. I'm not the only one who wants to know. How you knew anything at all, how this ESP works—and why you didn't know right from the beginning. Give it your best shot, Bluebell."

Blue stood and paced in the small office, stopped to stare at and prod the crinkled Mylar surface of the wallboard. Looked in the shiny surface of the bookcase doors.

"Will you fucking *stop that?*" Grey snapped.

"I'm sorry," said Blue. "I don't mean to make you more angry. I am angry too. I do know why I never felt it. Because he never touched me before. He never actually put his hands on me at any time, ever. Such a small thing, and we didn't notice. It seems so stupid. I told Morgan this but she made sure you weren't listening then; I couldn't hear everyone the same."

"But you had this flash of insight. It's even on the tapes. 'So *that's* who it is.'"

"No. When we understood, just before he attacked, it wasn't because I heard him. It was easier than that. We just remembered everything he had said—and figured it out."

"Figured it out," said the grey man softly.

"Yes. Like you did. If he said that, did this other, lied about yet another thing, and we finally knew what he had said and done with each of us—it meant he must be—well—even pathological liars lie for a reason. But it was clear that he cared for no-one, and that he didn't care if what he did caused pain."

"Do you mean he is a psychopath?"

"Maybe. Or that he is just evil. The effect is the same. He thinks he is the king of the world."

"God?"

"Oh, no, John doesn't believe in God. He believes in vid."

✿   ✿   ✿

Later that week Andris saw Mac going by in the hallway and called him into his office. "I want you to remember the discretionary powers our watching brief gives us. I've been informed that this case is not to come to court."

"That's vigilantism," said the grey man.

"It's vigilantism if civilians do it. If we do it, it's *realpolitik*," said Andris. "Those are my orders. If you refuse to deal with it, I will have to, or else someone will supplant us."

"No," said Mr. Grey. "I understand you. This is my responsibility." He carried on from Andris's office to the lab.

A few days after that, he went to see John Lee again in his secure cell. He watched the monitor covering John's cell for about half an hour before he leaned over and turned off the central breaker. The whole floor was plunged into unrelieved darkness for a second until the emergency solar kicked in and the hard bleak emergency lights came on. The self-contained cell locks still glowed active, but the monitors stayed dark. Jeffrey Bryant, the tech on duty, nodded, leaned back in his ergonomic chair, looked at the ceiling, and turned on the chair's built-in massage function, which like the locks ran independently of the main power grid.

"Later, mon," he said tranquilly, and closed his eyes. The grey man went across the dim open space between the cells and stood before John's cell. Without opening his eyes, Bryant—Jeffrey; now that Salomé was sleeping with him, Mac supposed he would have to call him Jeffrey—buzzed the grey man into the cell.

As he had been doing for the last half hour under Mac's view, and for hours every day as Jeffrey and the others had reported, John sat in the corner making notes about his documentary. With no paper or pen, and knowing he was being recorded, he was merely murmuring them in a clear, low voice. He did not seem to have noticed the change in lighting.

"You might as well stop," said Mr. Grey. "The camera and tape are off because of the power failures."

"What about my civil rights?" said John.

"Dream on," said the grey man. "That was when you were civil. You are now in my hands. You have no rights." He thought of Rahim, his last *disparu*, who still cooled his heels down the hall; there was an eerie similarity of sociopathy, though as far as they could find out, Rahim had not murdered anyone in the service of his art.

"Time to tell the truth," said Mac. "And you don't have much time at that. The power outage will be over in ten minutes or so. What kind of shape you're in afterward depends on how fast and how smart you talk now, off the record."

John looked alertly at him. "Tough guy."

"That's what they tell me. Start with why you attacked Morgan."

John's look sharpened and a wily slyness infused it. "Ooh, I see. It's *Morgan* you care about. Not Blue at all. You have a case for Morgan! Don't you? You're not an otherfucker at all!" Seeing something in the grey man's expression, though Mac was sure he hadn't moved a muscle, John began to bluster. "Don't you do it! You're alone in here with me, you know. The odds are—"

Mac picked him up by the throat and the belly, his small hands like iron claws. "—even," John finished weakly, voice still on autopilot.

"You are lucky," said the grey man, "that I *am* civil, and that I am governed more by love than hate, and more to the point that I am in a hurry. I could kill you right now, but I don't have the patience for a cleanup. But I'll do it anyway if you jerk me around. I have absolute power over you. Do you believe me?"

John shook his head minutely before converting it to a nod—not very practiced at hard interrogations, where his wits and his charm weren't the only ingredient of success, Mac thought coldly. Mac slammed him a couple of times against the flaking pink bulkhead, almost idly. John was struggling now, so Mac tightened his left hand's grip on John's thin throat. John calmed gratifyingly. Mac let him drop back onto the pallet. "Do you believe me?" he repeated.

John nodded.

"Fine. Begin now." The grey man reached into his pocket and keyed the remote, so that at the desk the monitors would come to life, the recording start again. "Why did you attack Morgan, and not Blue?" he began.

"I didn't want to. I liked her. She was cute. Kinda mean, but I like that in a woman. She would have been good, once we got together. She was getting normal, too, with Sal, but Sal was threatening me, had to go. Luckily she went with Russ. But then it all fell apart. Russ started with Jakob, so she was going to get dumped for a guy. I got rid of Jakob but it didn't make her go back. She went to Delany. Then when Russ went with Delany instead of her, she had nobody else but me or the bug. And she didn't . . ."

"She didn't like you. But why not kill the bug?"

"There's always another bug if you do it that way. This way, she's dead, I don't have to worry about her, and bonus, the bug goes back home mad. Icky aliens stay away, etc. Besides, Blue had to be there at the end. For the documentary."

"You had it all thought out."

"Yeah. Sell it on vid and virch. Make me rich. It's a good plan."

"Ending with you rotting in jail for life."

"It'll be poignant. Within two years, there'll be a Free John Lee lobby. Six years, max, I'll make you a bet, I'm out."

"Except you killed a cop. If we let you get to a public court, you get capital punishment for that, even if not for Jakob and Yuji-san."

"Appeals, no problem. Cap-pun has been back for ten years, everybody's still hung up in appeal."

"You'll be on death row. How do you suppose your documentary will get finished and marketed? Criminals aren't allowed to profit from a crime."

"Oh, there are ways." John's eyes flicked sideways slightly, then steadied again, but with the tell, the grey man knew where John didn't want him to look—at the wall near where he sat, where with the plastic cutlery, he had been carving the plaster away from the lines of the cell's vid and power feeds. The feeds were starting to emerge from the wall like an addict's tormented vein. Mac's hand was still in his pocket, and he pressed the remote again, sending the recording back into the dark.

The grey man reached into the inside pocket of his suit, pulled out the syringe case. The injector inside it was one of the new type, far more secure than a needle. Easy to administer, and negligible risk of detection, or, he should be thinking, of infection.

John was suddenly still and, for the first time, showed himself afraid. "What is that, man? What are you gonna shoot into me?" He scooted back into the corner of the sleepshelf, pulled in his arms around his bent knees.

"I don't think you'll be making your vid," said the grey man. He reached out, pulled one of John's legs. John tried to kick him away, but Mac's hands were strong.

"Hey, come on, I got a news permit, I kept your stupid code of silence, I did everything right, I did it all by the book!"

The injector hissed. "When you learn how to read again," said Mr. Grey quietly, "I hope you read different books."

He pocketed the syringe and toggled the remote again. "Bryant," he said, "call the doc. He's going into fugue again. We can't get anything out of him in this state."

"Mr. McKenzie, the surveillance cutting in and out in the power failure, but I think I got some footage of him talking about who he killed."

"That will do. Buzz me out," said the grey man, and he walked out of the cell, leaving the door open for the doctors. Behind him, harshly lit by the greenish emergency floodlight, John still pressed into the corner, shaking, blinking, and safe.

At the desk, the grey man too was shaking. He reached for the breaker again, but Jeffrey gently pushed his hand away, turned the switch himself. "Look, mon," he said. "Power come back on with just me flicking the breaker. What's wrong with this system today? Just when you need it, a system break down."

Behind him, John, safe from capital punishment, blinked and swayed.

"Thanks, anyway," said McKenzie, and went up to pack for a country holiday.

❀   ❀   ❀

At the end of their time, Morgan wanted to make every moment with Blue count, make something special for her memories. She and Blue took Russ's white car and drove into the spring landscape, Blue in pinkface to avoid notoriety, Morgan with her hair severely in a bun and wearing sunglasses covering most of her face, and Mr. Grey a kind of Mr. Talbot in the car behind, with his bevy of angels to watch over them from afar. After a few hours, Blue drove. Another human regulation broken, Morgan thought.

She was tired, and very sad. She had had everything, what more did she want? *I want to keep it,* she thought. *One last obstacle to grace.*

I'm not practical, she thought.

"It seems to me," Blue said, "—or maybe these are thoughts that came from you, because I remember floating through them while we were tangled up in making love—that this state of being human has a built-in paradox. If I look in one direction, I can encompass infinity. If I look in another, I come up against my limitations immediately. It all made sense then, but now I think: so what is my capacity? Infinite, or bounded?"

"You ask easy questions! What do you think philosophers and skeptics have been studying for all of human history? That's why so many mystics try to transcend their bodies," said Morgan. "They want to leave the limitations behind. For me, there's an essential problem in that: we are what we are because of what we are. The infinite grows out of the bounded. Our minds and souls exist because our bodies exist, and our bodies are inhabited by our psyches. Leave one half behind and we are no longer human, and not inhuman in a way I admire. I want to integrate, not dis-integrate. Not that I'll have time in this lifetime, but I'm working on it."

At the lodge in the foothills where they would be staying the night, they sat on the deck and watched the sun set behind the mountains. The interface of earth and sky was so sharp that it looked like stage scenery against a cyclorama, a skycloth. She said this to Blue.

"But it *is* dimensional," Blue said, smiling.

"Oh, I know. You can ride forever and not reach the horizon. That's the 'infinite' in your equation. Think of it as a Cartesian grid. One axis is bounded at 1. The other goes out forever."

"But Cartesian grids are two-dimensional. Where's the third dimension?"

"In chaos." At Blue's quizzical look, Morgan held her hand up in the dusk. The golden lamplight from inside the lodge limned one side's contours. "Interfaces." she said. "Look. Three dimensions. Think of that figure in chaos theory—remember, I showed you the triangles accreting like crystals onto the side of that triangle bounded in a circle—remember its infinite coastline? We fill only the space we displace, yet our skins are the coastline. We are finite in displacement, yet we have an infinite interface with the universe."

"You are saying we are infinite beings."

"I guess I am. I sound like an evangelist."

"Well, it's good news to me."

Later, they snuck into the hot tub after the other guests were in bed. The sky was clear and the stars' light was unimpeded by human light sources. The aurora borealis played across the light-smear of the Milky Way.

The tub was large enough that they could float between the edges. Blue dragged the bubble-plastic cover across the water and told Morgan to lie atop it. The edges of the tub disappeared behind the periphery of her vision. Blue began to pull her around in a circle.

Suddenly she was afloat in the dark sky, spinning slowly amid the stars, falling into infinity, surrounded by the void: she was at peace.

✾   ✾   ✾

In the early morning Morgan and Blue went trail-riding with the other guests and Mr. Grey, who was being minder in a light-handed, distant way, on placid horses trained to put up with the vagaries of citified tourists. They were led by two wranglers from the ranch, a slim, wordless woman Morgan would under other circumstances have tried to flirt with, just to see her blush, and a tanned, compact man who only last night had been showing them his new computer equipment—but today he looked the perfect cowboy from a century ago. The woman and the other guests chose a shorter trail and the groups divided. Blue and Morgan decided, despite Morgan's awareness of the disadvantages of her small size and wretched condition of fitness when straddling the back of a mammal as large as this, to go on to the lookout at the top of one of the mountains that last night had been just two-dimensional cutouts. They were certainly real now, every bump and gully, Morgan thought wryly. But she was hoping the view would be worth it.

At some point in the ride Morgan realized that she was happy.

It was a state she had enjoyed so seldom in the last few years that she was like a bad swimmer come up for breath—she took a great gasp of this air that smelled only of musty spring grasses—and, of course, horse. The man who rode beside her, however, didn't notice that she had moved up a level. He was riding in a curiously balletic posture, with one gloved hand loosely holding the reins, the other reached backward to the rump of the horse, resting there. She wanted to ask him if it was unconscious, or just a friendly gesture to the horse, or if he was doing something calming, horsey and wise. She didn't speak.

Ahead, Blue rode with the same lumpy rhythm as she, but Blue learned faster, and even as Morgan watched she saw the alien looking attentively at the wrangler then adjusting seat somehow. Morgan envied the facility, aware as she was of the sharp impact of buttbones on saddle. Sitting down wouldn't be easy for Morgan tomorrow.

Morgan thought that the wealth of Earth humans had to offer Blue was all in this moment. *We become concerned with the artifacts we create to last past our deaths,* she thought, *but we lose these moments. We lose the integration of our souls within with our souls without.* This gentle motion through the stands of softly surrounding trees and thickets of bush, this was the cosmic motion.

What was civilization really but a relentless drive to conquer all this, subjugate it, prove human mastery over the inhuman beautiful supramundane? And when we have despoiled it, what do we have?

Her optimistic belief in the effect Blue's visit would have on the world was not based on the apocalyptic model. More the stone in the placid pool. Already everyone who knew Blue had changed, and the process was spreading. Something like it must have been happening with each alien, in at least twelve other places in the world. Soon, she thought, everyone who knew everyone who knew . . . and so on.

But she let even those thoughts slip away, impelled by the insight of wind and the inspiration of leaf into a state close to what she expected pure consciousness to be; the state was modified by the stiffness growing in her right leg, the superficial pain whenever she urged the horse to trot, to catch up with the others. Because of that pain, she kept her horse to a walk, amazed—with a city-dweller's easily-won amazement at mastering a simple physical skill—that she had learned how and did it so easily. She was also amazed to feel she liked the horse, leaned to pat its neck. She had never thought a horse would be likable. Now she knew better. She snorted slightly at herself.

The rest of the riders had long since passed through a distant gap in the ridge, and even the grey man had not looked back. There were only three of them now in that magic landscape: the rich carpet of grasses and flowers growing on the water flat, the surrounding trees, the glades of willow, the sluggish gleam of silver creek water, the sun through the pattern of cloud, rays in the distant smoky/dusty air. The horses were walking steadily at a rhythm that reminded Morgan of cowboy music; the man beside her was humming to himself or his horse. Blue was ahead, also quiet, also walking the horse.

The wind blows, the grass grows, the Shadow knows . . . Morgan laughed out loud and the guide turned a tanned, lined face to her and smiled. She felt the current of humanity run between them—and whether it was sensual, spiritual, tactile, whatever, didn't matter. They were together in their solitude.

Ahead, Blue glanced back, the make-up not masking the mobile smile, then looked ahead and pressed the horse into a canter, disappeared into the trees. The flurry of motion only deepened the peace.

"Are you cold?" said the guide. "You could wear my jacket."

"No, thanks," said Morgan. "I like the way it is."

His brown face turned to the trail. Whatever she felt, whatever he felt was not written there. Yet she felt they had said something. They rode on in silence.

✿　　✿　　✿

334

Home from the mountains, they settled into the house again. It was desperately quiet, without Jakob, Russ, and John. "There are ghosts everywhere," said Blue.

"Yes," said Morgan. "After a while, if you live long enough, the whole world is made of ghosts. Layers and memories, shapes that aren't there any more. I used to be so angry about that. I hated entropy."

"And now you are reconciled to it?"

"I don't think so," said Morgan. "But I'm reconciled to something. Being human?"

"Me too," said the alien.

That night, drying the dishes, Blue dropped one of the blown-glass glasses that had been Morgan's mother's. It shattered on the floor, and Blue stood amid the shards, visibly shaken.

"What is it?" said Morgan.

"I feel so old," said Blue. "Part of me is very tired. I think, Morgan, I think I am wearing out. I think there is a—statute of limitations, perhaps we could call it—on this body. My hands are aching. Like you said was arthritis. Like the grey man said. Maybe I should have let them test my body."

"How long do you have here?" said Morgan. "Can we count on a certain amount of time?"

"I don't know," said Blue.

That night, they moved together again in their ecstatic journey of discovery. Morgan felt like each touch of Blue's hand to her, each touch of her lips to Blue, each moment that their minds swirled gently below that event horizon, was a manifestation of the essence of their connection. "This is such an important part of how I love you," she said. "Embodied. In your self. A body. Like me."

"This is not the end," said Blue. "It is just one answer."

"Let us dream while we can," said Morgan. "Eventually it will be memory and imagination. I want to store it up."

"Now that we admit to all this love," Blue asked, voice that innocent inquiring alien again, light, "pastel Blue" thought Morgan with an inner chuckle, "will you mourn for me with the self-hate that you did for your parents?"

Morgan shook her head. "No," she said. "I have learned some-thing about love these last two years. I will not forget it."

"Memory will serve us both," said Blue with satisfaction. "My whole life has been learning you."

"Learning Earth," said Morgan, alarmed.

"It's the same thing," said Blue. "Go to sleep. I want to dream."

Their days were a delicate balance of waiting.

✿   ✿   ✿

"What will we do for money?" Delany asked. "Your maintenance allowance from the Atrium probably lapses with Blue's departure, and my disability's been cut again."

They were six today at dinner: the diminished household of three, Katy who was still with them for now, the grey man, and, of all people, Aziz, who'd dropped by with flowers and stayed to help make the rich clam chowder they were eating with toast and cheese.

"I don't know," said Morgan.

"I have a severance allowance," said Katy. "I could stay here for a while more and pay rent."

"But you want to move on," said Blue. "You have found that nice apartment."

"Yes, but if I can help . . ."

"Thanks, K., but I don't think you need to sacrifice your plans," said Morgan. "But I do admit it's been worrying me. There are fewer of us than before."

"Nancy wants a place to stay," said Aziz.

"But that has its problems," said Delany.

"Russ will be out on bail after the preliminary hearing Friday," said Katy. She looked sideways at the grey man but he said noth-ing. Delany turned to him.

"Come on, Mr. Grey, you can't keep us on the hook forever. Did he squid the home vid as well as the government channel? Will he end up charged as an accessory to murder?"

"No. The home vid was John all the time," the grey man said slowly. Delany sighed with relief and Morgan leaned forward. He continued reluctantly, "Russ has an unconscious signature that's not present on the house squid, and John liked to sign his handiwork with some pretty characteristic flags. Hester McKenzie and Jeffrey Bryant—our experts—have made their depositions to that effect. Russ did the gov vid though. He's proud of it. So, he'll be fine until the trial on the sedition charge."

"But he'll be unemployed," said Morgan. There was a short silence. The grey man laid his napkin beside his plate as if preparing to say something, but before he could, the alien spoke.

"You could sell your story to the tabloid media," said Blue. "You know. The videorazzi?"

They looked at the serene pale face in shock. "Well, is that wrong?" said Blue. "I will be gone."

"It's a point," said Delany.

"True," said Morgan. "They'll be plaguing us anyway, once they find out. Might as well get something besides aggravation out of it."

The grey man cleared his throat. They all looked at him.

"You were not willing to have CSIS pay your garbage fees but you will take a living from the slag media?" he said sternly. Morgan was about to speak when Blue laughed.

"That's funny!" said Blue.

"Yes," said Mr. Grey, and smiled. "But in fact, I have already given some thought to this problem. Unstable though the situation may seem, I have made an arrangement that I hope will transcend politics. You won't have to sell your story to the media—unless of course you want to. There will be a—service pension, shall we say. Commencing on Blue's absence."

"I won't be dead," said Blue brightly. "Make sure it isn't a survivor's pension, or you will have to wait seven years to claim it."

Morgan, Delany, and the grey man chuckled along with the alien, and Katy looked at them in shock. "The things you people find funny are so—" she said.

"Funny?" said Delany. For the sake of Katy's dignity, Morgan managed to stop laughing only a few moments later.

❀   ❀   ❀

"Morgan, is that you?" The voice on the telephone was Robyn's, sounding very far away.

"Where are you? You sound like you're at the bottom of the ocean."

"Not quite. I'm in Tibet, on a land line."

"Tibet?"

"Well, actually, we've just crossed the border into India. Twylla and I are helping get the new Dalai Lama out."

"You're *what?*"

"Oh, her grandfather is some kind of Buddhist guy. Priest. Whatever. So they needed some people with some money and goodness knows I have some, since that Tumbrel Stones deal."

"What on Earth are you talking about?"

"It was a stock market thing, never mind. I put some of your trust money into it too, though, so you have some money. I'll tell you all about it later. I just wanted to let you know the wedding is still on. You and Blue still coming?"

"You sound like you're wired."

"Yes, I *told* you I'm on a land line. I'm just really happy to be alive, you know? So I thought I'd tell you I was."

"I thought you were in Saskatoon."

"Well, I'm not. Can I talk to Blue?"

"Sure." Bemusedly, she turned the phone over to Blue and walked into Delany's room. "Robyn has just been in Tibet with the new little Dalai Lama. Tibet. That is so weird."

"So, he developed a secret life after all. I knew he couldn't be your brother and be so—"

"Boring?"

"Well, a little staid anyway."

"I am totally astonished. Apparently he has also made me some money on some stock exchange deal. Now *that's* tainted money!"

Delany chuckled. "But I'm sure it will come in useful. For little junkets to Tibet, sometime in the future."

"You think I'm going to develop itchy feet?"

Blue appeared in the doorway, grinning widely. "He says it's my fault he's there and not in his office. He says that meeting aliens makes you look at the world differently. He says—"

"I'm sure he does," said Morgan. "He just wants you at the wedding."

"If I'm here," said Blue. "If not, I already got his present. It's in my bottom drawer."

"When did you have time to shop?"

"Never mind," said the satisfied, secretive alien.

✿   ✿   ✿

One cool night they built the fire, and sat before it quietly. "I have loved this so much, Blue," Morgan said. "In case you don't know."

"I know," said Blue. "Thank you for saying so. I am so used to thinking that you gave me everything. I like it when you remind me that you think I have given to you also."

"But that is what is so complete," she said, thoughtfully. "I didn't know at the time, but I was getting as much as giving."

" 'Is this love?' " Blue quoted gently, and they laughed.

"A course of loving," said Morgan. "Not perhaps what the bureaucrats expected."

"Your bureaucrats or mine?" Blue said, and Morgan laughed.

"And a sense of humor to boot. I really do love you, Blue."

"I love you too," said Blue. "May I have some more of that juice, please?"

Blue reached out a hand with the other blown glass in it: Morgan's act of faith, after the other day, had been to make sure that was the glass Blue used every time. Morgan poured dark red juice into it from the pitcher on the table. The iridescence of the glass in the firelight, the darkness of the contents, made it look like melted rubies flowing as Blue drank deeply of its cool beauty. Blue settled back in the armchair and carefully set the glass on the flat arm of the chair. Marbl jumped up on Blue's lap and settled down, purring under the long blue fingers stroking her.

Delany wheeled in and Morgan poured more juice and handed over the plate of lemon cake.

"Thanks, love," said Delany, and they sat in companionable silence, watching the fire.

"Interesting," Blue said at last. "I have enjoyed this evening very much, even though we did little but sit and think."

"So have I," said Morgan.

"Tomorrow maybe we can—"

There was a pop, as if a fireplace log had released a reservoir of pitch. The cat's purring stopped. "Can what?" said Morgan, and looked up to see an empty chair. Delany drew in a shocked breath. The glass, pulled by the wind of a silent, subtle implosion of air, slid in from the arm of the chair onto the seat, then rolled off. Miraculously, it didn't break as it thumped onto the hearthrug.

Blue and Marbl were gone.

❀   ❀   ❀

"Gone? Gone where?" asked Salomé.

The grey man was silent.

"Gone *back?*"

He nodded. "As suddenly as the arrival. The ships were behind the moon or something. If we ever meet these people, the first thing they'll have to explain is that lovely *Star Trek* effect. Better than on vid. And not a trace in the air. The boffins are in ecstasy. How the bloody *hell . . .*"

He was sitting on the edge of his comfortable armchair, unable to lean back in it. He sprang up, began to pace.

"Dad. Dad! What is it?"

"I don't know. Well, I know, but it's stupid. Envy. Jealousy. Whatever it's called. Of what they had, of the possibilities. In the end, Blue actually wondered if there was a way Morgan could go too. But clearly there wasn't. Morgan's still here." He was silent for a moment. "But Earth has sent an emissary after all. Besides Blue, I mean."

"Blue was the alien. The emissary to us. How can it be an emissary to its own people?"

"That's a long story, kiddo, but believe me, Blue's only choice was to be human."

"Just like the rest of us."

"Yeah."

"But what do you mean about another emissary?"

The grey man looked at his clasped hands, then laughed a little and reversed them, pushing intertwined fingers, palms out, away from himself to hear the joints crackle. Then suddenly, he did laugh, throwing his arms wide, and if it was a bit hysterical, so what, he thought—but Salomé looked worried, though, so he relaxed a little.

"The cat," he said. "Blue took the cat."

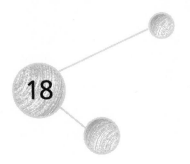

Finale, benedicte

18

Cast into the void again, Morgan struggled to regain her center. Sick, lonely, tired, and bereaved: she had been here once before. Then, it took years to come back. Now she had had only a few stormy days, but though she could foresee the end of the process, she could not teleport to that glimpsed resolution, had to live through the center of the storm.

Morgan had slept alone since Blue and Marbl left, her body unused to the absence of the small warmth against her back, the large warmth against her mind. The last few nights of Blue's body curled against hers had reassured them both against the coming departure, but she had thought she would have something left, even if it was only a small purr against the night. That Marbl could go where she could not go was another in the series of envies, losses, and challenges to accept.

She thought of Marbl's small absence to avoid Blue's large one; eventually the world would come rushing back to fill the emptiness. For the moment, however, she had the task of listening to the empty space, of encircling it with her mind, of deciding, in this infinity of loss and completion, where she would float, how she would remember, what she would accept, and how she would continue to live.

The difference between now and the beginning, when Occam's Razor had carved her hollow, was that although the void was as always the void, and she knew it with a deep and abiding and essential knowledge, yet she was empty no more. She had become an entity, a human, an alien, completed by everything she allowed herself to give to Blue. Everything she allowed herself to feel. She knew that the center would be there for her to find when she exhausted her pain with this wild and careless flying through the clouds of her grief.

She was lying on her bed, looking at the light through the circle of stained glass, reflecting on the changeless prairie and the landscape of change; Furbl, the new cat from the SPCA, was sitting on the trunk by the window, watching her, reflecting on whatever cats consider. *Probably wondering what he's been drafted into*, she thought wryly. Morgan would never share Blue's ability to listen to cats think, *so, what else is new?* she asked herself. *I couldn't talk to cats in a common language before, I can't now, what have I lost, really?*

Cheered and amused by this thought, she was smiling when Delany wheeled her chair through the door. She turned her head to extend the smile to her friend.

"How are you?" said Delany.

"I'm very sad, but I'm living," said Morgan.

"The thing I remember best," said Delany, "is a dream of flying. I was laughing at myself for having it. Even asleep I knew I was a fool, but I didn't care. I saw you below me. Your head was surrounded by blue dreams. I was so sad. I thought, after I woke up, how far you were from me. I knew I could never reach you."

"That was a true dream, a gift," said Morgan.

"Will I ever reach you?" said Delany.

Morgan felt a wave of exhilaration sweep her feet from some sandy shore. "Never," she said, her lips curving into a grin despite herself. "The question you want to answer is, does it matter? What a lovely time we'll have, trying."

Delany grinned too. "No, I don't think it matters."

"What will it be?"

"It's worth taking a chance on this."

"I don't know the future," said Morgan, "except in all the ways I don't want to. Knowing what they're going to do to me now. Knowing the media will give us no rest. All that."

"You don't have to make excuses to me. You always did want

to protect me from this darkness in you. Don't you think I know you? Don't you trust me?"

"You don't mess around," said Morgan.

"You have evidence that's not true," said Delany. "Think on that. Look at you. You think I don't know you're an existential fool, and you think I don't know that you love every solitary minute of it."

"But if you—"

"I can live with that; I never did want to be part of anything else. What autonomy means to a cripple—or as much of a cripple as I'm left after Blue's repair job. But I won't be patronized. You'd better open the lonely human race now, and let me in, or we won't last a second."

"We've lasted years already, my friend," said Morgan, "and we'll keep on. We are always faithful to something, in our fashion."

"Oh, well, that," said Delany dismissively, and Morgan laughed aloud.

"Well, *you're* gonna be all right," Delany said. Morgan laughed more.

"Nancy is downstairs," Delany said, "waiting to have the same conversation with you."

"And?"

"She wants to know when it's okay to come in."

"Oh, for crying out loud," Morgan said impatiently, "am I supposed to hold court? Have hours of reception? Turn into the queen of the moon?"

"Do what you want."

"Don't be cute," said Morgan.

This time it was Delany who laughed. "You'll be just fine. And to think we all worried about you."

"Come along, my friend," said Morgan. "Lets go down and commence our ambiguous future."

"Will you let Nancy rent the other room?"

"I don't know. It might be fun to take a crack at living with the younger generation. But she takes everything too seriously."

"What's going to happen with Russ?" Delany asked as they

walked and wheeled down the hall. "I miss him. This recent walk-about . . ."

"Well, tempting as it is to do a tidy wrap-up and say, he'll be back, I really have no idea. I don't know at all. The grey man says that he might get away without a jail sentence. But really I don't know. I hope we see him again."

"I'd like that," said Delany wistfully. Morgan looked down at her sharply, but Delany was intent on maneuvering her chair into the elevator.

"Come on," said Morgan, "I told you not to be cute."

"Russ and I spent a lot of time together the last few weeks. I seemed to him to be a lot like him. So, I just made it clear to him how I was and how I wasn't." Delany grinned. "It was kind of nice. Not that he really noticed. But that was what I liked. He was so wrapped in his own fog that he didn't bother to worry about how fragile I was. Yes," she repeated reflectively, "it was nice." And she smiled, not at Morgan.

"Well, well," said Morgan, and she reached down and lifted Delany's hand, and kissed it, fingers and palm. "The magic healing fingers." And she bent and kissed Delany, and thought, *the world is full of fools like me*.

Which by a backward wynd confirmed to her that the world was full.

The elevator bumped to a halt, Morgan pulled the door open, and she went out ahead of Delany to the living room where Nancy sat, where Nancy rose to meet her, and to smile and hug her tightly.

"I was afraid you'd go away again," said Nancy.

Morgan felt Nancy's arms around her, not as a shield against adversity, but as a symbol of the responsibility involved in rejoining the human race. Delany she knew would be fine, Delany in fact insisted on being independent, but Nancy had already once demanded salvation from Morgan in a form Morgan couldn't give. She felt the tension just below the surface, the tension that lingered beneath the comfort, which meant: *If I let my arms remain around her too long, as long as I would with a friend when I needed to cry or be comforted, Nancy would take that moment as an invitation to camp again in the middle of my life. No, I don't think I will be able to find a safe space for her here.* Morgan had the weight of all her life ahead of her, to keep making these tiny adjustments, these minute compensations, these gestures in deference to reality.

"Again?" said Morgan.

"You know what I mean."

It was the human paradox again, the infinite along one axis, the other bounded by one—one step, one vision, one real world.

So she opened her arms and thus signaled that Nancy must let her go, and only Morgan felt the double meaning.

"It doesn't matter," said Morgan, "everything is going to be all right," and felt the doors opening in her heart.

"I know that," said Nancy.

"I wasn't telling you," said Morgan.

     ✿   ✿   ✿

Morgan still floats in the void. It has always been there; she will always live there. Like the intimate other alien who is now away in the vacuum of space Morgan is nowhere, everywhere, and alone—

—but she remembers, and she can see and dream. She will not dream with Blue again, and she will have her time of mourning as she feels Blue taken apart until no trace remains of that beloved consciousness, that pale strong fire. She cries for Blue, for the void, but not for herself. She has stopped blaming the cosmos for her pain, she has taken it into herself, she has eaten its bitter flavor beside the sweet taste of understanding. She had taken them both for her daily fare, she is content.

Content in a way where she does not lose her anger, her sorrow, her pain, her love, but gains it instead, along with the rest of her alien, her all-too-human birthright.

     ✿   ✿   ✿

The doorbell was unusually *deus ex machina*; Morgan knew who'd be there before she opened the door. Her Mr. Grey was wearing

347

a sweater and corduroy slacks this time. Morgan was almost shocked to see him like this, somehow expected the suit again, as at their first meeting. She stood looking at him and his companions without speaking.

"Hello," Blue Suit—Kowalski—said nervously.

"Shut up," said Morgan's friend, enemy, or ally. Which? Friend, she supposed. He was silent too for a moment.

The stranger with him said, "Are you ready for us now?"

"This is Andris," said the grey man. "He's my boss. He'll be taking care of your debriefing."

"Debriefing? What about you?"

"I have . . . too personal a relationship with you. Someone objective has to take over now."

"Don't worry," said Andris. He was a solid, square-faced man with wavy black hair and beard, both heavily shot with white. He looked like a lion photographed in black-and-white. He looked like the patriarch of some prairie religion. He looked trustworthy. On principle, Morgan didn't trust him—but she would have to learn how.

Morgan walked out onto the porch. "Come here," she said, and walked down the steps and across the grass. From behind the wrought-iron fence they could see the city. She opened and led them through the ornamental gate which was kept closed now that the tall weeds had been cut away and the hinge repaired, all no doubt by the minions, faceless to Morgan, who answered this grey man's powerful word.

She walked across the road until she stood on the brink of the valley. Andris and the grey man walked beside her silently, Andris giving Kowalski, trailing them, a piercing look to stop comment.

"Look," said Morgan, and swept her arm across the decorated horizon's plane. "What do you see?"

"What do you see?" said Andris.

"When Jakob first saw this," she said, "he said, 'It looks fine, from up here!' That was why he came to stay with us. He felt safe. In the end, he learned the hard way that there's no safety. That's what I learned. I wanted to live quietly, but I made one motion in the direction of life, and my resolution exploded. Now I've got nothing to keep me safe."

"Do you want a guarantee from me?"

"What would it be worth?"

Kowalski started to speak, but the grey man said, flatly, "Nothing. Come with me, Ko," and they walked back across to the car.

"Yes," said Andris.

"Well, that's about what I expected. Don't worry, I'm very reasonable really."

"You can't go around with a chip on your shoulder," said Andris. "Neither can I. My people and I have jobs to do."

Morgan looked out at the city. "So do mine," she said, "all of them. Can't you see them? Every life in its balloon of context, all living tangled up in one another. Everyone looking for the answer. Caruso's voice teacher couldn't sing a note, you know."

"Probably had perfect pitch, though," said Andris. "You have to know what you're listening for, as well."

"I'm not a rebel," said Morgan. "I'm not. I just can't live any other way."

"You know I can't promise to understand," he answered, "but I'll try to listen. But you have to try to talk."

"That's very formal," she said, " 'A limb for the risk of a limb.' "

"I'm trying to be fair."

"I'm trying too."

"Yes, you are trying, sometimes. Mac has kept me posted. Do you think," Andris said, looking out as she had done, "that you are responsible for all this? That you control something there?" His hand snapped at the city skyline.

"As much as I ever did," she said. "Do you see where the city police have a cordon and a tape line down there? A woman was taken at knifepoint and raped there last night, and then he cut her, and she was lucky to get away with her life. They were within a stone's throw of the greatest show on earth, and all he cared about was to revenge himself on her for the ills of his life. Maybe you or I could have told him why that wouldn't work, but would he care? Maybe he enjoyed how that knife went like butter through her throat—and now I know—" she waved her hand with its hairline scar—"that it feels exactly like that stupid analogy, from her end. Maybe it worked for him, in the short run. But she wasn't saved by the New Consciousness that was supposed to follow the millennium, nor by whatever human transcendence is supposed to follow First Contact. We can barely save our own lives these days. But we manage."

"Are you so angry?"

She looked at him directly. "Of course I am. Do you expect peace on earth, or even in my heart? Just because a few aliens were sent down to become human for a while, and one came down here? Blue wasn't a Messiah, whatever parallels the tabloids made. Everyone's life is the stuff of which myth is made, when you look at it close enough."

"What do you want?"

"Everything," she said simply. "Just what I always wanted, but I was afraid to admit it before. Now I accept that I couldn't go with Blue; I'll never even walk on the moon. But I want it. All of it. From Goddess to green cheese to grey rock. And everything that comes with it. And while I am still alive, I wouldn't mind being able to walk with a lover down the street hand in hand no matter what sex we were. I know that would have made my father happy. He said that all human ills were caused by one bunch of people trying to make the others think like them. What do *you* want?"

"I learned to want as little as possible. So as not to get disappointed too much."

"It's a hard creed around which to live your life."

"Well, life isn't easy. What's wrong with that?"

"Nothing," she said, and stepped up to him so she could put her fingertips to his face in an unconscious parody of Blue's touch which she would use for the rest of her life to emphasize what was close to her heart. "But I have had a dream come real for me, and live in my house, and become as close to me as I am to myself. When I've had a moment like that it's hard to remember even the moment of my own death."

"Do you want special treatment on that account?"

"Do you think we have to make deals? Can't you just accept me on the riverbank here, let me tell you how I see the view?"

"I'm not the only person who wants something from you, you know that as well as I do. If it was only you and I we would soon talk ourselves around to some kind of understanding, as you and Mac have done. But you know you'll be different things to everyone, and they're not all likely to be tolerant or even friendly. You aren't exactly what some people think of as an ambassador for Earth."

"I appreciate you making that clear." She couldn't help the edge in her voice.

"I'm trying to be honest. Don't make fun of that."

"I'm not making fun of you. But do you think we'll ever meet across this valley?"

"I don't know. Is that what's vital? Today, I mostly care about what happened when the alien was here. I want to know what went on. Not what's recorded. What really went on. *That's* what makes you different, not your sexuality or your roommates or your *philosophia.*"

He walked a little farther, then turned back to her. "When I was first in the force, I used to have to take down reports of UFOs. We used to put them on file and now and again we'd correlate them with other files and in the end we had a great big pile of nothing. If you and I argue about this, we'll end up with a great big pile of nothing. I can't pretend I couldn't make it hard for you. You know the generous mandate that went with Mac's job? Well, I gave it to him. I have discretionary powers he only dreamt of having. But I'd rather use them to make things easier for you."

"That's fine as long as I do what you want. But if I get out of line?"

"Can't you trust me?"

"When you are doing your best to convince me we come from different worlds?"

"Do we?" He gestured around the horizon as she had done. She laughed.

"Well done!" she said. "Okay, I agree that if this has any point at all, it's that we're now one world whether we find it comfortable or not. I spent a year learning the lesson: eschew comfort."

"You speak so well. These tapes should be a helluva fine production." Andris gestured to the grey man and Kowalski, and Mr. Grey walked back across the street to join them.

"Maybe we can make a hit movie of them. After all, there's all that footage of John's that Mr. Grey here confiscated. Hester McKenzie can direct."

Andris laughed out loud. "She's Mac's daughter, you know. And she's already had some truck with those tapes. All right, Ms. Morgan, world citizen, here we go. You without the chip on the shoulder, me without . . ."

"Without preconceptions. Maybe we could even learn to like each other."

He smiled, tidily as a cat. "You hate being an optimist, don't you?"

Morgan grinned. "You got it, mister. But it's a fate forced on me . . ."

"As if fate could force you to do anything, on balance," he said, "I *have* been listening to you for two years," and Morgan laughed and laughed. He went on, "I'm the one who sent Ace here, you know. I thought it might be good for her."

"Was it?"

"I don't think it made much difference," said the grey man.

"We'll see," said Andris. "She's young. There's still time."

"I think," said Morgan, "that I *am* ready for you now. For what it's worth."

"We'll decide what it's worth."

"No," said Morgan, looking out into the empty air of the valley, "no, we won't. We're not that important."

Morgan jerked a thumb at Kowalski. "Keep the queer-bashers away from me. If you can."

"I can't promise," said Andris. "After all, it's the real world."

"You said it," she said. "Welcome."

✿   ✿   ✿

The grey man watched Andris and the man in the blue suit get into the car and drive away. After the car had hummed out of sight he turned to Morgan.

"With Andris and Ko fighting over you, I might have to move in here," he said. "To protect you." And for the first time since he had known her, he smiled at her fully, grinned even: not the puckish smile of the manipulator, but an openmouthed, relaxed grin of joy. She smiled back with the same fullness, said lightly, "There are a lot of empty rooms."

"I'd have to have Blue's rooms, if you don't mind. I don't want to live where John lived."

"No one does." They walked back toward the gate.

"My name," he said, "is Roger Terrence McKenzie. A.k.a. Mr. Grey."

"Welcome. Do I have to call you Rog now? Or Mac, like the rest do?"

"I'm like the rest of you: starting again. Maybe I should go by a new name now. Terry should be ambiguous enough to fit in, don't you think? Though I suspect I will have to bow to the inevitable and let you call me Grey for the rest of our lives."

"That will be fun," she said. He made a face and she laughed at him, her small face looking for a moment like a laughing river otter. "Give over," he said then. "You're teasing me."

"Yes, Grey, my friend, I always tease you. The world teases you. The Universe is a tease."

"I have to go. There is work to do. Wolves to keep from the stoop. I have to deal with the paperwork on John. Set things up for your tête-à-têtes with Andris. Deal with the flood from the outer world."

"Before you go . . . Where did John come from?"

"We don't know yet. He's in fugue now, and can't tell us. They say he might never recover. He certainly isn't John Lee. John Lee was a gay Chinese video technician in Vancouver."

"Was?"

"Died, of AIDS they thought, fifteen years ago. He was about twenty-five at the time. Back when people were still dying of it."

"Instead of living miserably in quarantine in government

health-care hostels," said Morgan automatically, then: "Fifteen *years?*"

"Yeah. Our boy would have been about twenty then—a bit younger. We don't know what happened, but we know that when Lee died his papers and his equipment were stolen, and his place ransacked, while he was still lying on the bed."

"Murdered?"

"No, the Medical Examiner's investigator went over everything about six times, just in case. But the scenario was that he died alone, and then his place was looted by his neighbors."

"Nice."

"Yeah. But this puts a different spin on it."

"Yeah, but . . ."

"But why?"

"Yeah."

"Getting away from something, or just—the obvious? Apprentice scenario? Or street kid taking advantage of a dying gay man who fell for the kid? Kid resents it, takes the stuff, gets interested? Shows a real hatred of the original Lee. Homophobia is just a kind of xenophobia, after all, same as misogyny. It would fit with what he did here. Let's just use the technical terminology. Nutcase."

"Yeah, we use that technical term in my line of work too. But if he's really in fugue, not faking it, it's not accurate, is it?"

"No, it isn't." Grey looked down, annoyed with the secret he'd be keeping for the rest of his life. "But he *is* a mess. If this case ever gets to court after the doctors are done with him, I'd be surprised. But I have to get the paperwork airtight, in case I'm wrong. I wish I could be wrong. I *want* him to be accountable."

"So do I, but maybe not the same way. I want him to understand what he did. Really understand."

"Which would have had the effect of actually *driving* him crazy, if it could happen."

"Which seems to be where we started." Morgan sighed.

"With a psychopath who wasn't crazy . . ."

"But on whom we wished both feeling and madness."

"Well, putting it that way . . ."

"Yeah. We live in a strange world, Grey."

✿   ✿   ✿

"Here's the list of people looking for an exclusive story, a book contract, an interview, an exposé . . ." The grey man threw an untidy, two-inch-thick file and a cube of memory down on the hearth rug. Beside it he threw another, thinner file in a tiger yellow folder. "And here's the ones you can't ignore. The meeting with the Prime Minister. The audience with the King of England and the Spanish Pope, as they call him, which always bothers the hell out of me."

"You have such an orderly mind," Morgan said wryly.

"He's from Central America, dammit. It's not Spain! People are so imprecise. Never mind. The Secretary-General of the UN wants to talk to you about Blue's sojourn, and about the activities of your brother in Tibet. As an expat Tibetan himself, he has sympathy with the new Dalai Lama's predicament."

"Predicament! Held almost a captive in that house in India. Can't even travel to the monastery where the old Dalai Lama lived. Poor little kid. He's so lonely. Robyn says half the people around him can't even speak Tibetan."

"Well, perhaps you can help your brother on this. This guy has made the UN into a world player again by sheer force of will, and he can probably do something useful about something as simple as that situation. He did win the Nobel Peace Prize, after all. Speaking of which, there's a letter here from them . . ."

"No. No." Morgan pushed her hands out in front of her. "Not me."

"No, not you." She looked at him.

"Us," he said, grinning like a cat with cream. "All of us. You, me, Delany, Russ, anyone with significant contact with Blue in this house. Including Aziz, the little twit. I must tell Rahim. He'll be furious. He'll think it should have been him."

"Are you ever going to let him out?"

"Oh, sure. I've got his cell fully wired for incoming vid now. I'm letting him catch up on developments. But I won't let him out until his part of the story is old news. I don't want him

355

catching the media wave and morphing himself into a hero. I'll wait until his *cousin* is a hero. The 'fucking dancer faggot' he hated so much. There is justice, after all, despite Heinlein's contention."

A few minutes later Aziz emerged from the attic studio he now called home. As soon as he opened the door, the light dull pounding they had been hearing all morning intensified. If they could hear it two storeys away, the music must be thunderous close up.

"He's going to make himself deaf," Morgan said. Aziz wandered downstairs and into the kitchen where Morgan and Grey were making sandwiches. As he walked he tugged earplugs out and tucked them into his pocket. Aziz was dressed in Jakob's workout clothes. He was letting his hair grow.

At least he's still combing it, not letting it dread, thought Morgan. *There's a limit* . . . "Hi, kiddo," she said.

"Hi," said Aziz, abstracted, rummaging in the breadbox. "What's the what's the?"

"Oh, nothing much. They're going to give us all the Nobel Peace Prize."

"Cool," Aziz said, opening the refrigerator door and leaning in. "Do we have any tahini?"

"He's already deaf," said the grey man, grinning.

"I heard you," said Aziz. "It's cool. I get it. Now I'm hungry. How about hummus? There are some pitas here, but there's nothing to put with them."

"Look at the back of the top shelf," said Morgan. "And here's a tomato to chop. Goodness forfend that a Nobel laureate-to-be should have nothing to put on a pita."

"Look, I *said* it was cool. What else can I say? I'm busy. I'm *working.*"

"See?" said Morgan, turning to Grey. "That's what it's really worth."

"Yes, yes, I get it too," he said. "Let's go back to work. There's a great deal more in that stack that you have to know."

✿ ✿ ✿

Later that afternoon, over tea:

"You know," Morgan said to Grey, "there has always been a part of me that wants to do something . . . different. Something . . . worthwhile. A small, stupid version of the Mother Teresa thing, if you like. Not the Christian part. The other part."

Grey looked skeptical. "As if what you did with Blue wasn't worthwhile? What version? Of what part?"

"I saw a movie of her life when I was about nine, and I only really remember one bit of it. She had just finished assuring a safe home for a bunch of multiply handicapped orphans. She had just calmed one of them from a terrified agitation with her rough, loving touch. And then she was sitting beside his bed and she glanced down and saw that the bedframe was dirty, so she picked up a cloth and began to wash it. I always remembered the simplicity of that moment. It made her a big hero of mine from then on. That's what I want to do. Go somewhere where there is that mindless need and begin washing things."

"Oh, you wanted to make yourself a saint? Oops, you became a secular hero."

"No, I said it wasn't a religious desire. I wanted to be invisible. Non-existent."

"In the mystical sense? I don't believe you. That is the opposite of who you are becoming. You are the probably most 'existent' person I know."

"Oh, exactly. I've completely failed to detach. That's what will make it so interesting to try. And after all, now that Blue's gone and I'm living on a pension—"

"Albeit a tiny government pittance," he teased.

"—which my brother has heavily augmented with ill-gotten capitalist gains. Anyway, now I am free. I can do anything now, you see."

"I don't see. You are about to become one of the most *visible* people in the world. You will be more famous than John Lennon."

She laughed, but he shook his head and went on, "You will be completely immersed in an existence that will be defined and constrained by others for a very long time, perhaps your whole life."

She scowled at him. He continued relentlessly, "Seventy-one book offers. One hundred and thirty-three vid and virch offers for exclusives."

"What are you talking about? We logged more than that."

"That's just for *me*. People are hungry for meaning. Hungry for—ecstasy if you will. Enlightenment. They will not be interested in helping you with the goal of spiritual non-existence or any other kind."

"Oh, bloody hell. That's so annoying."

"But it's true."

"No, I mean it's annoying that you're so—right. I can see my next few months looming—each day more insane than the other. Thank heavens the world has a short attention span. And all of this so unnecessary. Watch and listen to the tapes. Figure it out. It's all so self-evident."

"To us maybe. We were here. The world will disagree with you. You will discover that a public figure can do a lot of capricious things, but be invisible isn't one of them."

Morgan looked at him sternly. "You know better than that. There will come a time, much sooner than anyone is likely to admit, when my actual presence will not be necessary to the machine."

"Yes, I suspect you may be right."

"And when that time comes, I have decided what I am going to do," said Morgan. "After all this is over."

"Is it ever going to be over? Unless you get amnesia." He squeezed lemon into his tea.

"You know what I mean. When the first frenzy dies down. As soon as I can, I am going to go around and meet the others."

"The others?"

"Stop that. You sound like a parrot. The others who were with the other aliens. Blue was one of many. They haven't found all of them, I bet, but I read about the rest after they were all taken back, and maybe—now—I'll be able to communicate." She took a long draught out of the mug she was nursing, and savoured it. "Unless Blue really was the only one who became so—well, you know."

"Yes, that's a possibility. For you to do, I mean. We know something about the others. Perhaps Andris and I can arrange for you to know also, and you can go on from there."

"That would be lovely, thank you."

"You have no idea how lovely—and how rare."

"Oh, I'm sure I do. Give me credit for paying attention all this time."

"Oh, I'm sure I do. You may as well know now. You are the only one who successfully formed a connection with one of the aliens. Four of them died, it turns out. Others were very ill before they were taken back. What you know will be needed."

"But I can't make it my whole life. There isn't enough there for that. I will have to move on."

"Would you like some company?"

She looked at the compact, slender, elegant grey man with his small hands. He was looking into the basket made of those hands intertwined, and his eyes were not visible to her.

"You?"

"Why not?"

"Part of your job?"

"I could pretend so."

"Is this a proposition?"

"We could say so. And wouldn't be far wrong." His small, charming, three-cornered smile was directed at his teacup.

"Yes," she said. "I would like company. But you're joking, right?"

"No."

"It's a little clichéd, don't you think," asked Morgan, "you and me ending up together?"

"And we may not, though I can't imagine why not," said Grey. "But who else but the people in this house have any idea what has gone on here?"

"Your job . . . ?"

"I won't have one by then. Arranging your debriefing and seeing you through these next stormy months will be my last assignment. I'm retiring while I'm ahead. Andris will support me from above, he would support anything I chose to do now, but his years on the job are numbered too. The old guard is being forced out from below. The new era, guys like Kowalski—Blue Suit, you call him, which is about all he is—and the late great Boy Wonder—you have a gift for naming these guys, it seems—and young guys like Ace are in favor of 'going back to the basics of policing'. None of them remember the injustices of that time—the young ones weren't alive then—and they find reminders boring. People like Katy and me are being pushed out, if not by conscience, like her, then by the exigencies of power."

"You are fun to listen to. Do you know, you often speak in complete sentences?"

"So do you. Of course, mine are more reasoned and considered . . ."

"And mine are more erudite. So, who wins?"

"You surprise me," he said. "Have you actually developed an ego?"

"I'm not sure. Are they catching?"

"I must introduce you to my daughter Salomé. You would find affinity. She's the video artist you talked about earlier to Andris. You know her as Hester McKenzie."

"John was always talking about her. But you said Salomé."

"That's her other name. She uses her first name professionally. She keeps Salomé for us; I don't know why, really."

"Ask her."

He chuckles. "That's what she said about you. *Tell her. Ask her.*"

"She sounds smart."

He laughed. "She is."

"Why did you call her Salomé? I mean, in the first place."

"Because she had unlimited power over us. Parenting does that to some people, makes you heartfelt captives of your children. It did to me. She could have had my head on a platter if she wanted. She still could. I hope she never finds out."

"You think she doesn't know?"

He glanced at her sideways, eyes narrowed. "She certainly never acts like it."

"Oh, don't give me that cop look," said Morgan. "When you

know you have that kind of power over someone you love, you work very hard to make sure you never even let on, let alone exercise that power. You should know that."

"I have never had that sort of power over anyone."

"Yeah, right. And I'm not queer."

"Except maybe my wife, and she died."

"You have it every day in your job."

"Oh, that." He waved a hand aside, dismissively.

"Yes, that. Absolute power. Life and death. Life and safety."

"But that wasn't over lovers."

"I didn't say lovers. I said over people you love. Can you honestly tell me there wasn't anyone you loved in this house?"

To her shock, he colored slightly and his glance flickered away from her.

"Oh, shit," she said. "I didn't mean . . . I meant Blue."

"Yes," he said. "Blue too."

She felt for a moment almost disappointed, at the thought that this one too, whom she had respected, might have fallen for the mystique that she, in this recent life as Morgan, not in her past life as merely Constance Shelby, seemed to have created without intending to. "I can't just be myself any more," she said irritably.

"Not in the slightest," he said, and stood. "Don't forget, you have done all the things for which we admire you."

"Oh, shut up."

"Come here," he said, "and I will prove to you that I don't hold any illusions about you."

"Maybe later," she said, but she walked hesitantly toward him. He simply put his arm around her and pulled her close to his chest. She could feel his chin rest on the top of her head. She drew her head back and he kissed her softly, his lips tender and closed against hers, so quickly she hardly had time to kiss back before he withdrew and pressed her head against him again. She sighed with the outflow of tension, or perhaps it was the inflow of another layer of peace.

"You *are* short," she said. "How did you ever get into the Mounties?"

"They changed the height and weight requirements to remove the bias against women and non-Caucasians. And short people. They're probably changing them back next year. Brand-new back-to-basics cops have to be big."

"More tea?" she said.

"No, thanks," he said, and she heard his cup click onto the Arborite tabletop before his other arm completed the hug; Morgan returned it. "Who knows?" he continued. "I'm not making any plans. Let's go around the world first. And perhaps I'd better get to know Delany better."

"Good idea," said Morgan, but she didn't move for a few moments. Then: "I have to get ready for the news conference."

Delany wheeled through the door. "The first of the camera crews is here," she said, and wheeled over to them.

After a moment Morgan pulled away from Grey, holding his hand, and, standing between her two lovers, put her hand on Delany's shoulder. Delany lifted her shoulder and lowered her cheek to press Morgan's hand for a moment. Morgan smiled at her, and Delany looked the grey man up and down, not quite smiling, but almost. "So it's going to be you, is it?" she asked softly.

"Me who does what?" he said.

"Provides the balance," said Delany.

"I hope so," he said, and he too didn't smile yet. Morgan, however, knew he would, and so, by her glinting glance, did Delany, wheeling her chair around on a dime to lead the way out of the kitchen.

journal:

How the aliens came to us and left again. What it was. I dream about that long pale face, those feverish warm hands. I dream of cats, that curl up on our chests at high summer, to warm themselves. That blue gaze, too open to be so enigmatic.

Like the cat that after many years learned to play, to turn my shoes upside down in search of demons, I am learning to see the demons, learning to play with them, thinking there is something vital in that change, something more innocent than passion, if only I could find it, turning the world upside down, hoping that whatever falls out will be fun to play with. Or even, will be the answer, the real reason why that blue touch on my face was burning, burning through all reasoning, burning away the demons.

Where am I bound? If Blue's emissary to the stars, I'll be emissary to this world. Hard work but not as hard as it was to trust when those blue hands came toward my face and I thought I would die if Blue touched me. Maybe I did. Don't some religions call pure consciousness "self-destruction" and long for it as fiercely as I longed to be alien?—and here I am, human again, and I don't even mind, strangely enough.

Sometimes I am tempted to write as if Blue were going to read my journal, or dream as if Blue were going to share my dreams, or live as if Blue were going to meet me when I am old, to share memories of our ordeals. But Blue is gone, and I am more alone than I ever prepared to be. Blue is gone, vanished into the dusky sky, vanished into the night the color of those eyes, the color of that hair, the color of that mind, the color of nothing. Gone along that path I cannot follow, even with death. Up there in that strange mothership they will take Blue apart more quickly than we worked together to put that beautiful person together, and I can only hope it is with as much love. Meanwhile here they will take me apart too, and not easily, and not with love, by and large anyway, and all I will have when I am left alone at last will be the common memories, the story I will have told until I have only memories of a memory. Of love. Of a lover.

Ah. Love, I will say, and they will think I mean sex. Well, we did try everything eventually, but there was a time in language when "lover" meant one who loves, and one who is loved, and that's how I want to use it. I did my best not to be trapped into admitting it, but for Blue I admitted that I love, that I love the world in all its strange and alien splendor. And now it is easy to admit it to anyone, for Blue is gone, and if I learned anything from what has been done by those who hate, I learned that there's no sense in keeping any secrets.

The only way to be strong is to be completely vulnerable—

—and if they believe that, I can tell them what it was like.

Acknowledgments

A work of fiction is always unconsciously pieced together in part from the ragbag of real experience, but that process can happen consciously too. In this book, I have taken a certain gleeful pleasure in salting the mine with some references to reality. Among others, the artistic works and contributions of (in no particular order) Edouard Lock and La La La Human Steps (especially *Businessman in the Process of Becoming an Angel,* 1984), Ferron, Leonard Cohen, Caetano Veloso, Earl Klein, Rachmaninoff, John Crowley, Bob Dylan, Colin Simpson, Jane Siberry, Jack Dorsey, Marie Dorsey, Jaclyn Dorsey, Michael Dorsey, Sara Dorsey, Robin Dezall, Bambino Farelinelli and his creator ("Love one another with a pure heart fervently . . ."), Ronnie Burkett and his Theatre of Marionettes, Judith Merril, Brian Fawcett (*Cambodia* and *Public Eye*), Ken Brown (*The Cambodia Pavilion*), Sarah Smith, Joanne Sydiaha, Ankie Engel, Greer Ilene Gilman (*Moonwise*), Zhauna Alexander (*Amelia's Aquarium*), Steeleye Span, Sima Khorrami, Peter Sutherland, Chantal de Rementeria, Gay Haldeman, Dede Weil, Dean Stoker, Guy Kay (*Tigana*), Evergon, Jon Lomberg, Ursula K. Le Guin, Ma Rainey, Samuel R. Delany, Doug Barbour, Derwyn Whitbread, Jane Duncan, Judy Chicago, Margaret Atwood, Maria Formolo, Edgar Meyer, Rickie Lee Jones, Ian Tamblyn, Rachel Pollack, Annie Dillard and even Ian Fleming have contributed to the tapestry, either through my references that can be caught by the reader or simply by inspiring at some point the spirit or intention of the work. Sharon Grant

Acknowledgments

Wildwind invented in a piece of fiction the idea of kids in the future having recycling routes, and I use it with her permission. A poem written by a fellow student in a poetry class in 1971 ("the energy needed to live / alone is so great") has stayed powerfully with me although I have unfortunately forgotten the author's name. I have also forgotten the name of the dance company in Winnipeg in 1994 whose brilliant adagio dance to Rachmaninoff's *Vespers* is paid homage in Jakob Ngogaba's *Night Through Slow Glass*. These are only a few of the influences on this book.

First Contact novels are common. We all know what we have to do. This is a book not about aliens but about love. Thanks to all whom I loved and who loved me through the years of its creation. You know who you are.

Thanks to David Hartwell at Tor for his breadth of experience, editorial persistence, and friendship; thanks to his assistants Jim Minz (then) and Moshe Feder (later). Thanks to a community of writers and readers, and especially thanks to all the people who offered or were drafted to read all or parts of this book while it was in progress, including but not limited to (in alphabetical order) Timothy Anderson, Peter Brand, Bev Estock, Pamela Freeman, Betty Gibbs, Amber Hayward, Nalo Hopkinson, Farah Mendlesohn, John Park, Ursula Pflug, Cordelia Sherman, Donna Simone, Michael Skeet, Gerry Truscott, Elisabeth Vonarburg, Mary Woodbury, and no doubt others shamefully forgotten: thank you all for important comments and support.

Thank you too to the Alberta Foundation for the Arts and the Canada Council for the Arts for providing financial support directly for the writing of this book or for my writing work in general. Such patronage is essential for the existence of artists in general and of Canadian culture on the world stage.